Adirondack Audacity

Thanks for your support of the 2016 New York State Probation Officers Association.

To the beautiful mountains and streams of New York State, what an amazing setting to start a story!

Enjoy

[illegible]

Adirondack

Audacity

By L.R. Smolarek

Adirondack Audacity is a work of fiction.

Cover design by Ron Turchiarelli

Printed in the United States of America

ISBN: 978-1499215991

To the beauty and freedom
Of wild open spaces.....

Acknowledgements

When I started this project, it was my intent to portray the Adirondack Mountains as a central character of this novel. The mountains with their grace, beauty and majesty are a treasure to the people of New York State and beyond. Many thanks are due to the dedicated individuals whose perseverance has kept the mountains "Forever Wild" and to those who live and work in the Adirondacks trying to eke out a livelihood in harmony with nature.

To my husband, who has not read a book of fiction since high school yet brought his engineering attention to detail and credibility to this work. To Ronnie Turchiarelli, who designed the cover graphics, I couldn't have done it without you. And to set the record straight, I have a step-mother who in no way resembles Helen. Lena is my shopping, gardening, and tea buddy. The character of Helen is a product of my *very* vivid imagination. To my daughter, Meggie, who has proved with determination and hard work, obstacles can turn into accomplishments. As a reading specialist, she became my editor.

To my proof readers: Susan Young, who lived and worked in the Adirondacks and where a part of her heart shall always reside. Janet Evans, dedicated teacher and fellow Adirondack enthusiast. Linda Thomas, who entered into the foray of romance novels after a sabbatical of many years, welcome back and thanks. Rick Hartman for a quick and timely review and a perspective only a man can give. Gerry Zahariev, your spot on critiques and humor keep me real. A disorganized true blonde such as myself, who can't remember her own name on a daily basis needs a friend like Donna Gastle, an organized feet on the ground lady with amazing analytical skills. And last, but certainly not least, Sarah Belotti Smolarek, our beautiful bella, who agreed to marry my son and make him the happiest man in the world. Sarah's comment when she finished reading *Adirondack Audacity* was.........I love it! And to future readers, I hope you do too!

May this book be as fun to read,
As it was to write,

Linda

50% of the profits from this book will be dedicated to wildlife and nature conservation projects.

Prologue

August 21, 2012

Okay, here's the thing, only copious quantities of alcohol coupled with unconditional maternal love could put me on a plane flying 30,000 feet above the Rocky Mountains. The trip mandated by the fact my daughter lives on the *other* side of the country…….I miss her and it's just too far to walk.

The mountains lie below with the heavens above, but for me, I'm in purgatory. Updrafts from the peaks combined with wind shear cause the plane to buck and dip like a rodeo horse on steroids. I hate flying. It's fallout from my childhood. I'd be playing with Barbie sitting all pretty in her pink Winnebago while my brothers built model airplanes out of Legos, and proceed to bash them into the wall, squealing with laughter as the plane exploded into a million pieces. Barbie and I cringed in horror as the little Lego people careened across the room, and my imagination added flames, the whole conflagration erupting into a fiery inferno. And that's the memory I choose to pull out as I wing my way across the country. *Great.*

My name is Ellen O'Connor, and I'm more of a-feet-on-the-ground kind of girl……..my interests tend to lie in the mundane adventures of life, hiking, gardening, or idling away the afternoon with a good book. But I'm still waiting for the pink Winnebago adventure to spice things up. Sure seemed to work for Barbie.

As a birthday gift, my children upgraded my coach ticket to first class in hopes better accommodations would lessen my fear of flying. It didn't……..first class simply meant……better alcohol and more of it.

So one drink leads to two, two becomes three….and three means I'm drunk. So why am I still white knuckling the arm rest? *Because*….. I'm in a pressurized steel tube streaking across the sky at warp speed, held aloft by the grace of God serviced by fallible, bored and possibly high on marijuana flight personnel. That's why my stomach clenches as the plane lurches downward dipping into an air pocket, only to lift and fall again. The walls of the cabin close in and my body tenses in rising panic. Overhead the "fasten seat belt" sign flashes on asking passengers to remain seated during the anticipated turbulence ahead. *Seriously,* we need a sign to state the obvious.

And the irony of it……..my husband was a pilot. Jack would roll his eyes and chuckle over my foolish behavior. Married to a pilot for over two decades; and here I am….afraid of flying. Odd, isn't it? Jack reveled in the pitches and dips of the plane, the excitement of take-off, and the thrill of landing in stormy weather.

Outside the window a dense blanket of cloud stretches in all directions, exactly how heaven should look. I wonder if Jack is out there, somewhere riding around on a puffy cloud playing the harp. A rather ludicrous thought if you knew Jack. Most likely he'd be trying to con St. Peter into a game of poker, or peeking under the angel's wings to see if they have real breasts.

It's been almost two years, and I still can't reconcile myself to his death. He was too young to die. And I'm too young to be a widow. I think widows are supposed to be old ladies with glasses hanging off chains, tunic tops, gray hair and sensible shoes…..?

Personally, I prefer blue jeans paired with a cozy

flannel shirt, and somewhere along the way, I've developed a passion for red dresses........ and stiletto heels. I'm currently coveting a pair of Manolo Blahnik's, only thing holding me back is..... money.

Jack was forty-nine years old, in the prime of his life. He ate well, jogged two miles a day and with his easy-going Irish temperament, the pressures of life never overwhelmed him. At the merest hint of a problem, he'd say with an exaggerated Irish brogue, "Darling, don't ye be worrying, things have a way of working themselves out. Who knows, we could be dead tomorrow, so enjoy today." And with those words of wisdom he'd kiss the top of my head and be off.............leaving *me* to deal with the crisis at hand. That was my happy-go-lucky husband, shrugging away the cares of the world, secure in the knowledge his good looks and charm would extricate him out of any dilemma life sent his way.

And it usually did, a golden boy, classically handsome, and confident of his place in the world. Jack was blessed with good looks, athletic prowess and charisma, a lethal combination in a man who recognized his talents at an early age and spent a lifetime honing his skills. He was a Kennedy without the curse, until that day in early December, when his body lay lifeless on top of mine. The spark, the grace, the wit, the sum that had been him was simply gone, like an eternal spirit summoned back to the nether world by the gods who clearly missed him.

One minute he's laughing and joking, making love to me, the next moment seized by a gripping pain in his chest, he falls dead on top of me. And it was just like him to leave me the way he did. In the middle of sex, he has the big O, I don't, and then I'm left behind, butt naked underneath him. I imagine him up in heaven lounging on a cloud, chuckling "Oh, darling, just leaving you with a little bit of love," waving his wings at me, "If I have to go, I might as well go happy." With little thought of how I was going to extricate myself from under his lifeless body. I'm sure the people who work on emergency squads have seen just about everything. Jack would have loved the fact when the ParaMeds arrived; I'm half naked desperately performing CPR on him. I can still hear one of the guy's comments, "He must be dead, because no man with any spark of life left in him could lay there with her bouncing up and down on him like that." *Very professional.* And they took their sweet time handing me my robe. And again I hear Jack……"Ahh, let the boys have a little fun." He turned the brogue on and off when it suited his needs. He was a charming devil of a man.

He treated me like a queen. I was the queen who took care of the king's duties while he went his merry way. He never questioned our family finances or discipline decisions for the children, and still chased me around the bedroom to the point I had to change in the closet if I wanted peace.

And Jack gave me the family I desperately needed, a large extended Irish family with brothers, sisters, aunties, uncles and parents who loved me like their own. All and all it was a fair trade-off; many women envied my marriage. I married the catch. The catch or the "but" in our relationship was………well, frankly, Jack was a bit of a…….shit. He had a weakness…. for women, all women….. any size…… any shape……..any age. I learned to look away from the lipstick smudge on the collar, a stray hair clinging to his jacket, and the occasional late nights without explanation. I was number one in his heart, but other women lurked in the shadows of our bedroom. He was a player, it was who he was, and he needed the constant validation of his manhood.

Tears and arguments to no avail; it was this way, or no way. That was Jack......take it or leave it. Life is a series of compromises.

The fasten seat belt sign blinks off; and I exhale a sigh of relief. About time, my wineglass is empty and my buzz is wearing off. Where is that flight attendant? Brought on by the altitude and too much alcohol, my mind continues to reminisce, I remember the day I met Jack. I was a senior at the University of Syracuse, studying elementary education, and receiving quite a tutorial in the realities of life from my eleven-year old inner city students. Jack was stationed at the Air National Guard base just outside of the city. He had graduated from Embry-Riddle College with a degree in aviation and enlisted in the Air National Guard to gain experience for his commercial pilot's license. He exuded boyish appeal in a man's body, wearing sloppy oxford shirts and slim khakis, a clean-cut boy in an era of longhaired hippies.

I met him jogging in the park; he came up from behind and started running next to me. What can I say, I was smitten. He devastated me with his smile of even white teeth that would make an orthodontist cry. He was black Irish, dark curling hair that tumbled in heavy waves, Celtic morning blue eyes sprang from his face in startling contrast.

The deal breaker was the dog; he was jogging with a golden retriever named Lucas. My collie, Gabby, took one look at Lucas and was smitten too. We had coffee and the rest is history.

Before meeting Jack, I was content on my own, thinking I didn't need another man in my life. After losing Vic, I thought my heart incapable of love. And I was fine except for the nights, the long dark nights I laid awake, tossing and turning, unable to sleep, barely holding loneliness at bay. But then Jack came along…..and it was another chance at life.

But….they say you never forget your first love and while that summer in the Adirondacks seems so long ago; to me it seems like….*yesterday*.

It's
funny, how one
summer can change
everything.
It must be something
about the warmth,
the smell of pine,
the morning
mist on a
mountain lake,
the charged air after a late-day thunderstorm.
A first love……
a summer love.
Everyone can reach back to one summer,
pause,
and find the exact moment when everything
changed.
That summer was my Adirondack Summer.

Chapter 1

Adirondack Summer-June 24, 1982

At seventeen, I've never been more than 50 miles away from home, never spent a night in a hotel, never crossed the state line, and now.........I'm on a bus heading to the Adirondack Mountains. To a place I never heard of until two months ago, Camp High Point at Cascade Mountain. What kind of name is that? Summer camps usually have long unpronounceable Indian names that twist and turn on your tongue. Camp names usually bring to mind Native Americans who wandered these lands years ago, constellations, a type of tree, or even a species of birds. Camp High Point at the Cascade sounds like the place British aristocracy ship their children off to for the summer. *Very posh.*

The reason I'm on this bus is simple........in my world I have two nicknames, labels that follow me and define my life, nicknames that change depending on the mood of the day. For example, when I fell down the stairs in front of the varsity football team......showing off my pink polka-dot underwear..... and by the end of the day instead of being Ellen McCauley, the whole school is calling me Dots........that's a Klutz-Ellen day.

Or when I'm forced to miss softball practice, *again,* and my coach swears he's going to bench me, he doesn't *quite* understand my stepmother, Helen. When you live with Helen, you live with her rules......and that means starting dinner, folding laundry, and babysitting my brothers is *far* more important than softball practice or a normal teenage social life. That's a Cinder-Ellen day.

I blame the Klutz-Ellen days on my blonde hair; I'm somewhere between a blonde and a red head, sort of like Lucille Ball running smack dab into Marilyn Monroe's chest. Only I didn't get the red hair or the voluptuous breasts.

The Cinder-Ellen days, truth be told…I blame Helen and her endless list of chores.

In addition to nicknames, I have demons. Who wouldn't? My mother died in horrific car crash when I was twelve, my stepmother tutored under the Wicked Witch of the West, and my father has never made an authentic decision in his life. In addition, I live with two little brothers apprenticed to be junior terrorists. The fact that my stepmother adores them, and loathes me, doesn't bode well for yours truly.

So when I saw an advertisement in the newspaper for a nature counselor at a children's camp in the Adirondacks, I jumped at the chance…….because in my mind that ad said one word……*Escape.*

So here I am on a bus to the mountains, sun light streaming through the open windows as a June heat wave grips the Northeast. My idea of getting away from it all…..did not include being smashed against the bus frame by the bulk of a woman whose girth exceeds the size of her seat by a factor of two, an 85 degree day with humidity somewhere between hell and the Amazon Rainforest…. no air conditioning, and no lunch. Helen left my lunch on the kitchen counter, a little farewell revenge. Dust motes float in the stifling heat, and the air carries the faint smell of disinfectant. Watching the scenery roll by, I'm mesmerized by the rising waves of heat shimmering off the highway.

Catching sight of my reflection in the window of the

bus, I wince. Like most seventeen year old girls, I'm obsessed with my appearance. I keep hoping someone will tell me I'm beautiful.......I'm still waiting. My father has blonde hair, my mother had auburn hair, and I fall somewhere in the middle. My hair is the color of a warm caramel in winter, streaked to coppery blonde by the summer sun. In fifth grade, I was the smallest girl in my class with hair hanging in curling ringlets down my back. By high school I'm weirdly tall, a collection of arms and legs that tangle and trip me at the slightest provocation. And the ringlets are gone. Could I have peaked in the fifth grade? I once heard an aunt say I have almond shaped eyes. I liked that, almond shaped eyes sound exotic and mysterious. We'll ignore the fact my eyes are....blue, just blue. Not aquamarine, sapphire, or turquoise like the heroines in romance novels. No, just blue. At seventeen I'm not attracting a lot of boys; and quite frankly I'm not trying. Boys my age are preoccupied with four things, sports, cars, beer and boobs, the order of importance changing with their mood. Don't get me wrong, I like sports. But I am not the least bit interested in beer or cars, and I'd like to keep my boobs intact from the groping and mauling that goes on in the back seat of parked cars. Not having excessively large breasts, just the standard ABC cup variety, I've decided I'm saving them for the right guy. I just hope the right guy comes along before I hit eighty and the boobs head south to meet my belly-button.

Squirming ever so slightly to avoid body contact with my seatmate whose snores threaten to overpower the diesel engine of the bus, I reach into my backpack and pull out a tattered pamphlet, corners curled and frayed from too much handling. *Camp High Point at Cascade*

Mountain is written in bold print across the top margin. The front cover shows campers canoeing on a lake, hiking through the woods, singing around a campfire, and horseback riding across a meadow……I've never ridden a horse.

Smoothing out the wrinkles of the brochure on my knee, I read for the hundredth time the list of camp promises…. and add a few of my own.

I'm seventeen and have done, basically, *nothing*. Never smoked a cigarette…….never drank a beer…….never kissed a boy. I'm not counting Mark Pinowicz. He only kissed me to see if he could French kiss with his braces on, and he wanted to try it out on me because I wasn't popular enough to count. To say the least it was a very unrewarding experience.

So maybe I'll go skinny dipping………not wear a bra for the entire summer………..drink beer………do something *illegal*….like smoke a joint….*hmmm*, the possibilities of summer are endless.

But truth be told, the real reason I've left home for the summer is…..it's been five years since my mother's death…and the night my mom died, part of my father died too. And life as I knew it ceased to exist. As much as I tried to fill her shoes and help ease his grief, nothing I did filled the void of her absence. My father was never the same, a combination of guilt and grief. He blames himself for the accident. My mother drove home from the party that night because he was drunk. He didn't notice she had been drinking too, and she wasn't wearing a seat belt. She ran a stop sign, collided with a utility truck and went through the windshield. She was dead upon arrival at the hospital.

The light in our family went out that night. My mom

was by no means a conventional mother. She didn't believe in stringent housekeeping, regular meals, starched and pressed clothes or punctuality. My mother ascribed to a rather carefree lifestyle, it was the age of the hippy love child, and she raised her children unencumbered by the established mores of society.

Magical and irresistible to everyone around her, she possessed an infectious laugh, quick wit and a love of adventure. She knew no boundaries, and schedules were a mere suggestion. She created her own rules on a daily basis. Dinner was likely to be peanut butter and jelly sandwiches with Twinkies in a tent made of blankets or a five course meal under the oak tree in the back yard. We ate when we were hungry, washed when we were dirty and cleaned the house when company was coming. And we were happy.

After her death, my dad shut down emotionally, leaving me to take care of the family. With the help of my grandmother, I learned to cook anything that was packaged, canned or thawed from the freezer. Face it, at the age of twelve; I didn't have a whole lot of experience to draw on. Using the owner's manual; I studied the dials of the washing machine and we wore a lot of pink underwear. Eventually I figured out how to separate whites from colored clothes and clean the house well enough to keep the health department away. My grandmother wanted to help and even though she was his mother, my dad's stiff necked pride wouldn't allow her to move in and take over the care of his family. As the only living grandparent, she came up with a scheme to cope with our motherless house. Hence, the beginning of my Cinder-Ellen saga, and life was good until Helen came.

Apparently my father and Helen dated briefly in high

school; my father dumped Helen to marry my mother. But Helen never gave up the torch for him, so as soon as it was socially acceptable she showed up on our doorstep wearing black and carrying a casserole. The rest is history, within a year he married her. My father is well over six feet tall, heavy set and blonde. Helen barely comes up to his elbow, and with her black hair and a body too thin to be healthy, they look like a pair of a cartoon characters. And Helen was the bipolar opposite of my mother; orderly, fanatically clean and had rules for everything. But it seemed to work for everyone….my dad played golf on Saturdays with no guilt, the house and children were neat and tidy. My brothers loved having real food on the table and baseball shirts that were the right color and size. Traitors.

It worked for everyone…..but Helen and me. We didn't work. See, I'm the walking, breathing, living image of my mother complete with my father's blue eyes and square jaw, just enough proof of their union to throw in her face…… everyday someone else was here before her. We despised each other at first sight. With my eyes on a scholarship for college, I'm plotting my escape and counting the days until I leave. Four hundred and thirty-two to be exact, this summer job between my junior and senior year of high school is step…..numero uno, baby.

…

"Sandwich, dear?" asks the lady in the seat next to me, breaking into my day dream. I realize my growling stomach announced the fact I'm slowly starving to death.

I take the sandwich with a dubious glance at the woman. "Ah, thank you." I say. She is plump wearing a cotton housedress, faded from too many washings.

The seams stretched taut over her large frame. The

faint scent of body odor lingers in the air. She has kindly blue eyes, and seems nice enough.

"I'm Vera Watts. What's your name, honey?" The lady asks, cramming half a sandwich into her mouth. Even with her mouth full she still has the ability to carry on a conversation......... how does she do that?

I look at her in awe. "My name is Ellen McCauley."

"So where are you headed for in the mountains?" She inquires taking another enormous bite of sandwich.

"Inlet." Is my muffled reply, my tongue contorted as it tries to pry the slick white bread from the roof of my mouth.

"Now where is that?" she asks, reaching into a paper bag taking out a can of soda. "Here, darling, you need this to wash down that sandwich. It's warm but better than nothing."

Gratefully accepting the tepid soda, I steal a peek into her bag, hoping a Twinkie will magically appear. No such luck. Taking a sip to wash down the glob of sandwich, I respond to her question, "Inlet is near Blue Mountain Lake." The bubbles from the soda tickle my nose. "I've never been there so I don't know too much about it."

"So are you visiting family?"

"No," I respond with a sigh. My first glimpse of the mountains against the backdrop of a vivid blue sky and I'm stuck talking to this nosy lady. "I'll be working at a camp as a nature counselor."

"Oh, how exciting! Tell me all about it. Are you going to trap bears?"

I look at her as if she's insane. Trap bears, what the heck is she talking about?

"No," I begin slowly, as if talking to a dull witted child, "No, more like take kids on nature hikes and teach

them about the plants and animals of the Adirondacks."
Jeez.

"Well, dearie, that sounds kind of boring. I like a little adventure." She says with an indignant sniff. "I'm going to visit my sister and her husband. They leave food out now and then so we can watch the bear come at night and feed. Then Frank, that's my brother-in-law, leaps off the porch screaming and banging a pan with a metal spoon. What a racket that banging makes. Lord, you should see the bears jump. We run back into the cabin nearly peeing our pants with laughter."

"Oh, really." I groan, wincing, and they call the bears stupid.

"Oh, speaking of all those kids at camp, did I tell you I have three grandchildren." She reaches into her enormous bag, pulling out a fistful of photographs and holds them reverently before my eyes. After an agonizing half hour on the glories of her grandchildren, Vera's considerable girth collapses back into the seat. "All that talking about those grandchildren has plum worn me out. I'm afraid I need a little nap. I hope you don't think me rude if I just close my eyes and take a rest."

"No, no, not at all. A nap sounds like a great idea." I hastily agree. Halleluiah, there is a God.

As Vera drifts off to sleep, her lips make little popping noises. I lean my head against the metal frame of the window watching the mountains rise up out of the fertile farm foothills, giant humps of granite and limestone reach for the sky. Towering white pine, spruce and balsam jut from the craggy mountainside. I smell the faint aroma of balsam as the bus rolls by sparkling lakes, cut and carved by the thick glaciers that covered the Adirondacks for tens of thousands of years. I feel a tremor of excitement, a sense of familiarity, of coming home.

Vera gives a little snort in her sleep pulling my gaze back to the dim interior of the bus. As I glance at my seatmate, I'm struck by the difference between her and my grandmother. As little kids we couldn't say grandma, it came out as "ran-ran" and "ran-ran" turned into Gran. Watching Vera sleep reminds me of my Gran falling asleep in her chair next to the fireplace, knitting needles resting in her lap, reading glasses sliding down her nose. But the similarity ends there. Where Vera is plump and slovenly, Gran's body is sparse and lean, her days filled with hard work. A long angular face dominated by a curving slender nose, reminiscent of a wary female hawk. Steel gray hair cut short with curled bangs she calls "Mame Eisenhower" bangs, a style popularized by former President Eisenhower's wife. Her blue eyes framed by silver rimmed glasses seem to magnify her vision to a piercing gaze. But for all of her foreboding appearance, she is a marshmallow with a big heart, and like my mother, she loves to have fun. Water bucket battles out on the lawn in summer, card games around the dining room table at night....with bonus points for the best fart jokes.

I reach into the backpack on the floor and pull out the nature journal she gave me years ago. A birthday present the year Helen moved into the house. The journal gave me an excuse to explore the outdoors, leaving responsibilities behind to spend hours collecting, sketching or just day dreaming under the willow tree growing alongside the pond.

Once I caught a mouse in a Have-a-Heart trap and put it in a box with air holes, hoping to keep it. I named the mouse, Oscar and tried keeping it for a pet. Until Helen met me at the door with her arms folded across her chest and ice daggers in her eyes. Not uttering a single word I turned and walked to the field next to our house and let the mouse go. I thought Oscar had a better chance with the feral cats in the neighborhood than he did with Helen.

It's because of my grandmother that I'm qualified to take on the job as a nature counselor. She passed her love of the outdoors on to me. I grew up spending afternoons wandering in the fields and woods around her house as she pointed out various plants and animal signs to me. In her world, the fields and forest are her church and Bible. This is where God lives.

Glancing at Vera to make sure she is still asleep, I brush away stray pieces of lint from the journal's cover. The front is hand-tooled, scrollwork blooming with flowers and leaves. The binding is broken and worn. At one time the pages smelled faintly of trees and sunshine. Now they smell of earth and dried leaves.

Growing up in a house that wrote its own definition of normal, I became introspective and quiet. Coupled with my stumbling clumsiness, the kids at school dubbed me with the nickname, Klutz-Ellen. It's no wonder I preferred playing with frogs and butterflies. It's not that I'm bad at sports; I'm just bad at life. It could be worse; Joey Thompson's nickname was Poopy Pants. Don't ask.

Turning a page, I run my hand over the delicate plants pressed in the peak of bloom, now faded and held eternal by a dab of glue. Colored pencils highlight or shade points of interest…

And there on the inside cover is my grandmother's firm handwriting.

Dearest Ellen,

Hold fast to your dreams; keep a still secret spot where they may go. Shelter those dreams so they thrive and grow, away from doubt and fear. Let the magic of nature work at will in you, and may your spirit soar. Be not afraid of the miles ahead, hold fast to your journey, stay proud and strong. Make the past your history, and not an excuse for the future. Embrace truth, banish falsehoods and never let darkness win.

Always my love,
Gran

The bus winds and climbs the steep roads, pushing through rocky outcrops of forests. Huge boulders bump through the forest green like gnarled knuckles and rippling spines of granite. Balsam fir gives way to red maple, white birch and towering white pines. And I can't help but wonder what this summer has in store for me.

My guide book said the Adirondack Park is one of the largest parks in America, larger than Yellowstone, Grand Canyon and Yosemite combined; the largest publicly protected area in the contiguous United States. The park contains forty-six mountains over 4000 feet, thirty thousand miles of rivers and two thousand lakes and ponds. In 1894 the Adirondack Forest Preserve was established and recognized as a protected Forever Wild area……..and my passport to summer freedom and new beginnings.

The sign along the roadside reads *Inlet* in carved gold letters poised above a painted loon. The bus turns into a parking lot and comes to a stop with a hiss of air brakes.

"Good bye, Vera." My voice muffled as I bend over

tying up the laces of my hiking boots.

"Whattt?" Vera blinks with bleary eyes.

"This is my stop. I get off here."

"Here, dearie, let me move so you can get out."

"I hope you enjoy your summer." I say, wedging myself into the narrow aisle of the bus.

She gives my shoulder a motherly pat before settling back into her seat. "Honey, don't you worry about me. I know how to have a good time."

Taking a deep breath, I head for the stairs. With a wave good bye, I turn to exit the bus and snag the toe of my boot on the ragged edge of rubber mat covering the steps, lose my balance and crash with a thump into the arms of the surprised bus driver. *Ouuu!*

"Whoa, little lady, you'll get there soon enough, no need to fly off my bus." He says with a chuckle helping me to my feet with his strong arms.

"I'm so sorry," I say to him, pushing myself off his chest. *Oh God.* While the driver retrieves my suitcase from the luggage compartment, I survey the parking lot hoping no one noticed my precarious flight down the stairs.

"Good luck, little lady." The driver gives me a salute as he boards the bus. "Enjoy your summer!"

The door closes cutting off my last link with home, leaving me in the cool Adirondack evening. My last sight of the bus is Vera wildly waving good bye from the window.

In the west the setting sun outlines the pines behind the town hall in streaks of orange and pink. Shading my eyes against the glare, I look around the parking lot for my ride to camp and stop dead in my tracks…..*it can't be?*

Chapter 2

Summer Friends

Placing my belongings on the blacktop, I stop and stare, shaking my head in disbelief. Am I hallucinating? The man striding toward me could pass for Vera Watts's twin brother….how is this possible…did they leave her behind? *Oh shit….*

"Ellen, come over here." The man gestures for me to join the group of teenagers lounging against a van in various states of boredom. I say a quick prayer, please tell me they missed my grand exit from the bus, unfortunately it looks like they had…nothing…else…to do.

"I'm Morris Erhart, Director of Camp High Point; we spoke on the phone last April for the interview. Welcome to the Adirondacks." Rocking back on the worn heels of his cowboy boots he continues, "You can call me, Morris, unless my wife is around, then it's Mr. Erhart. She likes a little respect between staff and management, but for me, I'm more of a down to earth kind of cowpoke." Morris Erhart is a large man weighing at least 270 pounds with a broad face, dark brown eyes that tend to vanish into the little folds of fat surrounding his eyes when he smiles. Faded blue jeans are held in place by a turquoise belt buckle and his plaid cowboy shirt strains against a spreading paunch. Atop his head is an honest to goodness Stetson cowboy hat. Not exactly attire for a mountain man. Vera Watts gone Texas style?

According to the camp information Morris sent me, the Erhart family was originally from Texas and involved in the oil industry. His grandfather fell in love with the Adirondacks while on a business trip to New York in the 1920's, and purchased a mountain retreat for his family to escape the dust and heat of Texas summers. Due to economic reasons in the 1950's the family converted their vacation property into a summer camp for children. Morris and his wife are the second generation of Erharts to manage the camp.

"Ellen, you're the last to arrive but before we pack up and head to camp, let me introduce you to some of the other counselors you'll be working with this summer." Morris rubs his hands together and continues, "Let me see if I have all the names and faces straight." He glances around at the group, tapping a finger against his cheek. "Once we get you buckaroos introduced, we can hit the road and head back to camp."

I notice a dark lanky kid leaning against the van roll his eyes skyward and silently agree with him. Buckaroos, seriously? This could be a long summer.

"This here tall fellow is Mac Luciano." Morris says. "He'll be the assistant director of sports this summer. Mac plays varsity baseball and even had a few college scouts check him out this spring." Mac is over six feet tall with straight brown hair that falls over his eyes, as if he were trying to hide something. He'd be good looking except for his large nose and acne marked face. As he throws a baseball back and forth, I can't help but notice he's missing half of the pinkie finger on his right hand. He stops throwing the ball and extends his hand to me, challenging me to touch his damaged finger. Little does he realize, I've grown up with two brothers who's sole purpose in life is to gross me out. I reach out and shake his hand, our eyes meet and I return the challenge…it takes more than a missing pinkie to faze me, buddy.

"Hey," he says, and with a mischievous grin, he leans in and whispers, "Fall much?"

Crap…..so much for no one noticing my exit from the bus.

Ignoring Mac, I turn my attention to Morris who is introducing a kid wearing a tweed blazer adorned with suede elbow patches over a white t-shirt, the cuff of his blue jeans are shoved into unlaced hiking boots. His blond hair is long enough to run a comb through, but considered short in this era of the long haired hippy. Looking at him, you can't tell if he wants to be a Harvard law professor or a farmer.

"Ellen, this is Ben Harmon," Morris points to Ben who is straddling a suitcase and strumming a beat-up guitar. "Ben will be in charge of creating the props and scenery used in our theater productions and bringing out the musical talents of our campers." Shorter than Mac, Ben is solidly built with a ruddy Irish face. I feel his keen, green eyes surveying every detail of my appearance, but in a nice way. His scrutiny is more curious than malicious.

"Hi, I'm Ben," he stands to shake hands. Flecks of paint stain his t-shirt, obviously an occupational hazard of one blessed with artistic talent.

"Nice to meet you, I'm Ellen McCauley." I return his handshake, thinking he has that cute, nice guy look about him.

A tall girl with straight, ash colored hair is Theresa Donaldson; she is perfectly groomed in carefully pressed pink shorts and coordinating button down shirt.

"Hi, call me Tee," she says, a welcoming smile on her face. "I'll be the tennis instructor this summer."

She swishes an imaginary tennis racket through the air

followed by a rueful laugh. My first reaction to her appearance......how is she so neat and clean? A glance down at my rumpled jeans, wrinkled shirt and scuffed boots confirms the bus company did not provide valet service to whisk away the grime of travel. I tug my shirt down in a vain attempt to smooth out the wrinkles and try hiding my hiking boots behind a suitcase. Maybe after a shower and clean clothes I can forgive her fastidious appearance.

"Now this here little gal is…Katherine Hunt. This is her second year. Katherine, oh yeah, I forgot you wanted to be called Kat," Morris shakes his head with a dubious look at Kat. "Anyway, *umm*…Kat is working in the theater program; she'll be working with Ben."

Kat flashes me the peace sign. "Just call me, Kat." This was uttered as a declaration, not a request. Her voice is sensuous bordering on sultry. Tall and slender, gypsy red curls tumble down her shoulders and her skin is the color of café au latte. Dark brown eyes, almost black are heavily rimmed with mascara and blue eye shadow. The denim shirt knotted at her waist has several buttons undone revealing ample cleavage. She looks older and exotic. Her appearance bodes a red flag of warning, a foretelling of wild bohemian ways, a beacon of impending trouble...I return her peace sign with the delicious anticipation of adventures yet to come.

"Here, you look like you could use one of these." A girl with long brown frizzy hair hands me an ice cold soda from the cooler at her feet. I'd forgotten how hot and thirsty I was until my hand touches the frosty glass bottle. I smile at her with gratitude. "I'm envious," she says. "You have such beautiful hair."

Really? Someone thinks I have beautiful hair. *Wow.*

But a closer look at her hair in the fading evening light reveals the reason behind her envy. If her hair were straight, it would fall to the middle of her back; unfortunately, it's a mass of tight curls coming to rest at her shoulders. *Sigh*…understated hair envy, so much for the complement. "Thanks, I'm dying of thirst." I answer politely to both the complement and the Coke.

"You're welcome, I'm Emi Jo Rodney." She says, laughing blue eyes peer out of glasses too large for her face. "I'll be doing arts and craft projects with the kids. There ain't nothing I can't do with a piece of boondoggle." To illustrate her point she wiggles a long cord of brightly colored strings fashioned into a keychain. Emi Jo's figure is lush bordering on plump. With a matching gingham bow in her hair, she is the personification of an arts and crafts counselor.

"And over here…" Morris gestures to a teenager lounging in the background, too cool and disinterested to join into the group introductions.

"This is Vic Rienz, our youngest counselor this year, he came highly recommended…. by me. Vic made it to the New York State Swimming Championship this year." Morris says to us. "Our families have known each other for years and we're thrilled to have him lifeguard for us this summer. No drowning campers this year?" Morris chuckles and ventures a lame attempt to engage Vic in conversation. "Right Vic?" I'm close enough to hear Vic mutter under his breath, "Yeah, if I don't try and drown myself first at this joke of a camp."

Youngest? I can't help think; you've got to be kidding me. Apart from the group, Vic props himself against the hood of the van, tall, lean with the air of a brooding panther locked in a cage against its' will. He looks better suited to counseling gang members on the streets of New York then coaching privileged upper class children. He reeks street savvy, not camp counselor. Hands slouched into his pockets, black hair loose around his shoulders, one errant lock tucked behind his ear. In a tough guy kind of way, he's handsome, cool, dark and private. Even in the dim light he has the most arresting eyes I've ever seen, dark brown with luminous shots of molten gold. They're gorgeous.

He has the well-defined arms and back muscles of a swimmer, wide shoulders tapered down to a narrow waist. His face is a study of angles, high carved cheekbones and a square jaw. He unfolds himself from the van and extends his hand, saying, "Hello *mia*, it is a pleasure to meet you, Ellen McCauley." I feel a jolt run through me at his touch. He holds my hand a moment longer than necessary, and leans in close as if to capture the very air around me. I see the change in his eyes as our hands meet; and feel the sudden tension in his fingers. Smoldering dark eyes look deep into mine…and I feel my heart begin a slow insistent thudding against my ribs. His voice a drawl with a trace of Spanish accent, warns me to beware. I can't believe he even heard my name let alone remembered it. His jeans are faded, worn through at one knee and he wears a hooded sweatshirt loosely knotted around his waist. Unlike the rest of us, clad in sneakers or hiking boots, he wears sandals. His presence unnerves me, yanking back my hand; I mumble a greeting, my voice husky with a slight tremor. *Jeez, who is this kid?*

Chapter 3

Mountain Silence

The van turns off Route 28 onto an unmarked dirt road. Almost instantly the left front tire hits a pothole with a jarring lurch. Outside, it's total darkness except for the twin tunnels of light coming from the high beams.

"Mr. Morris?" asks Emi Jo, hands braced to prevent involuntary ejection from her seat. "What kind of road is this, I mean, is it even a road?"

"Of course it's a road, little lady." Morris replies. His hands clutch the steering wheel as he swerves back and forth in a vain attempt to avoid the crater like potholes. "We're just a few miles from camp."

"Sir, exactly how many miles is a "few" miles?" Ben asks; not appearing too upset over the rough ride. Emi Jo now has a death grip on his arm and each jarring bounce crushes her ample breasts against him. The smile on his face confirms he's enjoying the trip. And Emi Jo is clueless to the source of his happiness.

"Well," Morris chuckles amused by our discomfort. "Last time I checked the mileage from Inlet to Camp High Point, it was about twenty-three miles on the main highway. I know y'all are in a hurry to get camp, being tired from your travels, so I took the short cut. This is one of the old corduroy roads, made from railroad ties years ago so travelers wouldn't get bogged down in the spring mud. This route cuts ten miles off the trip."

And just when I think the lurching and bouncing can't get any worse, a moan comes from the back of the van. Kat calls out in a panic stricken voice, "Hey, Up front! Morris, pull over, quick! I'm going to throw up!"

There's nothing like a sick camper on board to shut Morris up. A quick twist of his wrist and the van comes to a screeching halt at the side of the road. Mac opens the door for Kat to make a quick exit. As she vanishes into the night, the rest of us step out to stretch our legs. As Vic climbs from the back of the van I hear him complain, "What the hell, nothing between my ass and a grizzly bear…" his voice fades away.

I look back at him in astonishment. What in the world is he doing here? He obviously doesn't want to be here, he acts like a condemned prisoner on death row. And he's an idiot; grizzlies don't live in the Adirondacks, only black bears, the chances of a grizzly bear coming along and eating his sorry ass are far and few between. We should be so lucky….probably give the poor thing indigestion. *Jerk*

Standing in the shadows of the high beams, Ben has a sad expression on his face for Emi Jo's breasts are no longer imprinted on his arm. A collective gasp goes up from the group as Morris turns off the head lights.

I don't think anything has prepared me for night in the North Country. Far removed from city lights, we're wrapped in total darkness. The stars overhead are hidden by a canopy of trees and the new moon sheds a meager sliver of light. The air is soft and quiet; it is so quiet. Silence like a cloak of night velvet surrounds us. The stillness is deafening to ears grown accustomed to city noise.

I'm enchanted by the darkness and silence. As a child I hid under my blankets, afraid of the dark, sleeping only if the door was open or a nightlight left on. But this was different, so calm, so peaceful, so serene.

And from out of the shadows comes an eerie tremulous howl wavering through the woods…what the hell?

"Oh, my God, what was that sound?" Kat hollers from the down the road. Apparently not everyone is enchanted by the darkness. "Where are you? Holy shit! It's too dark, I can't see anything! Where did everyone go?! Heeelp!"

"Over here." Morris calls. The van lights come on illuminating the road, banishing the darkness.

"Who turned off the lights?" Kat wails. "I thought you fricking left me in the woods. What's howling out there? Is that a bear, a *mountain lion*?" Her shoes kick up little puffs of dust from the road as she runs back to join us. "What was I thinking coming back to this wilderness!"

"That was a loon, a duck that hunts by diving for fish in the lakes." Morris explains calmly. "You should remember them; they're on the lake by camp. That's a mating call. Listen, there it goes again."

And actually, after knowing it's only a duck and not some Sasquatch stalking us through the woods, the sound is hauntingly lovely. I step to the side of the road to hear better, and notice Vic standing outside the circle of light, listening, he turns his head, and I can feel his eyes on me.

Morris opens the van door and ushers everyone back inside. "And by the way, I have to caution you about your language. There is no cussing or swearing around the campers or my wife. She does not tolerate foul language and lewd behavior from our counselors."

And what does he mean by lewd behavior? The image of the staff chasing each other around the campfire, naked comes to mind…..I don't think that's going to be a problem….being a Christian based camp and all. And the only reason Helen let me come was her hope that a summer filled with Sunday church service and prayer would save my immortal soul. Like there's ever a chance to tarnish my soul under her watch…..

…

The sign announcing the arrival to Camp High Point is fashioned out of woven tree branches, like a huge cobweb hanging in the glow of the headlights. The camp is deserted and shrouded in darkness. Is this what the camp brochure meant by pristine mountain experience? Or is pristine just another word for primitive…

"Where are the lights, why is it so dark?" asks Mac peering into the night, trying to get a glimpse of the buildings.

"Well, we had a little problem with the electrician." Morris says looking back at us, a guilty expression on his face. "In the fall we turn off the electricity to save money over the winter and then switch it back on in the spring before the campers arrive. The electrician wasn't able to come until tomorrow. So I'm afraid your first night at camp will be in the dark. And no electricity means no water. Sorry."

Terrific……no lights, no water, no food, *and* no evidence of people….what *if* Morris is a deranged serial killer with a particular appetite for teenagers…….*oh boy*…

Chapter 4

Camp High Point at the Cascade

Sunrise comes quickly in the North Woods. Golden rays of morning sun spill through the web of tree branches causing streams of light to play across the hardwood floor. Stretching in my sleeping bag, it takes a moment to remember where I am. Snuggling down in the warmth of my bed, I survey the room with interest. I wasn't dreaming. It's as charming in the daylight as it was under the flashlight beams last night. Morris might be nuts, but he's not insane. After feeding us; and providing flashlights he conducted a moonlit tour of camp, dropping us off at our respective cabins.

The walls of the cabin are unstained wood coated with a single coat of varnish, mellowed to a soft yellow patina. The beds are placed between long narrow windows that swing in like a set of small French doors when opened. Each window is covered in screening to keep out the voracious black flies and mosquitos.

Curtains and bedspreads are made of a faded green plaid material. Tattered braided rugs in tones of green, rust and burgundy are randomly scattered over the knotty pine floors. Four wooden dressers are lined up on the wall opposite the beds, the drawers chipped and worn with age. And best of all…..it's clean. No dingy cabin with smoke-stained walls smelling of mildew, crawling with spiders, mouse droppings, and bats flying overhead at night. At least I didn't see any bats last night; a cautious glance at the ceiling confirms the absence of bat life. *Whew*. Helen tried selling me on the idea that bats live in cabins and try to nest in your hair at night. Knowing a little bit about nature, I didn't buy it. On one hand she wanted me to leave, on the other hand she hated losing her free slave labor…Cinder-Ellen. Viewing the cabin from my snug nest, I decide…this is way better than a summer with Helen. Through the panes of glass I can see a chickadee flitting from one branch to another, calling out, *chick a dee, chick a dee, dee,dee.*

A strident knocking at the door breaks the morning silence, followed by a commanding voice. "Girls, rise and shine, the sun is up and we have work to do." The apparition standing in our doorway begins shaking a cowbell, the clanging of the bell is deafening.

Four pairs of bleary eyes appear from the depths of flannel sleeping bags looking at this woman as if she were an escaped lunatic from a mental institution. I can hear Kat mutter under her breath, "What the F…?"

"Ladies, I'm Mrs. Sally Erhart, Mr. Erhart's wife and Camp Director. You may call me Mrs. Erhart. I pretty much handle the day to day operations of the camp. You girls will report to me until your senior counselors arrive. All camp matters of discipline and finances are handled by me. Is that understood?"

Heil Hitler, what happened to good morning and welcome to camp?

"Yes, ma'am." We chorus as dutiful schoolgirls, sitting at attention under the woman's steely gaze. We thought Mr. Erhart was Camp Director. We were just told otherwise.

While Mr. Erhart is jovial and generous, his wife, *Mrs.*Erhart, is all business and apparently…no nonsense and no fun.

"I have breakfast started and I'll need some help.

Here is a jug of water to brush your teeth and wash your face." She says setting down a jug on the dresser. "Take it with you to the latrine. I'm sure the electrician will be here soon and we will have water before noon." I think the almighty has spoken, and no one dare question *her* authority.

She has the athletic build of a tennis player, tall and slender, arms cut with well-toned muscles, blonde hair styled in a short bob. Her high cheekbones and thin nose suggest the essence of former beauty, now faded. Her blue eyes are cold and determined in a face devoid of makeup. I guess she is somewhere in her late forties. Mrs. Erhart reminds me of the women at a country club I once visited with a friend from school. She has the air of good breeding and wealth, but the look of her worn clothes and the fact she runs this camp suggests the family has fallen on hard times. And the firm set of her mouth shows she never forgave life for the injustice.

Her blue eyes scan the room to ensure everything is in order. The gaze then turns to study each of us. Squirming under the inspection, we push sleep-flattened hair in place, smooth rumpled pajamas attempting to appear alert and awake. With an upward flick of her eyelids and a shake of her head, we are dismissed as lacking…but adequate. Her scrutiny put us in our place, we are the help…and she is the mistress of the manor.

Turning to leave, she pauses at the door. "I'm going back to the kitchen. I expect to see everyone at breakfast in a half hour. Don't be late."

"The witch is back!" Kat exclaims, untangling her legs from her sleeping bag as she peers out the window watching Mrs. Erhart retreating back. "Ugh, I have to pee!"

"Oh, holy shit!" Kat exclaims as her feet hit the cabin floor. "It is freezing in here." She leaps back into bed, pulling the sleeping bag over her head.

"How cold can it really be?" Tee asks, craning her neck to peer at the thermometer mounted outside the window. "Oh, goodness, you're right. It's only 43 degrees. This is the end of June; shouldn't it be warmer than this?" Looking at Kat she wags her finger in disapproval. "And must you use that word. It's vulgar."

"Yeah, get used to it." Kat's muffled voice comes from the depths of her sleeping bag.

"Come on, let's go, I'm starving." I say. "We don't want to keep Mrs. Erhart waiting. God knows what punishment she'll exact on us, turn us into forest pumpkins or something." I dig down and retrieve my socks, pulling them on before getting out of bed.

"I'm ready." Tee says twirling around, showing off her perfectly pressed jeans and sweatshirt. Her hair is brushed and pulled back with a matching ribbon. The sleeping bag on her bed, straightened; pillows fluffed and stuffed animals lined up in a row. How did she do that, I just turned my back for a minute? Wow, she's good.

"It's too early, too cold and too far to walk to the bathroom. I'm going back to sleep." Emi Jo whines, sliding back into her plaid cocoon, earning her a volley of pillows thrown at her head. *Get up!*

. . .

Within twenty minutes we're standing on the porch of the dining hall, a large building constructed of cedar bark, majestically rising out of a clearing in the woods. A carpet of green lawn rolls down to the lake's edge, anchoring the lodge between the forest and water. The porch wraps around the front of the building, curved and bent branches provide ornamentation and support for the steeply pitched roof. The porch rails are fashioned of cedar branches spelling out, "Camp High Point." Traditional Adirondack chairs are scattered across the lawn facing the lake.

"I can't imagine how much it costs to send a kid to this camp," Emi Jo whispers. "This doesn't look like the dump I went to as a kid. I've never seen a camp this nice. Most of them are pretty crummy."

"You're right." Tee says, also whispering, "The camp my parents sent me to three years ago was not cheap by any means but it sure was nothing like this one."

I've never been to camp, so I have nothing to use as a reference. But even I knew this is pretty ritzy for a kid's camp. It makes me wonder what kind of snotty nosed little brats come here.

As we walk up the porch steps Mr. Erhart rings a huge bell used to call campers to meals. The smell of coffee assails our senses as we enter the dining room through a set of double screen doors. The inside of the dining hall is a wash of sunlight streaming through multi-paned windows, reflecting off the wood panel walls. There are no curtains on the windows to obstruct the view of the lake and a crisscross of exposed wooden beams hold up the roof rafters.

Suspended from the center beam is an Adirondack guide boat, a cross between a rowboat and a canoe, it moves across the water using two oars instead of a single paddle like a canoe. The focal point of the room, the boat looks more suited to an art gallery than navigating lakes and rivers.

Mr. Erhart gives us a brief description of the dining room procedures. The door to the kitchen swings open and Mrs. Erhart comes bustling through, setting down a huge platter of eggs, home fries, and bacon on a large table that acts as a buffet serving station. Stopping to wipe her hands on her apron, she commands, "Everyone dig in, we have a lot of work to do, so we need a good breakfast to keep up our strength. Right, Sweetie?" She says tickling Mr. Erhart under the chin....psycho woman.

I head to the coffeepot, noticing Vic right behind me. I hand him one of the heavy enamel coffee mugs commonly used in restaurants. There is something about picking up a nice heavy mug, the aromatic steam of coffee wafting up, filling your senses. Add a little sugar and cream, take that first sip, it's a little bit of morning heaven. As I take my first sip and sigh, I see Vic looking at me.

"What?!"

"That's a lot of cream and sugar." He says, pouring himself a cup of black coffee. "Hate to see you get fat."

Jerk. "Well, black coffee is too strong for me." I say with a faint shudder, tipping my mug in the direction of his cup. "Ladies don't drink black coffee."

"What does drinking black coffee have to do with being a lady?" He leans against the table crossing his arms over his chest, cocking his head to one side, an amused look on his face. Wearing jeans, hiking boots and a flannel shirt, he looks more like a logger than the tough punk kid of last night.

"I don't know; black coffee seems harsh and bitter." I lift my mug in a mock toast to him, laughing. "Something a lumberjack would drink on a cold mountain morning."

"What? You don't like my clothes?" He makes a grimace. "My mother picked them out. I knew I should have checked my duffle bag before leaving home."

He seems so tough and independent; I wouldn't think he even had a mother, let alone one who picks out his clothes. I try slipping away from him but Ben blocks my exit. "Hey, how's the coffee?" he asks, rubbing his hands together, chasing away the morning chill.

Vic reaches into the pyramid of mugs, hands one to Ben. "Here, try some." Ben hesitates, his face momentary registers surprise at the friendly overture from Vic.

Ben fills his mug from a large urn, adds a healthy dose of cream, takes a sip and proclaims. "Not bad."

Vic leans back against the counter top, his dark eyes glinting gold in the morning sun as he surveys my body... up... and... then down, leisurely taking his time, as if I'm not aware of what he is doing. *Excuse me.*

His voice dripping like dark melted chocolate says, "Oh, the coffee is *very* good." The corner of his mouth turns up; as he stares appraisingly at me.

I find myself blushing, the temperature of the room rises or maybe it's just me. I've had enough of his once over. In turn, my eyes run up and down the length of him with a look of total disdain, I say in a scathing voice, "The coffee is.....*quite* ordinary. Nothing special." And with that pronouncement, I set down my mug, turn on my heel and walk away. I can hear Ben and Vic giggle like twelve-year old school boys and clink their mugs together in camaraderie. Ugh..... Why does he have such an unnerving effect on me?

Heading out to join the girls on the porch, I yank the screen door open and run smack dab into a wall of muscle, clad in a cotton shirt smelling faintly of starch and a summer clothes line. Small pearl headed buttons lead my vision higher and higher to the heavens, where haloed in the morning sun I meet the most stunning blue eyes I have ever seen. A square jaw stretches into a slow smile of even white teeth, in stark contrast to ruddy bronze skin. Small crow's feet crinkle in laughter as his eyes look down on me. He must be in his early twenties; sun bleached curly blonde hair peeks below a cowboy hat, long enough to graze his shirt collar. *It's true, angels do exist.*

"Hold up there, little lady, you're running out here like a buffalo stampede on a Saturday night." The blonde god says to me.

I'm struck mute.... cat got my tongue...can't find an intelligent word in my head...and I believe the technical term is.... gob-struck. He is the most gorgeous thing I've ever seen. I feel dizzy and faint. I reach out a hand to steady myself against his chest, and just stand there... staring at him........not uttering a single word.

"Well, you must be one of the new gals on the ranch. Welcome," he chuckles. "I'm Scott Branson. I take care of the horses around here. Hope to see you down by the barns." He pats me on the shoulder as I stand blocking the doorway, causing him to walk around me. I turn and watch his broad shoulders saunter away in butt perfect Wrangler jeans, a body made taller and leaner by the two inch heels of his cowboy boots. *Oh, My God, I'm in love....* come down to the barn, *I'll move into the barn.* And with that the screen door slams, hitting me in the face...*Ouch!*....... I think I just brush burned my nose.........and my ears ring with the chorus of male snickering from across the room.

Chapter 5

Misplaced Affection

We were hired as junior staff counselors, the terms of our employment included arriving at camp a week before opening to help "spruce things up". Being a naïve, trusting soul, I assumed an extra week of camp without the encumbrance of parents, young campers and older peers, a teenage dream. That dream turned into a mini-nightmare of slave labor. Mornings started with Morris waking us to the sound of Scottish bagpipes wailing over the loud speaker, and the little camp "spruce up" proved to be five days of grueling work. While the girls cleaned the inside of the cabins, the guys tackled the outside work, painting, nailing down loose boards and repairing the mortar around cracked chimneys.

At the end of the day we dragged our weary bodies to dinner, too tired to move. The evenings spent sprawled on faded couches in the recreation building. The rec building holds every indoor activity created to wile away a rainy afternoon with the exception of ……a television. One of the first revelations discovered upon our arrival was the lack of television. It dawned on us, ten weeks of semi-forced confinement in the wilds of the Adirondack Mountains, with no television and a radio station that plays only classical favorites from the 50's. Music from our grandparent's era… translates into we're forced to rely upon our own devices for entertainment. And that spells trouble with Kat and Mac in the lead.

Even though exhausted, there is still energy to fuel raging teenage hormones. The relationship game begins, who will score and who won't. Or is it *whom* will score?

The pairing off begins, Emi Jo and Ben commandeer the couch, discussions over the evening newspaper turn into debates, the debates become a wrestling match or better described as a grope and fondle. Mac and Kat sit cross-legged on the clean but faded rug, playing poker. Instead of poker chips, they use peanuts; the peanuts will turn into dollars after their first paycheck.

Tee, Vic and I play *Scrabble,* or as we call it, *Battleship Scrabble,* most nights ending in an argument over a Spanish word Vic insists he can use. Tee's mother is sending us a Spanish dictionary.

Vic remains a mystery. At first, quiet and aloof, he preferred staying apart from the group, too cool to join in, but slowly the loneliness and isolation of the woods, combined with the necessity for socialization made him realize, he was stuck with us. We are his only options for age appropriate human contact this summer. And to our surprise, a mischievous devil lives inside of him. Even though he's hired as the lifeguard, he's hell bent on drowning us. Especially the girls…and more *specifically* me. And I'm running out of clothes. The dunking, dousing, spraying and splashing have taken a toll on my meager wardrobe. Did anyone say wet t-shirt contest. I refuse to wear white anymore. Tee says don't worry she has enough clothing to last the two of us the entire summer and into early fall. The thought of wearing pink, preppy shorts with a matching shirt and headband…makes me want to puke.

Vic's methods of dunking and drowning vary, depending on his mood, either a bucket suspended over a door jam, one tossed from behind a corner or a casual push off the dock.

This afternoon I made the mistake of walking out to the end of the dock, crouching down to study a patch of water lilies when suddenly from behind, I found myself propelled head first into the lake.

"Vicente Rienz," I sputter, my head braking through the surface of the water. "You stupid, immature idiot! What if I can't swim!"

He cups his hands in front of his mouth, mimicking a megaphone, calling out to me. "You have those beautiful long arms and legs, of course, you can swim."

"What!" He can't possibly be serious, my arms and legs make me look like a stretched out Gumby with boobs, he's insane. "You suck as a lifeguard." I call back to him. "I'm drowning! Look, I can't touch bottom." I scream, flaying my arms in a parody of a drowning victim, bobbing my head under water for extra effect. Except maybe this is not a joke.... and I am drowning, the water is cold and deep. I can't feel my toes, I'm freezing to death. That obnoxious shithead from the Bronx or God knows what ever portal of hell Morris and his wife dug him out of .....is trying to kill me. I fume even more as I watch him stretch out on the dock, his head resting on his elbow, his expression soft and amused..........watching me thrash and flail away, giving an award winning imitation of a drowning victim. His baseball hat cocked jauntily to the side, a smug smile on his face. He reaches one long arm to me saying in a sickeningly sweet voice, "Ellen, darling, just grab my hand." He wiggles his fingers enticingly over the edge of the dock. "I'll pull you in, just surrender to my masculine superiority."

So help me, if I grab his hand, my righteous anger will haul his sorry ass under and drown him. "Over my dead body will I give you my hand, I'll drown first!

"Well," he says, watching my pathetic attempts. "I guess I'll just have to assume my duties as lifeguard and save you." In one swift motion, he bounces to his feet, pulls his shirt over his head and starts to unbutton the top of his cut-off jeans… his hand reaches for the… zipper.

Oh my God… I realize with horror……he is going to strip down in front of me. And if the growing patch of white skin above his cut-offs is any indication, as he slowly and tantalizingly eases his zipper downward, he's not wearing underwear. My options dwindle to watching him perform a strip tease on the dock, being saved by this junior water terrorist or hauling my butt out of the water on my own. No way in hell is that Spanish Casanova gringo chasing me through the water.

"What are you doing?" I holler in disgust. "Stop it, stop it, right now. Leave your pants on for God's sake." At this point he has slid the zipper all the way down and begins wiggling his hips to help accelerate the decent of his tight shorts. The shocking display of white skin just below his waist band is getting larger. Ben is rolling on the grass, howling with laughter. Kat and Mac shout out burlesque taunts to encourage him. I hear them yelling, "Lower, lower, save her, Vic." Emi Jo is torn between her bond of friendship and giving into hysterical laughter. Tee, the only loyal one of the entire group, has come running down the dock with the buoy ring in her hand. God bless her heart, she really thinks I'm drowning.

"Vic! Stop taking off your clothes and go save her!" She screams flinging the life ring in totally the wrong direction, trips over the rope and proceeds to fall onto the dock in a tangled pink heap. "What is wrong with all of you, can't you see she's in trouble!"

At this point I realize my performance will not win any Oscar nominations so I kick off to shore, each stroke fueled by every curse word I've ever known, hurtled at Vicente Rienz's head... shouting at top of my lungs....so *everyone* hears. And who is there to greet me at the shore but ....Morris with a stern look on his face and Mrs. Erhart. "What's going on here?" They're standing at the edge of the lake, Morris has his hands on his hips, and his wife looks really pissed. *Oh, my God, damn it.*

"Maybe we need to assign more work to keep this group out of trouble." Mrs. Erhart says, riveting her cool blue gaze on me. "I'm shocked at you, Ellen."

Morris continues, "Ellen, I'm surprised. That kind of language is not acceptable, you should know better. Your reference letter was from a priest. What would Fr. Oligano say if he heard you?" *Ohhhhh boy,* plenty I'm sure. My mind groans.

"Ellen, this could be grounds for dismissal. Do you understand?" Mrs. Erhart continues with righteous indignation.

I mutely nod my head, water dripping down my nose, mixing with tears of frustration.

"Tomorrow the senior counselors arrive, followed by our campers." He frowns, shaking his head at my pathetic appearance. "Ellen, get back to your cabin and change before you freeze to death." Dismissing me, he turns his attention to the rest of the group. "I expected a little more maturity; we have a long summer and a great deal of responsibility ahead of us. So get back to work." With a disgusted shake of his head he stalks off in the direction of the administration cabin with his wife leading the way.

Vic comes running after me. "Ellen, wait, slow down,

I'm really sorry." He holds out his gray sweatshirt. "Elle, tossing you in the lake was a dumb idea. I didn't mean to get you in trouble. Take my sweatshirt before you freeze. Keep it," his voice laden with remorse. "I don't need it, please take it. I'm so sorry."

Over my dead body!" I hiss at him, turning on my heel, running down the trail in the direction of our cabin, dripping and shivering all the way. "I would rather freeze to death than take anything from you." I hurl the words over my shoulder.

My mind whirls with worry as I walk back to the cabin. I can't go home to Helen. I'll run away to the mountains, survive on nuts and berries. Anything is better than living with Helen. What will I do if the Erharts fire me? God, I hate Vic Rienz.

Chapter 6

Burt

The gossip at breakfast this morning centered on my boss, Burt, the chief naturalist at Camp High Point. Apparently he arrived late last night. I'm anxious to meet him, but the stories circulating around the breakfast table leave me filled with trepidation. Apparently the man is eccentric to a fault. Rumor has it; he owns property just outside of the camp boundaries and lives in a tree house, preferring to spend his time with the trees and animals, instead of people. Okay, I kind of get that….I'm trying to keep an open mind.

I strike out on the trail to the nature cabin unsure of what will meet me, following the winding path through the woods along a small stream. My shoes damp with morning dew as the shaded trail journeys deeper into the woods, the path bordered with hobble bush growing under dappled shafts of sunlight. Patches of pink sorrel are scattered throughout the ferns and moss that make up the forest floor.

The nature cabin sits isolated under a canopy of trees, about a quarter of a mile from the main camp, at the edge of a small lake. The rough-hewn building is constructed of hemlock logs with a pair of old-fashioned lead glass doors opening onto a small covered deck.

Knocking softly on the door I peer inside the cabin. "Hello, anyone here?"

"Helloooo," I call out again, taking a deep breath I venture into the dim interior of the cabin. Instantly I'm assailed by the scents of wood smoke and mildew.

I wrinkle my nose. "Hellooo! Anybody here!"

"Hey," booms a voice from the shrouded corner behind me, causing me to yelp in surprise. Instinctively I grab for the nearest object at hand, planning to ward off the unknown assailant. Glancing down I realize… the nearest object at hand was not my best choice.

"Sorry, did I scare you?" says the faceless voice.

"Yes!" Unfortunately, I startle easily. "Come out where I can see you. Is that you, Burt?"

"Who else would it be? The *boogie* man?" A small middle aged man walks out of the shadows carrying a crate. He sets the overflowing box down and reaches into his back pocket pulling out a red bandana to wipe off his hands. Leaning against the table he crosses his arms and observes me with keen green eyes. His eyes twinkle with good humor. Nodding his head in my direction he asks, "So Rambo, that's your weapon of choice? You might take out an unsuspecting butterfly with that thing, but it's no weapon of mass destruction." He shrugs his shoulder nonchalantly. "Gee, I didn't realize I was so *scary*. A whole butterfly net, am I *that* menacing?"

Okay, in my haste, I grabbed a butterfly net off the table. Looking at the slender pole with the dainty lace netting attached, it's doubtful I could fight off a mouse with this thing. I give the net a couple of quick swishes in mock display of my power.

"Oh, yeah, you wouldn't be so smug if you were a Monarch butterfly." I challenge. Great, I've just made a complete fool of myself in front of my new boss. Yes, I'm afraid of the dark and things that goes bump in the night…but there's no point admitting that to him… until absolutely necessary…preferably never…I've always had a soft spot for the Cowardly Lion, kindred spirits and all that.

"Oh, I'll be sure to put out the word; beware of the butterfly dragon queen wielding her net of death and destruction." He chuckles. "So, Dragon Queen, I *assume* you must be Ellen?"

His reddish blonde hair, thinning on top is tied back in a ponytail, forming a halo of loose ends framing his face. Pale green eyes wink out from small wire-rimmed glasses. His mouth turns up in a hint of a smile, as he studies me, taking in the details of my appearance. He seems amused.

"Yes, I'm Ellen McCauley; it's nice to meet you." I return his inspection. He is lean like a wild animal, not a spare ounce of fat on his body, and he moves in graceful silence. The story around the campfire is he can stalk and touch a deer before they even knew he's there. Based on my recent experience… this is no rumor. The companion freckles of a red head stand out in stark relief on his pale face.

With a laugh he reaches out to shake my hand, "I'm Burt Burganey." Dressed in a drab green shirt and rumpled khakis, he blends into the background of the cabin, except for his hiking boots, which are tied with neon green laces. "Hey, do you know how to make *falafel?*"

"What?" I think this man is a little crazy. Is this some nature term I'm supposed to know? I've noticed he has the habit of emphasizing certain *words* in a sentence to stress his point. Strange.

"You know, *falafel*, the fried chickpea balls you eat at a Lebanese restaurant. I had some last night and I want to try making them."

"Uhhhh, well," I proceed cautiously. "I've never been to a Lebanese restaurant or tried…what did you call it?'

"Falafel, I'll get some and we'll make it for lunch. Just thinking about them makes me hungry."

"Sounds great." I respond with enthusiasm…not. Fried chick pea balls, it can't possibly taste good.

He stands with his hands on his hips surveying the disarray of the cabin. "This should be the year we get organized. I have no idea where any of our equipment is located. My assistant last year was a *diaster*. He just threw things in boxes without regard to labels or sorting. Why don't you start pulling down the boxes from the shelves? Check to see if the contents inside match the label on the outside of the box." He scratches his head, looking around the room. "ehhhh, first, I guess we should *sweep* and clean up a little bit in here…broom and dustpan are…ummm, somewhere around here. I'm sure you'll find them. I, eh, have to check on…..um, something with Mr. Morris. It won't take *long*. I'll be right back to see how you are doing." With those parting words he turns and walks out the back door to his car. The vehicle is so tightly packed it's impossible to see out the rear view window. Gear spills out the open doors onto the dirt road looking like a yard sale gone bad. He pushes or pulls the extraneous gear into place, slams the doors, and disappears down the dirt road in a cloud of dust.

"Okay, the we, just became me. I'm not sure the assistant was the messy one, Burt seems a little disorganized." I mutter to myself looking around the dim interior of the cabin. The dark wood walls are bare. Cobwebs hang from the ceiling beams, and the windows are streaked with dirt. A set of raccoon tracks lead across the dusty floor to the chimney, its winter den. And it looks like the raccoon used the cabin as his personal latrine. *Ugh…* Equipment lays strewn about on the tables and benches as if the campers had walked out in the middle of a project. Morris said Burt liked to do things his own way, he wasn't kidding. *Whew, what a mess.* Looks like Cinder-Ellen to the rescue.

I sweep up small piles of dirt from the floor, and wash the wooden planks with oil soap until they gleam. Gagging, I clean mouse droppings and dried insect carcasses from the shelves before scrubbing them with pine disinfectant and hot water. Once started, I enjoy the task. Burt joined me half way through the job and we swept, scoured and polished in companionable silence, broken by a joke or a riddle he "insisted" on sharing with me.

After several hours, and countless buckets of water and cleaning supplies, the cabin sparkled. "Wow," Burt says, stepping back to survey our work. "I don't think this place has ever looked so *good.* You're a hard worker, Ellen. You did a great job."

Against my better judgment, I can't help but feel a glowing sense of pride over my accomplishment and his praise. The cabin gleams with the radiance that only comes from a good scrubbing. The air hangs heavy with the scent of oil soap and pine. Now it feels more like home, a sanctuary for the summer. And Burt is beginning to grow on me…

"That's enough for *today.*" He says handing me a can of what appears to be some kind of hippie juice.

"I agree. I don't think I could face another cobweb." I eye the can with suspicion, but I'm thirsty, and it's cold. And to my surprise, it's sweet and quite tasty.

"I'm glad to see you aren't afraid of spiders, it's *really* stupid to have a nature counselor afraid of bugs."

"I've had a few counselors over the years afraid of snakes, spiders, and mice. I even had one in a panic over a moth. Afraid of a *moth*?! Give me a break." He tilts his head back, and I watch his adam's apple bob up and down as he swallows. Wiping a hand over his mouth, he shakes his head, "It makes for a long summer and it just *freaks* the kids out when they see the nature counselor dancing on the table as a mouse scurries across the room." He looks at me in question. "You aren't afraid of mice, are you?"

"No." I giggle over the idea of me dancing on the table over a silly little mouse. "So where do you work when you are not at Camp?" I ask, tossing my soda can into the nearest garbage bin.

"I'm a biology teacher at a high school in Ohio. I teach college level field ecology during Christmas and Easter breaks." He pauses, chucking his can after mine, missing the trash bin completely; we watch it spin in circles on the floor, neither one of us moving to pick it up. "Last year I took a group to the rainforest in Costa Rica. It was the *best* week of my life." He picks up the can from the floor and mimics a jump shot into the garbage. "What about you? How do you spend your time when you're not in school?"

"Costa Rica. Wow. I've never been out of New York State. Coming to camp is the farthest I've been from home." I fumble for something interesting to say. "I go to school, hang out with my friends, hike in the woods, play basketball, the usual kid stuff." In other words, just call me lame and boring.

"Radical," he says looking at his watch. "I'm starving. It's time for dinner; did Hank and Marsha arrive yet?"

"Oh yeah, the chef and his wife, they came in last night. I haven't met them." I answer over the rumbling of my stomach. "Are they good cooks?"

"Yeah, if you're into that kind of food." He gets up, shutting the windows.

"What do you mean that kind of food?" My hungry stomach grumbles in panic. My mind conjures up images of mushrooms, Brussel sprouts, liverwurst, cheap hot dogs and canned spaghetti. "What do they cook?"

"Oh, normal stuff, meat, *potatoes* and vegetables." He replies with a shrug of his shoulders.

"And the problem with that is?"

"Well, maybe fine for you, but I'm a *vegan*." He answers as casually as if he said his favorite color was blue.

Putting down the stack of identification cards I was organizing, I look at him with suspicion. What the hell is a vegan? I think to myself. Sounds like something voodoo. Okay, he's weird……and I was just starting to like him. I close my eyes and sigh; what the hell did I get myself into, spending the summer working for some hippy nature nut who lives in a tree house. *Great*…...

Chapter 7

Head Over Horse Tail

The big day has arrived. Starting at one o'clock the gravel driveway leading into Camp High Point is packed bumper to bumper with cars and minivans bursting with campers eager to begin a summer filled with Adirondack adventures.

Activity counselors such as myself; escort the new arrivals to their proper cabins while resident counselors, who bunk with their charges, assist incoming children unpack and organize their gear. Each cabin bears the name of an Adirondack High Peak. Mt. Haystack is for the youngest group, followed by Santonini, Colden, Whiteface and so on until the highest peak in the Adirondacks, Mt. Marcy, is designated for the older campers.

After the majority of the children have arrived, I notice a little boy standing apart from the others. His parents gone, he looks lost, tears streaming down his face. I start to make my way over, when Vic appears, kneeling down beside him. I see him comforting and joking with the little boy, trying to ease his fear over being at camp for the first time. Gosh, I'm surprised he isn't offering the kid a cigarette….I watch as the two of them walk away hand and hand toward Haystack cabin, the little boy looking up at Vic, laughing at some silly joke, adoration shining from his eyes. *Hunh, go figure.*

…

Camp settles into a routine. Morris wakes us in the morning blaring horrendous music over the loud speaker ranging from bagpipes to opera, symphony, and even Israeli folk songs. Breakfast follows a flag ceremony and morning meditation. Returning to their cabins, the campers ready themselves for the day ahead, and the activity counselors hurry off to their respective stations. Resident counselors heave a sigh of relief and fall back into their bunks for some much needed morning R & R.

Days with Burt fall into an easy rhythm, morning hikes, paddles across mist shrouded lakes or up meandering streams. Afternoons devoted to nature related projects, collections, games and stories.

The silver lining in the slave bound existence of a junior staff counselor lies in our one afternoon a week off…free from kids…free from bosses……free from kitchen duty……free…free…free! And did I say free from lunch with Burt. Due to the schedule of programs and hikes, lunch with Burt is part of my job. Let's just say it's been a learning experience. A vegan learning experience.

Burt insists on bringing lunch from the tree house. It's true; he lives in some wooden structure high up in the tree tops just outside of the camp boundaries. Our daily fare includes delicacies such as tofu, almond milk, bean casseroles, hot dogs or cold cuts made from tofu. Along with brown rice, carrot juice, wheat bread, fruits and vegetables, some I don't even recognize. And God forbid no meat and no sugar. Apparently, a vegan is someone who consumes no animal protein. Reluctantly, I must admit some of the food is quite edible or my taste buds have gone into mountain mode. Along with the food is a dose of *the* Burt Burganey philosophy of life, stewardship of the earth, not getting hung up on material goods, working to make the world a better place. His moods change like quick silver, one minute he's serious, the next, telling jokes and outlandish stories. For instance, he claims one day he was standing so still in a field, a skunk walked right over his feet. And he swears, scouts honor, that he's touched a deer grazing in a meadow by using the slow stalking techniques of the Native Americans. He seems so sincere, I believe him. A little crazy, eccentric, moody, exasperating, messy and often late but I like him.

As much as I enjoy Burt's company, an afternoon off means…I can do what I want with no discussions to hurt my head; eat regular lunches of peanut butter sandwiches on white bread, chips, brownies, and a cold soda. *Ahhhhhh,* a little slice of heaven. And having an afternoon off means I can pursue that good looking object of my heart's desire… Cowboy Scott. Scott Branson. His family owns a ranch in Texas near the Erhart's. A professional rodeo rider, he broke his leg on a bucking bronco last winter. He's taking the summer off to run the stable at camp and recuperate from his injuries. Being older than me only serves to enhance his desirability.

What a hunk…..I've spent my afternoons off hanging around the stables, in hopes he will become infatuated with me, and we spend the summer holding hands looking into each other's eyes.

It's amazing how far fantasy can be distorted from reality. My scheme backfired……*big time.* In the fantasy, Scott adores me. In reality…I'm simply one of the annoying gog-struck girls tagging behind him. The man's shadow consists of a stream of worshipping little girls. I just happen to be the biggest one.

Oh, he lets me muck out the stalls, saddle the horses, tag along on a trail ride but his eyes gaze right over me…like I'm dead space.

So here I am on my day off, standing in a stall with a pitchfork, up to my ankles in you know what, and not a trace of Scott in sight. A clean stall with a bedding of yellow wood shavings, warm and glowing, a soft breeze blowing through an open window, air sweet with the scent of horse, a clean stall is a pleasant place to be. But with several layers of days old manure….it stinks. Sunlight streams into the stall, as I breathe in the dusky rich scent of horse, and my adolescent girl's version of infatuation deflates. I'm beginning to think my plan to attract Scott stinks….literally. With my mind busy formulating a new strategy; I heave a wheelbarrow full of manure toward the door and who should appear? *Terrific*……just what I need. Vic walks into the stall carrying a full bucket of water.

"Hey, you look like you could use a hand there, Cowgirl." That annoying lock of long hair falls across his forehead shading his eyes, but not before I see the smirk and mischievous glint.

"Thank you, but you're a little late." I reply primly, wiping the sweat from my brow on my shirt sleeve.

"What are you doing here?" Pretending not to know Vic and Scott became friends based on their mutual interest in horses. Vic's family has a ranch somewhere in Mexico; he worked as a *ranchero* since he was old enough to ride a pony. "Shouldn't you be throwing some unsuspecting girl in the lake, hoping to get her fired?"

He sets the bucket down on the stable floor. "Nope, I've sworn off throwing damsels into the lake, bad for my social life." He stops; a small smile plays across his face. "It's my afternoon off, so I stopped to check on a horse with a lame leg. Scott and I think she needs a rest and shouldn't be ridden for a while." He points at the pitchfork. "And what are you doing mucking out stalls on your afternoon off? Burt not working you hard enough?"

"I like horses."

"From where I'm standing, looks more like you like horse shit."

"Why don't you just mind your own business, go mug a camper, burn down the forest with that cigarette hanging out of your pocket, start a gang war, rob a bank, there are so many opportunities for your juvenile delinquent behavior than here in this stall with me."

"Why do you want to get rid of me? I could help you clean this stall. *Or*…is there someone else you wanted to help you?" He leans back against the stall door with a smug smile on his face.

Ohhh…..He is such an infuriating little creep. Except…he's not little…..by any stretch of the imagination. I can't help but notice how his broad shoulders fill the stall door….. and the sun streaming through the window lights up the dust motes floating around him like flecks of gold. And his eyes, dark chocolate caramel, amber gold. *Aggggh!* He is so annoying…..

"I could be *nice* to you, if you gave me a chance." He cocks his head sideways, voice steamy, laden with hot Latin undertones, and his eyes twinkle with mischief as they travel over my sweaty, dirt streaked body. His eyebrows dance up and down in a suggestive samba. "Very….nice."

He can't be serious, I'm a mess. Then I glance down and cringe, in the heat my shirt clings to my body like a drowning man on a life raft, a button or two undone just for extra effect. *shit*…

"I don't need your help." Pulling away the snug

garment in an attempt at modesty, I glare at him and point at the cigarette sticking out of his shirt pocket. "What are you doing smoking? If Morris catches you, you'll be fired. How stupid can you be?"

"I can take care of myself. I don't need a mother, I already have one. I have two packs for the entire summer so I can't exactly kill myself on forty-eight cigarettes." *Darn.*

"Suit yourself. No skin off my back. Why don't you get lost, I have a job to finish." I see his face wince at my callous brush off. God, he has the most beautiful eyes, dark, deep……and I feel myself falling into them. Whoa….pull in the reins…what am I doing, he's only playing me.

Straightening my shirt, I give him a withering look and assume a dignified pose, trying to forget I'm pushing a wheelbarrow of horse poop. "I can do the job myself. I like being around the horses and the……..exercise." I finish lamely.

Snorting, he gives me a speculative glance, "So why are you dressed in new jeans judging by the tag hanging off the back pocket, and your hair tied back with a pretty ribbon? The horses aren't going to notice."

"Crap," I curse, pulling off the offending tag. Groaning inwardly, I look like an idiot sporting the name, brand, price and size of my jeans.

"I can wear whatever I want. Why do you care?" I turn my back on him, setting the rake against the wall wishing him away by the sheer force of my will.

"Fine, have it your way," his face moments ago, teasing and laughing, closes to a hard edge devoid of emotion. "I would hate to keep you from your precious muck raking. I see how dedicated you are to the task." He spits out the words, thrusting the bucket of water into my arms. "Here, you want to learn about horses, finish filling the buckets and make sure each horse has a flake of hay. Rule number one: Horses need water and food. You know what comes out of them, now learn what goes in." He turns on his heel to stalk away when Scott's head appears in the doorframe.

"Euuuu," I sputter repressing a stinging retort, instantly changing moods and fixing a sappy-sweet smile on my face for Scott.

"Well, little lady, haven't you done a superb job. Hey Vic, look at how hard she's worked cleaning these stalls. Ellen, you must be exhausted." Scott kicks the shavings with his boot, smiling up at me. Oh, there is hope yet. He noticed me. Scott drawls "This stall looks more comfortable than my mattress." I glance over his shoulder to give Vic a smug smile as if to say "Told you so, smarty." Unfortunately Scott finishes his complement with this parting sting, "You work like a little heifer, a little she cow with a strong back and hunches."

Heifer!! My mind screams at the unintended insult, picturing a large black and white Holstein dairy cow placidly chewing her cud, over inflated udders swinging as she saunters back to the barn. She cow! Is my butt that big? I give a dubious glance at my behind. I hear Vic snort, choking on his laughter.

That's it, I'm done here. I turn to place the bucket on a hook, and as luck would have it, in doing so I step on the rake propped against the wall. The rake handle springs forward, whacking me on the head, and with the heavy bucket in my arms, I lose my balance…and fall sideways……. into the loaded wheelbarrow… full of "you know what"……followed by the bucket of water crashing over my head. *Splat!*

I'm sitting in manure, wet smelly disgusting horse poop seeping into my new jeans with a bucket over my head… Please God, let me die now, if you love me you'd grant me this one wish. I cannot face Scott and Vic Rienz covered with horse shit. Howls of hysterical laughter echo in the tin bucket. Well, there is nothing to be done for it; God refuses to grant my death wish. I can't sit in a pile of horse shit for eternity. And obviously, there will be no help from the two of them. I pull the bucket off my head; wipe the hair out of my eyes only to smear manure down the side of my face….sending the two of them into further bouts of laughter. Slumped on the stall floor, Vic rocks back and forth laughing, "Oh my God; I've never seen anything so funny in my entire life. She's covered with horse shit."

"Wet shit, no less!" Scott says in a fit of laughter. "Here, let me help you get out." Scott wipes the tears from his eyes as he sees me struggling to my feet, trying not to bury myself further in the muck. "I'm sorry, we shouldn't laugh but you look so damn funny! Like a little heifer that slipped coming into the barnyard." This only sends Vic into another bout of laughter as he staggers to his feet, leaning against the wall, hands on his knees trying to catch his breath. *I hope he chokes to death…*

As much as I'd love to be a good sport…some things are beyond humor. Lying in a pool of filth in front of the man that fills my fantasy dreams….and the jackass who has become my new nightmare, I just want to cry. So help me if I cry, I will personally hang myself.

Taking Scott's hand to pull myself out of the black fetid muck, I turn on them, my voice dripping in venom, "If either of you…..so much as breathes a word of this to anyone…….and I mean anyone, I will haunt you every day for the rest of your miserable lives and the lives of your children and grandchildren." Pointing my finger at them with a vengeance, I intone, "Do you understand me." The two of them nod, biting their lips to keep from laughing. *Jerks!* I turn with as much dignity as I can muster to stalk out of the barn, but not before I see Scott trying to wipe his manure covered hands on something other than his clothing, thus sending them into further hysterics.

*Ughhhhhhh…*there aren't enough Twinkies in the world to make this feel better.

Chapter 8

On Second Thought....

Returning to the barn after the "wheelbarrow" incident is out of the question, and besides, my ardor for Scott has cooled. Extinguished....doused...smothered.... not a spark left. Nothing like landing in a pile of horseshit to bring a girl to her senses.

I've spent the last week pleading with Emi Jo to switch with me so Vic and I don't have the same day off. Her sweet nature wants to say yes but her crush on Ben says no. I offered Scott as bait, but she wrinkled her nose and said horses stink. Apparently Ben takes her out in the canoe and practices his latest love songs as they paddle across the lake. She says it's all very romantic. Fine then.......

Upon consideration, spending my afternoon off in the woods, beside a quiet, peaceful lake, reading, sketching in my journal and swimming...sounds like a good thing...I like it.

The day dawned with no wind, the blue sky overhead broken only by the occasional puffy cloud scuttling across the horizon like a slow lumbering turtle. Two miles down the trail from camp a large rock juts into the lake, a perfect spot for a leisurely afternoon. Spreading my beach towel in a pool of sunshine, I stretch and breathe in the fresh mountain air, peace at last. Opening my pack...I wonder what to do first, swim, read my book, sketch,take a nap or eat my lunch.

Decisions......decisions......decisions. I see a chipmunk scurry across the rock and stop, his nose twitches in anticipation of sharing my lunch.

"Oh, no you don't." I laugh, wagging a finger at him. "That's my lunch and I have no intention of sharing it with you." I put the lunch back into my pack, away from his greedy little eyes. The chipmunk rubs his paws together, wiping them over his mouth in a vain attempt to make me feel guilty.

"I don't care how much you beg," I admonish the little critter. "It's not good for you. You need to fend for yourself. Now, shoo!" He chatters angrily at me, scooting off into the woods.

Walking to the edge of a boulder that stretches into the lake, I dive straight into the freezing water. The first contact numbs my skin as I burst to the surface but it's wonderful and I feel painfully alive, charged with energy. The swim washes away the heat and cares from the week; my body relaxes floating on the water's surface, watching the clouds slowly dance across the sky.

Finally, the goosebumps on my arms signal it's time to return to shore. As I doze on the towel, the warming rays of sun gently massage my skin into a state of relaxed languor, interrupted by the quiet movement of something creeping out onto the rock. The chipmunk.

"Back again, I see. Hungry?" Sitting up I reach into my pack for lunch, the little creature keenly watching my every move. "Me too." Placing a sandwich and apple on the towel, the chipmunk rubs his paws together in anticipation. "Fine then, just a nibble, don't tell Burt on me. Feeding wild animals is not a good idea. But your eyes are killing me and it's nice to have a friend."

Pulling a corner off my sandwich; I hold it out to him, quick as a flash he steals the piece and flees into the woods. "Ouch!" He didn't really bite me but his quick attack on my sandwich startled me. Serves me right.

"Careful, you can get a nasty bite from those little monsters."

"Aggggh!" I squeak in surprise. Who's standing at the edge of the woods……. but Vic. *Oh goodie*, just the company I was hoping for….an arrogant asshole. *Terrific.* There goes my peace and quiet.

"Sorry," he says, dropping down on the towel next to me, uninvited, I might add. "Did he bite you?" He picks up my hand examining my finger for injury.

"No," I say, snatching my hand back, but not before I feel the glowing heat of his touch travel up my arm. What the hell…..? "He just startled me when he grabbed the sandwich." I hasten to add.

"Does Burt know you are out here feeding the wildlife?" he teases.

"No, and you're not going to tell him." I retort. "Shouldn't you be at the stables rescuing damsels in distress from manure piles?"

"Na, did that already, gets boring. See one damsel in a manure pile, they all look the same after a while." He smiles, leaning back against the rock.

"You're not staying are you?" I make a shooing motion with my hand. "I was looking forward to some peace and quiet. The constant laughter and chuckling from this week are not welcome here. Now go."

"Sorry about that," he says. "You have to admit, it was pretty funny. Truce? No more laughing." He holds out his little finger for a pinky swear.

"How can I trust you?" I wave my hand dismissively at him. "I let my guard down and next thing I know you throw me in the lake or you're off tattling to Burt."

"I swear and I'm a man of my word," he says. Against

my better judgment, I hook my finger with his; and as our eyes meet, something inside of me melts. *shit*.... His arms are muscled and brown from the sun, he takes my breath away. I can't take my eyes off the patch of smooth skin showing through his open shirt collar. *Damn it.*

Still holding my finger, he says, "I'm sorry to disturb you. I wanted to finish this sketch of the lake and didn't see you until I was on the rock." He lets go of my finger..... and I feel bereft. "I'll be less of a bother than that chipmunk. I won't even mooch your lunch. I brought my own." He holds up his pack as proof.

"Umm," Sitting cross legged, I pull small pieces off my sandwich and chew slowly, ducking my head to hide the blush creeping across my cheeks. My heart whispers, *he likes you.* My mind screams, *I don't like him.*

He takes his sketch book and begins moving his pencil over a blank sheet of paper with quick sure strokes. I watch, fascinated by the fine articulation of muscle on his arm and shoulders.

Brushing away the stray crumbs, I stretch out on the towel, head propped up on my hand, aware he's watching me. His gaze appreciative of the new blue checkered bikini, not one of those shapeless bathing suits we're forced to wear in gym class. I saved my allowance for a month to buy it, without Helen's approval. She said it was not modest for a girl my age, and she sure wouldn't approve of me stretched out in front of Vic Rienz. He was the type of boy mothers warn their daughters about: sensual, magnetic and dangerous. He's forbidden fruit.

"Can I ask you something?" I question.

"Sure, what do you want to know?"

"How old are you? Morris said you were the youngest counselor. I find that hard to believe. You seem older, maybe not more mature, but older."

He shrugs his shoulders in a nonchalant way. "I'll be seventeen in the fall."

"Oh…so why did you take a lifeguard position when you seem to love art and photography?"

His eyes slide over to me, amused. "Well, Miss Twenty Questions, I like to swim." His hand makes quick slashes on the paper, occasionally glancing up. "And for me, my art is private. I rarely show my work to anyone."

"I can understand that, I keep a journal of nature sketches and whatever strikes my fancy on a particular day. My work isn't very good, and I live in horror one of my brothers will find it and publish excerpts in the local school paper." I sit up, pulling my knees to my chest. "So that's the only reason you took the lifeguarding position?"

"Oh," he raises his head from his drawing, a quirk to his mouth, a tightening of his lips. "I got in trouble at school this year. My father thought a summer in the Adirondacks would be a fitting punishment."

"Bad trouble?"

"Bad enough. My father used it as an excuse to keep me away from our ranch. When he heard Morris had a lifeguard position at camp, he signed me up……so here I am."

"Can you tell me about your life on the ranch?" Curiosity propels the question out of my mouth. "Do you have horses, brothers, sisters…..or come from a lair of dark demons?" I see him stiffen, knowing I've treaded on deep and murky waters. Everyone at camp babbles on and on about their parents, brothers and sisters, what Uncle Fred and Cousin Steven will be doing this summer. On and on to the point you want to blow your ears off.

Vic and I contribute very little about our families, apparently like me, there's very little he wants to share.

"Well........" He says with pensive look on his face, dark eyes probe deeply into mine, weighing how much to trust me. "Okay," he says slowly. "But someday, I'd like to hear your story. One would think a long-legged stork dropped you from the sky, and you grew up in the swamp raised by river otters or something."

"I'm not a big talker." I look at my hands, nervously averting my gaze. I become suddenly embarrassed and blush for the second time today under his steady scrutiny. I came to the mountains to escape my home life. It's not that bad, I know kids are abused and have all kinds of awful stuff happen to them. I just have Helen, a modern rendition of Cruella DiVille. This summer I vowed to erase her from my thoughts, not only a summer vacation, but a Helen vacation. And I'm not going back, not yet.

He notices the rising anxiety on my face, not wanting to push; he leans over and gently puts his finger on my lips. "Don't, I understand. I'm actually a patient guy." I nod against the pressure of his finger on my lips, and wonder how his lips would feel there.

He puts the sketch book down, throws the crust of his sandwich to the chipmunk, and gazes out over the lake before he speaks. Without looking at me he begins, "My full name is Vicente Esteban Menendez Rienz. My family is from Mexico, going back many generations, a bit of ruling dynasty in the local area. They own many businesses; foremost is the Rienz Rancho, a huge cattle ranch." He hesitates, thinking before he continues, "The Rancho has many buildings and family houses where my aunts and uncles and cousins live. I spent my summers riding with the *vaqueros,* that's Spanish for cowboys."

I sit quietly, fascinated by the story of his life. As he talks, I prop my head on my elbows and listen.

"My cousins and I prefer hanging out in the bunk house rather than the main complex with our families. You see, my father is a stubborn bullhead and so are his brothers. It's rare they agree upon anything." He taps the pencil against his sketchpad in a staccato rhythm. "Because my father went to college in the United States he handles the business end of the ranch and exports products to the U.S. In addition, he negotiates business deals for other wealthy families in Mexico. We have an apartment in New York City which he uses as his international base and where I went to high school. And until I screwed up last semester, I was allowed to spend my summers in Mexico. And for further punishment, my father insists I finish high school in Mexico this year." Vic pauses, looking at me. "Am I boring you?"

I shake my head hastily. "No, not at all. Mexico. Wow." God, my life is *so* lame and boring.

"Okay, I gave you a chance to save your ears." he continues, "I grew up fast and learned to be tough." He pauses. "I have three older brothers. Carlos and Juan finished school and work for the family in Mexico. Manuel is studying at the University of Southern California."

"Your mom lives with you in Mexico?"

"My mother," he sighs and shakes his head, "No." He pauses looking over the lake then back at me, his eyes haunted. "My mother lives in New York City, which is why I wanted to go to school there. Best of both worlds.

She grew up in Chicago; her family money is from the meat packing industry. She became a vegetarian in her teens and then married my father, whose family raises cattle for a living." He gives a sarcastic chuckle. "How ironic is that? Between her family and mine, she didn't have a chance."

"How did they meet?" I'm intrigued by the story.

"My parents met in New York City. She studied art at N.Y.U. He was in town for business and they met over cocktails at a bar. I never understood how the two of them got together, talk about opposites attracting. She is blonde, elegant, and sentimental. My father is a workaholic with a quick temper. I asked her once how they came to marry. She said it was love at first sight. They married and moved to Mexico before they even knew each other. She never fit in with my dark Spanish aunts; my uncles felt my father married beneath him because she was not of Spanish blood. She felt isolated on the ranch and after my little sister died of leukemia a few years ago, she gave up and started drinking." Vic pauses, tugging his lower lip between his teeth.

I lay a hand on his arm, "Don't say anymore, I understand." The loss of my mother still haunts me.

"No, I like to remember how she was before my sister died," he says, letting out a ragged breath. "She was different back then, laughing, and very talented. Her paintings were exquisite; with practice and the right environment, I think she would have been an accomplished artist. But the drinking went from sporadic to a daily habit. She's not the same woman. Now her talent swirls around ice cubes in a glass of vodka."

Vic drums his fingers on the sketch book. "My father refuses to divorce her. He is old school Catholic, it would create a scandal. Instead, he keeps a mistress in Mexico."

He cut his eyes to me, regretting his words. "I'm sorry; I shouldn't be telling you that," he apologizes.

Really, I try to keep the shock from registering on my face, I've never heard of anyone having a mistress. I blink my eyes several times to focus on his words. I'm not sure I even know what a mistress is.

I nod. "I'm so sorry."

"Don't feel sorry for me, Elle," he admonishes me. "I don't want anyone's pity. It's no big deal. If anything, I'm stronger because of it." He scrunches his shoulders forming an armor to ward off my empathy.

"Vic, I don't feel pity for you," I say, angry he misinterpreted my meaning. "I'm sorry because I can relate to your story."

"Enough of the past," he shakes his head ruefully, looking out over the lake with a wistful expression on his face. "God, it's beautiful here. Don't you wish we never had to leave? I can imagine building a little cabin in that clearing over there, like that old hermit Burt was telling us about the other night. Living off the land, hunting and fishing, never have to worry about anyone else."

"Sounds tempting," I agree. "But I'm not sure how long I would survive without hot water, cheese doodles and Twinkies, basic necessities in life. A girl has needs, you know." I roll over onto my stomach, trying to keep my tan lines even.

Vic wags his baby finger at me, teasing, "Pinky swear on that and I'll provide the Twinkies and cheese doodles."

"There has been enough pinky swearing for one day." I reach for his sketchbook. "Let me see that picture of yours, we can decide where the cabin is going."

He chuckles; handing over the book, and to my astonishment, there is no mountain lake scene, but a perfect likeness of me stares up from the page.

"Oh." Surprised, I ask, "What happened to the lake?"

"I like this scenery better," he tilts the corner of book, studying the picture, "You're very beautiful, Ellen. You just don't know it yet."

"Beautiful, me?" His eyes darken, and I get the feeling he wants to be the one to show me.

He holds out his hand and pulls me to my feet. How natural and easy his palm feels against mine, like I've held his hand often, that familiar. His eyes dilate deep and dark, the corners of his mouth soften into the hint of a smile. Against my better judgment, but as natural as breathing, blinking and sleeping, I reach up to touch his face and run my hand through his hair. He leans his cheek into my hand and pulls me against him. "Elle," his voice is soft and seductive. His hands move up my back to the nape of my neck. He bends and kisses me gently, waiting for my response and I melt against him. Wrapping me in his arms, he holds me close for a few moments. He kisses my forehead, and to my great disappointment, releases me. *ohhhh……..I was right… deep, dark chocolate with lots of warm caramel….*

And I realize cowboys, horses, and Twinkies are for little girls…big girls want deep, dark chocolate eyes, black hair kissed gold by the sun, teeth white as shaved curls of coconut against skin the color of vanilla-coffee cream, and the smell…… exotic, like a roasted spice from the rainforest….

He smiles, his eyes wide and serious, and the atmosphere between us changes, the animosity vanishes, replaced with something new, something so much better.

He nods in the direction of camp. "We'd better go; Morris will kill us if we're late for dinner."

Chapter 9

Raisin' Olde Glory

Holding up her flask of vodka, Kat proclaims, "It's tradition, we'll be camp legends." A summer rite of passage. What could go wrong? Oh, so wrong…..

Kat, keeper of hidden whiskey, forbidden cigarettes, and living life on the edge decided to expand our horizons beyond illicit alcohol and cigarettes to thievery. Yep, thievery. Goods stolen in the dark of night without prior consent of the property owners.

And what are we stealing……underwear….men's unmentionables, gotchies……briefs……and boxer shorts. Are we nuts? Yes, not quite certifiable, but well on our way.

And the question that begs to be asked is……Why? A combination of alcohol from Kat's flask and a crushing defeat in *Pictionary* called for retribution. It was guys versus girls in *Pictionary* last night and the guys annihilated us. Apparently Vic's artistic skills put our stick people to shame…….. and this morning, they couldn't let it go. The teasing and taunting lasted throughout the day. So the mood is ripe for…revenge. Nothing says vengeance like a woman scorned, and the more alcohol we drank, the more we were scorned.

"You want us to sneak into the guy's cabin and steal their underwear!" Tee squeals. She looks at Kat as if she has lost her mind. "Mr. Erhart will fire us on the spot and if his wife catches us, she'll burn us at the stake." Tee needs to drink more.

"Don't worry," Kat says as she passes the small silver

flask to Tee for encouragement. Where she gets the alcohol …we've yet to figure out. A still in the woods?

"We're too far into the summer for him to fire us and still keep the camp running." She waves her hands dramatically. "And besides he'll never know who ran the underwear up the flagpole. We'll sneak out under the cover of darkness and hoist them up the rigging. By morning the guys' boxers will be proudly waving from the top of flag pole. Done deal. They will be so pissed off."

"I don't think this is a good idea." I say.

"Oh, Ellen, grow up and stop being such a baby, for God's sake." Her mouth twists in disgust as she levels a withering look at me. "Sometimes you're afraid of your own shadow."

"Fine then, we're in." I throw back at her. No one calls me a baby, especially Kat.

The next thing I know, we're standing outside the guy's cabin, tonight was their turn to clean up the dining hall. We need to hurry before they get back. Hunkering down in the bushes surrounding the cabin we decide our plan of attack. The crickets send up a battle cry from the depths of the grass.

"Okay, the only fair way to do this is to draw straws. We'll pick to see who gets the shortest stick." Tee says. "One of us will go in the cabin, and the rest will stand guard outside. We don't have straws so I collected sticks."

"This is Kat's idea; she should go in and take them." Emi Jo insists.

"No way, I'm the brains of this operation. I shouldn't have to do everything." Kat says.

"That's why we'll draw straws." Tee has an innate

sense of fairness. "We're in this together. All for one and one for all." She gives a nervous giggle.

Except for the person who gets caught, I can't help but think as I draw a stick. That unlucky person will take the blame, possibly lose their job and at the very least, earn an unwanted trip into the lake if discovered by the guys.

Tee thrusts a small bundle of sticks out in front of her, like a warrior holding a shield going into battle. "Now," She commands. "Each of us takes a stick and I will keep the remaining one. The person with the shortest piece goes into the cabin. If caught, you have to swear you won't tell on the rest of us. There is no point in all of us getting in trouble. It will look like a one person operation." Who suddenly became the brains behind this mission? Next she'll be handing out poison capsules to take upon capture. With bated breath, we each draw a stick holding them in fisted hands, until Tee turns on the flashlight to compare lengths.

"Oh, come on!" I cry out. "Damn it!" In the small circle of light, it's obvious… I hold the shortest piece. My mind wanders to the sentence the judge will pronounce upon me when caught……death by hanging with a noose made of boxer shorts……..trampled by runaway underwear…brief electrocution.

"Oh, Ellen," Emi Jo pats my shoulder in sympathy. She glances at the dark cabin as if it just became a troll's lair.

"She won't go. She's afraid." Kat says in disgust.

"It's not a big deal." Tee hands me the flask. "You'll be fine. Drink up and get going before they get back." I fire a look at Kat, wishing her reduced to a pile of ash.

Damn it, I need more eye of a newt, rabbit gonads,

rotten monkey brains……or whatever, to cast an evil spell on her. I think she has gypsy blood in her that is pure witch evil.

Tee continues her instructions, oblivious to my hesitation. "Take the flashlight so you can find their shorts quickly without making a mess of the cabin. And be careful not to do anything to alert them that someone has been in. Go." With her hand at my back, Tee propels me down the path leading to the cabin. Twigs snap under foot, my heart hammers in my chest, and a dull roar fills my ears. A police siren would be quieter.

"We'll be right here and if we see them coming, we'll give a warning so you can escape." Tee promises. Her voice reassuring, but her eyes glance furtively about the woods.

My feet fly up the porch steps. I push open the screen door and run through……trip…crash ….and fall… flat on my face…...entangled in an ocean of dirty laundry.

"Quiet!" Kat hisses, "What the hell are you doing in there?"

"What do you think I'm doing?" I hiss back at her. "Going to a pajama party!" Picking my head up, I flash a beam of light around the interior of the cabin. Oh, my God, what a mess! Clothes litter the floor, covering every piece of furniture including the beds. And smell! Haven't they done laundry all summer long? The stinky toe of a sock bunched under my nose confirms the verdict. Ugh!

"These guys are pigs." I yell out the window. "They have clothes thrown everywhere."

"Well, just grab some and get out!" Emi Jo entreats. The urgent sound of her voice galvanizes me to my feet. The flashlight beam dances across the darkened room.

"Turn off the flashlight, do you want to give us

away!" Tee instructs from outside the window screen. Give us away? Us? Ummmmm.......who's standing ankle deep in smelly guy underwear. The worst kind of stink.

I flash the light low to the ground and collect shorts from different parts of the cabin. If luck is with me, I should have a pair from each one of them.

Outside the window, I hear Tee utter, "Oh, no!"

What do you mean, *oh, no!* Turning to leave, my hand on the door, I hear a muffled scream outside the window and the sound of running feet crashing through the brush. *Ohhhhhhh, shit!*

Switching the light off, I watch in panic as the dark silhouettes of Mac, Vic and Ben come up the porch steps. What are they doing back so early? How the hell did those female knuckleheads miss three noisy guys walking down the trail? I know they're drunk, but are they deaf and dumb as well? Aggh...they're on the porch! I'm caught, stuck, trapped....no place to escape. I am so screwed!

The door opens and the only means of escape is blocked except for the screened windows. And it's too late to unlatch a screen and jump out. In desperation, I dive under the nearest bed clutching my stash of underwear. I dare not breathe and recant every prayer I learned in Catholic grade school....Hail....Holy...Blessed ......Glory....Praise........Oh, Holy Hell, I can't remember any of them. I'm doomed to death by underwear suffocation hidden under a bed in a guy's bunkhouse. My tombstone will read......Here Lies an Idiot. Mac flips a switch and the room is flooded with light. With relief, I realize my hiding place is safe.

My heart is hammering so loud the whole camp must hear it screaming, "Here she is, here she is. Thief! Thief!

"I'm beat," Mac says throwing a T-shirt onto the floor, mere inches from my foot. "That camp softball tournament for tomorrow has been a bitch to plan. Rick and I have organized the teams to include the smaller campers with the older kids, spreading the skill level of the players throughout the teams to make them even. It's been a hell of a lot of work. I'll be glad when the whole damn thing is over. Hey Ben, I thought you were hanging out with Emi Jo tonight?"

"I had a few things to go over for tomorrow's awards ceremony, so I told her to go back with the girls." Ben says. I see his hand grab a towel off the floor, and his feet head for the door. "I'm going to take a quick shower."

Mac turns on Vic. "Hey Vic, I see you making eyes at Ellen." Mac's leering voice assaults my ears. "I wouldn't be wasting my time in here if I could be out in the woods with her." I gasp, smothering the noise with the dirty clothes, and then gag at the smell. Ugh, he is such a pig.

"Yeah, I heard she wasn't interested in spending time with you." Vic says. *Yea, Vic!* My mind shouts.

"She didn't protest that much if I remember correctly." I can hear the zipper go down on Mac's pants, squeezing my eyes tight as I hear them hit the floor. Please don't let me see, please don't let me see…...

"Don't worry about Ellen. Her neck isn't sporting hickeys like Emi Jo, cuz gentlemen don't bruise their ladies." Vic opens one of the windows and cool night air streams into the cabin. The thought of Vic nuzzling and kissing my neck sends tingles down my body, all the way down to…..oh……oh *my*……

As he turns from the window, his eyes lock on mine underneath the bed, his face registers a what-the-hell-are-you-doing-here look. I scuttle further back under the bed.

I will never listen to one of Kat's plans ever again, as long as I shall live. So help me God.

"Ah, she doesn't know what she's missing." Mac says. He lets out a long, disgusting belch. "I have several satisfied ladies in camp." I shudder in disgust under the bed….to think I ever let him touch me. *Ugh…*

"Why don't you just shut up and let us get some sleep. I'm beat and tomorrow's a busy day. I have to coach fifteen groups of swimmers." Vic flips the light switch off, plunging the cabin into blessed darkness.

"Hey man, what are you doing? I can't see." Ben comes back in, letting the screen door bang against the frame. "I'm too tired to take a shower. I'll take one in the morning."

"Good night, Ben." Vic calls out, walking over to the bed I'm hiding under and flops down, making the mattress sag, causing me to hug the floor. Thank God, I jumped under his bed instead of Mac's. He rolls over and pulls the blankets to one side as a curtain, concealing my hiding spot. "Just get into bed and shut up. What do you need to see anyway? All you do is drop your pants and fall into bed."

"I was flossing my teeth." Ben protests, as his belt buckle hits the floor followed by the protesting squeak of his bed springs.

"Floss them in the dark, go to bed!"

With the lights off, silence fills the dark cabin except for the rhythmic sound of relaxed even breathing.

Now what should I do? The cold night air is seeping up through the floor boards. I can't stay here all night, I'll be found in the morning, frozen in the fetal position on the floor. I'll just wait. Once they're deep asleep, I'll crawl from under the bed and slip out the door. Vic saw me but he didn't give me away. What a predicament.

After what seems like hours, I feel Vic move in the cot above me. He rolls onto the floor still wrapped in his blanket. I can't see his face only the gleam of his white T-shirt in the dark room.

"What the hell are you doing under my bed?" he hisses in a whisper. I shake my head frantically, waving my finger to hush him.

The clouds part in the sky overhead, sending a shaft of moonlight through the window. The light illuminates Vic's face, a mischievous twinkle gleams in his eyes. Muffled snores from the cots compete with the hoot of a lonely Great Horn owl off in the distance.

"If you wanted to get in my bed, there's an easier way." He murmurs into my ear.

"No, *Jeez louise*, I don't even know you that well."

"If you look under the covers, you'll know me better."

"Are you crazy?"

"You're under my bed, after lights out, with a fist full of dirty underwear crammed up against your face and you're asking me if I'm crazy?" I groan in reply. "All you had to do was ask. Always happy to accommodate a lady's wishes."

"Shhh," I hiss in panic as I hear a bed creak across the room.

"Don't worry; a herd of moose won't wake them up."

"Just get me out of here!"

"It might cost you." He shifts his weight and leans in closer.

"Anything, get me out!"

"A kiss."

"Now, are you nuts?" I push against his chest in a

feeble attempt to crawl out from underneath his cot. While the idea of a kiss is tempting, the location leaves much to be desired. "This is not my idea of romance, stuck under your bed with an armload of smelly underwear!"

"Just what are you doing with the underwear? Kinky….if I do say so."

"Nothing, it was Kat's idea."

"Oh, that makes it sane."

Ben moans in his sleep and his noisy snores cover our whispered conversation.

"Come on." He slides out from under the bed, pulling me to my feet. My legs cramped from lying in the same position give out as I try to put weight on them.

"Oww,"A small cry escapes as pins and needles of pain shoot through my numb limbs; luckily his arms catch me before I crash to the floor, causing certain disaster. Hidden by his body, we creep past his sleeping bunkmates as he half carries me across the room. The door swings open and he sets me on my feet, giving me enough space to place both hands on his chest and shove him backwards into the cabin where he trips, falling in a pile of laundry. "Hey!" He hisses at my back. "You owe me a kiss!"

"Kiss yourself." I taunt through the screen. And turning, I run down the steps onto the path leading through the woods, pumping my fist full of underwear in triumph over my head………mission accomplished.

I hear Ben yelling from inside the cabin. "Vic, what the hell are you doing? Close the door, you're letting the bugs in!"

Running through the underbrush, I hear Vic's voice echo through the trees. "I was letting a bug out, a pesky bug, who owes me an explanation in the morning."

...

By the time I reach our cabin, I'm so mad; I fly up the steps in a rage.

"Where were you!" I yell switching on the overhead light, pulling sleeping bags off my former friends, who henceforth shall be called traitors.

"I thought you were going to watch out for me! General Patton and his fifth army could have swooped down on the three of you in broad daylight and you'd miss them coming."

"What happened?" Tee asks. Her voice carries a note of horrified thrill.

"What do you think happened? I was this close to getting caught." I hold my fingers out measuring a barely discernible distance under her nose. "I almost froze to death lying underneath Vic's bed. Thank God, he was the only one who saw me hiding there." I throw the underwear on the floor, and kick it for good measure. "You didn't even wait for me! You deserted me, leaving me behind enemy lines! What kind of friends are you?" I pull Kat in her sleeping bag across the bed, glaring at her. "You're supposed to be so smart! You couldn't come up with a plan to divert them? Yell free beer, naked women in the woods, Yankee tickets! Anything for God's sake!

"Well," Emi Jo begins, "It got cold and we were trying to fix Tee's zipper and next thing we know, they were walking up the steps. It was too late, what could we to do?" She makes a face. "We feel bad for leaving you."

"Look you're fine, what's the big deal." Kat stretches and yawns, annoyed at the interruption to her beauty sleep. "Can't you just go to bed?" She burrows down into the cozy warmth of her sleeping bag.

"No!" I smack her over the head with a pillow. "Here is your stupid underwear, the three of you can figure out how to get them up the flag pole. I'm done. I had to lay on that cold damp floor listening to Mac brag about his sexual conquests. Ugh!" I shiver at the memory. "And just so you know, Emi Jo, Ben farts in his sleep."

"Oh, dirt, tell us more." Tee says, sitting up in bed always eager for gossip.

"Get your own dirt. Good night." I say, flopping down onto my bunk, turning my back on the three of them. I can't help but think…..maybe adventures aren't so glamourous.

…

As dawn begin its slow creep over camp, seven pairs of underwear fly from the flag pole rigging, gently billowing in the morning breeze. Assembled outside the dining hall for morning salute and meditation, the entire camp enjoys the spectacle of boxers and panties flying in place of old Glory. A great deal of laughter and pointing accompany the question of who put them up the flagpole.

"Could someone explain why our underwear is up there with the guys?" I whisper in Emi Jo's ear. Of course, my favorite ones are up there. I knew sleeping in while they finished the job was a bad idea.

Flying from the pole interspersed with the boxers, hang Kate's red lace panties more fitting for a lady of the evening than a camp counselor along with Emi Jo's white briefs, Tee's days of the week undies and my perfectly innocent pink panties. Tee wears days of the week underwear, what would you expect. And of course, being Wednesday, Wednesday's panties fly from the pole.

"Shh." Emi Jo says, staring straight ahead with a look

of innocence on her face. "Don't let them see us talking. Act like this is just as much a surprise to us as the rest of the camp." She raises her voice. "Wow, who could have done such a thing?" She's a terrible actor. We need to shut her up or we're busted.

"We added our personal contribution to throw Erhart off," Tee whispers smugly. "Pretty smart, huh?" *Just brilliant.*

I can't look in the direction of the Erharts. I fear guilt is written across my face in bold neon letters. *She took them!*

Mr. Erhart is beyond furious and then some. He walks to the pole, tugging down the rigging, removing the contraband. He turns to the assembled group and in a tight voice fumes, "This type of immature behavior will not, I repeat, *Will not* be tolerated at Camp High Point." He walks through the campers and counselors, his hands behind his back like a prison warden, looking intently for the slightest speck of guilt. "If these pranks continue I will start canceling activities. We can spend the rest of the summer cleaning or reading in our cabins." This announcement is followed by a chorus of groans. "If another prank occurs, the activities of the day will be canceled. I will continue canceling activities as I see fit to protect the safety of the campers. Is this clear?" He glares at the group. "These pranks get out of control and people get hurt. Is there anyone who fails to understand me?" A chorus of "No, Mr. Morris" rises up on the morning air from the assembled group. "Now everyone go into breakfast and that will be the last of this nonsense." With that pronouncement he stalks to the trash can and tosses the underwear into it. *Damn, my favorite pair.*

"Look at the trio of fools standing over there, they're

furious." Kat, the voice of wisdom suppresses a giggle, shoving her hands into the pouch of her hoodie.

"Yeah, especially Mac, he recognizes his boxers." Emi Jo says. "Ellen, you did a great job taking a variety of colors and sizes. Those are Ben's, second ones down the line."

"Shh," I look at her with shock. "How do you know which ones are his?"

"It's not what you think, gutter mind." She starts to explain when three pissed off faces come stalking in our direction. "Oh, boy, here they come, play it cool."

"Good morning, my dear ladies." Ben says. He looks at the four of us with feigned devotion etched on his face. "Lovely morning for a little flagpole activity, isn't it? My, my, I wonder how those smelly boxers from our cabin got up there on that little bitty flagpole."

"I don't know how you did it, but you'll pay." Mac takes a menacing step toward us.

I look at Vic, he shakes his head ever so slightly, indicating our secret is safe.

"Beats me, underwear just don't fly up flagpoles." Kat shrugs her shoulders.

"I think it was the four of you," Mac shoves his face close to Kat. "So watch your back."

"Fuck you." She shoots him the bird. I'm going to faint. Flying hand gestures are not condoned at camp.

"And the same goes for you, that looks like our underwear up there." Tee gets in Mac's face. "How do we know you didn't do it and you're just bluffing?" Apparently Tee has a taste for intrigue, she's enjoying every second of this dialogue.

With the fun over, everyone heads to the dining hall; tagging behind I prefer to be last in line. Until this incident blows over I intend to avoid social contact for….ever. And then I notice Vic standing behind me. He slips his hands on my hips and breathes these words softly into my ear, "Ella, Ella, my mia bella, the next time you see my underwear, darling, they aren't going to be flying from any flagpole. And just for the record, I don't wear any." And with that he gives the hollow space of my hips a sensual squeeze and walks away………

Oh my God, what have I got myself into? I'm paralyzed with a titillating fear running up the back of my spine……fueled by the possibility of a delicious threat……and the implications of his whispered words.

Chapter 10

A Little Illegal

A few days after the "boxer incident" Vic saunters across the dining hall, stopping to pour a glass of water from the pitcher on our table. He leans over whispering in my ear, "The Erharts are going out tonight. It's a secret; no one is supposed to know. But after lights out, a bunch of us are going down to the beach for a moonlight swim. Why don't I come by your cabin and we'll walk down to the lake together." Behind the cover of my hair, I feel his tongue lightly fleck over my ear. "I think you owe me something, and I'm ready to collect."

Jeepers creepers. Sneaking out after curfew…….against all the rules…….. into the dark……. lions and tigers and Vic…..*oh my*. Everyone else has been creeping around camp at night, except for yours truly and Tee. And Vic wants to collect……..the kiss. Something about him suggests…he has kissed more than a few girls and I'm suspicious he knows *stuff*. I feel anticipation titillated by fear, a flavor new to me, but rather yummy…..

…

Temperatures hovering in the eighties call for one thing, a clandestine moonlight swim. The night is cast in the light of a full moon, the lake bathed in the soft sepia shadows of black and white. With the Erharts off for the night and the campers snug in their bunks, it's time for operation S.W.I.M. (Swim Without Informing Morris) Eight pairs of shorts and T-shirts litter the bushes lining the shore as we shuck down to bathing suits and dive into the inky black depths of the lake, surfacing amid suppressed squeals of laughter, giggling, and splashing. The water feels exhilarating against our hot skin. Only Mac eases into the lake carefully, holding a small baggy over his head; swimming a slow one handed crawl out to the raft. Kat climbs up the ladder jeering at him to "hurry up, slow poke".

To avoid detection we swam out from the west end of camp, making the distance to the raft a longer swim than if we had left directly from the beach. Emi Jo almost didn't make it; but Vic swam along beside her and brought a life jacket along in case anyone needed help.

The barrels under the raft make gurgling sounds as we take turns diving off, slicing though the midnight black water causing the raft to lift and fall in our wake. At last exhausted, we collapse onto the swaying raft forming a circle of heaving chests and spent muscles. We're momentarily struck silent by the beauty and solitude of the lake on this sultry evening. An island afloat, cast in the light of the moon. We're moon bathing, in beams of moonlight that throw cooling rays onto the rough tarmac of the raft.

With my head cradled on Vic's shoulder, my chest heaves with the exertion from the swim. I fume looking over at him.... he's hardly breathing........all that swim practice, he's in such good shape...maybe I should have eaten fewer Twinkies over the winter........ taken track practice more seriously.......learned tennis.........well, let's not get crazy here.

On sudden impulse, I lean over and plant a quick kiss on his wet lips. "There we're even, debt paid." He smiles, shaking his head. "Later, *caro*." My lips carry the faint taste of a recent cigarette. He brought two packs stashed in his duffle bag to last through the summer, only one a day……he can be very disciplined…. sometimes.

At last cool, replete from the rigors of swimming and diving; everyone stretches out, watching the stars create a luminous moment in the sky overhead.

"Come on, Mac, what are you waiting for?" asks Patti, one of the resident counselors and Mac's newest conquest. A voluptuous dark haired beauty, although older, she appears quite taken with him. There is no accounting for taste.

"Let's get lit," she urges him.

I exchange a look of trepidation with Vic, light up what, remembering the baggy held aloft as Mac swam out to the raft.

"Yeah, sure, okay, who hasn't had a joint before?" Mac asks looking around. No one wants to admit to being marijuana virgin. Everyone just shrugs their shoulders like "no big deal." Personally I'm freaking out. *Oh, boy…….what am I going to do?* I've never smoked before, let alone *pot*!

"I have three joints. That should be enough for everybody to get a little buzz going." He holds the baggy over his head, shaking it as a long lost treasure reclaimed. Reaching in the bag he takes out matches, carefully laying the joints side by side on the top of the plastic bag. Suddenly all conversation on the raft stills, every eye focused on the dim outline of the joints.

"Holy shit," I mutter under my breath…..*Dorothy, we're not in Kansas anymore.*

"I have some vodka." Kat rolls over, revealing a silver flask tucked into the back of her bathing suit. What is she? A Girl Scout of calamity and disaster? Her motto, be prepared to get her friends shit faced and into trouble.

"Hey Mac, how about we smoke only two of the

joints and Kat's vodka." Vic says, sitting up, alert to a potentially dangerous situation. "We have to swim back across the lake. Even if we take the short way, the water is still deep. I don't want to play lifeguard tonight. Let's take it easy and save the rest for another time."

"Aw," Patti whines, looking like a disappointed child at the candy store who can only have one lollipop instead of the whole jar. "I was looking forward to getting high." The reason for her attraction to Mac becoming clear as she greedily eyes the joints. How and where does one get pot, unheard of in my circle of friends….along with a number of other subjects……I think the only kids in school more lacking in worldly experiences than myself….was the chess club.

"You're probably right." Mac puts one of the joints back in the bag, leaning down to kiss Patti full on the mouth promising, "We'll finish the other one when we get back on shore, I have plenty more stashed away for safe keeping."

"Oh, my summer hero!" She gushes. *Oh, please!* Superman he's not, Wiley Coyote, maybe…

Mac strikes a match. The flare momentarily blinds our night sensitive eyes, turning the end of the joint into a glowing ember, enticing the taste of the forbidden. He holds the roll to his lips and pulls a deep draft into his lungs. I watched in fascination. Kat and Patti pass the joint between them, taking deep breaths with practiced ease. Closing their eyes, they lean their heads back to send the fumes deep into their lungs, then exhale, the smoke hanging like a curtain in the night air.

"I'll pass," Tee says, waving her hands to fan away the sweet smelling smoke screen. "Just the smell makes me nauseous." She hands it to me.

Looking at the joint in my hand, I stall…I'm not sure what to do with it. *Marijuana virgin, oh boy…*

Vic whispers in my ear, "I'm going pass, you try it. I've done it before and I want to stay alert so everyone gets back to shore safely." He puts his arm around my waist, pulling me closer, "Just relax and take a slow long breath into your lungs. Don't hurry, hold it there for a few seconds and exhale."

I crane my head back to look at him in astonishment. His list of accomplishments never ceases to amaze me. I'm sure on that ranch in Mexico, he and the vaqueros probably grew marijuana, rolled their own joints and had nightly pot parties. Ho hum….another day on the ranch…

Leaning back against his chest, I pull the pungent smoke down into my lungs, trying not to cough or choke, hold for a few seconds and exhale. A few minutes later a sweet sense of euphoria begins to snake and curl through my limbs, relaxing and exhilarating at the same time.

Emi Jo takes the joint, and inhales too quickly causing her to cough and choke.

"Here, try again," Ben says, holding the joint for her until she regains her composure. "This is good shit."

"I wouldn't know." Emi Jo says and tries again, inhaling without a problem. "I think I like cigars better." Several minutes later, "ohh…….maybe not, this feels pretty good."

"Told you," I say, as the silver flask comes around the circle, catching and reflecting the sparse light. I take only a small sip, not liking the bitter taste of vodka. "Mac, where do you get all this stuff?" I ask as the joints are passed back and forth. They say you don't get stoned the first time but I feel the stars moving closer to the raft.

Taking another hit off the joint, I pass it to Ben.

"For me to know and you to never find out." Mac takes the flask and salutes the sky.

"Why did you come to camp?" Tee asks him, sampling the vodka after wiping the top of the flask with her shirt tail. "I thought this kid stuff would be boring for you. You seemed to live a pretty fast paced life back home."

"I don't know," he gives a careless shrug of his shoulders. "I want to go into professional coaching or teach phys-ed so coming up here gives me some experience. I like the woods, the money and …..a little bootie." He pulls Patti into his arms, lowering her down on the raft, covering her body in a passionate embrace.

The raft bobs in the water like a lazy cork, as we point out constellations, giggling, making up our own names for the star clusters.

"Donkey's butt"

"Three little pigs"

"Looks like a guy's…anatomy?"

"Knock, knock," Someone calls.

"Who's there?"

"Star light, Star bright."

"Star light, Star bright who?"

"Star light, Star bright, wish I may, wish I might, aren't you glad you got lit tonight."

Finally Kat can't take it anymore. "I'm freezing my ass off. I'm going to swim back to shore, anybody else ready?" She shakes her head in disgust or jealousy at the moans coming out of Mac and Patti. "You're disgusting, get a room," she admonishes them. Kat's on again, off again relationship with the boyfriend back home is temporarily on hold, and the lack of male companionship this summer is making her crazy......causing those around her to suffer....greatly.

Ben leads the exodus off the raft with a cannon ball, soaking the passion entwined couple. The raft pitches and rocks threatening to throw them off as we follow Ben into the water.

"You bastards!" Mac yells over the lake.

Tripping and giggling, we stumble over the slippery rocks lining the water's edge and fumble in the dark to retrieve the shorts, shirts and sneakers left behind. Shivering, we share the few towels that only Tee thought to bring along, but this does little to dispel the chill from our wet bathing suits.

Vic and I lag behind, letting the others lead the way down the darkened path to the cabins. "Here, take my sweatshirt," he says, noticing the goose bumps on my arms. He pulls his swimming hoodie over my head. The shark mascot on the front shines in the moonlight, the word captain spelled down the left arm.

Damp tendrils of curls form as I shake my hair free of the rubber band and wiggle into the warmth of his oversized sweatshirt. Pushing up the cuffs, I help him smooth his shirt down, running my hands over his torso. Feeling mischievous, I stand on my tip toes, giving him a quick kiss before sprinting away, daring him to chase me.

I have rather long legs and ran track this spring, but barely cover ten feet when two strong arms grab and scoop me up. The giddy feeling from the joint only intensifies the maleness of his presence.

"Thought you'd get away, didn't you?"

Truth be told, I didn't try very hard.....a slow turtle would have caught me. The same thought on our minds as he pulls me in close. His heat contagious, warming my skin, seeping into my chest, and slowly working its way south. His lips slowly meet mine, soft and tentative at first, seeking my response. As I lean in craving more, his arms coil around me molding our bodies together. I tilt my head back, loving the rough texture of his cheek and jaw beneath my hand. I whisper, "I didn't really want to get away."

"Too many Twinkies this winter?"

"What!" I squeal in righteous indignation. I can feel him chuckling against my hair.

"Elle, I don't care how many Twinkies you eat. I'll always catch you."

"Promise?"

"Promise."

He lets out a ragged breath touching his forehead to mine. He pushes my hair to the side, kissing the tender hollow of my neck, sending delicious tingles down my spine. His mouth works its way up my jaw to my lips which part under the demands of his mouth and our tongues entwine. Trailing up my back, squeezing, kneading, his hands sweetly caress my body. I groan and tilt my hips against him. *Wow and double wow!* So much for kissing the boy next door……..now this is a kiss.

"Hey, you two, break it up." Kat hisses, appearing out of the dark. I jump two feet in the air and smack my head on the trunk of a tree.

"Ouch! Kat! Sweet Jesus, just give me a heart attack, why don't you! What!"

"Morris is back and prowling the camp." She pulls us apart, dragging me down the path to our cabin. "Hurry up before he catches us. What the hell were you doing necking out in the open? How stupid can you be, at least hide in the bushes." She looks over her shoulder in the direction of the raft silhouetted in the moonlight. "Sure hope Mac and Patti are fast swimmers. It would be a shame if they got caught…" She cackles in delight. Sometimes she can be downright *scary*.

Chapter 11

Rock Jumpin'

Today the camp counselors have the day off. We're between sessions with a new load of campers arriving tomorrow. At breakfast this morning, I found a note in the back pocket of my jeans. The message read, *Meet me by the old boathouse and wear your bathing suit.* Signed, *you know who*. I'm seriously considering registering my butt with the United States Postal Service. Vic has declared the back pocket of my jeans his own personal message depot. I find little love notes; invitations to meet him in the woods, jokes and riddles to share with Burt and even camp gossip left in my pocket. Personally, I think it's an excuse for him to feel up my ass, but what do I know, except the back pocket of my jeans is getting more mail than Santa Claus at Christmas. And just for the record, his hand lingers a little too long on my butt. Isn't that like defacing government property, or something?

...

At the far end of camp sits the boathouse. Neglected for years, the building has a decided list to one side with the shingles weathered to a silver grey. The roof, entirely covered in green moss, is home to small ferns and baby pine trees sprouting from the emerald turf. The dock is more a suggestion than a reality, laying half in and half out of the water. An old aluminum canoe is turned upside down on the dock; sides marked with dents and the gunnels mottled with chipped paint. Vic discovered the canoe in the boathouse when he was searching for buoys to rope off the swimming area. The name, *Polly*, is scripted in faded black letters across the bow. Considering the canoe was abandoned under a pile of old moldy lifejackets, it looks surprisingly seaworthy. Not a gaping hole to be seen.

Our destination is a group of islands on the opposite side of the lake. The canoe paddles crafted of ash wood are signed and dated by a local carpenter. They feel smooth and sleek under our hands as we dip them into the lake. Small dotted trails follow in the water as drops spin off in the rhythm of lift, dip, and pull. We paddle along in companionable silence, happy to be together, no responsibilities, and the entire afternoon stretching out in front of us. Vic pauses occasionally, putting his paddle down to pick up his camera, trying to capture the mountain images reflected on the lake. Off in the distance a loon's head pops to the surface from a dive.

"Ella, Ella, my mia bella," he calls, pointing his camera at me until I swivel on the seat, laughing at his persistence and strike a silly pose. *Snap,* clicks the shutter over the lens. My hair bleached to a honey blonde by the sun, lifts and floats in the gentle breeze. Skin tanned to a peachy golden glow, toned by hard work and hiking.........today for the first time in my life.....I feel almost pretty.....somehow worthy of his attention.

The warmth of the sun seeps through the thin cotton shirt covering my bathing suit. Cicadas call from a distant shore and an osprey soars on the thermals above, alert to the fish living in the shadowed waters below.

Vic points to a small J-shaped island, the center covered with trees, the shoreline broken by a small beach and at the far end a secluded cove bordered by rocks, flat and open, perfect for sunning. The island is dotted with small scraggly pines and blueberry bushes, while moss and golden lichens coat the rock surfaces. The western side bares a steep jagged slope that falls off quickly into the deep water below.

I smile, giving him the thumbs up, and sink my paddle into the water, eager to explore the island. The bow of the boat scrapes against the rocky shore, wading into ankle deep water; I hold the canoe steady for Vic to climb out. Securing the boat to a dead tree branch, we turn to survey our own private retreat.

I lead the way over to a flat rock, "Why don't we put our towels down here, I think there is enough room." The boulder has a smooth edge sloping down to the water for a perfect sunbathing spot.

Vic tousles my head affectionately and dives into the water swimming away with strong, clean strokes. Momentarily distracted by the sight of his powerful back cutting through the water, I stop, gazing in admiration.

Shading my eyes against the glare of the sun, I watch Vic hoist himself out of the water and begin scaling the steep cliff rising straight out of the water. "What the hell is he doing?" I watch with mounting dread, if he falls, it's straight down to the water. How deep is it there?

My heart pounding, a cold chill grips my spine even in the heat of the afternoon. As he reaches the top of the summit about twenty feet above the water, he stands up and waves.

"Vic," I yell out in fear. I watch in horror as he trips on an exposed tree root, loses his balance, and with arms flaying…. plunges down the cliff toward the rocks below. The scene clicks in slow motion frames before my eyes as I watch him plummet into the water.

Frozen in horror, I can't move. Then with a scream, I dive into the water, my eyes trained on the spot where

Vic went down; praying with each stroke. Swimming alongside of the cliff I will his body to come up, choking back a sob when he doesn't surface. As I reach the area, the water erupts in a torrent of bubbles, followed by a head of black hair and dark eyes alight with golden sparks of mischief. I throw my arms around him like a drowning victim clutching a lifeline.

"Hello love, decided to go for a swim, did you?" he asks, gasping for air to fill his heaving chest.

"Are you all right? You could have been killed!" I cry, clutching his neck.

"I'm fine. It's a cliff jumping rock. All the local kids come out and go jumping. Ben and I ran into a group of them hiking through camp the other day. They call it Osprey Island and they told us where to jump without crashing onto the rocks. There's an X carved on top of the rock where you start your dive. Did I scare you?" he asks with feinted innocence, whipping his long hair, sending streams of water spinning out to break the glistening surface of the cove.

"Yes! I thought you were falling to your death." I exclaim. "This was a joke?" My voice remains low with barbs of venom. "You jerk! You're going to wish you had drowned, mister!" I yell, grabbing his head, pushing him under with little success due to his broad shoulders and strong forearms. I push, shove, sputter and swear. My clumsy attempts to drown him only result in him giving *me* mouth to mouth resuscitation……of the romantic type.

"Elle, I shouldn't have teased you. I'll show you how, it's easy. Trust me, mia, come on," he pleads, leading me toward the cliff. The rocky shore casts a shadow over the water.

I protest, "No way."

"It's easy. Really, follow me."

With caution, I climb the steep rock face trailing several yards behind him. At the top I mentally take the three running steps that would launch me out over the lake….plunging into the cool depths to surface, exhilarated by the experience. *I don't know…..*

Tentatively looking over the edge to the water below, I think to myself…why does it always look higher when you're at the top looking down, than from the bottom looking up? *Holy crap*. I start backing up, only to run into the solid wall of Vic's chest as his hands cradle my elbows. He pulls me close, leaning his head in to brush the side of my face as he gives me instructions, "Just watch and follow my lead. Start back here, take three running steps, you'll be flying. It's awesome, trust me."

"This is waaay coool!" Vic whoops in pure joy as he plunges over the edge, landing in a clean splash below.

"Come on, Elle, you'll love it," his voice echoes up the side of the rock face. As he watches me hesitate, he stretches out his arms wide singing, "Ella, Ella, my mia bella, come on! Trust me, I'm right here, I won't leave. Come on, baby, fly!"

He extends his arms, an invitation and like the siren song calling to ancient sailors of the sea, his voice beckons and, willingly, I go.

Taking a deep breath, I push off, take three running steps and leap off the ledge…….down I plunge…..the breath whizzes out of my lungs with a scream, my stomach drops, my heart races and I've never had so much fun in my entire life! *Yahooooo…*

…

The adrenaline rush fades after several more jumps.

Spent, we lay on our towels listening to the hum of cicadas chorusing, *summer, summer,* through the treetops.

With a few hours before we have to be back at camp, I breathe in the peace and solitude of the island. Peering out from under the sheltering brim of my hat, I hear the *click* of a camera shutter, aimed directly at my half hidden face.

"Don't you have anything better to waste your film on?" I ask, rolling over to my side, watching as he continues to click off frame after frame.

"Nope," he says aiming the lens in my direction, adjusting angles and changing position to catch the available light. "I'll enlarge these and hang them on my bedroom wall."

"It's going to get crowded in there with all of us. *Jeez, I've never been a pin-up girl for a guy's bedroom wall.*

He moves the camera from his face, a wicked gleam in his black eyes, those eyes that catch and hold flirting lights of gold, dazzling the very air around them. He's not excessively handsome, yet there is an arresting quality to his face, the light plays off his sharp angled cheekbones, long generous lips rest above a slight cleft in his chin. The eyes, by far…….totally his best feature. At first I found the gold surrounding the dark iris, disturbing. What was once disturbing, translates into irresistible. I'm powerless to resist this alluring attraction to him.

"Hey, fair is fair, let me take a few pictures of you. I'll add them to my collection of boyfriends. All those boyfriends, their pictures cover my entire bedroom wall." I stick my tongue out at him reaching for the camera.

"Careful with that tongue, or was that an invitation?" He cocks his head; the leering look in his eyes suggests he has other things on his mind than taking pictures.

"Hand me the camera, Romeo," I take the camera, surprised at the heaviness of the cool metal resting in my palm.

"Now come over here and show me how to work this thing." I hold the lens piece up to my eye and view the lake and surrounding shoreline.

I feel him come behind me and steady the camera. The warm touch of his skin against my back, his breath tracing curls of desire down my neck…and suddenly I have *other* things on my mind than photography……..*oh*, so many other things.

"Concentrate," he commands. *Spoil sport.* And how can I concentrate with him only wearing cutoff jeans, brushing his naked shoulders on my bare skin? *And I know what he wears under those cutoffs…..nothing!* He persists, showing me how the various dials and lenses work until I'm able to bring an object in from a bleary image to sharp focus.

"Go sit over by the rock." I brace the camera in my hand, point to a rock framed by the trees and lake.

"I'm not posing like some girly model," he says. *Click*, goes the shutter of the camera. "Hey," he says with a disarming grin. *Click* goes the shutter again. "Fine, where do you want me?" He flops down, assuming a cheesy model pose. I indulge in a moment of unabashed ogling before depressing the shutter. *Yum.* Where is that sweet innocent girl who came to camp? My inner good girl sighs in disgust……long gone.

"Just look at me, pretend the camera isn't here, let me see your eyes." I suggest, adjusting the lens, realizing the camera loves the angles of his face, and use the zoom to focus on his eyes. Little do I realize but years later these pictures will be a treasure of memories, taking me back to this summer in the Adirondack Mountains.

The film runs out along with his patience. Laying the camera aside, the time for looking is over, I want to touch…"Vic," I reach out holding my arms open, an invitation, and some invitations don't require an R.S.V.P.

Passion flares in his eyes and with a quick leap, he's beside me nuzzling the hollow of my neck, his arms slip along my bare skin, pulling me ever closer, waves of heat intensified by the summer sun course through our bodies. My teeth tug; teasing his lower lip followed by nips and light kisses until with a groan his mouth seeks mine in a feverish meeting that borders on assault. I love it……and want more…..the chocolate…caramel….vanilla….slivers of pure white coconut…..exotic spices. I want it all….*now*. I thrill to the power and intensity of his hold on me. His head bows kissing the curve of my breast. In a strangled breath he says, "These damn blue ruffles on his bathing suit have been driving me crazy all summer long, wiggling, waving, taunting and teasing with the promise of what is underneath." He slowly lowers the strap on my bathing suit with a sensuous movement followed by his tongue and the slow exhalation of his breath. All conscious thought leaves me as I give in to the heady intoxication of his hands laying ownership to my body. With a deft twist, I feel the hook holding my bikini top give way. He lowers his head, plucking the offending ruffles away with his teeth, leaving my breasts bare and rejoicing in the afternoon sun. It feels wonderful, free and sensuous. I arch my back, squirming with pleasure. My eyes fly open as his mouth circles my nipples, sucking gently causing spasms of white heat. I'm beyond myself with desire, no thoughts of denying him, if anything encouraging him with soft whimpers, wiggling my pelvis against him, begging for more of this unspoken ecstasy. He moves with practiced ease from one breast to the other, kissing, licking, teasing while taunting the other breast with his fingers. My very bones melt into the sun soaked rock.

As his hand slides down the edge of the bikini bottom, he looks questioningly, his eyes half hooded with desire. Conflict plays across his face as his fingers slowly slide under the fabric and into my very being. My body lights up with longing. His lips continue their slow torture, sucking hard, nuzzling softly…oh please….slowly he eases the bikini bottom off. I'm lying naked in his arms.

"Elle, open for me, *quierda,*" he murmurs against my ear. Before I can confirm or decline his offer, he slides a finger inside me, then another and he moves them with agonizing slowness in and out.

"Just here," He breathes as his fingers work their magic. And just when I think I can't stand the exquisite torture a moment longer, he rolls on top of me, holding my arms out to the side of my body, I can feel the sharp outline of his manhood pressing into the soft pillow of my stomach. *Ohhh……my !*

And suddenly he is gone. With a desperate groan he flings his body off me. "Elle, Elle, I'm sorry, I'm so sorry."

My lust addled brain fumbles, *Sorry?sorry…for what!* My body feels bereft without his touch.

"We can't, we just can't. I have to stop." Sitting up, he holds his head on arms propped against his knees, his breath coming in ragged gasps. "It's too soon, I shouldn't have done that. I'm sorry," he caresses my cheek. "I don't want to hurt you." *Trust me; I wasn't feeling any pain, exquisite torture, maybe.*

I'm alone, skin bare to the gentle breeze blowing over

the island. The only sound is the hum and buzz of a dragonfly hovering above. Shivering without his warmth and the sun sinking into the horizon, I wrap myself in a towel to cover my nakedness. Leaning into him, I stroke his hair seeing the torment deep in his eyes. "I trust you," I say. "I know you would never hurt me. And just for the record, *oh my,* I wanted it to go on forever."

"We can't, it's far too risky." He brings a knuckled fist up to his mouth, rocking slightly back and forth on his haunches.

"How do you know so much about, you know, making love?" I ask.

He glances over at me, sighs; and looks away, shaking his head. "You grow up early in Mexico, especially with my father."

"How so?"

"At fifteen he expects us to be men, run cattle, hunt, shoot and….." At this he looks at me, shakes his head, his jaw clenches, "and whatever."

"What do you mean…whatever?" I ask, not sure I want to know, but plunge ahead anyway. "Have you had sex, Vic? I mean like real sex with a woman?"

"As I said, you grow up quickly in Mexico." Not looking at me, he takes my hand, tracing the inside of my palm with his finger, stopping to place a kiss on the tender hollow. He looks deep into my eyes, "It was different, not like with you. She was just my father's………she wasn't you," he finishes with vehemence, running a hand through his hair. "Please don't ask me anymore. Just trust my feelings for you are real. I don't want to hurt you. Tell me no, you have to tell me no."

In truth, I don't want to know more, the thought of

him with some strange woman is like a stake in my heart. I pull the edge of the towel closer, resting against the heat of his body as a shiver of apprehension runs up my spine. The sun sinks slowly toward the mountain ridge painting the sky with slashes of pink, purple and lavender gray. And I realize the folly of what he asked of me. No, such a simple little word, how can I say no, when every fiber in my being wants to say…..*yes.*

…

Later that night back in my bunk, all is black as pitch. The light of the moon imparts a dusky glow. The cabin makes queer nocturnal noises, the rustling of mice and batting of insect wings against the window screens. Tossing and turning, I pound my pillow for the hundredth time. My mind is a jumble of thoughts; precluding sleep. Lacing my hands behind my head, I stare out the window. When I came to camp, I envisioned new friends, adventure, and maybe romance. But love? There was a moment, I suppose, when I may have entertained the idea but I've never had a real boyfriend, never really liked anyone, never felt that surge of feeling or the fall from loves grace. I've only watched others weather it from afar. How could I be in love?

But I don't care about how tall I am, or how I klutz up everything. All that matters is to have his arms around me, the soft tender feel of his kiss, how I feel when I am with him. The truth is undeniable….I'm in love with Vicente Rienz. One day I hate him and, now… He is dark and mysterious, far too dangerous for a girl like me. But with him, I'm someone else, someone bold. My only thought is putting distance between me and my old self and what I left behind, because the truth remains, I love him. This summer, Vic Rienz is just what I need.

Chapter 12

The Hermit

Last night Burt invited our group to a dinner party. The rumor is true. He lives in a house high up in the boughs of a large maple tree. A tree house, he calls it his den. I swear the man is part bear with a little elfin magic thrown in for good measure. It's amazing the comforts that can be found in a ten by twelve dwelling. The cooking area consists of a propane stove, a cooler which he stocks with ice from the camp freezer, shelves fashioned from rough hewn planks of wood, the bark still showing on the outer edge. A set of fiesta wear dinner plates brightens the room in a blaze of orange, yellow, deep blue and green, sunshine even on a rainy day. A scattering of pillows cover the floor in a kaleidoscope of color. A sky blue rug causes the room to appear upside down, the sky at your feet, and the ceiling painted black, stenciled with shimmering stars. A small circular staircase leads up to a sleeping loft above. Two walls of the tree house are taken up with windows overlooking the forest floor below; it's like living in an eagles' aerie.

Burt made a delicious vegan enchilada dish and served Mexican beer. And even though we're underage, Burt gave us a beer, one….no more, with the threat of death if Morris found out. It was a magical evening.

…

And today feels like heaven, a humid day in midsummer; the afternoon off, a backpack filled with picnic supplies and a hot boyfriend…… whose butt heading up the trail in front of me is…….rather…

delicious. Add a blanket and a few stolen beers, all the ingredients needed for a perfect day.

We plan to hike up the mountain crest that overlooks the camp and lake below. There are no marked trails leading to the summit only an eroded creek bed as a guide. By summer the creek is reduced to a slow trickle. Rocks worn smooth by the rushing water of spring are skeletal remnants of the stream's former glory. Water striders break the still surface of small pools caught in the eddy of the stream.

Bathed in golden shafts of light streaming through the tree tops, the scent of the forest is like that of a hothouse with its door just flung open. The light is dreamy, the air soft carrying the piping calls of birds. As we climb higher the world below vanishes, distant villages and lakeside cottages disappear under the canopy of forest as civilization gives way to wilderness. The whine of tires on the highway and the drone of a passing plane fade to the sound of hiking boots crunching over loose dirt and rock, and the occasional grunt of pain as our feet trip over exposed tree roots.

The journey up the mountain seems endless as I struggle to keep pace with Vic's long legs. Finally, stopping to rest, I drop my pack to the ground and stretch my aching back. As I pluck the clinging shirt away from my sweaty body, I sigh in disgust. To think I washed my hair and put on make-up this morning. I probably look like a factory worker getting off the third shift, the feminine allure lost two miles back down the trail.

"Hey, look at this. What the hell is this place?" Vic slips the pack from his back onto the matted ground and glances around with a confused look on his face. Tucked into the trees on the edge of a meadow is a camp of some sort. Not an ordinary camp, no tent, picnic table, neatly stacked Coleman supplies or folding camp chairs placed around a fire ring.

This camp consists of a lean-to made of pine logs and a crudely constructed workbench covered with animal pelts in various shapes and sizes. A beaver skin is stretched across a drying rack. The heads and scales of fish litter the ground underneath the bench. Rustic stools made from stumps sit around a campfire ring of stones. A dirty worn jacket hangs from a hook protruding from the lean-to.

"It looks like someone lives here," I say. A sense of foreboding makes the base of my spine tingle. Something about this place doesn't feel right. We're intruders, entering into someone's private domain. There are no posted signs warning against trespassing but the omen is in the air. A passing cloud blocks the sun, casting the meadow in shadows.

We've walked into a scene from an 1890's Adirondack guidebook, a picture from one of the reference books kept in the camp library depicting the early days of the Great Camps. At any moment I expect to see a group of wealthy guests on a hunting party come striding out of the woods. Laughing, singing, carrying a creel heavy with fresh fish caught from a nearby mountain stream. A world from the past. Whoever resides here has fallen from another place in time with no desire to enter into the entrapments of modern day civilization. Almost every article in camp is constructed of natural materials.

"You think someone is living here?" I ask, "Maybe it's one of those civil war reenactor types, trying to live as you would in the 1800's."

"Yeah, it could be. Let's look around a little more."

"I don't think we should snoop around someone's camp."

"We won't touch anything," he says walking along the perimeter. "But this is really cool. I just want to check it out and then we'll leave."

I glance to my left. A coffee pot and matching tin cup along with a pile of mussel shells lay scattered outside the fire pit……messy eater.

A deer hide stretches between two trees, drying in the sun. I give a little shudder, animal carcasses everywhere. An Adirondack pack basket filled with small sticks of kindling wood hangs from a hemlock tree. Off to the side strung on a rope between two small sapling trees I recognize the roots of Queen Anne's lace, chicory, cattail, sassafras and wild calla. All these plants have edible or medicinal properties, valuable for anyone living off the land. Maybe we've stumbled on a real life Henry David Thoreau. Burt will be so jealous.

A large red maple with a fork down the middle dominates the clearing. Several sturdy branches are placed in the V of the tree, spreading out like rungs of a wagon wheel. Only the tips of the branches are visible from under a huge mound of leaves. It looks to be some type of crude shelter or burrow.

A sense of unease washes over me….. I want out of here. Whoever lives in this camp cherishes their privacy. We have no business being here.

"Vic, let's go."

"Just one more sec, I gotta crawl in here. How awesome is this." Unable to contain his curiosity, he drops to his knees inspecting the entrance.

"Cool." Wiggling in on his belly soon only his denim legs are left exposed.

"What are you doing?" Squatting down, I tug at the leg of his pants. "What if there is a bear or coyote in there? Get out!"

"Rrrrrrrrr," a growl comes from inside the leaf mound.

"You are so not funny. Get out of there before I leave you for bear bait."

"Trust me, no animal made this hut." His voice is muffled by thick layers of leaves. "You're the naturalist, you know that. Come in, this is really cool. There's a bed constructed of pine branches covered with a Hudson Bay blanket, pillows made with deer hide, and a few pieces of clothing." He slides further into the gaping black hole, his legs disappearing. "Come on."

"No way. My mama raised no fool to go crawling around in dark little holes in some wacko's camp."

I run my hands up and down my arms glancing back into the forest expecting the owner to appear at any time. "I know all about making shelters, my brothers and I played in the woods behind our house. Every fall we raked leaves and made huge leaf shelters." I kneel down next to the opening peering inside. "My mom and dad allowed us to sleep in our fort as long as it wasn't too cold or raining. We quickly learned the more leaves the better for keeping us warm on damp October nights." I smile at the memory.

"Sounds a little drafty for me, I like my down comforter."

"Burt talked about making shelters with the kids this summer, using branches and leaf litter from the forest floor. He had some crazy idea of them sleeping in the shelter and earning a survival badge."

"Uhuh, I'm coming out. Just the thought of sleeping in here is making me cold."

"Come on, City Boy, let's get going before Big Foot returns."

As I stand up a darker, more menacing presence approaches, I smell him before I see him; the rank smell of an unwashed body assails my nose. Fear rises in my throat as the claw of a hand bites down on my shoulder yanking me to my feet.

I attempt to twist away from the vise-like grip. A blood-curling scream rips from my throat. My fear escalates into terror at the sight before my eyes. The man is huge with hair black as a moonless night. A long beard covers his entire chest. His dark hair is plaited in two thick braids that reach to his waist. He stares down with blood shot eyes. He says nothing, lifting me off the ground with one hand; the other hand a raised fist, deciding whether to punch me or toss my body off into the woods.

"Put me down!" I scream, squirming in his grasp. His lips curl back in a snarl.

"Elllllleee," I hear Vic calling out to me.

"Viccccc!" I struggle to break free, causing his grasp to tighten, pulling me closer to his filthy body.

"Ellen, what the hell is going on out there?" Vic yells thrashing about in the hut, attempting to escape. In his haste instead of crawling out the entrance hole, his head bursts through the roof of the shelter. Without the interwoven support, the structure tumbles down, pinning him beneath the framework of branches and wet leaves.

"Son of a bitch!"

"Put me down, oh please, put me down, sir. I'm so

sorry we didn't mean to intrude on your camp. We were just curious." I plead. "We didn't hurt anything."

The blood shot eyes glare at me, he lifts higher, the toes of my boots fail to touch the ground, I'm held pinned against his unwashed body.

"Who is out there?" Vic yells, pushing away the branches obstructing his view. "*What the hell!*" he exclaims staring in disbelief at the sight before him. He tries jumping over the entangling branches and only succeeds in tripping and falling face first in the dirt.

Gasping for breath, he hollers, "Put her down! What the hell is the matter with you!" With his free hand the man whips a hatchet out of his belt pointing the blade at Vic. I whimper, daring not to breath or move.

"Okay, mister, let's…slow down here." Vic stands up slowly, holding his hands out in a placating gesture. "We were wrong to intrude on your privacy. Why don't you put down that hatchet and we'll fix your house. I'm real sorry, truly I am. Please don't hurt her."

To our shock and amazement the man starts rocking back and forth on his heels with a loud booming laugh, his entire body shakes, causing me to bob up and down like a fish struggling at the end of a fishing line.

"Ahaa, got you." He says, placing me on the ground, releasing his grip. I dive behind Vic, clinging to his shirt, peering around his back, staring at the apparition before us. I don't know if I have ever been so frightened in my life.

"I wouldn't hurt the little lady. I was just having a little fun with you. I don't receive many callers up on the mountain. And certainly none as pretty as this damsel." His voice hoarse and raspy from disuse but his words have a cultured, well pronounced clip to them.

He obviously has some education.

"Vic, get us out of here," my voice squeaks as I burrow my hands into the fabric of his shirt.

I feel his chest heave as he takes a deep breath, attempting to communicate with the huge man. "Hi, my name is Vic and this is Ellen. We work at the camp down on Lake Cascade. I'm real sorry about the leaf hut; we will fix it and be on our way. No harm done, right?"

Raising his arm, our "host" flings the hatch at a tree behind us, the razor sharp head embedding in the tree trunk. I feel Vic's muscles tense under my hands, I bury my head against his back praying….Hail Mary……wacko…….full of grace…..nut case…..the Lord is with thee…..lunatic, ………Blessed art thou amongst women….. clinically insane……and blessed is the fruit of your womb, Jesus……..Please Jesus, save us….

"What if I say no?" He glowers down at us.

"If we don't return to camp by dinner time, everyone will wonder what happened to us. The camp director will call the police and search parties will be sent out. You don't want anyone to find your camp, do you?"

"Do you have food in those packs?" His eyes wander greedily over our backpacks.

"Yeah, sure," Vic leans over scooping up the packs handing them to the man. "You're welcome to them. We have sandwiches, apples, cookies and a couple cans of soda. Even beer."

"Coke?" he asks, unzipping the pack, eager to examine the contents.

Pepsi, Vic shrugs his shoulders. "Almost the same."

"Not really," the man mutters in disappointment, and then brightens as he holds up the beer cans. "The beer makes up for not having Coke."

"Here's the deal," the giant offers sitting down on a rock placing the packs between his legs. "You share your food with me, we fix my shelter and you go on your way. I'm tired of eating deer meat and opossum. God, those opossum are stupid creatures. Deal?" He extends his filthy hand for us to shake, sealing the agreement.

Vic grasps the hand with a firm grip while I snake one hand out and shake his finger, making as minimal contact as possible. One would think with all the water and lakes in the Adirondacks the man could find one to bathe in.

"Let's eat first, my name is Jolib Freeport," he hands us our backpacks as a gesture of good will. "You find the food." We dig into our packs as Jolib licks his lips in anticipation.

"Here," I say, arranging the sandwiches and fruit in front of him, seeing how desperate he is for the food. He is tall and lean, and looks half starved. "You eat this, we had a large breakfast and dinner will be waiting for us when we return. Please enjoy this as our way of apologizing for disrupting your camp."

Under my breath I hiss at Vic, "I told you we had no business snooping around here." He lifts his eyebrows, jerking his head in the direction of Jolib, warning me to be quiet.

"Are you sure?" Jolib hesitates for only a moment before grabbing a sandwich, eating half of it in one bite. What's the name of that camp you work at again?" His mouth is crammed full of sandwich.

"Camp High Point at the Cascade," Vic answers, sitting cross-legged on the ground a little too close to the giant for comfort. His curiosity will be the death of us yet.

"Ah, the fancy one, eh?"

"Yeah, some of the kids are pretty wealthy."

"I went there as a kid." A supercilious grin spreads across his face.

"Get out!" I exclaim. The words rush out of my mouth in shock over this announcement. I immediately regret them as he turns glaring at me with those blood-shot eyes.

"Yes, my dear, I was not always a bum living off the land." He takes another bite of sandwich. "My family built one of the finest Great Camps around here. My grandfather was William George Freeport. Did you ever hear of him?"

Of course we recognized the name, anyone who knows anything about Adirondack history has heard of William George Freeport. He was a lumber baron, logging the Adirondacks in the late 1800's. To this day his name is a dirty word to environmentalists for his clear cutting of the forest.

"Sure," Vic and I answer. We nod our heads in agreement, hungry for the rest of the story.

"Well," Jolib says, his eyes getting a faraway look as he warms to the subject. "My grandfather along with J.P. Aster and Durant turned the Adirondacks into a playground for the wealthy." The can of soda opens with a squirt; we watch his adam's apple bob up and down as he swallows. "Ahh," he says wiping his mouth on a ragged shirtsleeve. "I do miss some things about civilization. Water and herbal tea just aren't Coke."

"Pepsi."

"Whatever."

Spellbound, we listen as the man continues his story. Common sense tells us to get out of here, screaming our heads off all the way down the mountain for special effect……but no, we just sit there fascinated…..with a hatchet buried in a tree behind our heads.

"If there is anything I've missed, it's an ice cold Coke, the downfall of growing up in the Pepsi generation," he chuckles. "Anyway, back to my story. My family had money, great gobs of money until, well, until…..never mind, something bad. I didn't understand it before but I sure as hell do now. Bad investments, alcoholism, suicide, I was born wealthy but now I live as a hermit. I prefer my own company. But after today it won't matter anymore." He looks at us and throws back his head to laugh uproariously at some private joke. "Here, I have a little present for you."

"No, no, it's not necessary." I protest, my mind shuddering at the thought of some filth riddled object coming from him.

"I insist," he raises a hand to still my protests. "It's impolite to refuse a gift from your host." He steps into the lean-to and begins rummaging through a wooden box hidden under a pile of pelts. "Here she is," he holds a small object up to the light, admiring the glittering display of color in the sun. "She is so beautiful," he says wistfully. "I hate to part with her, but I must." Vic and I glance at each other, shrugging our shoulders in puzzlement. What does he have in his hand? She?

We gasp in surprise as he turns to us holding a dazzling diamond broach. The sun reflects off the multicolored gems set in a circular starburst. The broach looks like a miniature eruption of fireworks resting in his hand, glittering in the afternoon sun.

"I want you to have it." He holds the broach.

"Ohhhh," I say in a whoosh of breath. "I..I…

couldn't take that. It looks far too valuable."

"Really, sir." Vic interjects. "It's not necessary. Thank you, but Elle is right. You must keep it. It looks like an antique."

"It belonged to my grandmother. My grandfather had it commissioned for her. It just makes me sad to look at now. It reminds me of a life gone by. I don't want it. The minute I saw this beautiful young lady, I knew it belonged with her."

I look at Vic with desperation, I can't accept this broach. The man is crazy. I start to protest again, "Jolib, this is very generous of you, but I wouldn't feel comfortable accepting such a g…" Before I can finish my sentence, he roars, shoving the broach in my face. "You will take it. Do you hear me?" Spittle comes flying out of his massive beard as he leans in closer to me. "Take it and leave now. Do as I say before I get angry."

Good Lord. I shrink away from him in fear. Before I get angry?…this isn't angry? I'd hate to see him on a bad day.

"Yeah, sure, it's okay. We'll take it." Vic reaches over to take the broach. "Watch, I'll wrap it up in this bandana to keep it safe." Vic places the broach in his bandana, starts to opens his backpack with elaborate care when Jolib roars again. "No! It's not for you. She has to take it. Put it in her pack." He gestures wildly at my pack. I grab the broach from Vic's hand and tuck it between the folds of my sweatshirt.

"Is this all right?"

"Yes, now go, I'm sick of you. Leave my camp."

"We didn't help fix the hut."

"I don't care….just go!"

A second invitation wasn't necessary. We practically

trip over ourselves, leaving in haste, literally running half way down the mountain before stopping to catch our breath.

"What the hell was that?" Vic asks bent over double, gasping for air.

"I don't know, but I never want to see it again." My heart hammering against my ribcage, lungs on fire, and my legs feel like rubber.

"That guy's nuts."

"That's an understatement." I glance over my shoulder, ears perked for any sight or sound of him following us. "I'm going to have nightmares for a month. A shower, I need a shower. Hot water, lots of soap and more hot water…..Ugh! He was disgusting."

"Come on, let's go. I don't want to wait around here in case he decides to follow us."

"I'm already gone." I hoist myself up, ignoring the burning sensation in my chest. Sheer will forces my legs down the trail. I've never been so scared in my entire life…..and I've been scared before.

…

The episode with Jolib and the broach was eclipsed by the near tragedy that greeted us back at camp. One of the six-year old boys almost drowned in our absence. The lifeguard on duty was distracted by some older kids fighting in the deep end and he missed the younger child wade out over his head. Thankfully Burt was near the beach conducting a pond study with a group and noticed the child struggling in the water. The irony is……Burt can't swim a stroke. On kayak trips he has on so many lifejackets he looks like the Michelin Man. The little boy wasn't in very deep water so Burt was able to pull him to shore and started CPR. A 911 call was placed and the child taken to the local hospital for evaluation. The mood at dinner was somber. Morris reported the little boy was in good condition, spending the night in the hospital for observation until his parents arrived. Launching a full investigation, Morris plans to understand how this accident happened and ways to prevent future incidents.

Vic is devastated. When Sean, the head lifeguard returned to college early, Vic was appointed head lifeguard for the remainder of the summer. In this position he felt it was his responsibility to ensure the safety of each camper in the water. His skin visibly pale under his summer tan, he refused dinner, just sitting with a cup of coffee in his hand. The muscles in his jaw twitching as Morris reviewed the water safety rules, admonishing the counselors to realize our grave responsibility to the campers left in our charge.

Later that night, I empty my backpack and the broach falls to the floor. The sight of it makes me shudder, recalling the events of this horrible day. I want to throw it out the window, but it looks expensive and antique. So I shove it in the back of my dresser drawer, out of sight and out of mind. Good riddance.

Chapter 13

A Night Under the Stars

The Perseid meteor shower occurs every year on or about the 11th of August, on nights when the earth's orbit passes through a band of space debris that comes too close to the sun. Each piece of debris is hardly bigger than a speck of dust, but when entering into the earth's atmosphere, it's transformed into a dazzling arc of light called a meteor or shooting star and then disappears.

Vic and I planned to hike up the mountain ridge and watch the meteor shower from a clearing near the top. So when the *ping, ping,* of small pebbles hits the cabin screen, I'm ready to go.

"Ella, Ella, my mia bella, won't you come out and play?" floats through the open window to my waiting ears. *Ping, ping!* "Come on, Elle, I feel like "Chicken Little" out here with the sky falling. The stars are incredible." His voice edged in impatience. Already dressed, I clattered down the steps and round the corner of the cabin where I'm swept into his arms. He spins me around in a circle, my feet fanning out like a carousal in motion. Placing me breathless on my feet, his lips capture mine.

"Mia, mia, bella," he murmurs between kisses.

"Why?" I pause to catch my breath, my feet barely touching the ground. "Why do you always call me, mia bella, isn't that Italian or something? You speak Spanish." I question him, softly peppering kisses up and down his face.

"Because Elle, Ellen, Ella," he laughs. "I just like the

way it sounds, you're my Ella Bella, *querida*." He runs his hands down, pressing the length of my body against him.

"Come on." he says, leading me down the path. Tucked under his arm is an old green sleeping bag, the lining covered with camping scenes highlighted on the red flannel. He found it in the old boathouse along with the canoe. "The stars aren't going to wait for you, slow poke; the bluff off Little Wolf Point will be a great spot to watch."

We walk through the dark forest as the stars overhead play connect-the-dots, forming images of ancient gods and goddesses. The new moon sheds little light to distract from the brilliance of the stars. Our footsteps hush the chorus of chirping crickets as they surrender to silence. Content, we walk in stillness feeling the peace and beauty of the forest night.

"Almost there," he helps me up over a fallen log. I trip into his arms, causing us to fall onto the ground in a giggling heap.

"Shhhhh."

"Who are we disturbing?" he asks.

"Ummmm….crickets?"

"Really?"

Coming out of the trees just above the lake, a bluff opens to reveal the heavens dropping down to play with the earth. It's a beautiful night, cool, fresh and clear. We stop at a small clump of pines, where seductively soft shadows provide a hidden cove, carpeted with skullcap moss, resembling a blanket made of small green stars, an invitation to touch and sink into the arms of the earth. Vic shakes out the sleeping bag to cover the moss and holds out his hand, bowing deeply in a gesture reminiscent of a prince inviting the princess to his humble castle. As a true princess I drop into a low curtsy and step lightly onto the soft carpet as if walking in dainty ballet slippers. I sit down onto the makeshift throne……and with one swift tug…….. pull the prince down with me.

Losing his balance, he tumbles down onto the blanket. I lean over slowly letting my hands run through his hair before resting on his shoulders, my mouth pauses inches from his curved lips, moving to the V of his open shirt. The solid warmth of him beneath my fingertips is intoxicating. I slant my lips over his and slide my tongue inside his mouth and, then he is kissing me back, his tongue exploring, sending delightful shivers down my spine.

"Ella, mia bella, make a wish upon a falling star," he murmurs in a husky whisper.

"Not a knock, knock joke?" I nibble at his ear.

"Nope, a wish."

I roll off his solid warmth and stretch out my legs crossing them at the ankles, head propped against his shoulder, watching the explosion of stars. The sky is a blizzard of stars, blurring the perfect darkness of the night. Horizon to horizon arrayed in a misted veil. A fireworks display, silent pops of light streak across the star studded sky, vanishing into thin vapor. If wishes were treasures, the wealth on this night would be untold.

"Star light, star bright, first million, trillion, stars I see tonight, wish I may, wish I might have the wish I wish tonight." I recite the nursery rhyme, adding a little meteor shower twist.

"What's your wish?" Vic asks, lifting his head, his fingers trace my face, tucking a lock of hair behind my ear. "You are so beautiful."

"You're distracting me," I argue, fighting the spell of his hands and mouth, as overwhelming desire threatens to invade common sense….he presses his body against mine, proof of his masculinity, evidence of his desire. His hand tugs the shirt out of my jeans and slips inexorably upward, causing tingles of anticipation. Trails of fire follow in the wake of his hands on my bare skin. Slowly he unbuttons the shirt leaving my skin bare to the night air as his fingers deftly unhook my bra, removing the offending article of clothing. His hand caresses the softness of my breast causing already hard nipples to throb and burn. His mouth paints a line of fire from my neck down. Using his teeth, tongue and lips, the effect is overwhelming, driving me wild with his touch. As his mouth closes over my breast, hot and warm, I'm spinning out of control with desire under the flood of shooting stars.

"What do you wish for Elle?" he murmurs against my mouth, his voice laden with desire.

I reach up to clasp his handsome face and kiss him gently, pouring all the love I feel into this one sweet connection. "I want you," the words are out, gaining a life of their own as the idea pulses, growing in the night air. "Make love to me," I whisper. His head rears back, and his nostrils flare in disbelief, eyes glitter with a feral light.

"Touch me. I can't wait any longer to be with you," I plead with him. "I want the first time to be under the stars on this mountain overlooking our lake. I want this moment with you." Life taught me tomorrow holds no guarantee and my mother's death proved tomorrow doesn't always come. I want today.

"Elle, Elle," his voice intones my name in a ragged

breath as desire fights with reason. A desire driven by questing hands, as I slowly unbutton his shirt slipping under the material to touch the bare skin above the waist of his jeans, stroking the soft down of dark hair causing his belly to clench in longing as he moans. Gently pushing me away, he stands up, reaches down and pulls me to my feet. Squeezing my face between his tan lean hands, he rests his forehead against mine, "Elle, please, I'm not that strong. Please don't tease me…." His voice comes out in a strangled whisper. I take a step back from him, the trees and stars forming a background canvas, a temptress of the night, I unzip, undulating my hips to slither out of my jeans and stand naked, skin a pearly glow in the luminous darkness, arms held wide casting a spell of enchantment.

With a resounding groan mimicking a gut punch to the stomach, he picks up my pliant body. My arms tighten around his neck and capture his dark hair. I will take this and give it to him, just this once, gather him close to me in love.

Bending down, he gently lays me on the faded sleeping bag. He trails his fingers up and down my spine as we gaze at each other. He brushes back the long mane of hair tumbling over my right shoulder, picking up a lock, inhaling the scent of summer sun. As I move to kiss the throbbing pulse at the base of his neck, he stands up, shucking off his jeans, tossing his unbuttoned shirt to the side, and stands gleaming in the faint light of the moon. I've never seen him completely naked before and gasp in surprise at the sheer masculine beauty of his body. A swimmers' body of wide shoulders wedging down to a chest defined with taut pectoral muscles tapering to ridges of abdominal cords cutting across his stomach. He bends down on athletic legs to lean over me, propping himself on one arm, as his other arm slides around my back pulling me close so I can feel the heat of his strength along my body. His chest is hard against my breasts making them tingle.

One hand cradles my head, stroking my cheek, as he pushes back the hair from my face. "I love you," he whispers, just before his mouth slides over mine, cutting off any response. A weakness seems to invade my body as I melt into him tracing the muscled ridge from his hip to the smooth curve of his spine. "Love you back," I say. His tongue slides seductively into my mouth to coax a response that is hot and scalding. I cling to him, devouring his kisses, catching fire as his hands rove up and down my body, creating a backlash of desire in their wake. His mouth slides down from my lips to my throat, nibbling at the hollow of my shoulder blade, then across my chest. Grabbing the damp tangle of black hair, I guide his mouth to my breast, searing pleasure races through me as his mouth closes over the nipple and my back arches in delight as my body writhes beneath him succumbing to a spiraling passion. "Vic," I gasp as exquisite tremors of pleasure race along my skin.

Unable to remain still under the onslaught of his hands and mouth, afloat on a frenzy of longing, the ground beneath me undulates like the waves of the ocean. He moves down my rib cage to my belly, a skim and glide of fingers followed by the trail of his moist tongue. His hands sliding down touching the triangle of curls between my thighs, then his fingers slide between my legs finding the tender bud, touching, pressing and driving me mindless with need. He moves down to kiss the concave hollow between my hip and stomach trailing kisses lower and lower. Pushing my knees apart he places small nibbling kisses up one side of my inner thighs then down the other. Running his tongue lightly over the core of desire, my body quivers in response. "Oh, yes," I gasp, pulling his head in closer, reveling in the pleasure of such intimate contact, weightless floating on his touch. When I can take the exquisite pleasure no longer, he rises to lie next to me, crushing me in his arms. Moaning with need, his lips come down to mine bruising with a ferocious possession. His voice thick with passion, he pauses above me, "I want you."

"Love me, Vic." For a moment he is above me, looking down, eyes deep and black as I pull his mouth down to drown in his kiss. Lifting his head, he cradles my face between his hands and whispers, "Let me in, *caro*." And with that he slides into me, deep, and deeper. Long, slow thrusts until a quick spasm of pain causes me to inhale sharply, he stops, waiting until I beg him to continue, carrying me spiraling upward mindless with passion, feeling more and more until the sky above me explodes into a million starbursts of delight. "Elle, Elle," he cries. Clutching my body to him, he groans in response finding his own satisfaction, thrusting deeper into my quivering body.

We are one dancing with the mountains under the sky of streaking stars in a noiseless display of fireworks. Fate or destiny, as desire blooms under the flare of a hot August night.

Chapter 14

Busted

The rustic boathouse tucked a mile down shore from the main camp, sets as a reminder of days gone by, slowly returning to the forest from disuse and neglect. A flight of rickety stairs leads to the second story, a large spacious room framed with small leaded glass windows and a French door which opens onto a small balcony. Years ago, guests of the camp seeking a place of solitude would come to the boathouse and sit, read, enjoy a cup of tea or an evening cocktail as the sun set behind the mountains. Once cleared of cobwebs and the accumulated dirt and grime of neglect, the boathouse proved to be a perfect meeting place for young lovers. Our night on the mountain meant to quell the fires of passion, served only to stoke the flames into smoldering embers of desire not to be denied. Desire overcame reason and we were headed toward a towering inferno of disaster. And on the nights we could sneak away, we made love in the boathouse with reckless abandon ….until Burt found us.

A thunderstorm had just passed over the boathouse leaving the sky pierced and shattered with trailing flashes of distant lightening pursued by the answering rumble of thunder. It's drizzling outside, not a downpour or a shower, just a slow steady sprinkling drizzle. The soft dancing of raindrops on the tin roof plays a steady tune in reverence to the falling rain. The French doors are open to capture the subtle breeze of the storm's aftermath. Small brown bats dip and weave using echo-location to hunt; darting past the open window. Up and down, back and forth streaking over the lake's surface chasing mosquitoes in the feeble light of the moon as it breaks through the thin veil of cloud cover. A foundation of old deck cushions bleached clean by the sun and zealous scrubbing, along with a couple of old sleeping bags makes for a cozy haven. Drowsy in the wake of spent passion, the tin roof symphony lulls us to sleep innocent in the belief of being safe and alone.

And that's how Burt found us. The beam of his flashlight cuts through the darkness of the boathouse, ravaging our sleep laden eyes.

"*Son of a bitch*," I hear the expletive explode, shattering the quiet of the night.

"*Damn* it, damn it, *Damn* it," Burt swears, enunciating his words even more than normal. "I knew the *two* of you were up to no good."

I scream in terror, pulling the sleeping bag up to cover my nakedness, while Vic pushes me behind him in a protective pose, saying, "What the hell?" Trying to shield his eyes against the glare of the flashlight's beam, he yells, "Who the hell is it?"

"Who the hell do you think it is? It's *Me*! You two dummies! You're not even up to knuckleheads anymore, you are both beyond *Stupid*." I groan to myself, I've never hated the way Burt emphasizes certain words in his sentences as much as I do at this moment. *Stupid*. He is bellowing his anger at us out into the night

"Burt," we groan, relief mixed with fear.

"Just what the *Hell* do you think you are doing?" He rants at us. I pull the sleeping bag higher, mortified, busted by Burt, ohh, this is not going to be good.

"Could you turn the flashlight off or direct it away from our faces?" Vic asks him, holding up a hand, shielding his eyes from the glaring beam.

"*Hell*, no!" Burt spits back at him taking a step closer, shining the light directly into our eyes with even greater intensity.

"Damn it," Vic growls, pushing his hair back, a pained expression on his face. He drops his head onto his hands, elbows propped up on his knees, exhaling a loud sigh. I nestle closer burying my face into his back, praying if I don't open my eyes Burt will vanish like a bad dream. No such luck, he is still there with a mounting temper to match his red hair.

"I want the two of you *dressed* and in the Algonquin Nature Cabin in ten minutes. If you choose not to show up, then I will be forced to go to Morris and report the inappropriate conduct of his two favorite counselors. Do I *make* myself perfectly clear?" He commands in a tone just shy of being beyond furious, punctuating his words with the flashlight. Bouncing the flashlight beam from my face to Vic's, weaving back and forth until we're dizzy from the rapid motion.

Blissfully, the light ceases the back and forth assault on our eyeballs as he pivots on his heel, disappearing into the darkness of the staircase. "Ten minutes and *don't* be late," echoes up the steep wooden steps.

"Oh, we are so screwed," Vic says, gathering me into his arms, burying his face in my hair. "Oh, Elle, I feel like I've been caught by your father. You know Burt adores you. I'm a dead man. If he punches me, I deserve it."

"We're in this together remember, he has to punch both of us." In the back of my mind, I can't help but think, Burt's not very big……… how hard can he punch.

…

Clad in jeans and sweatshirts, our hair damp from a quick swim in the lake, we mount the steps of Algonquin cabin holding hands in a white-knuckle clasp. Burt shakes his head, looking away from us as we come through the door, a pinched look of pain scrunches up his face. I hear him mutter under his breath, "God, I wish I didn't care so much about what happens to them."

The cabin is bathed in the dim glow of candlelight. Being so far removed from the main camp, it is impractical and expensive to run electrical lines. Therefore, the cabin exists in the rustic state of light furnished by candles or lanterns. The rough wooden table in the center of the room is covered with a vintage flowered tablecloth I found in the boathouse. At the end of our workday, Burt would make tea while I set the table using our favorite mugs. It was a small ritual we shared, taking a quiet moment to reflect on the activities of the day and plan ahead for tomorrow.

Two pillar candles imbedded with bits of pine needles and wood chips flicker in the dark casting golden shadows on the walls. Our teapot, the one with the chipped lid sits on the table. Steam wafting from the spout fills the room with a minty aroma. Burt remembered mint tea is my favorite, but tonight, three mugs sit on the table, and he's standing there with a thunderous look on his face, arms akimbo. He flashes a look of murderous venom at Vic. Okay, so this isn't going to be a proper English high tea.......

"I *really* want to punch you," he fumes at Vic shaking his head vigorously back and forth.

"I understand, sir." Vic replies nodding his head in agreement. "I deserve it."

"You do not." I butt in with rising indignation.

"I'm just as much to blame for this as you."

"*You*, be quiet," Burt says, stabbing his finger in my direction to emphasize his point. "I've been trying to talk to you all summer. I begged you to trust me, let me help you. Do you know the consequences of your actions? *Do* you really understand what an unwanted *Pregnancy* could mean to your futures? Do you? *Do* you?" he repeats as he whips into a tirade about the statistics of teenage pregnancies, early marriages, suicide and just about every pitfall that can happen to stupid kids who don't stop to think about the future.

"I could see this coming since the beginning of summer. I tried to intervene, make you understand that *You* are too young to be having sex. Just… too… young!" His voice rises on each word. "*Seventeen* years old, shit, you have your whole lives ahead of you. You wait until you're in college, at the very least."

"*What* do you have to say for yourselves? Huh?" He flops down onto a bench, chest heaving from the exertion of his rant.

I think he simply ran out of breath, unable to yell, rant and rave at us any further. What did we have to say for ourselves? Well, there's not a lot to be said in our defense. We've been like small children playing with matches, hoping not to get burned. So we stand looking sheepish, nodding in agreement with his assessment of our wrong doings. As we sit in that peaceful cabin in the woods, he's right, we've been playing a game with consequences too dire to imagine.

"Sit down," he says in a weary voice, pouring the now cooled tea into our mugs, passing a small plastic bear of organic honey. "What am I going to *do* with the two of you?" he muses shaking his head.

"What are you using for *birth* control?" He asks.

Vic and I glance over at each other with a pained expression on our faces.

"Oh, Sweet Jesus, Mary, *Mother* of God! Don't tell me you haven't been using anything, anything!"

"Well, the rhythm method. Kat said if you count back fourteen days from your period…" I start to explain before he erupts, his voice shaking with disbelief.

"The rhythm method! Do *You* know how many good Catholic families of eight kids are running around in the world because of the rhythm method? Millions, my parents for starters, I have five brothers and sisters. It doesn't work very well."

"And we used……." My voice trails off in embarrassment, looking at my feet, unable to continue.

Vic finishes in a tight voice, "I had some condoms."

"Of course you did!" Burt fumes. His voice lowers to a hiss as he slams the table with his fist. "You should know better," he points an accusing finger at Vic. "She's innocent, I can't believe she let this happen, but she loves you. But you *know* better, Vic, I know you do. You know how the world works."

"Innocent?" I squeak in disbelief. "I'm not an innocent baby. Kat said…." I weakly try to explain but confusion and doubt cloud my words.

"You chose to talk to *Kat*, Queen of Camp Wild Life instead of me! I'm a biology teacher, my life is teaching about reproduction, but no, you talked to your eighteen-year-old girlfriend. Ask her about *her* abortion last year," he says, dropping this bombshell in our laps.

Our eyes widen in horror at the thought of Kat having an abortion. Oh, God, abortion, babies.

"Yeah," he continues, "No one is supposed to know

about *it*, she came to me at the end of the summer last year, scared and wanting to know her options. Some guy back home."

"Oh my God," I say, the breath escaping my lungs replaced by a quaking fear. A tremor starts at my spine working through my body to a quavering chill. I clutch Vic's arm in a vise-like grip. He straddles the bench, pulling my trembling body into the hollow of his arms, kissing my forehead saying, "We'll be all right, mia, Don't worry."

"A little *late* for that," Burt says getting up from the chair he was straddling. "Stay here," he commands as the screen door bangs behind his retreating back.

"Where is he going?" I ask, the warmth of Vic's body doing little to quell the rippling fear gripping me. "What's he going to do?"

"I don't know," Vic says with a deep sigh, "I'm so sorry, Elle."

The screen door squeaks on its' hinge announcing Burt's return. He tosses a small box on the table. "Here," he says pointing to the box.

Vic and I look at the box in confusion then read the word, *condoms.* Condoms. I can't look at Burt's face, I pray the floor will open up and swallow me; even China won't be far enough.

"Oh, shit," I whisper into Vic's shoulder.

Vic instead chooses to look directly into Burt's eyes, a man to man in agreement.

"If you're going to have sex, have it *responsibly*. Count your days and use the condoms, better yet don't have sex for a year or two. The pill works the best. Ellen, make an appointment with a doctor, but you may need your parent's permission being under the age." I look at him in disbelief and horror at the mere suggestion of involving my father and Helen, is he *nuts!!*

"Consider talking to Noreen, the camp nurse, she may be able to give *you* some advice."

"It won't be an issue in two weeks," Vic says, rubbing his hands up and down my arms in agitation. "My father is sending me back to school in Mexico. He wants me to finish my high school education there, it's tradition for the men of our family. And when my father insists, no one stands in his way." The muscles in his jaw twitch, his arms pull me tighter into his embrace. "I don't know when I will see Ellen again."

"I see," says Burt. "I'm sorry, but maybe it's for the best, try looking beyond next year. College will open many doors for you. I'm sorry I came down so *hard*, but it had to be said. You know I care for the both of you," he shrugs his shoulders, stifling a yawn. "Look, I'm going to bed. I'm *exhausted*. I'm too old to be running around all hours of the night. I don't think I have the energy to climb into the tree house. Maybe I'll just sleep on the ground, like a bear."

"Burt, wait." I call out, leaving Vic's arms to give him a hug as he stands at the open door. "Thanks for caring."

"Hey, I was young once, believe it or not. Blow out the candles when you leave."

Chapter 15

Farewell

Summer is over on the mountain, Pegasus retreats south as Orion climbs higher in the night sky. The early fall reds and yellows of deciduous trees pepper the otherwise green mountain slopes. The golden rod is thick with bees as the sun ebbs ever closer to the equator and night time temperatures bring the foreshadowing of winter.

A hillside meadow stretches to the mountain lake, dotted with a tide of black-eyed Susans. The yellow daisies wave in the early afternoon breeze. Our last day at camp. A sense of melancholy pervades our hike up the hill. Thick tufts of cumulus clouds give relief to the heat of the day. Shaking out the faded sleeping bag, we fall wearily onto the cushion of daisies, cocooned in a sheltering ring of tall wildflowers. We are surrounded, hidden by a wall of purple knapweed, blue chicory, and Queen Anne's lace, overshadowed by the vivid Tuscan yellow of black-eyed Susans.

I clasp Vic's hand across the worn flannel, the sun warms our bodies as we stretch out on the sleeping bag, relishing the quiet mountain solitude. Summer on the mountain is ending. The buses leave for home tomorrow.

"*Querida,*" Vic murmurs, rolling his body on top of mine, his fingers spilling the sun bleached locks of my hair onto the grass, creating lines of molten gold. Blue eyes meet smoky dark eyes that glint with amber light; his eyes are mesmerizing, almost hypnotic.

"Umm," I sigh in contentment, running my fingers

with a feather touch along the edge of his jaw pausing to outline the shape of his finely chiseled lips. Tilting my head deliberately, I give him the invitation to lean in and take possession, complete and total surrender as desire meets desire. I melt into him as his arms wrap around me, drowning in the natural scent of him.

Stopping to lean back on his elbow, his eyes study my face as his long fingers caress the hollow of my collarbone stroking the swell of my breast, the heat of his touch sends quivers of delight racing through my body. *How am I to live without him?*

His lips move slowly and lingeringly from my mouth to my earlobe. "*Caro, caro*," he says, burying his face in my neck while his hands rove up and down the length of my body. Waves of pent-up passion begin to build, craving fulfillment. We've not made love since the night Burt discovered us in the boathouse. I can feel the stirring in him as his hands move exploring every curve and hollow through my thin cotton shirt and shorts.

"Did you bring Burt's "presents?" I manage to eke out in a ragged breath as I struggle to overcome the dizzy spiraling need growing in my gut. His hands still their exploration as he gently brushes the hair back from my face looking deeply in my eyes, "Elle, are you sure?"

"How do you say, make love to me in Spanish?" I whisper, my voice trembling as I kiss the small indentation in his chin. "Is it *Harcerle el amora* ?"

"Close enough.........close enough." The low dusky notes of his voice are the quiet melody of a distant thunderstorm, echoing the slow reverberation in my chest, as my heart beats the low bass notes, *thump, thump.* "Love me, Vic." I repeat in a throaty whisper, teasing the lobe of his ear, lifting his hair allowing it to slither through my fingers like fallen black silk.

"Do you know how much I love you?" he asks.

"As much as I love you back."

"Forever and ever?"

"Always." There is one person in world for each of us, one worth the risks and pitfalls of love. For me, it is him.

He kisses my hair, eyes and face and the pulse that beats in the hollow of my neck as his mouth forges a burning trail down to my breast. His fingers undo the buttons of my shirt…one by one. I feel his mouth teasing my nipples until I groan, a strangely incoherent sound. Slipping his hands to my waist he slides the lower half of my clothes off, tossing them into a careless pile on the grass.

My hands tug impatiently to pull the shirt away from his body, slipping needy fingers under the smooth fabric to knead the ridge of muscles along his ribs and abdomen. With one quick move I shuck the shirt from his body, hands roving slowly over his flat, muscled stomach, I feel him suck in his breath and soon his jeans join the growing pile of clothes.

The molding of body against body, as heat and desire fuel flames of passion not to be denied. His hand is on my breast as his movements quicken and my body moves in response, matching his pace, pulsing and arching to forgetfulness, fulfillment and back.

Lying there against him, his arms holding me close as beads of perspiration glisten on satiated skin, evaporating in the noon day sun. Turning over in his arms to face him, I watch the sunlight create a halo effect on his jet black hair, hair that tumbles over his forehead in careless disarray. I kiss the roughened skin covering a scar on his shoulder. Those vaqueros again. His hands run over my body trying to memorize each line and angle, pausing to kiss the mole on my inner arm, tracing the outline of a birthmark on the lower edge of my butt, caressing the scar on my knee from a bicycle fall when I was six. Using eyes, hands and mouth, following every curve, we create a remembrance to hold against the barren loss of the future.

"I can't stand the thought of leaving you," he reaches out running his hand down the length of my hair.

I nod as tears well up in my eyes. I brush them away with the back of my hand.

"I don't know how, but we'll find a way to be together. I've never met anyone who makes me feel the way you do. I'm in love with you, Elle. That first night when I saw you trip down the steps of that bus, falling into the driver's arms. I just knew I would love you."

"I love you, Vicente Rienz," I tease. "But I have to admit, it took me a little longer to warm up to you."

"Yeah," he says, running his thumb over my knuckles. "I was a pain in the ass when I first came here. I was so pissed off at my father, forcing me to take this job, and now it's the best thing that ever happened to me. Between finding you, Ben, Emi and the others, being in the mountains, I don't want it to end."

I nod, reaching up to tuck that gorgeous black hair behind his ear. "I know; I feel the same way. I dread the thought of being apart from you."

"We'll think of something, I can hop a bus or hitch-hike." Tilting my chin up with a gentle touch of his hand, our eyes lock. "I'm afraid you'll go home and find someone else."

Not bloody likely. My prospects at home are dull,

boring and *very* limited. Frankly, the captain of the football team hasn't exactly been knocking down my door. And once you've tasted dark, deep Spanish chocolate, the captain of the football team is……..rather *mundane*. "Not much chance of that happening." I squeeze his hand.

"You are so beautiful; I can't imagine every guy in school not wanting to be with you." *Really*….. he needs his vision checked when he gets home.

I venture, "Maybe we could be exclusive, you know, how everyone exchanges rings and promises to be true to each other."

"I don't have a ring to give you." He turns his hands over, indicating the ring less state of them.

Okay, sometimes I have great ideas and sometimes I get caught up in the enthusiasm of the moment, swept away by the emotion, beguiled by the romanticism of a gesture or a symbol….and sometimes that idea is *really* bad. This is one of those times. While Vic's thinking of a ring to symbolize our commitment to each other, I pull from the recesses of my memory, a story I read years ago. The image is still fresh in my mind.

"Ummmm, I read this book," I begin tentatively. "A story about a pioneer girl growing up in the 1870's and her friendship with a young Cherokee brave. My favorite part of the story is when they make a friendship pact. They cut the palms of their hands and hold the wounds together, symbolizing the blood bond between them, a vow that bridges the differences between family and culture. The story ends years later when he spares her husband and family from a raiding war party." At the time I thought it was so romantic……and Vic reminds me of a Cherokee brave, tall, dark and handsome. In my mind I can picture him riding across the plains, bareback on a painted pony rescuing me, tossing me on the back of his horse. And somehow I think I would look cute in a poke bonnet……….and gingham. Very *Little House on the Prairie.*

"I like it," he chuckles, squeezing my hand saying, half serious and half in jest, "We'll make a vow, a sacred pact, sealed with our own blood." Reaching into his pack he brings out the small pocket knife he carries with him all the time. The blade glitters silver in the sun. My stomach clenches, maybe this wasn't a good idea; I just remembered, I don't like blood…..or sharp objects.

"Really?" I look at him with trepidation.

"It's kind of a Native American sacred custom. We cut each other's palm then hold our hands together, mingling our blood, the ultimate bond." But before I protest he whips out the blade and makes a quick slash across the palm of his hand. Jeweled drops of ruby red blood seep out, forming a small crimson line. *Sweet Jesus, does nothing faze him?* I hide my hand behind my back, I've changed my mind.

"Elle, give me your hand, it doesn't hurt much, just a quick sting." He reaches out, and turns my hand over gently so the soft palm lies open. *Oh boy…*

With a quick sure stroke he runs the blade over my hand, a slash of red springs to the surface, vivid against the white of my palm, a quick sting of pain. The pain fades quickly as my gaze shifts from the wound to his eyes. Sparks of light explode from his eyes as he hold his hand up, I place the open wound against his, our fingers intertwined, the warmth of his blood mingles with mine, creating a bond more consummate than most marriages.

Holding hands together, our lips meet, warm, soft

and deep. His lips don't just brush or nibble, they absorb my entire being, leaving me dizzy and breathless. A shimmering heat wave starts in my toes, rising as he pulls me into his lap, draping my limbs over his while that wonderful mouth continues to move over mine causing a tremor to travel down my spine.

"Relax, Elle," he commands, a slightly amused look on his face, lightly running his fingertips over my mouth.

"Oh," I exhale in surprise, realizing I forgot to breathe. I hasten to comply, much to my awaking pleasure, his tongue gently probes, traces and dances in duet with mine. I feel him tremble against my own shiver of response. My hands tangle in his hair, fisted while I nibble one corner of his mouth, then the other, my breath exhaling like a torn sob. His hand roves the length of my body, igniting shots of white heat.

Later still drowsy in the aftermath of love, watching the clouds scuttle overhead, "Elle?" he murmurs against my ear.

"Umm?" I answer with a sleepy reply.

"You smell like the forest."

"What?" I look at him as if he has lost his mind.

"The forest, pine trees, ferns and moss. I think all that time you and Burt spend in the woods has seeped into your skin."

"How can moss smell, sounds like I need a shower."

"No, you smell clean and fresh, like opening the windows after a summer rain."

"You're silly." I'm distracted by his hands that have strayed from tickling to concentrating on more intimate areas. "Stop, stop, stop, let me catch my breath, you brute!" I holler in mock protest.

"Fine, fine, you're nothing but a woodland temptress

disguised under that sweet innocent face." He rolls onto his back resting his head on his hands, squinting up at the sun. "Oh, I almost forgot, guess what I have in here?" Vic sits up holding his pack over my head with a teasing come-and-get-it wag. "Mac gave us a going away present."

Oh, boy, I think to myself, anything from Kat and Mac is bound to be illegal.

Sure enough, Vic unzips his pack and takes out a small baggie with a marijuana joint in it.

"What do you think," he says shrugging. "Should we?"

As I lay here gloriously naked with nothing between me and the sky but bare skin...... is this really a good time to ask if I want to be prudent? Seems a little late for conservative thinking. "It's a shame to waste a perfectly good joint." I answer with a sweet innocent look on my face. "Light it up, baby!"

"Yes, Miss Bossy Pants," he shakes his finger at me as if admonishing a precocious child. "Or rather Miss Bossy without her pants."

"Yes, sir," I respond, giving him a mock salute.

Vic takes out a small packet of matches advertising a restaurant in New York City and lights the joint. He inhales and passes it to me on delicate fingertips.

Lying in his arms, the heady sweet smell of pot, combined with the warmth of afternoon sun, causes my body to melt on a tide of relaxed euphoria.

"Elle, pose for me." Vic asks in a lazy voice holding up his camera with a quizzical look on his face.

"What?' I rouse from my languor to look at him.

"I want your picture in the black- eyed Susans."

"In the daisies? But I'm naked."

"Nude, its art."

Drunk on the sun, high from the joint, inhibitions cast aside under the loving reverence coming from his eyes, I ask tentatively, "Can I wear my hat?" As if the hat somehow makes it less nude.

"Sure," he replies, changing the lens on his camera, turning the dials, checking for light and focus.

The camera in the hands of a skilled photographer can open doors into a person's soul as angles and shafts of light pierce though hidden veneers, little revealed secrets exposed onto film, images held frozen in time, captured, then bared to witness. Vic has the gift of understanding light and color, blending the shadows to a whole, drawing the eye to an image of balance and pleasure. We play hide and seek with the camera between the stalks of black-eyed Susans. His eyes making love to me through the shutter, *click, click* as I bask in the glow of his affection. Flowers placed strategically with careful posing preclude the pictures from being lewd, art graced by golden flowers dancing in the breeze. The photographs capturing innocence on the brink of womanhood, tasting the first fruits of adulthood while still cloaked in the quintessence of youth.

As the sun sets in the western horizon, we swim in the icy cold current that feeds the lake from an underground spring, the cold shocking us back to reality. With a towel snitched from the camp laundry, we buff off chilled skin roughened by goose bumps, the dry air of late summer holds the hint of autumn. We dress each other slowly from the pile of clothes left in a careless heap. Loving hands smooth down shirts, buttons slip through holes… a kiss left with tender care as a collar is folded into place. Taking the last cigarette from the crushed pack, Vic smiles, "That's it, summer's done." He crumples the wrapper into a tight ball, and with the whisper of a match, the cigarette glows. We share that last cigarette, slowly exhaling, staining the night air with rings of smoke. Holding our scarred hands together, we sit watching the sunset turn the sky pink, grey and vermillion and fade to twilight as the stars appear on the horizon's edge. Morris will be furious…..we've missed dinner and have no excuse, because summer is gone…..and only the abyss of winter lies ahead.

Adirondack Lost

Chapter 16

Helen

"Welcome home, Ellen," my stepmother, Helen, says without a trace of warmth in her voice, turning her cheek so I can dutifully kiss her. "It is certainly good to have you home after your little vacation to the mountains. Starting tomorrow we're cleaning the house from top to bottom. It's entirely too much work for me. I've been patiently waiting for you to come home from all that camp foolishness." In a snit of jealousy, she pulls my brothers away before I can hug them. "Boys, leave your sister alone, I'm sure she's too grown up from her camp experience to want your attention." She says *camp*, as if it were a dirty word. As I look at my brothers' sun-kissed freckle faces, I realize how much I've missed them. I do want their attention. At one time we were everything to each other.

As my father extends his arms to hug me, Helen commands, "John, get Ellen's bag so we can head for home." She nods to me. "I told your grandmother not to come knowing you would be too tired from the bus ride." And like three little puppets on a string, my father and brothers jump to do her bidding. My heart sinks, some things never change.....

...

Just before Halloween at dinner one evening, Helen casually mentions my brother Rory has a hockey tournament in Pennsylvania the weekend of November 15th. An idea bursts in my head like a Fourth of July fireworks display. Vic's school is on holiday that week, something about the patron saint's feast day. He was hoping to come back to New York to visit his mother. The timing is perfect. No one knows about Vic, not my friends at school, certainly not my father or Helen, not even Gran. I can't bring him to Helen's house and the thought of meeting him in a hotel is gross...it's time to tell my grandmother.

....

Convincing Gran to let Vic stay for the weekend while my family travels to the hockey tournament was……a piece of cake. Barely able to contain her curiosity, she readily agreed to the visit. And in her no nonsense, blunt vernacular she said, "You tell lover boy to get his ass up here so your grandmother can meet him."

So on a cold November day, the rain drumming against the pulsing windshield wipers, we drive to the bus station. Graciously, Gran waits in the car while I go meet Vic. The large white clock on the wall shows I'm fifteen minutes early. I pace back and forth by the arrival dock for the bus, my stomach a twisted coil of nerves, hands thrust in the pockets of my jeans, staring anxiously at the arrival ramp. Imagining our reunion, I see myself running to him in slow motion like in the movies, flinging my arms around him, embracing him with a mad passionate kiss. That was my image until I see him get off the bus…….he stops half way down the steps, scanning the waiting crowd for me. Our eyes meet, his dark eyes glitter hungrily. I blush and he still stares. A crooked smile plays across his face. *Holy cow*. He's grown taller, he's now maybe, six two, six three. Skin tanned, carrying a hint of bronze left over from the summer. His hair so long it skims the collar of his black leather jacket, unzipped showing the denim work shirt layered over a white T-shirt. His worn jeans slung low on his hips are cuffed over scuffed hiking boots. He looks….*fantastic!* Kind of that "dirty" boy look with the wrinkled worn clothing, shaggy hair, day old growth of beard, a look that is so, so sexy. I can't move. I'm paralyzed with the thought…this is him……he is gorgeous….and he is coming home with *me*! He smiles, waving as he trots across the station zigzagging around people toward me. I just stand there, rooted to the spot with a silly grin plastered to my face. Dropping his backpack at my feet, he's so close, but he doesn't touch me. His proximity is overwhelming, exhilarating. The familiar pull is there, all my instincts goading me toward him, staring at the patch of skin showing in the V of his shirt, I bite my lip, helpless, driven by desire. I want to taste him there. *Damn him.*

He sweeps me up in a huge hug. I reach up, diving my fingers in the unruly waves of dark hair at the base of his neck, pull his head down to meet my lips, blushing at the brazen intensity of my kiss. The sight of two teenagers kissing draws stares of amusement and some of outrage. I don't care who sees us kissing and less of their opinion……until I hear behind me, "Et, hm, I was wondering if there was a problem." Turning in Vic's arms, my stomach drops, it's my grandmother, looking both amused and outraged at the same time, if that is possible. *Oh, I am so screwed….*

"Oh, Gran," I cringe in embarrassment.

Before I'm able to gather my wits, Vic extends his hand to Gran with courtly grace and Old World charm saying, "Hello, Mrs. McCauley, I'm Vicente Rienz. Thank you for your hospitality and allowing me to stay with you for the weekend. I am honored to be invited." His accent seems even more pronounced than usual. "Call me Vic."

I look at him in alarm, who is this Spanish grandee straight off the hacienda trying to charm my grandmother. And charm her he does, I watch in amazement as my sixty-eight year old grandmother melts beneath his gaze.

"Hello, Vic. I'm Ellen's grandmother, Bernice, but everyone calls me Bernie, you should too." Gran accepts his outstretched hand, sizing him up for character content and flaw. Their eyes meet over the handshake, approval sealed with a nod.

...

Gran's house is a small red cabin at the base of a steep hill. In the summer, the surrounding gardens are glorious with flowers. Now, the small porch sadly overlooks the remains of her flowerbed, only lifeless stalks of seed heads encased in frost hold promise of spring and life again. The entrance to the house is crammed with pots of geraniums to "winter over" on window ledges. Gran directs Vic to leave his duffle bag in the living room where the fieldstone fireplace dominates the room under a ceiling of exposed beams. The room is rich in color, wood paneling mellowed over the years to a reddish cherry hue. Plaid fabric on the couch and chairs harmonizes with pillows and rugs covered in matching earth tones make for a cozy retreat from the weather.

Outside the security of the snug cabin, gusty winds out of the west rattle the windows and rain beats on the roof with the promise of snow by morning. The fire in the grate glows red, popping and spitting bits of gold embers against the hearth.

We eat dinner on the floor in front of the fireplace. Vic tells Gran about his life, how his family moves back and forth between Mexico and New York City. From his duffle bag he brings out photographs of his family and country along with the ones taken over the summer.

"These are really good," Gran says holding the pictures up to the light, stopping when she sees one of me. I'm sitting in a canoe, legs dangling over the edge, a smile peeking out from under a straw hat. The colors and composition of the photograph are nearly perfect almost professional quality. "Do you have any more?" she asks.

Before Vic can answer, I try changing the subject and suggest, "How about playing some cards?" I'm nervous some of those "naked daisy day" pictures might be lurking in his pack. The last thing my grandmother needs to see is my naked butt in a field of daisies. Jumping to my feet I say, "I'll get the deck." Knowing fully well Gran can't resist a game of cards. "You decide what we should play."

Vic and Gran's eyes light up and in unison they yell, "Poker!" I groan. I'm a terrible poker player. I couldn't bluff my way out of a convent full of nuns. For the next few hours, Vic and Gran are in their element, dealing cards, checking their hands, betting, folding, and scrutinizing each other under hooded eyes, expressionless faces, impossible to know who's bluffing who. If my Grandmother lost a hand, she smacked her cards down with a resounding *slam* and called him a "horse's ass." By the end of the night he has his baseball cap on backward, saying to her, "What's the matter, Granny, 'fraid to put your money where your mouth is?" He finishes the insult by stealing one of her cigarettes, leaning back in his chair to blow smoke rings in the air above her head.

"You, little shit, take that," she'd counter, laying down a winning hand. Banging the table with her fist, she swept in his dwindling pile of peanuts, the accepted currency of the night and cackle like an old satisfied hen on a brood of eggs. At midnight a truce was called, Gran having the slightly larger pile of peanuts. I vow never to suggest cards again. Gran asks where he learned to play so well; Vic admitted the cowboys on the ranch in Mexico taught him…….and what else did the cowboys on the ranch teach him? Combat guerilla warfare, drug smuggling, possibly cattle rustling, counterfeiting……

After Gran goes to bed, Vic and I curl up in each other's arms, a movie playing in the background, but we're oblivious to the television screen. The hours pass by, hugging, talking and kissing. At two o'clock in the morning Gran calls down from her bedroom, "Hey, you two, how about getting some sleep. Ellen, you go upstairs to your room. And lover boy, you had better not leave that couch or your ass will be out in the cold, hitch-hiking your way home……...no one tells it like my Gran.

…

A light snow fell overnight, blanketing the grass with a carpet of white. The temperatures hover in the thirties. The day is spent hiking and exploring the creeks and ravines that traverse the steep slopes behind Gran's cabin.

I've missed you, mia bella," he stops, leaning me against a tree. I feel the rough bark through my wool jacket. Shoving his gloves in his pockets, his hands warm my cold cheeks, and slowly his lips lower. Gently at first, then with increased intensity devouring my lips, his mouth traces the warmth of his hands along my cheekbones and down my neck. Pulling the hat from my head, his hands run through my hair catching the lingering rays of afternoon sun. His breath glazes my hair as he whispers in my ear, "Elle, I can't tell you how you torment my dreams." Strong, sinewy arms gather me close, the warmth from our bodies dispelling the chill of November air.

His chin rests gently on top of my head. My mouth posed at the hollow of his neck allows me to place small kisses along the curve of his collarbone. His hair having lost the gold sheen of summer is darker, longer, brushing the collar of his plaid flannel shirt. I gather it up in a ponytail, luxuriating in the silken feel teasing at my fingertips.

"Oh, before I forget, I brought you something." He taps his chin playfully. "Let me think, where did I put it?"

"Really? You didn't need to bring me anything."

Looking skyward, he shakes his head as his right hand reaches into the front pocket of his jeans…….those jeans so tightly stretched across his slender hips, and he extracts a small manila jeweler's envelope. "Sit down, Mia," he points with boyish eagerness to a tree stump.

He shakes the envelope and a shiny object slides into his fingers. "Close your eyes and hold out your hand," he instructs, placing a soft kiss on my forehead. Slightly suspicious, I cocked my head to one side, but dark eyes shuttered by long fringed lashes give no clues.

"This had better not be a frog or snake…"

"Seriously, look who you're talking to….I don't do slimy things."

"They're not slimy."

"Be quiet and close your eyes."

With eyes closed……he places a delicate object with a chain in my hand, my fingers close around the gift as he whispers, "Okay, open your eyes."

Resting in the palm of my hand is a delicate silver chain with a small heart-shaped locket, the etching on the outside of the locket shines in the weak sunlight. A gasp of astonishment escapes my lips at the beautiful workmanship lying in my hand. The locket looks antique.

"Oh, Vic, this is beautiful." I turn the locket over examining the clasp, "Help me put it on."

"Here," he takes the piece and the hinge springs open revealing two miniature pictures. "You, on one side of the locket and me on the other side, two hearts come together as one." He turns the locket and the words *Cor te reducit* are inscribed on the back. "It belonged to my grandmother on my father's side."

"Oh, Vic, I can't accept this, it belonged to your grandmother." I shake my head vehemently. "It's too precious. What if I lose it or something? I'll be afraid to wear it."

He holds up a hand to silence me. "Mia, mia, it is for you. It's mine to give. Please accept it."

I tuck a lock of hair behind my ears. "Thank you." I say softly, rubbing my finger over the raised surface of the engraving. "What do the words mean?"

"The words are in Latin, translated it means, the heart leads you back." He takes the locket from my hand and his fingers undo the top buttons of my blouse, leaving a trail of heat between my breasts. Holding up the silver locket from his grandmother, he says, "My heart will always lead me back to you." The words weigh heavy on my chest like an unspoken vow. Quietly, I take the chain and slip it over my neck, holding my hand over his heart and say, "I will wear it always." Our lips meet, forging a pledge.

Snowflakes like soft white petals fall from the sky landing on our cheeks, with infinite care he kisses each melting flake, sending sparks through my body where cool diamonds lay. With my face in his hands, his kisses deepen, in a voice hoarse with emotion he says, "I love you." And while daylight fails and night falls, the snowflakes drift and blow, lift and fly, I tenderly kiss the inside of his palm, our eyes lock, "And I will always love you, Vic."

Chapter 17

The Jig is Up

The slashing snow and rain of December scold in the dormant days of winter. The bullfrogs retreat to the bottom of the pond and marsh cattails explode into powder puffs leaving naked stalks of brown scattered across the shore. Fallen leaves cast adrift whirl like cyclones to rend and smash against stationary obstacles in their path.

Time is running out, time is running out, soon your secret will be out, out, out…..

I lied to Vic; it wasn't mono, making me feel so tired. I'm not feeling better, if anything, I feel worse. Fatigue plagues my days…….because I'm pregnant.

As much as I try to deny the reality of my situation, this morning I marked off December 15 on the calendar. It's been over four months since I've had a period.

The cold truth permeates my bones chilling them as the frost outside the window encases the trees and grasses in a suffocating hold of ice and snow. Trapped, my mind not allowing the word to form, even thinking the word pregnant condones acceptance of the impossible. How could I have been so stupid? My mind rails in a tirade of self-recrimination.

…

January ushered in the New Year with a flurry of blizzards. The winds from the west blowing lake effect snows off Lake Ontario with a vengeance, dumping five to seven feet of snow, non-stop for three days. Living in upstate New York, blizzards are a natural occurrence, taking place any time from November through the early part of April. While the storms raged outside, I battle the need to confide in someone about the baby. Desperate for help, I decide to tell Gran. As much as I want to tell Vic first, I need a plan. There must be a way we can graduate from high school and keep our baby. As terrified as I am over the prospect of having a child, I want our baby.

And I had a plan; it was a good plan except for one major flaw. On the final day of the blizzard, my independent grandmother decided to climb up and shovel the snow off her roof. She's done this for years, but she turned sixty-eight last July. My father insisted it was too risky for her to climb up on the roof. He would do it from now on. Well,....no one...and I mean no one....tells my grandmother what to do. She climbed on the roof, slipped and fell. She lay unconscious in the snow for several hours until a neighbor stopped by to check on her. He found her lying in the cold and called the emergency squad. The ambulance rushed her to a local hospital, where she was treated for frostbite and spent eight hours in surgery to mend a broken hip and place two pins in her right leg. The surgeon predicted a long stay in a rehabilitation facility before she'd be able to live independently again.

Devastated over Gran's injury and the fact I have no one to trust. I feel the bile green color of the hospital walls close around me, my thudding heart rises in my chest and threatens to choke me. Like an animal caught in a trap, I freeze......incapable of thought or action.

...

And the noose tightens around my neck....Helen is suspicious. Even though I am tall and thin, wearing baggy sweatshirts and jeans does not conceal six months of pregnancy. Tonight at dinner with a smirk on her face, Helen announces she's made an appointment for me with Dr. Richards next Tuesday. She claims I have not been "right" since returning from camp this summer; her face wears the predatory gloat of a cat ready to pounce on a cornered mouse. The jig is up …….. she knows. I feel my cheeks flush with color as I hide my trembling hands under the table. Mustering my courage, I look her in the eyes and calmly tell her I would be happy to visit Dr. Richards. *The bitch.* Her eyes widen in surprise at my acquiesce. I smile smugly at her though I fear I may throw up…….all over her favorite table cloth. Serve her right.

There is no other choice; I need to be out of this house by Tuesday. To give Helen the satisfaction of a confrontation is pointless. In this house she is absolute power, dominating the will of those who lived under her roof. I'm simply a pawn in her web. I will leave on my own terms before she makes me abide by her terms. I have to tell Vic but first….

…

"Burt?"

"Hey, what's *Happening*?"

"Is this Burt?"

"Of course it is, who else would you be calling at this number? Who are *You*?"

"Burt, this is Ellen." I cringe; this is the man who's going to be my savior, but just hearing his voice lightens my heart, even if he still *emphasizes* his words.

"Ellen *Who*? My sixth grade math teacher, Ellen or my Aunt Ellen with the bad breath or are you, my favorite Ellen, the little one from camp, infamous underwear thief?" Oh boy, he knows me too well.

"Burt, it's your favorite Ellen, you goofball."

"*Hey*, did you figure out how to make Falafel yet?" I groan in despair, thinking some things never change.

"No!"

"Well, I guess you're still my favorite, but you're on waivers, maybe my aunt started using mouthwash, so you're treading on thin ice. What's *up*, Kiddo?"

I hesitate; looking out the scratched window of the phone booth, making sure no one is listening. "Umm, Vic is coming to town this weekend. We thought it would be fun to see you. We'd take the bus to Ohio. If you're not busy, could you pick us up at the bus station?"

"Sure, I'd love to *See* you." His voice sounds puzzled. "Are your parents okay with this plan?"

"Oh, yes, absolutely." I gush. "They thought it was a great idea." *Damn.* Too much information, Burt knows our parents and the idea of them being thrilled over our little road trip is preposterous.

"Really? The two knuckleheads are traveling alone? Are *You* okay, Ellen?"

"Yes, yes, just fine."

"Okay," he starts slowly. "*Mi Casa est Sous Casa.* Or whatever the hell Vic would say in Spanish."

"Oh, thank you, Burt." Relief floods through my voice.

"Ellen, do you want me to come and pick you up?" Concern clouds his voice. "It's not a *problem.* I could use a break from the sabbatical research.*On the Road Again* and all that Willie Nelson bullshit. I really don't *Mind.*"

And here at this moment, I make a decision I will regret for the rest of my life. "No, Burt, really, we'll be fine. I'll call when we get close."

Chapter 18

Confession

San Miguel Academy, Mexico

The ringing of the phone in the hallway shatters the pre-dawn silence at Saint Miguel Academy. As the sun approaches from the east, the morning birds roosting in the trees open their throats to warble in the day. One of the boys annoyed by the unanswered ringing of the phone stumbles into the hall and snatches up the receiver, brusquely demanding, "What the hell do you want?" He leans on his elbow against the rough stucco wall listening to the response on the other end. "Vic, it's for you, some girl. I don't know, I think she's speaking English." He announces as he lets the receiver fall and bounce off the wall swaying from the cord, shuffling back to his room scratching his butt through his pajama bottoms.

Vic lifts his head from the pillow, suddenly wide awake; his adrenaline response at full alert, knowing an early morning call can only mean trouble. Kicking aside the bed sheets, he hastily dons a pair of sweatpants lying on the cold floor and stumbles to retrieve the phone. With his heart in his throat he answers, "Hello?" There's no reply from the other line, so he repeats, "Hello?"

"Vic," comes the sound of Ellen's voice weeping.

"Elle?" He asks, pulling the stretched-out cord of the phone into his bedroom, shutting the door against the prying ears of the other students living on the floor.

"Elle, what's wrong, talk to me, *querida,* why are you crying?" he asks, confusion clouding his voice; "Is something wrong with Gran?"

"No, Gran is doing fine, it's not her. It's me." Ellen tries to explain. "I'm calling from a phone booth. I don't want anyone to hear." She is weeping uncontrollably, huge gasping sobs, almost hysterical.

"Ella, tell me what's wrong." Vic demands, running a hand through his hair, pacing as far as the cord will allow, moving in a confined circle. "Elle, please talk to me. I'm here, *caro*. Take a deep breath, calm down. Whatever it is, we can fix it."

"I don't think so, Vic……I'm pregnant," she gasps out the words between sobs and only stunned silence comes over the line. "Vic? Are you there?" There is a thud as the receiver of the phone bangs to the floor.

"Vic! Answer me," she shouts into the phone when he makes no reply. "Vic, say something, you're scaring me."

Vic picks up the receiver, trying to control the trembling in his voice. "Elle, did you say, pregnant?" he asks in disbelief feeling his heart hammer a hole through the wall of his chest.

"Vic, I'm pregnant with our baby."

"*What!?*" His breath grows ragged as he slides down the door frame, sitting with his head cradled in his hands, panic coursing through his body. " Are you absolutely sure? I don't understand. My God, how many months pregnant are you?"

"I'm six months pregnant, Vic. I know how stupid this sounds. I just kept hoping it was mono or something…." In a ragged whisper she says, "I can feel the baby kicking, I'm definitely pregnant."

"Why didn't you tell me sooner," he asks, incredulous she would keep this secret from him. "Why did you keep this from me?" Anger seeps into his voice as shock mingles with disbelief.

"Please don't be angry with me, I haven't told anyone." She sounds almost apologetic. "I was going to tell Gran. I know she would help me, but she had the accident. And…and I didn't want to worry you."

"You didn't want to worry me!" His voice rises in consternation. "I think I had damn well better be worried, like about five months ago. What the hell were you thinking!"

"I don't know!" Her sobs come in heaving gasps, desperately needing his reassurance not this shocked wraith. "I was afraid. I didn't know what to do."

"How could you keep this from me?!"

"Vic, I wanted to tell you so many times, but I was afraid. I didn't want you to leave school." She pauses, trying to regain her composure. "We *have* to finish school this year. How else can we go to college? It's our only hope."

Vic leans against the wall, closing his eyes as the enormity of their situation becomes a reality.

"Vic,' Ellen whispers into the phone. "I'm frightened. I need you so badly."

Vic takes a deep breath, stands tall, straightening his shoulders to the responsibility ahead of him. "Oh, Ella, Ella, mia, forgive me, *querida,"* his anger vanishes, as he leans his head against the door for support, wishing he could slip through the phone line and take her in his arms. "I'm sorry. I didn't mean to scare you. It's just such a shock, that's all…..Let's both calm down and figure out what to do. Have you seen a doctor?"

"No, Helen made an appointment for me to see one next week, I think she knows. Vic, I'm starting to show."

"Listen to me carefully," he says aching to touch her face, wipe away her tears and fear. "I love you very much."

"I love you." Snuffling through the tears, relief floods her voice as his anger is replaced by concern.

"I'm coming to get you." His voice takes on a reassuring tone as his mind races from one plan to the next accepting and rejecting possibilities in a matter of seconds.

"Vic, I called Burt," Ellen says. "I didn't tell him anything. I only said we wanted to come for a visit. I think he was suspicious, he even offered to come get us, but I didn't know when you would be able to get here."

"Good thinking. Burt will help us." he sighs, pausing. "Go about your normal routine. I'll leave immediately; catch a flight to New York and then a bus to you. When I arrive in New York City, I'll call and let you know approximately what time the bus will get into town. Try to bring as much money as you can get together." He rubs his forehead to stop the throbbing in his temples.

"Gran started a joint account for me several years ago; she called it my nest egg, just in case I needed money for an emergency. I went to the bank after school today and withdrew the money. There was about two thousand dollars in the account."

"Thank God for Gran, that will get us to Burt and still have some left over. Then we'll think of another way to come up with some cash," he says, squatting down on his hunches. "But we can't plan too far ahead, let's just worry about the next few days."

"Once you're here, I'll be okay. I just need you to hold me."

"I wish I was with you now." Vic closes his eyes,

picturing her in his arms, safe from harm. "I had better get going, the sooner I start traveling the sooner I'll be with you. Can you hold out until I get there?"

"Yes, I feel better already."

"I love you."

"Love you back." And the phone lines go dead.

Chapter 19

The Bull is Unleashed

Pushing open the door and switching on the lights, Vic's father, Ramon Rienz walks into the chic New York City apartment, no sound of warm greeting welcomes him home after a long day of business negotiations. Without looking, he knows his wife is passed out across the pale blue comforter in her separate bedroom, another day of wooing the vodka bottle.

Shaking his head in disgust he walks to the wet bar, tosses a few ice cubes in a tumbler and pours himself a shot of whiskey and a splash of water. Surveying the main living space of the apartment his face twists in a grimace of distaste; his wife's decorating style evident in every single piece of furniture and fancy whatnots. The thick white carpet is soft in contrast to the azure blue walls and sofa, accented with pale shades of yellow. Her artistic taste apparent in the Impressionist reproductions hanging from ornate picture frames throughout the apartment. The room too formal and feminine for his taste, he prefers the rustic atmosphere of the ranch. His idea of comfort is not silk pillows edged in lace. He loosens the tie around his neck, and tosses his suit jacket across the back of the couch. Pulling at the cuffs of his French tailored shirt, he takes out the cufflinks and rolls up his shirtsleeves. With a manicured hand, he smooths back his hair, touched at the temples with just the right amount of dignified gray. Sighing, he takes a sip of whiskey, still a handsome man at the age of fifty-four; he has no problems attracting women. He just doesn't like keeping them; inevitably they turn into whining nags and shrews. Except for Maraposia, his mistress back in Mexico, together not out of love, maybe lust, they understand each other. She is also ruthless in pursuit of her needs. One of the few women in his life tolerated for more than a casual fling. She serves a purpose, but if need be, she can be discarded without remorse. Feeling restless he walks out onto the balcony overlooking the city inhaling the cold January air, clearing his head of the tension nagging at his temples. Setting the glass on the balcony railing, he reaches up stretching his back releasing muscles cramped from hours of meetings.

Through the open balcony door he hears the sound of a phone ringing. Glancing down at his watch in annoyance, he thinks, who the hell calls this late at night? Not relishing the prospect of further business dealings this late, he idly contemplates ignoring the irksome ringing. He casts a wistful glance at the television where he planned to relax and watch the basketball game. But his sense of duty sends him into the study; the phone sits atop a leather blotter on the mahogany desk. A family picture of his wife and children taken at the ranch stares up at him as he answers the phone with an impatient, "Hello, Ramon Rienz."

"Mr. Rienz," an apologetic voice replies. "This is Louis Salvatore, the headmaster of St. Miguel's School. I'm sorry to be calling so late at night, but I thought you would like to know."

Yes, fine, fine, what do I need to know, what has Vicente done this time?" Ramon has grown wearily of dealing with the mischief his four sons have created over the past two decades. Vicente is the youngest and Ramon's patience has worn thin, with little tolerance for the antics of adolescence. Vicente's life has been mapped out for him since he was a young child. It pleased Ramon his son agreed to finish high school at St. Miguel's and Ramon planned on enrolling Vicente at the University of Mexico in the fall. After he finishes the pre-requisite four years, he will return to the ranch, marry his betrothed Isabella Martin and work in the family business. It has been decided. There will be no deviation from the plan, the other sons obeyed the family wishes, and Vicente will do the same.

"Umm, Mr. Rienz, I regret to inform you that Vicente has left school." Mr. Salvatore voice waives over the phone line.

"What do you mean he left school?" Ramon asks irritably, he despised the current head master of the school thinking Salvatore was an impotent fool. Ramon shakes his head in disgust. The man's appointment to the position of head master was based on academic merit not his administrative skills. As a member of the school board, Ramon had expressed his disapproval over the appointment of Salvatore. It rankled him the school board chose to override his veto and appoint the man to the post. Now the reality of this thin, balding incompetent fool calling him at his home, informing him that he'd lost his son was more than his patience could bear.

"You've lost my son!" He rebukes in a voice dripping with sarcasm.

"No, Mr. Rienz, the school did not lose your son, your son chose to run away from school."

"I leave him in your care and he just disappears, seems like a case of incompetence to me. I want an explanation on the where abouts of my son and I want it now." Ramon slams down the tumbler of whiskey causing a fine spray of droplets to mar the smooth surface of the desktop.

"The nurse was told he had the stomach flu and wished to stay in his room for the day. A staff member went to check on him at dinnertime and was unable to locate him." Mr. Salvatore explained, knowing fully well that Rienz would not accept this accounting of what had happened.

"So you waited until dinner time to check on the condition of my sick son, he damn well could have been dead by that time!" Ramon bellows into the phone.

"His cousin, Hector, assured us that his condition was not serious. Vicente just needed to rest, and we trusted the judgment of an immediate family member." Mr. Salvatore replies in an even tone of voice.

"Where is Hector, I want to talk to him."

"I am sorry to say once we discovered Vicente missing; suddenly Hector was no longer available for questioning. We believe he is covering up for your son's disappearance and doesn't want to be questioned. I'm sure he will turn up shortly."

"So now, you blundering fool, you have lost both my son and my nephew, and you expect me to be calm about this situation."

"No, I was hoping the family would have a reason for the boys to be missing from school." Salvatore responds realizing the possibility of losing his job over the incident. And as much as he despised the boy's father, he genuinely liked Vicente and hoped the boy was not in serious trouble.

"What time was my son last seen?" Ramon voice snaps over the phone.

"He was at dinner last night. When he failed to show up for dinner this evening a staff member went to check up on him and discovered him missing. One of the boys living on the floor said Vicente received a phone call from a girl early this morning, but couldn't identify the girl."

"A girl?" Ramon asks; dread snaking through his empty stomach.

"Yes, the boy said it was definitely a girl. I'm sorry there is no further information at this time, but I felt you should be called and informed."

"Thank you so kindly for nothing!" Ramon bellows, slamming down the receiver, storming down the hall toward his wife's bedroom.

"Elyse, damn it, wake up!"

Elyse Rienz lifts her head from the pillow, blinking at Ramon standing in her doorway. The presence of her angry husband sends a tremor of fear down her spine. Filling the doorframe to her bedroom, Ramon Rienz is six foot two inches of raw fury, with the body of a linebacker. He was a boxer in his college days and not against using his fists on occasion to persuade his sons and once even his wife to see his point of view. This dogged persistence made him the heavy weight champion in his senior year at college and the core of his bulldog attitude in business dealings. No one liked to cross Ramon Rienz, least of all his wife.

"What's the matter, Ramon?" She asks, sitting up in bed reaching to turn on the bedside lamp.

"Vicente is gone from school. Do you know anything about this?"

"Gone, what do you mean gone?" She questions pushing back her shoulder length blonde hair, concern for her youngest son penetrating her drunken stupor.

"Gone, God damn it, left school and no one knows where. Hector is covering for him and now he's disappeared. Something is up, supposedly some girl called this morning asking for Vicente and then he left shortly after. Do you know anything about a girl?"

"No, he's never mentioned anyone in particular that I can recall."

"As usual you don't know shit." He turns on his heel, stalking off in the direction of Vic's bedroom. Elyse follows behind him pulling on a silk bathrobe, hastily knotting it at her waist.

"What are you doing?"

"I'm going to search his room to see if I can find any clues as to where he could possibly be going. That idiot at the school had no idea where to start searching." He marches into the room, pulling open drawers, tossing the contents onto the floor with little regard to the mess he was creating. He flips over the mattress, searching under the bed then flings open the closet door to rifle through the clothes and art supplies neatly arranged on shelves.

"Nothing, what the fuck!" Ramon curses. He stands with his hands on his hips, breathing heavily from the exertion of his demolition, surveying the room for the slightest trace into the hidden life of his son. "There has to be something here, a kid doesn't leave school for no reason. Who is this girl and why has he left school? Damn it!"

He pulls the dresser away from the wall and there taped to the back are two manila envelopes containing all the clues he needs. Ripping the envelopes from the dresser he crosses the room in two strides tossing the contents on top of the bed. Letters from Ellen written over Christmas break spill across the bedspread and reveal to his prying eyes the relationship she shared with his son. The second envelope contains the pictures taken over the summer including the ones showing her naked among the black-eyed Susans that hot August day.

"I'll be a son of a bitch. God damn it, I'll kill him when I get my hands on him. Who the hell is this little *punta?* Nothing but a whore, look at these pictures." He throws the pictures on the bed and snatches up one of the letters. "No return address, damn it." He marches from the room calling over his shoulder, "I'm calling Morris Erhart and then Carl, head of our security division, time to call in some favors and find my son before he becomes anymore involved with this whore!"

Elyse sits down on the bed and with a shaking hand picks up the pictures, looking at them closely one by one. She doesn't see a whore. What she sees is a beautiful young girl not quite a woman with vivid blue eyes shining out with a look of all-consuming love for her son. She looks at the pictures with the eyes of an artist, observing the carefully rendered photographs that use light and angles to portray his love for this girl captured on film. The letters open her eyes to the loneliness and longing she had no idea existed in her son, a mutual loneliness the two young lovers shared. She carefully gathers up the letters and pictures and hides them away in her room before her husband destroys them in his fury.

She stands hesitantly at the door to his den; one hand placed tentatively on the doorjamb watching him gesture wildly in the air with his free hand as he shouts orders into the phone. When he hangs up she enters his den timidly and he looks up at her with a glance of disgust.

"Throw those letters and pictures in the trash, do you

hear me." He commands in a menacing tone.

"Yes," she lies refusing to meet his eyes. "Ramon, I read a few of those letters, maybe we should slow down and talk to Vicente. They sound like two kids who have fallen in love. Do you need to call in the police and security people? Why don't we try to keep this private?"

"Bullshit, I talked to the girl's parents and apparently she's gone also. They had no idea she was seeing anyone, but the step-mother thinks she's pregnant. Obviously, they're on the run."

"Oh, Ramon, Vic knew you would disapprove of him seeing anyone but Isabella. So of course he hid his relationship with this girl. He must love her very much. Let's give them a chance to share their side of the story."

"Why don't you just shut up and I'll handle this, the way I have to handle everything in this family. Look what falling in love did for the two of us. I should have followed my father's wishes and married the woman he picked out for me. But no, I had to have you and look what that has gotten the two of us, nothing but misery. I won't let my son make the same mistake. He is betrothed to Isabella Martin and that is who he will marry." He turns away from Elyse shaking his head in disgust. "Why don't you go and find your bottle because that seems to be the only thing you are capable of doing. You're nothing but a drunk. Fine mother, you turned out to be." He pushes past her nearly knocking her to the floor in his haste to leave the room.

Chapter 20

Revenge

Sitting with hands jammed into my pockets, I look down at the floor as fear burrows a deep hole in my gut escaping in shuddering bursts of trembling. Vic, please come, I pray to myself. You said you would come, no matter what. Please get me out of here, I'm going to disintegrate, explode into a million pieces, panic only moments away.

The cold concrete walls of the bus station close in; the bright orange chairs with chrome legs became an anchor to focus on as nausea and dizziness whirl before my eyes. The smell of diesel fumes hangs in the stale overheated air. I hug my backpack to my chest as desperate eyes search for him to appear. Panic threatens to overwhelm me……where is he, he should be here by now, what if something happens to him. What will I do? Oh, God…….

Placing a protective hand over my stomach, my anxious thoughts race on…..okay, baby, we have to stay calm, he'll be here soon. Everything will be all right. I repeat this mantra over and over to myself. Once we're in his arms, nothing can happen to us. In answer, the baby gives a soft kick to the right side of my ribs to reassure me.

And suddenly….he's there beside me. Vic slowly slips the backpack off his shoulders and opens his arms to me. I flung myself at him. His embrace nearly crushes me as his mouth seeks mine.

"Ella, Ella, my beautiful bella," He croons against my

hair, smoothing the coppery blonde strands back from my forehead, enfolding me against him. He opens his jacket so I can reach my arms around his waist, pressing into him, drinking in the encompassing warmth of his body heat trapped beneath the jacket. He grasps my face between his hands as if to stop the outflow of pain from a wound, his thumbs gently caress my cheekbone, and he kisses me for several long seconds. His lips taste like sunshine; and his mouth hot and cool at the same time, and I hear him say my name over and over again.

"I'm so sorry." I apologize as if the whole situation were my fault.

"Shhh, we'll be fine. Everything will work out as long as we're together," he nods "We'll think of something." But I hear the worry in his voice, his frown and the tense line that furrows his brows lets me know he's afraid. I've never seen Vic afraid and fear is written on his face. My heart begins a slow, insistent thudding against my ribs….we're in serious trouble.

"Did you call Burt?" He asks, squeezing his arms around me as if I'll disappear if he loosens his tightly clinched grasp.

"Yes." I burrow my face into his shirt inhaling the exotic scent of him; resting my head against his chest. Everything will be fine, with him I'm safe.

He waits a moment and asks, "What did you tell him?"

"Well, I didn't want to say too much over the phone. I was afraid someone in the house would overhear the conversation." I begin with a sigh, "I told him you were on your way."

"What did he say?"

"He asked if the Knuckleheads were in trouble."

"Knuckleheads, eh?"

"Yep," I say with the first smile to cross my face in days, "He asked if we needed him to pick us up. I told him we'll call from the bus station in Cincinnati." My hands revel in the feel of his back through the denim shirt, it feels so good to touch and hold him. I could stand here all night with my arms wrapped around him. With regret I lift my head and point to the sign announcing the arrivals and departures. "There is a bus leaving for Erie, Pennsylvania in fifteen minutes, if we hurry we can be out of here and on our way to Burt."

"Perfect, let's get this road trip started." He takes my hand leading me toward the ticket booth. I don't want to stay here. It's too close to your home."

...

The bus station in Erie was a smaller darker version of the one in Syracuse; it appeared older but cleaner. The walls painted the same impersonal colors, furniture chosen more for function than comfort. We sit huddled on chairs exhausted and disappointed. The next bus leaving for Cincinnati departs at six in the morning. It's ten o'clock at night. We face the prospect of a long night on hard chairs and no food.

Unfortunately, a wet sloppy January snowstorm blew in across Lake Erie making travel treacherous; calling Burt to pick us up on such a miserable night is not an option. We'll have to wait the night out.

I feel Vic take my hand. His fingers slip around mine, and I squeeze my eyes shut as I feel his lips brush my knuckles. He opens my jacket slipping his hand in the front pocket of his old hoody sweatshirt touching my stomach reverently. "Our baby… here, inside of you."

I nod, "its okay, you won't hurt it." I slip his hand

under the sweatshirt and cover it with my own, feeling his warmth seep through my skin, a penetrating glow inward to the baby, who kicks in response.

"Did you feel it?" I ask delighted by the look of amazement on his face.

"Holy shit," his eyes widen in awe as he stares at his hand hidden under the sweatshirt. He lifts his gaze to my face. "Ours," he whispers in a voice almost too quiet for me to hear.

"Are you angry?" I whisper, holding him still with my eyes.

"Elle, *querida,* no. How could I be angry with you?" He gazes at me, listening.

"I was so afraid. I didn't know what to do, so I did nothing." My throat closes in on me. "I felt like an animal frozen in the headlights of an on-coming car. I couldn't tell anyone or do anything. It was almost like if I ignored the baby, it wasn't real."

He leans back, looking deep into my eyes and says, "It's the three of us now, I don't know how or exactly what we will do, but we'll make a plan as we go along. Together. We love each other. We'll get married and somehow finish high school with Burt's help. Hopefully get scholarships for college and student housing with childcare. Keep the baby, we'll be a family."

"I love you." I smile into those dark eyes alive with amber glints of hope, trusting him. I desperately want to believe in the possibility. "A family," I repeat aloud. It sounds too good to be true. For as long as I can remember, I've yearned for a family, a normal family. Mom, Dad, siblings, a dog, a cat, the white picket fence. The total package. I run my hand along his jaw line, "Vic, you are my family."

We kiss sealing a pact over our unborn child, falling asleep in each other's arms, forming a protective tent of love over the baby.

. . .

A curling chill at the base of his spine wakes Vic with a start, his eyes open, horrified to see his father striding through the entrance doors followed by two State Troopers and what must be Ellen's parents.

"No!" He exclaims in disbelief. "Elle, quick wake up, they're here, we gotta run." He grabs my arm, yanking me to my feet. I gave a small scream, tripping in my haste as my eyes meet Helen's, she gives me a look that sends a chill through me like a rush of frigid arctic air.

"Run for the other door," I cry, picking up my backpack, making a dash for the exit at the far end of the terminal.

Just as we reach the exit, two young men, darker and heavier versions of Vic burst through the doors, his older brothers, Manuel and Louis. We're trapped, no place to run, as the seven of them close in on us.

With heaving chests and pounding hearts, Vic pushes me gently behind him in a protective gesture, and holds his hand up imploring them, "Listen, let's just stop and talk. I know you're angry with us. But please, just let us explain, we don't need the police."

"Angry isn't the half of it, you son of a bitch," my father yells at him. "You bastard, knocking up my daughter and trying to run off with her. Take your filthy Mexican greaser hands off of her." I stare in shock and disbelief at my father.

"Well, well, Vicente." Ramon Rienz says to his son with a sneer. "You certainly know how to pick them, charming people, just charming."

"Dad," Vic says with pleading eyes. "I know this a shock. Yeah, we made a mistake, but we're willing to accept the consequences. We want to get married and raise our baby. We have a friend who will help us, we'll be fine. We can do this, please just leave us alone."

"That solution is unacceptable to both families," His father states emphatically. "You are betrothed to Isabella Martin and your little *punta's* family does not wish to dirty their family honor with a *greaser* for a son-in-law."

Isabella Martin, who the hell is she? My brain screams.

"I don't love Isabella. I love Ellen. We won't be separated; we have to stay together. Please try and understand for once in your life."

"We're going home and you're coming…. alone."

"Mr. Rienz," I beseech him, moving alongside of Vic trying to keep the fear and fatigue out of my voice. "Please, can we talk, our friend is a teacher; he is older and responsible." Well, maybe, Burt is sort of responsible….echoes in my mind. "Burt will let us stay with him and then next year we can start college. Our grades are good enough to get scholarships, so we won't need any money. Please let us stay together. I'll die without him. Please don't do this to us." My plea ends on a sob. Anxiety mixed with frustration rises in my throat choking off the flow of oxygen to my lungs; I feel faint and lightheaded. This can't be happening.

"You little *punta*, you should have thought of that before you spread your legs for him like a common slut." Ramon Rienz says with vehemence, spitting at my feet, like I was a whore off the street. I reel back as if I'd been slapped.

Seventeen years of repressed rage erupts in Vic as he reaches back, and slams his fist in his father's face, blocking my father's enraged charge at Ramon. The collision sends my father crashing into the terminal wall.

"You, stupid bastard." Ramon says through a clenched jaw, wiping the blood trickling down his chin from the bruised corner of his mouth.

"Hold him, boys." He commands Manuel and Louis who seized Vic, preventing his attack against the man who bullied and repressed him every day of his life.

I watch in horror as Ramon's huge boxing hands slam into Vic's body with a sickening thud, "Noooo!" I scream, "Stop, stop it!" Turning to the police I beg, "Please make him stop before he kills him."

I lunge for Ramon's arm hoping to stop the punch only to be catapulted backward by the force of his swing. The older trooper catches me, breaking my fall, while his partner steps in and grabs Ramon's arm saying, "I think that is enough, Mr. Rienz." Both of the troopers looked embarrassed and uncomfortable over this display of family violence. Apparently this Mr. Rienz has friends in high places and tonight, he called in his favors and they were the unfortunate ones on duty.

In the confusion over my fall, Vic manages to slip from his brother's grasp, his hand snakes forward and with a quick deft motion flips the leather security strap from the younger trooper's holster and slides the gun out. He stands with a shaking arm, pointing the gun at his astonished audience; no one more startled by this unexpected turn of events than I. *Sweet Jesus, Holy Mary, mother of God, what is he doing?!*

"What the hell!" The younger trooper sputters spinning around as he feels the gun lifted from his belt.

"Nobody move." Vic says, in a quavering voice, wiping the blood out of his eyes, holding the gun in a steady aim at the stunned group.

"Elle, come over here, quick," he commands.

"Vic, what the hell are you doing?" I cry out in disbelief staring at the gun in horror.

"I haven't a clue, babe." he says with a half sob, shaking his head, chest heaving while his teeth catch his trembling lower lip. "They didn't leave us much choice, did they? I'm not leaving you."

What are we going to do? My mind races as seven pair of eyes watch our every move. "We can't shoot them for God's sake!"

"Son, you better put that gun down, you could go to jail for assault with a deadly weapon. Let's not have any more trouble here tonight." The older trooper appeals to Vic, "Come on kid, give me the gun before someone gets hurt."

"Can you guarantee they'll let us go?" Vic asks, raising his eyebrows in question, nodding as he watches the trooper shake his head. "I didn't think so."

I watch the scene play out before my terror filled eyes. "Vic! Look out behind you!" The station security guard dives at Vic from an exit leading to the loading platform. The gun flies from his hand spinning in crazy circles as it slides across the floor. The two troopers jump on Vic in a flash, handcuffing his hands behind his back, standing him up against the wall, searching him for concealed weapons. I watch aghast as the older trooper reaches into the pocket of Vic's leather jacket and draws out a small baggie with two joints sealed inside of it.

"That's not mine, Vic protests in disbelief. "I didn't have any pot." He turns to his father, his voice scalding with loathing. "You planted that shit on me, you son of a bitch!"

"Well, well, Vicente," His father smiles smugly. "You have been a very busy boy this evening, one pregnant girl, assaulting a police officer with a deadly weapon and now possession of an illegal substance. It's difficult to keep up with you, Son. Sounds like a little time in jail may cool your ardor and help you get your priorities in line, doesn't it?"

"Sir, it's not necessary to press charges." The younger trooper says shrugging his shoulders. "The kid felt he had his back up against the wall and had no choice, we could look the other way and let this go."

"Mr. McCauley," Ramon asks in a voice dripping with sarcasm, looking at my father with raised eyebrows. "What would you like to do?"

"I hope he rots in jail for what he did to my daughter." My father hisses, his face screwed up in a mask of hatred aimed at Vic. I never knew my father capable of such emotion. Unfortunately, I can't help but feel the sentiment is misplaced pride rather than love or concern for me.

"Daddy, please don't do this, please don't send him to jail." I beg him, tugging on his arm trying to have him just once look at me and realize that I'm real, not just a shadow in his life.

"I'll sign the papers tomorrow." My father answers with finality through clenched jaws. "Show up on my doorstep and next time I'll have the gun." He points his finger at Vic's chest. "And I swear to God, I'll kill you."

"No!" I wail, "Please, please, I beg of you." I'm screaming as hysteria courses through me, throwing my arms around Vic's waist, refusing to be separated from him.

"Officers, I'll meet you at the station house to help

process the paperwork. I'll make sure arrangement can be made for him to be extradited to Mexico." Ramon Rienz says smoothly. His trap baited, set and sprung. "There is no reason your government should bear the financial responsibility for the incarceration of my son. I'm sure Mr. McCauley doesn't mind where my son goes to jail as long as he serves his time and the farther away from his daughter the better."

"That's fine with me; get him the hell out of here." My father retorts with a contemptuous wave of his hand. "I don't want him anywhere near my daughter ever again." He looks Ramon in the eye. "Are we in agreement over this matter?"

"Totally." Ramon gloats with a smile of satisfaction. "Louis, you go with the McCauley family to make sure the arrangements for the girl are properly taken care of with as little fuss as possible. I'll meet you back at the apartment in the city."

"Arrangements! What arrangements?" Vic cries out, frantic as he struggles almost breaking free from the hold the troopers have on him. "What the hell are you talking about? What are you going to do with her? So help me God, if you hurt her or the baby, you will live to regret it."

Helen gives Vic a dismissive glance, a small smile tugs at the corner of her mouth. "Your little friend will be going to a lovely remote convent for wayward girls. I've known Ellen was pregnant for some time. I took the liberty of finding just the right place for her to finish out her confinement." Helen speaks in a calm soothing voice for the first time, looking impeccable in her Chanel suit, not a hair out of place even though it's six o'clock in the morning. To look at her one would think she dressed for a celebration and in her mind it was, she was finally vindicated in her revenge against my mother. My humiliation and downfall into disgrace is sweet revenge for her. Yes, revenge can be sweet, sometimes the longer one waits the sweeter the taste. She sniffs in disdain, "It's such a shame that it had to come to this." She says coolly, glancing down to check the perfect finish of her polished nails. "But Ellen knows sins must be atoned for through prayer and sacrifice, only through the help of the good nuns, may God forgive and help redeem her soul." Her face glitters, breaking in a thousand shards of hatred spinning off toward me as she stares into my eyes with unmistakable malice and says, "May God help you, my dear, you have always been a difficult child." I look beseeching at my father who shakes his head in disgust, turning away from me.

I spit out at the two of them, beyond caring. What more can they do to me? "I hope the two of you burn in hell, I will *never* forgive you for this!"

"Elle, I'll come back, I promise!" Vic shouts as the State Police drag him handcuffed through the station door into the early morning, the sky streaked pink with the coming dawn, shoving him into the back seat of the waiting patrol car.

The world spins around me as I sink to my knees, supported by Vic's brother, Louis. The finely honed trap our families planned for us overwhelms me. The enormity of their convoluted warped concern is a front for the deep-seated resentment that we dare flaunt their dominance over our lives. We were going to pay. Oh, yes, we were going to pay. Not God and his legion of angels can help us now. We're going to hell.

Chapter 21

Lost

March through May 1983

Oh yes, Helen had her revenge. She laid her plans for me carefully. A meaner more dogmatic place was not to be found. An austere old mansion donated to the church, encircled by an eight foot high wrought iron fence. Our Lady of the Immaculate Conception, what an ironic name to call a home for wayward girls. My room, a hole, a cell, everyone hates it here, even the nuns. The next few months, a prison term, days divided between work, prayer and school. Determined to graduate high school in June, my studies a distraction to the misery of my days. Awakened at dawn, the bells summon us to the cold, damp chapel for prayer, to atone for our sins of earthly pleasure. Obey the church and confess your sins. I don't care what they say; my love for Vic is not a sin. This baby growing in me is not a sin. We made a mistake, a reckless abandonment of the rules. How could a loving God be so angry with us?

I dream Vic will fly down and take me out of here. But I don't know where he is.....in jail...here or in Mexico? The uncertainty, the fear of not knowing keeps me awake at night.

I'm allowed no contact with the outside. No letters, no phone calls, no visitors to deter my time for reflection and prayer for my immortal soul. I thought I heard Burt down in the lobby one day, yelling. I swear it was his voice. But the doors between the entranceway and dormitories are kept locked. I was told it was a figment of my imagination, part of my condition, but I know it was Burt.

Our baby was born in May, and they stole it. Helen and my father signed my child away for adoption. Saying I was too young and I would later thank them. After eighteen hours of labor, I was not even allowed to hold my son. They said I would thank them……..only on a cold day in hell will I ever thank those bastards for what they did to me. I never knew I was capable of such hatred.

I returned home with the single minded goal of finishing up my senior exams and finding Vic again. My grandmother was not allowed to see me. Helen said she would taint me with her liberal ideas. I have no idea what that meant…..Gran?

I barely recovered my strength from the baby when a phone call came from Mexico. Helen called me to the phone, saying it was Vic's aunt. Overcome with joy I snatched the phone out of her hand,…… the woman on the line was sobbing into the phone, her voice making no sense, the words refusing to register in my stunned brain. "I don't' know how to tell you this, senorita, but there has been an accident. Last night, Vicente, our beautiful Vicente, was riding his motorcycle, he had just gotten out of jail and we knew he was planning to find you. His father forbade him to do so and they had a fight. He got on that motorcycle, furious at his father, driving too fast; he went around a mountain curve." She stops to blow her nose, gasping with tears. "The bike slid out from underneath him, he went over the embankment into a tree." She pauses, "He was dead on impact." I dropped the phone with a wordless scream, by the time I reach my bedroom, my world went black. I curled up in the fetal position on my bed, refusing to eat, drink or talk; for all intents and purposes, I died that day with Vic.

My depression so deep, and not knowing what to do, my father and Helen asked the family doctor to sign papers committing me to the county mental institution. Only by the grace of God, Doc Winkle….. our family doctor for years, treating everyone in town, regardless of age, creed or money, knew me well enough… and Helen…..to realize this was not the right decision. So behind my father's back, he went to Gran. Armed with her cane and Burt by her side, Gran stormed the house, marching up to my bedroom and held off my father and Helen with a string of profanities that would scorch the hide off the devil, himself while Burt picked me up in his scrawny sinewy arms and carried me away.

Only through the sheer force of their will and determination did they nurse me back to health. Filling my days with the things I loved, flowers, books, opening the windows of my bedroom to the fresh summer air, and the sounds of birds, frogs and toads in their early summer chorus. Tempting food, not one ounce of tofu or any crazy vegan concoction, just fresh wholesome foods gathered from the local farmer's market to whet my appetite.

Butterflies in jars during the day to keep me company until dark, then Burt would release them and replace them with fireflies at night. Music, jokes and light hearted banter combined with the care they bestowed upon me, cracked through the darkness of my nightmare and they taught me to live again, laugh and eventually they taught me I could love again……..…

Adirondack Found

Chapter 22

Adirondack Found......August 21, 2012

The flight attendant works her way through the first class section of the plane, refilling wine glasses. Thankfully, the turbulence subsided and the captain has turned off the fasten seat belt sign. I tell the hostess, no thank you. Two glasses of wine made me happy but by the third glass I was melancholy.

I admit to being lonely, my children are grown, Lani living on the west coast, Trey off to college, and my friends involved in their own lives. I've been asked out by a few men since Jack's death, but no sparks. It sounds selfish, but the idea of dating and the far-fetched notion of remarrying seems impossible after loving Vic and Jack ....I've had magic.......and nothing else will do.

I shake peanuts from the foil snack bag, and idly arranging them in a pattern, a habit from my days as a kindergarten teacher. I muse, it's August and I'm heading in the wrong direction. Instead of heading west to visit our daughter, Lani, in Los Angeles, I feel the familiar tug, north to the Adirondacks. I crave a walk in the forest, just to smell the balsam.

Every August, Jack and I rented a camp on Saranac Lake for a month, inviting our family and friends, including the dogs. Our gatherings were almost tribal. It was a wonderful month of quiet mornings spent on mist shrouded inlets with loons calling from the cove, fishing from a guide boat almost too beautiful to be put to common use. And evenings of lavender sunsets, turning the lake into a silvered mirror, as the ground gives up the last held heat of the day. Porches, front and back, deep and wide served as a backdrop for the loon's echoing cry.

Friends and family scattered over the house and lawn forming a human strand of colored twinkle lights as jumbled pockets of laughter and camaraderie blink on and off across the property illuminating the house with cheer. I can still smell Jack's famous barbecue sauce filling the air with its tantalizing aroma. We were never sure if everyone came back for the sauce, the house, or the cooler full of beer. But every year they came, the numbers swelling as nieces and nephews grew and brought families of their own. The lean-to by the lake was filled, tents popped up across the lawn under the cover of hemlock trees. It was wonderful, hectic………..and a hell of a lot of work. But I loved it and Jack thrived on the attention of his family.

I haven't rented the camp since Jack's death. Without Jack it wouldn't be the same. I can picture the family standing around looking lost and sad, the loss of his presence the missing hole in the fabric of our family. It would be that ghastly funeral replayed again. Once was enough. Maybe next year…..they say time heals all wounds.

Lani invited me for a visit this month, hoping to fill the empty gap in my summer. I have a few weeks before returning home to help my son, Trey, pack for college and start the new school year. The last sweet days of summer spent with my daughter. And…….I will meet her new fiancé. Is my daughter old enough to have a fiancée? I'm a widow?! *Damn*…I want to pinch myself asking if this is some kind of sick joke. I take out a compact mirror from my purse and check for new wrinkles. It's becoming a compulsive habit. I don't look *that* old……blue eyes stare back at me, a nose inherited from my father, coppery blonde hair from my mother, currently maintained with a little help from my hairdresser. At five foot-seven inches, my figure could be described as athletic more than voluptuous. I wanted voluptuous, God said no. I have great teeth and hair; attributes for a good horse. I'm thinking men like me for my smile and easy going nature……. Jack said it was my great ass.

The sky stewards are preparing to serve lunch, thank goodness, another glass of wine without food, means walking off the plane under my own accord on four inch stilettos…. highly doubtful. High heel shoes and excessive wine consumption do not make for graceful exits.

The last thing I need is to meet Lani's fiancé, drunk. They say first impressions are lasting. Jason's from the Midwest, wholesome, family values and all that. At least I wouldn't be boring. Although sometimes boring can be good…..and then again…sometimes not. Children prefer their parents fade into the background opposed to…..being the center of attention. To this day, my daughter has not forgiven me for the time I brought cow bells to her championship soccer game. It seemed like a good idea at the time. The other moms loved it, my daughter…..not so much. It didn't help I painted our large white poodle, blue and gold, the school colors. The paint turned out to be permanent, and the damn dog was the talk of the town for the next month.

"Excuse me, are you ready for lunch?" The flight breaks into my reverie by setting down an artfully arranged Caesar salad on a pale peach placemat. Steaming hot bread sticks in a small wicker basket covered with a matching plaid napkin are placed next to plate.

"Yes, thank you, it looks delicious."

"Would you care for another glass of wine?" She's an attractive, middle aged woman with short brunette hair spiked with highlights of auburn, giving her a youthful athletic appearance.

"Yes, thank you, just a small glass." I smile at her, liking the look of her short hair. Maybe I should cut my hair and go for that buff, toned female jock look. Unfortunately, Jack would rise up out of the lake where his ashes are scattered and haunt me. He loved my long hair, never allowing me to cut it. So I never did and it seems sacrilegious to his memory to do so now.

The flight attendant returns with my wine, her name is Annette. She leans over to set down the glass and asks, "Are you enjoying the flight?"

"Yes, thank you. I'm on my way to see my daughter in Los Angeles." I slide the silverware from the confines of the napkin, placing it neatly on my lap.

"Oh, what fun, my daughter lives outside of San Francisco. We always have the best time shopping, dining, sightseeing, or taking a morning jog in the park. I'm sure you'll have a blast."

"I'm really looking forward to it." I say, companionably leaning back to take a sip of the chilled Chardonnay. "I've never been to L.A., and I finally get to meet her fiancé."

"A new fiancé you haven't even met? That should be interesting."

"I've spoken with him on the phone several times. She's known him for quite a while as a friend and then after six months of dating, they're engaged."

"That is fast. But when you find true love, I always

say, grab it with both hands." Annette re-corks the wine, placing it in an ice bucket. "Does she have any adventures planned while you're visiting? Not that anything could top a new fiancé." She sits down in the seat next to me, and relaxes for a moment as we chat.

Warming to the subject, I can't help confiding. "Actually, a movie premier. Lani was the assistant costume designer on the movie set of *FireBrand.* And when the head costume designer was unable to attend the premier and after party, she gave Lani her tickets. So Lani called and asked me to go with her. Who could resist such an invitation?" I shrug my shoulders in delicious anticipation. "She picked my dress out from the wardrobe of the costume design department. It sounds so glamorous."

"What!! *FireBrand?* The new movie with that hunky Spanish guy, wait a sec."

Annette jumps to her feet, walks down the aisle to the magazine rack and selects a glossy issue of *People* magazine. "I knew I had seen something on him and the movie. Look! A full cover story. His name is Esteban Diago. Before this movie he had a few supporting roles in major films. He was a big deal down in Latin America, but now he is "all the buzz" around Hollywood." She makes quotation marks with her fingers, "This will probably be the first of many starring roles for him. He's from somewhere in South America, don't you think he is the most gorgeous thing you've ever seen. He was married to Sophia Delong and I think they have a child. He doesn't go in for all the publicity stuff, supposedly the quiet type. I'm surprised to see the full magazine spread, must be PR hype for the movie." She gushes, a flush of excitement causing her cheeks to glow. "I would *love* an invitation to the premier. What an opportunity to rub elbows and *maybe* a little something else against him; if you get my drift?"

I laugh over her bawdy confession and pick up the magazine for closer inspection…..and for a second I think my heart stops.

"Oh my *God!*" My breath escapes in an astonished gasp.

"What?" asks Annette in alarm, "Are you okay? You look like you've seen a ghost."

If she only knew…………I stare at the cover of the magazine. My breath coming in short panting gasps, prickles of shock run up my spine while my fingers trace the outline of Esteban Diago's face.

"Are you all right? Annette touches my arm in concern for my health….. or sanity, not sure which worries her the most.

"I'm sorry, this Diago looks…..he looks…." I shake my head to clear my thoughts, peering at the magazine picture closely and then laugh with a chagrined expression on my face…mistaken identity. I notice Annette looking strangely at me and hasten to explain. "He looks like an old boyfriend of mine." Pointing at the picture, I explain, "But the nose and cheekbones, the overall look of his face, very different. And Diago has no hair, or very little. His hair is blonde and close shaven, and he has a beard. The person I was thinking of had black hair, and lots of it." I look up at Annette with a shaky smile. "Sorry, I didn't mean to startle you, but the person I was thinking of, well, it couldn't be him." I dismiss the likeness to Vic with a depreciating laugh.

"You dated someone who looked like this?" She asks, holding up the magazine for a closer look, then peers back at me in disbelief.

"Yes! It was many years ago." I reply almost defensively. I can look hot, it takes a little work, but I can do it. I actually thought I looked pretty hot now. Okay, I'm not a fabulous cook. I don't always balance my checking account to the penny, and I never wear a watch which means, I'm perpetually late. I've learned to live with these shortcomings, but I always thought once in a while I could look really hot. Well, maybe not *really* hot…just hot. Fine then tepid….but above average. Who am I kidding?

"Well, I can tell you," Annette says with a knowing wink and an evil lift of her eyebrow. "I wouldn't mind slipping this one under the sheets for a night of play." Chuckling over her honesty, I look at the dark handsome face smiling up from the cover of the magazine. "He is some kind of delicious, isn't he?" I add my own leering wink and suggestive eyebrow wiggle, enjoying our bit of girl banter.

"Yes, madam, I'm going to leave you with this magazine, so you can do a little *research.* You're going to see him in the flesh. Who knows what might happen? He's in his forties, so it wouldn't be like robbing the cradle, apparently he loves the ladies. He is plastered all over the tabloids with a different woman each week." she says gleefully rubbing her hands together. "Men with experience are sooo much better."

"Why you dirty, old lady," I tease her in mock retort.

"Like a fine wine, darling, women……. and *some* men, improve with age. The Europeans feel a woman hasn't reached her peak until her forties. Honey, we're just beginning to live. My grandmother lived to ninety-three; I could live for another forty-three years." She places her hands on her hips and gives a saucy wiggle. "And I don't intend to live them as a nun. And neither should you, I don't see any wedding band on that hand holding you back." With a saucy tip of her head, she pats my arm, "Enjoy L.A., honey, check out Diago for me. Now I need to collect a few trays, and there's a very attractive business man in A-4 who has my name written all over his weekend agenda."

I admire her bravado. She's right, there's no wedding band holding me back. I took my rings off as I packed, placing them in the jewelry box, abandoned, but not forgotten. Holding up my left hand framed against the window, I can still see the pale circle against the tan of my fingers. An echo of my wedding band.

With thoughts of being on the prowl darting through my mind, I remember the box of pink condoms my friend, Kat slipped into my purse as she hugged me good-bye at the airport.

"Pink and textured, they're more fun." She sang into my ear as she unzipped my purse slipping the box discretely to the bottom. Kat never changed, going from the queen of trouble at camp to a thriving business woman, managing a chain of liquor stores in the Albany area. She's divorced, it was a brief marriage and she had no children, claims she doesn't have time for that *shit*. She along with Emi Jo and Tee came to my house for our annual girl's weekend and to see me off on my trip to California.

"What! Are you crazy!" I gasped in horror. "Get those things out of my purse. What if someone sees them? Like my daughter!"

"It's time you got lucky. Even Jack would say enough of the Irish wake." Kat snorts. "You can't be a nun forever. A girl has to be prepared these days."

"Prepared!" I hissed at her. I remember looking over my shoulder with trepidation, hoping no one was close enough to hear the conversation. "What about the security check?"

"They are small and discrete; they'll pass right through." Emi Jo said. The voice of wisdom. She married Ben and is now the mother of four children, adding ten pounds with each child. She exudes happiness and contentment. Tee left early to get back to New York City, something about an important deposition at her law firm that needed immediate attention. She is still pressed, starched and imbibed with the ambitious vestige of her former innocent self.

"I don't want them." Reaching into my handbag I tried shoving the offending box back at her.

"Lord only knows, you're too cautious to have sex without protection. And I know you'd never buy your own raincoats, suits, rubbers, oh, whatever they're called now. So just leave them in your purse. Look they even match." I look down at my pink purse appreciating the good-natured intent behind the gift. I had planned on tossing them into the nearest trash can….which I forgot to do, and now the offending objects are staring up at me from the depths of my purse. *Shit.*

Pink condoms, raincoats, boots … Good God, I wouldn't know what to do with them. I repress a snort of laughter imagining the scene. Oh, here honey, just put some protection on, as I hand my lover a hot pink rubber. And what self-respecting man would wear a pink condom……… a horny one. Maybe Annette can give me some pointers. A glance over my shoulder shows Annette flirting with the handsome businessman a few aisles away.

Upon closer inspection, he is kind of cute…..and I'm not dead. At least not the last time I checked my wrist for a pulse. Yep, still here.

With a rueful expression I turn my attention to the cover of *People* magazine.

Damn, Annette is right, that Diago is some kind of gorgeous and so was the woman hanging off his arm, looking up into his face with adoration, as if he had just uttered the most scintillating remark. Vanessa Leason.

Sipping my wine while picking at the salad, I step into the lives of the star and co-star of *FireBrand*.

I run my hand over the glossy picture of Diago standing in the foreground of a meteor shower, tracing the star points etched against the sky. The movie plot centers on a meteor shower that forces the inhabitants of earth to seek shelter in the mystical land of *FireBrand*.

The Perseid meteor shower in the Adirondacks. The memories come flooding back in a torrent. The Perseid meteor shower, a spectacular explosion of stars shooting across the sky, made even more fabulous in the dark night of the mountains. Shaking my head, a small smile plays across my face at the chain of events sparked by this earthly marvel.

August. The Perseid Meteor Shower and Vic. They go hand in hand. It's been a few years since I've paid my summer homage to him, a memorial of our brief love. A time shut away and sealed in the recesses of my heart. Yet, once a year I would bring it out, allow it life, light and air and remember…….Vic laughing, standing on a mountain boulder framed by the lake, black hair burnished ebony by the sun.

When Jack and I rented the camp in the Adirondacks, I'd choose a night when he was away flying somewhere, no guests, my children asleep, a brief respite of calm amidst the flurry of guests. On such a night, I'd take out the old moth eaten sleeping bag, riddled with holes and spread it on the dock. With reverent hands, I opened a battered scrap book filled with pictures, pressed flowers, faded letters, bursting with sketches and watercolors painted by Vic. A legacy of his artwork.

Pulling on his old team sweatshirt, I swore it still carried the faint lingering of his scent, impossibly so, as if his presence joined me on the dock those nights.

The scrapbook opened only once a year, on a summer night, a sacred bond of fidelity to Jack binds the lock the rest of the year.

On either side of the album, a sanctuary of balsam scented candles lined the dock. Shaking out a cigarette from an old crumbled pack, I'd light it from the candle flame, and watch the shreds of tobacco catch fire and glow, inhaling deeply as my body filled with calm. *Psssst,* hissed a beer can as the tab was pulled back, an offering to the past, wishing the beer and cigarette were instead a joint, for the blessed anesthesia it would bring to this bittersweet reunion. Leaning back on that old sleeping bag, slightly drunk and high on nicotine under the moonlight, I imagine Vic next to me gazing up into the stars, taking me into his arms.........I still ache for him; the loss dulled but never vanished.

The images in the scrapbook pressed upon my mind, I see the shiny, peeling, scotch tape, no longer strong enough to keep the wild flowers intact and pressed. The flattened flowers of the journal entries turned brown, becoming transparent with age. Time not only discolored the contents of the scrapbook, but had begun the task of decaying. The volume filled with remembrances, friends from camp, faces smiling with eager anticipation of all life has to offer. Photos pressed and anchored to the pages, recording a summer, memories too precious to let go. Without the pictures, I can barely remember what Vic looks like. I often wonder, nothing happens by accident, I learned this the hard way. I grew to fear the power of consequences and found myself powerless to avoid the treacheries of fate.

My favorite picture…..Vic sitting on a rock, mountains in the foreground, wearing faded denim jeans with a hole in the knee, a plaid shirt open over a chest of rippling muscles, long black hair, dark eyes flecked with amber lights, his slow easy smile filled with a love that still sends tremors of desire through my body……….*Vic.*

Chapter 23

Around and Around We Go.....

A trip to the west coast begins early. Like 6 a.m. early. Followed by a layover in Chicago, and I didn't say no to the wine being offered....so.....by late afternoon....I dozed....okay, slept like the dead. Ahhh....the benefits to flying first class: wide leather seats, fleece blankets, soft pillows combined with complimentary champagne and a window seat worked their magic...I may have lost my fear of flying.

"Travel much?" A tall man in his forties with the chiseled good looks of an athlete raises his wine glass in a mock toast. "First class is the only way to fly. I wouldn't be caught dead back there in coach." Annette's hot businessman from a few aisles away has slipped into the seat beside to me.

"Umm, yes, I guess." I stammer, struggling to sit up, caught off guard by his sudden attempt at conversation. Smoothing my hair into place, I pray I haven't drooled down my chin while I slept.

"I'm Frank Norris." He extends his hand.

"Ellen O'Connor." I accept the handshake from a hand too well manicured and soft to have done manual labor......of any sort......ever.

"Spending time in L.A.?" He asks.

"Actually, I'm visiting my daughter for a few weeks before school starts." I answer politely. "And you?"

"I'm in town for the next two weeks. I enjoy the restaurants, theater, and try to catch a ballgame or two between business meetings."

"Sounds interesting," I reply.

"My company is located outside of Minneapolis. I like changing gears from the Midwest to the West coast, get my fill of sun and fast paced California lifestyle."

"This is my first trip to California, so everything will be new and exciting." *God,* How provincial can I sound?

"Perhaps you would consider joining me for dinner some evening?" He cocks his head in askance; a wry smile creases laugh lines into the corners of his eyes. I'm thinking he's had loads of success with that lazy grin in his lifetime. "Meet me in town, and take a break from your daughter," he cajoles. "I'm on a first name basis with the maître des of some of the best restaurants in town. Think about it. Business travel gets lonely; I'd enjoy the company of a lovely lady."

Boy, this guy works fast. Lovely lady? I almost turn in my seat looking for the lovely lady. It's been a long time since I flirted with a man, especially a stranger. I've forgotten what it feels like…..actually……it's kind of nice. This guy has "player" written all over him…...but at the same time he is tall, handsome, crew cut silver grey hair with broad shoulders tapering down to a narrow waist. Crisp white button down shirt, tie slightly askew, suit coat casually tossed over the seat, this boy is the poster boy for expensive, high end business attire. And possibly the bluest eyes I've ever seen. *Okay, I'm tempted.* No evidence of a wedding band, not even a tan line. I cringe inwardly as I remember those pink condoms going to waste in my purse. My girlfriends will kill me if I let this opportunity pass. The question is, *is he condom worthy?* I can't believe I just thought that, I feel my cheeks blush.

"Maybe," I take a gulp of wine. I'm beginning to feel light-headed, and don't know if it's the wine on top of the champagne or the charged atmosphere created by the handsome man sitting across from me……or just sheer panic. I lean back in my seat, smile, trying to appear relaxed while sizing him up. What do they say, no time like the present to get back on the horse? Or is it get back in the saddle……..I'm not even sure how to find the barn, which end of the horse to saddle, and as far as taking that horse for a ride……let's just say…….. it's been awhile. And my dating experience is well…limited. Vic and Jack, the sum total of my love life……. and with them, love just happened. No dating required.

…

But by the time the plane starts it's decent into the LAX airport, and a half hour of witty conversation later, I'm holding Frank Norris's business card, with *all* of his contact numbers, promising to call him for dinner sometime within the next week. As he handed me his card, he held my hand longer than necessary, brushing his thumb across my knuckles, looking deeply into my eyes, his expression sincere as he whispers, "I'd like to see you again, Ellen, soon, show you the sights of the town."

"*Oh*, okay," I croak, voice caught in my throat.

Frank Norris may be a player………but he certainly is a smooth and practiced one……..I know he is an outrageous flirt……but for the first time in a long time I feel that flutter of attraction, that slow delicious sensation spreading outward like rippling waves from the lower center of my body that says………..*oooh my, maybe…yes.*

…

It was no small feat squeezing my feet back into the four-inch stiletto heels. What was I thinking, nothing says stupid like a pair of high heels to go dashing between terminals and humping luggage ungodly distances over uncertain terrain. I'm coveting the sensible white sneakers on the lady standing next to me as we wait for our luggage to be unloaded. In my vain attempt to appear young and chic for my fashion designer daughter……I may have done irreparable damage to my feet. How dare I break my stiletto code of operation, I know better. Never walk more than fifty feet, be dropped off at the restaurant door, make an entrance, find a chair, sit and assume the Kate Couric crossed-leg pose.

I spy my bag coming around the turnstile, easily spotted by the colorful designer name tag Lani sent as a birthday gift in anticipation of the trip. Balancing on pencil-thin heels I make a grab for the sixty-pound suitcase as it moves down the belt. Ouch, damn it, I curse to myself, stomping my foot as the suitcase handle slips from my grasp, careening off for another spin around. Why didn't I pack two smaller bags? Because that's what smart women do…

Okay, here comes the bag again. I stand in place, planting my heels for balance and make a grab for the suitcase. *Shit,* it hardly budges. And there it goes again. I venture forth giving chase on heels that have turned into wobbly stilts of tortured hell. This is turning into a comedy routine and now I've broken a nail. I scan the terminal in hopes of seeing Frank Norris……knight in shining armor…….ummm, no such luck.

Realizing I'm on my own, I set down my purse, push up my sleeves, concentrate on the bag making its way toward me and taking a deep breath, grab and pull. I swear the thing is stuck. So this time instead of letting go, I plant a foot on the conveyor belt for leverage and yank. The next thing I know I'm hopping on one foot alongside the carousal, tugging and heaving…… to no avail. I decide to abandon the failed attempt, when to my horror.........the thin heel of my shoe is wedged in a crack of the conveyer belt and bent at such an angle so I can't get it out. *Oh, my God,* I'm hopping....and hopping...and hopping...I can't get it out....*shit, shit, shit.* I'm going to lose my balance and fall, dragged along by a luggage carousel! What to do.....but swing the other leg up and on. As the motorcycle commercial says, "Let's ride." I'm now on the conveyor belt straddling my suitcase like a monkey to the amazed stares of the other passengers. *Help,* I mouth mutely while people step back, confused by the apparition rotating in front of them. I furiously work at the heel of my shoe to extract it from the vise like grip of the belt. Not budging. Glancing ahead shows I'm heading toward the plastic curtain into the unloading dock from the planes. Look out!.....I'm going through, baby.

I duck my head in anticipation of the small space and see behind me, not more than twenty feet away the horrified face of Frank Norris. His mouth agape, no sympathy or compassion for a fellow traveler, actually, disgust is written all over his face. He snaps his jaw shut, turns on his heel and flees the scene. *There goes that date.*

As I flap through the plastic curtain, Frank's look of horror is mirrored by the baggage handlers. They stop, caught in the middle of swinging bags from a luggage cart onto the belt and stare with wide eyed shock. Apparently a woman winging along on a baggage carousel is not an everyday occurrence. Go figure.......finally finding my voice, I shout, "Help me! Turn this damn thing *off!*" One of the handlers comes to life and streaks to the stop switch, just as I'm about to go back through the curtain and take an encore tour of the lobby.

"Hey, lady, what the hell do you think you are doing?" A stocky dark haired man demands.

"What do you think I'm doing? Going for a joy ride!" My eyes shoot lightning bolts at him. "My shoe is stuck, I can't get it out." I hear a collective whoop of laughter erupt from the workers.

"No shit?" One of them asks wiping the tears from his face.

"Seriously, help me get it out!" I demand realizing my short shirt has ridden up my thighs, giving the "gentlemen" an ample view of my legs and a possible sampling of my Victoria Secret underwear. Coral pink…..with the matching bra…..of course….they were on sale, I couldn't resist.

…

Twenty minutes later, I exit the baggage claim area with damaged pride, a badly mangled shoe and a suitcase that goes *wibble, wobble* down the concourse. Authorized personnel only……..yeah, right….not if you're Klutz-Ellen.

A glance at the clock on the wall tells me the plane arrived early. Thank God, Lani didn't witness my *joy ride.* Checking my cell phone for messages, I see the business card from Frank Norris peering up from the bottom of my purse. So much for that possibility, I take the card out and tear it into tiny pieces and watch it flutter like discarded confetti into the trash bin. The box of pink condoms seems to wink up at me with mocking glee…..better luck next time, loser.

And then I see her, Lani, striding confidently down the concourse, her father's smudged coal black hair falling in tumbling curls down her back. Her blue eyes twinkle with mischief as she calls out, "Ellie Jane!"

I cringe with embarrassment over her perversion of my proper name, Ellen Jane and call back in retort, "Fiona!" her hated middle name after Jack's grandmother.

Lani was christened Delany Fiona O'Connor. When she was three weeks old, Jack's ancient grandmother, Fiona, bent with age, picked up the diminutive baby. Her gnarled hands, swollen knuckles of arthritic pain from working on the coast of Ireland held the baby aloft and pronounced, "This child has a will and spirit of her own, she won't be tamed. Be careful how you treat her, a heavy hand will destroy you both." Grandma Fi was held in awe within the O'Connor family for her throw back to the old Celtic ways and beliefs. She's what they called a Black Catholic; she played both sides of the spiritual fence attending daily mass while at the same time retaining a few pagan traditions.

My cramped toes along with two broken fingernails are forgotten as I enfold Lani's five-four frame into my arms. I breathe in the scent of vanilla laced with a hint of jasmine. Lani, strong in spirit, sweet in nature.

At first glance, she appears like the girl next door. But her almond shaped blue eyes stand out in stark contrast to the tumbling curls of black hair. She designs her own clothing and her appearance always garners a second look. At an early age she had a knack for combining colors and texture. That talent landed her a prestigious job as a design assistant to one of the most influential costume designers in Hollywood, right out of college.

"Ellie Jane, you're suffocating me." She laughs in mock fear, yet shows no signs of loosening her embrace.

"Darling, let me look at you. You are some kind of gorgeous, as your father would say." Standing back, I admire how healthy and fit she looks, her lean body brushed a golden bronze by the California sun.

"It's so good to see you." I hug her again and whisper in her ear. "Don't ask me about my flight until we've had a glass of wine."

"Anything to do with your shoe?" She points an accusing finger at my foot.

"Casualty of battle."

"Must have been a hell of a fight, cuz that poor shoe looks like it deserves a proper burial."

"With honors."

"Mom, this is my Jason." Lani proudly takes the hand of a tall young man whose been standing off to the side. "Jason this is my mother, Ellen O'Connor, and if you're real nice, you can call her, Ellie Jane."

"Jason, it's a pleasure to meet you, and call me Ellen." I stretch out my arms to hug him. "One person calling me, Ellie Jane in the world is enough. Lani's roommates in college were convinced I was born and raised somewhere in rural Tennessee. Please…just call me Ellen."

"The pleasure is all mine, Mrs. O'Connor." Returning my hug, he chuckles and says, "Lani has told me so much about you, I can see now every word was true." *Good God, what has she told him?* He has the long, thoughtful face of a scholar with brown eyes that hide behind the dark rim of his glasses. Honey brown hair is streaked California blonde and he has the body of a surfer. His manner is respectful with the easy going demeanor of his Midwestern upbringing. Sliding an arm around Lani's waist, I sense a comfortable ease between them, friends turned lovers. Slipping her arm through mine, Lani includes me in the circle asking, "How is Trey?"

"Your brother is fine, in fact, better than fine. He has the house to himself, a stocked refrigerator and all of his friends are home with two weeks to celebrate before they leave for college." Rolling my eyes, I continue, "I pray I find nothing worse than a pile of dirty laundry and a sink full of dishes when I return. I threatened him. If our home looks like a frat house gone wild after a holiday weekend, I'll visit him at college armed with naked baby pictures, home canning, and decorate his dorm room with Grandma Fi's hand crocheted dollies." I blow out a deep sigh. "I'm not optimistic, remember last time I left him? I found beer cans in the gutters and bottle caps in my flower beds for a year."

"I hope you're hungry?" Lani says changing the subject before I can lament any further on the exploits of my son. "I've booked us a table at this fab little restaurant on the beach; it overlooks the ocean and has the best seafood around. We can catch up while enjoying the scenery." Still holding Lani's hand, Jason grabs the handle of my suitcase and stops after a few steps, "What happened to this wheel?" He bends down with a puzzled look on his face, inspecting my suitcase, trying to find out what's causing it to go *wibble, wobble,* down the concourse.

Apparently my catastrophe was a series of mishaps, starting with a cracked link in the conveyor belt, causing my suitcase wheel to become wedged, followed by my high heel, compounded by the champagne and wine consumed on the flight. I should know better…..Klutz Ellen and alcohol don't mix. *A.A., where were you?*

"It's a long story; you do have a sense of humor?" I ask Jason, watching him try to pull my unbalanced bag, thinking, boy; you're going to need it. His face splits into a grin, "I hope it's as good as some of the other stories

Lani's told me. You're a riot, Mrs. O'Connor."

"Ellen, please." I wince. It's not my fault…and pray with fervor, please God, no more fall outs with Klutz-Ellen. My life needs a vacation from her….

Chapter 24

Enchantment

A dog barking brings me out of a long complicated dream of hot steamy men. First there was Frank Norris, the businessman on the plane, then along came the handsome black bartender with the wicked smile and sexy wink from the restaurant last night followed by the hot movie star on the cover of the magazine. All of them, all night long, chasing me around the luggage carousal…..three hot men chasing *me*…..at the same time……yeah, that's called an impossible dream.

Where am I? Sitting up in bed, I look around at the unfamiliar surroundings and remember I'm staying with Lani and Jason, in their adorable bungalow….in California. Where garbage trucks wake you before the sun rises, followed by the recycling truck and then the neighbor's barking dog. I didn't sleep well last night, probably due to the time change from the east coast, the excitement of seeing Lani, meeting Jason and *too* much wine.

The aroma of coffee perking downstairs draws me to wakefulness….Lani and I have plans today. I think she said something about hiking, a farmer's market, shopping, meeting a few friends….and tonight is the movie premier. Boy, I need coffee…and lots of it.

…

Looking into the mirror, I barely recognize the reflection gazing back at me as late afternoon sun slants through the window shutters. A transformation has taken place since this morning. Lani took one look at me over coffee, blurry eyed from lack of sleep, no makeup, hair pulled back in an untidy knot, chipped nail polish and cancelled our plans. Insisting, no *mandated*.....a girl's day at a spa owned by her friend. Oh, the burden of having a fashionista for a daughter.

And now buffed, polished and pampered to womanly perfection, fortified by an afternoon nap, what can I say but…W*ow*!…….like magic……..I've never looked better……….at least not since I was twenty-two.

My daughter selected a few gowns from the stock production wardrobe at the studio. Her boss insisted I borrow one for the evening. I knew Lani excelled at her work as a fashion designer, I just didn't know she was a miracle worker. The minute I step into the blue dress, there is no doubt, it's perfect. The long sheaf of vivid turquoise undulates, sparkling with color as I walk across the room. I spin and survey my reflection in the mirror. My slim ankles flirt and dance beneath the diaphanous hem. The gown clings to my body and long limbs; the bodice presses what little I have upwards until I am precariously close to overflowing its bounds.

Instead of twisting and teasing my hair into a fashionable coiffure, I leave it down to fall in soft waves around my face and spill over my shoulders. I tuck one side behind my ear, the copper highlights glitter in competition with the diamond studs dangling from my ears. I wear the necklace Vic gave me years ago and a bracelet from Jack, the simplicity of the jewelry works with the extravagant dress.

…

The premier of *FireBrand* is a huge success. After watching the movie, I have that feeling, the one, after a great movie, where the audience sits in stunned silence through the credits, unable to leave the theater and break the spell. *Movie magic……*

Tonight *FireBrand* joins the ranks of classics; everyone there knew it. The air snaps and pops with jubilation. And yes, I have to admit, Annette was right, Esteban Diago is *hot……..Whew!*

Sitting in the limousine on the way to the after-party, still mesmerized by the movie's hypnotic hold, Jason and I congratulate Lani on the extraordinary details of the costumes. Creating characters of the underworld, turning mere mortals into surreal beings of middle earth and underground seas through the simple use of fabric, color and texture is true artistry. We talk in hushed tones as the driver pulls into a line of expensive cars, slowly inching forward. Tall King palms form an arch of rustling green branches over the drive leading up to the portico of the Sodoma Hotel.

The legendary costume designer, Julia Ward, invited Lani to represent the design staff, quite an honor, and sent along her limousine and driver. Lani's flushed cheeks and sparkling eyes give testimony to her excitement. Pulling up to the entrance of the hotel, Ms. Ward's driver jumps out of the car and quickly opens the passenger door onto a green carpet. Feeling like Cinderella alighting from her coach of finery, my foot touches down on a velvet green carpet. Glowing lanterns lead the way into the sumptuous entrance of the hotel.

Jason proudly escorts us down the runway. We follow the green carpet with a steady stream of Hollywood's elite dressed in their finery. Two photographers marshal the guests to pose against a waterfall draped in tropical plants. Our arrival at the end of listed celebrities and dignitaries gets little notice, but we're on the list.

I can't help but feel a kinship with Judy Garland walking down the yellow brick road, catching her first glimpse of the Emerald City. Stopping to take it all in, I clutch Jason's arm whispering, "Oh, my God," and try not to gape as we walk into the venue. My eyes alight with child-like excitement.

Decorated to mimic *FireBrand*, the room is a mythical land of the netherworld, peopled by the lost tribes of the earth, vanquished to the inner realms. A world of vast inner earth oceans, islands of climatic forests ranging from tundra to deserts. Inhabited by a race of people, proud and stubborn governed by religious tribal law. Based on a book by the bestselling author, Hamish Bodawanna, *FireBrand* exploded on the screen using state of the art cinema photography under the creative genius of a brilliant director.

The dim lights of the hotel lobby illuminate the play of blue and green beams arching from a fountain into glittering rainbows, creating the illusion of passing from the realm of this earth into the land of *FireBrand*. Under the stream of blue green light the fabulous gowns of the women designed by names such as Vera Wang and Valentino glow like jewels on parade.

Golden bubbles float out open doors to a garden where exotic plants perfume the night air. Out on the flagstone patio a spread of tables are decorated to resemble the twelve islands of the *FireBrand* legend. Tables simmer in the moonlight mimicking a coral reef dappled with shafts of afternoon sun, vast outposts laden with food beyond imagination in a sea of people. Ice sculptures tower from the tabletops depicting characters from the movie, dripping and melting in the humid night air, a mist of silver steam.

Chains of paper lanterns hang throughout the gardens, a white pergola is strung with loops of green gauzy material cascading to the ground, resembling an underwater kelp forest, twisting and turning in the pale light. Beneath the stars, a dance floor swirls under blue lights, surrounded by columns sculpted to resemble coral heads.

Enchanted, I barely notice the waiter offering a tray of azure blue glasses in the shape of an underwater blossom, filled with *ambulla*, a pink tinted beverage, the drink of mythical gods in this underworld fantasy. I take a sip, anything pink with bubbles…what's not to love. Clutching the glass stem to still my trembling hands, I *ping* the rim of the glass with a lacquered nail, the sound brings me back to reality…. because I must be dreaming.

It isn't just the grandeur of the surroundings that feel surreal, but the people are like aliens from some distant planet, well known but little visited. The next hour is a whirlwind of introductions. I've met four Hollywood actors, two producers, and several people involved in costume design and film graphics. Lani keeps me close to her side; the sheer lavish scale of this event is exciting and intimidating. I've never been to anything, *anything* even close to this in my life.

Needing a quiet spot to sit and rest my feet, I shoo Lani and Jason off to the dance floor. Seeking a private nook to watch the party undisturbed, I risk a peek into the tent set for dinner. *Oh my*. The visual display is stunning. Four enormous chandeliers strung with sparkling netting cast the ceiling into a kaleidoscope of ocean color. There must be twenty tables set with crystal glasses, crisp coral and green linens cover the tables and chairs. Climbing vines clamor up the center columns of the tent and spread throughout the netting covering the ceiling. Brilliantly colored birds and fish co-exist among the greenery, land and sea as one. In the center of each table a miniature fountain bubbles over with azure colored water. Stealing a glance at the seating chart, I can't help but wonder who will sit at our table, the possibilities are endless…..

Chapter 25

Shattered

Standing on tiptoes, my eyes impatiently sweep the room hoping for a glimpse of Jason and Lani. They're nowhere to be found, probably off necking in a dark corner under a curtain of kelp. I tug nervously at my lower lip, searching for a path that would allow me to move through the room without actually having to stop and talk to people. At times like this, I really miss Jack. With his good looks, Irish charm and quick wit leading the way, social engagements were a breeze. He always knew what to say. I'd simply hold on to his arm and we'd mingle, engage in conversations, and move from group to group, conducting our own private party. He'd whisper in my ear, whether the well-endowed recent divorcee across the room was natural or fake, who got the latest promotion, or cheated on their golf score, at times it was hard to keep a straight face. It was party banter, our own little social commentary.

I wander along the edge of the patio, stopping to inhale the scent of a pale peach rose. My fingers marvel at the silken feel of the petals against my fingertips. Chewing nervously at a hang nail on my left thumb, my earlier false bravado floats away on a golden bubble, evaporating in the night air, leaving me feeling very much…. alone.

I hear hear, "Excuse me," from a deep male voice behind me. *Oh….*the sound causes me to whirl around in surprise and ill-concealed relief to be noticed and sought out.

Drat. ….it's only a waiter carrying a tray of empty glasses trying to pass through on his way to the kitchen. As I pick up the hem of my dress to clear a path for him, the thin strap of my purse catches the edge of his starched French cuff. And we watch in horror as the tray topples off his out-stretched hand, crashing to the floor.

The sound of shattering glass causes every eye in the room to turn in our direction.

"Oh, shit, I'm screwed, so screwed," the waiter mumbles under his breath. He is a short well-muscled young man who looks like he works as stunt man by day. "I may as well quit now before they fire me. Damn it!" He curses, stooping down to pick up the pieces of glass littered across the floor.

"I'm so sorry. Let me help." I insist, hitching up my dress, kneeling to help him clean up the scattered wreckage.

"Ouch!" He cries as a bright red bead of blood oozes from his fingertip. Sucking the tip of his injured finger he fixes his eyes on me with a malevolent stare.

"Are you all right?" I ask, reaching out to touch his arm in concern. "I'm so sorry, this is my fault. Maybe I can talk to someone?" If looks could kill, I'd be dead on the spot; this guy's eyes are shooting daggers at me.

"No, lady, seriously, what are you doing. Leave me alone." He hisses. "You're a guest; get up before I get in more trouble." He shakes his head in disgust at my stupidity.

"I'm not a guest, a least not like the *rest* of them." I protest. "I'm just a regular person, like you." I proceed to launch into a full-blown explanation until his mean little eyes compounded by a snarl of "Get the hell away!" cause my head to snap back in shock …….and I shut up.

Holding up my hands in surrender, I can't help suggest just one more thing, "Let me get a napkin to bandage your hand." The maternal instinct kicks in, even if he is a rotten little prick. As I reach for the napkin on the edge of the table, he stands up abruptly, our heads bash together; the force of the collision sends us careening to the floor on our butts. "Shit!" We say simultaneously. I feel all eyes in the room upon us.

"Mother!" I hear hissed from behind my left shoulder. Lani. She's *really* pissed off, she never calls me, *mother.*

Busted! I breathe out cringing. So much for the two of them off necking in the kelp forest. *Oh Lord, just let me die now.*

"What the hell are you doing down there?" her voice dripping with mortification.

Go away, I try sending her a telepathic message, save yourself, no one knows I'm related to you. Run, don't ruin your career.

"Lady, just go, now!" The waiter pleads.

These Hollywood people; try and act like a decent helpful person and they get all bent out of shape….they think everyone has an ulterior motive……

Brushing my hands to shake off any stray fragments of glass as well as the social mores of this town, I feel a hand on my elbow helping me to my feet.

Standing up, I look with astonishment into the eyes of Esteban Diago, *Esteban Diago!*......my mind screams as my jaw drops in a very unglamorous gape. *The Esteban Diago* has placed a trembling hand on my arm, helping me to my feet, looking as if he has just seen a ghost.

His tan face visibly pales; beads of perspiration dot his forehead. His breath coming in short ragged gasps from a heaving chest, the trembling of his hands increases as his eyes focus on the locket around my neck. His gaze swoops upwards from the locket to my eyes like a hawk after its' prey with such intensity it causes me to step back.

"*Dios mio,* Elle?" his voice rasps out in a hoarse whisper.

Who is this man, what is wrong with him? Is he on drugs? I think to myself in confusion. Elle, why is he calling me, *Elle*?

His face is so close, I can see the pupils of his eyes pulse, the eyes familiar, but the voice starts a chill at the base of my spine, moving through me as if I had just swam through a cold current. The air around me seems to shimmer. I'm seized with unreasonable panic that the next breath I take may choke me. My blood runs cold as a sense of familiar gnaws from the recesses of my subconscious. Deja vu, I've been here before, this feeling repressed, buried for years. Diago's eyes.....dark deep eyes, gleaming with flecks of gold...the black hair ....skin the color of melted caramel.......tall and lean..........*it can't be.........*

He misinterprets the shaking of my head to mean no, a look of bitter disappointment crosses his face. "I'm sorry. You look so much like someone I once knew." He whispers.

"*No, no*," I say desperately, wildly, confusion clouding my mind, "You called me, Elle?" He nods his head, his eyes tempestuous. "Only one person has ever called me, Elle. He's dead. He died many years ago, in a motorcycle accident."

A soft moan escapes his lips, the pallor of his skin deepens, and with a trembling hand he reaches out to trace the intricate carving on the locket. The warmth of his hand against my chest causes a slow steady flush of heat rising to my face.

Closing his eyes, almost grimacing in pain he runs a hand across his forehead through locks of black hair, gleaming with strands of sun bleached copper. Exhaling audibly, he appears to struggle for control, his body in a state of agitation. Tears well in his eyes as he tries to speak, but can't seem to get the words out, he stops, and whispers, "*Ella, Ella, my mia bella, won't you come out and play tonight?"* As the words leave his lips the chill in my spine creeps ever higher as those glorious dark eyes bore into mine. Up close, the face is different, *but* the eyes and hair, it can't be. I whimper; my knees buckle underneath me as I grab hold of his arms with both hands for support, my eyes wide with shock.

As Diago stares into my face, he traces a finger down my arm. The hint of a smile begins to take life, he removes his hand and looks at the inside of his palm, holding it up to my face for inspection. I knew what I would see. And there it was, etched across the inside of his palm, the thin line of a scar, a pale crescent against his swarthy skin. As clear today as it was thirty years ago.

The rush of blood in my ears turns to an incessant buzzing. My body trembles under his hands; I can't seem to bring air into my lungs. *I can't breathe.*

As if seeing it for the first time, I turn my right hand over, looking at my palm, wearing the identical scar. The scar carved into our palms as dumb seventeen-year-old kids, hands pressed together, blood mixing and mingling to form a pact, in our eyes a sacred oath.

With a thudding heart, I match my scar to his, the nails of my fingers biting into the back of his hand. The other hand slides up the satin lapel of his tuxedo jacket, the top button of his shirt undone and I can feel the heat rising from his chest as I am drawn closer to him. Our eyes locked in disbelief.

His left hand moves from my hip sliding up to touch my back where fabric ends and skin begins; his touch a brand on my flesh. And we stand staring, drinking each other in, the atmosphere charged between us, almost crackling, neither saying anything, just looking. Then he leans down and kisses my lips softly, igniting my blood. I moan into his mouth and one of his hands moves into my hair, pulling my head back as we kiss savagely. The room spins, bright spots of color appear before my eyes, my knees buckle beneath me. I feel him scoop me into his arms as I faint and the world goes black…..*Vic*…….

Chapter 26

Reckoning

Reality returns with the flash of a camera, the feel of strong arms cradling me against a warm, hard chest. I want the flashing to go away, to burrow deeper into the safety of his arms. My mind jumbled by the confusion unfolding around me, exclamations of surprise and shock, the high pitched hum of many voices talking at once. The *click, click,* of a camera shutter shooting frame after frame. My dazed mind slow to comprehend the turn of events, am I really in Esteban Diago's arms? Is Esteban Diago really Vic? Is Vic, Esteban? Am I *crazy*? The impossibility of these thoughts causes my head to whirl…and I feel faint again.

"Jackson, have Ike meet me at the back door with the car." Vic…..Esteban…whoever he is, calls over his shoulder to a short balding man, as he turns down a hallway. "We've got to get out of here before the paparazzi goes crazy."

"I can walk; you don't need to carry me." I protest yet tighten my hold around his neck. Who am I kidding? Whoever this guy is, he's hot and I'm holding on… Nuzzling my face into the starched front of his shirt……the smell……is Vic.

"I'm not letting you out of my sight." He says, picking up the pace. "Look what happened last time."

"Excuse me, Mr. Diago!" I hear Lani calling from behind, her high heels clicking down the tiled corridor. "Slow down! Stop! *Excuse me*. Sir? Just where are you taking my mother? Ellie Jane, are you hurt? Mom!"

"Lani! It's Vic!" I try to reassure her.

"Vic? Who the hell is Vic!"

"My boyfriend, the one from the Adirondacks."

"He's dead! What does that have to do with Esteban Diago carrying you off into the night?" She says panting with the exertion of keeping pace with Vic. "Diago, slow down, damn it!" She explodes.

"Mr. Diago, maybe we could stop and talk for a minute." Jason implores from the background.

"Sorry kids, we have to get out of here or your mother's life as she knows it will be over. The paparazzi are vicious. We'll explain later, but for now trust me."

"Lani, meet Vic. Vic, meet my daughter." I gesture weakly with one hand between the two of them.

"What are you talking about? Mom! How much did you have to drink? This is Esteban Diago." She demands tugging on Vic's arm. "Are the two of you drunk or high? Put her down! *Mom!*" She wails, "I leave you alone for a few minutes.......!"

"Lani, I wish we were meeting under better circumstances, but my real name is Vicente Rienz. I only use Esteban Diago for my acting roles." Vic says extending his arm from under my butt to shake Lani's hand, chuckling at her bewildered expression. "Your mother and I have a lot of catching up to do. I promise to return her with no harm done, but we need more privacy than is offered here."

"Oh God, this is insane." Lani looks dubious as Vic sets me on my feet, keeping a protective arm around my waist. Lani looks at Jason in askance as a large black limo speeds around the corner. "I guess, Mom, are you sure you want to go off with him?"

"I'll be fine, if Diago is trying to kidnap me, with that

horde of photographers following him," I point down the corridor at the photographers trying to get past the security. "He isn't going to get very far." I take my purse from Lani's hand. "I have my cell phone, I'll call you when I wake up from this crazy dream…..cause this must be a dream." I look up scrutinizing Diago's face, my hand automatically running up and down the fabric of his sleeve, trying to convince myself….is this really Vic standing here?

"Hey *amigo*, we had better go." A tall lean man with russet red hair, sprinkled with grey, holds open the door to the limo. "I don't know what kind of shit you got yourself into this time. But those paparazzi heading this way are looking for blood."

"Lani, Jason, Don't say a word to them." Vic warns as he tucks me into the car. "Every word you say will be splashed crossed the morning's tabloids." He raps on the roof of car signaling to Ike. "*Vamonos!*" He calls out.

As the car door slams shut, I settle back into the leather interior, closing my eyes to still the whirling throbbing in my head.

Vic takes my hand and gently skims his thumb across my knuckles as the limo speeds away from the hotel. "Elle, *querida,* are you all right?" He asks his voice laced with concern.

I open my eyes and smile. "I want to touch your face," I see surprise reflected in his eyes. Lifting my hand, I caress his chin, run my fingers across his high cheekbones, trace the outline of his lips, the broad plane of his forehead and finally I run my fingers through his hair. In the pictures from the movie, his hair was cut very short, in a blunt military style. With a sob of disbelief, I finally realize the truth. This is Vicente Rienz sitting next to me. Different…….but oh, so much the same.

"Kiss me, and then I'll know for sure." I wrap my arms around his neck, pulling his head closer to me. His proximity is overwhelming, exhilarating. The familiar pull is there, all my nerve endings goading me toward him, my inhibitions fading. *How can he still do this to me?*

His mouth is on mine, that gentle, persuasive, slow simmering warmth patiently unlocks every shred of doubt. My resistance melts like wax, rekindling the spell he put on me so long ago.

When he draws back, his hands outline my face, fingers skimming over my cheekbones, then down, trailing lightly over my throat. Remembering it, experiencing it, is like being offered a cool sip of water before you realize how desperately thirsty you are.

"Elle, is it really you?" His eyes search my face. "I can't believe you are here. How can this be happening?" He leans in kissing me softly, whispering in my ear. "Where have you been all these years?"

And that's when it hits me. *Bam.* Right in the gut. "*Where* have I been all these years!" I cry out with indignation. Suddenly all the pain and pent up heartache comes pouring forth in a rush of anger. I feel a well of fury rise up so quickly I nearly choke on it. I'm livid, incensed with rage. *Look out every wronged, scorned and cheated on woman in the world…….cause here I am, ready to avenge.* I draw my hand back and slap his cheek with all the hurt and rage I have repressed for so long.

"Wh…Wh….Whereee!" I sputter. "Where, have I been!! You, bastard, you left me behind with a baby. You left me with those horrid people who wanted nothing more than to steal my baby and put me in a mental institution. *You said you would always come back!!* You take off to live your life as some glamorous movie star without a thought to those you left behind. You, lying, cheating, no good son of a bitch." I'm hysterical….Okay, I am *way* beyond hysterical. Great heaving gasps of sobs rack my body. My fists pound his chest as I scream insults against the injuries he inflicted on me so many years ago. "I thought you loved me!" I gasp. "You swore you would never leave. Never leave, ever! Then you run off and leave me with our baby. They *stole* our baby. I had no one to turn to, you were gone. Then a month later your aunt calls. She regrets to inform me that you *died* in a motorcycle accident! You asshole!" I slug his chest once more for good measure. "You look pretty alive to me!"

And I'm just warming up, this guy needs body armor. "What kind of heartless bastard are you? How could I have been so stupid? All these years I've loved you….. never, ever, stopped loving you. A husband and two children later and I still loved you." I scream flinging myself back against the seat in agony. "What kind of idiot am I? The classic dump and I never saw it." I'm into the ugly cry now….and not a Kleenex in sight.

"Hey, buddy," Ike's voice comes over the car's intercom system. "Everything all right back there? Do you need some assistance?"

"No, he does not need assistance!" I shout at the partially opened Plexiglas window separating us, flinging my purse at it. "If he is not man enough to hear what a rotten piece of pond scum he is, he deserves to be beat up by a woman." I launch into another barrage of fist pummeling against Vic's chest. I swing my hand back to slap him again when a steel grip closes over my wrist.

"Elle, we need to talk." Vic says in a tight voice, attempting to calm my agitated state. "Ike, I need you to pull over as quickly as possible. I'm going to be sick."

"Sick, oh please," I fume; "Give me a break, what kind of girly excuse is that."

"Sure thing." Ike responds. The car swerves off the road, thumps over a speed bump and comes to a screeching halt in a deserted parking lot. "Here is a beach, hop out."

As soon as the car comes to a stop, Vic vaults out the door to the concrete wall separating the parking lot from the beach. I hear him retching onto the sand below, as I step from the car.

"What's he doing?" I stupidly ask Ike, who's standing next to me with a chilled bottle of water and clean cloth in his hand.

"I believe it's called vomiting." He says sarcastically.

"I know that," I say defensively. "Just because I yelled at him? The weak bastard!"

"When Vic gets unhinged, his stomach goes." Ike glances at me with disapproval, the street light overhead illuminating his amber eyes. "I only heard part of what you said to him, sounded like a lot of yelling and screaming. If there is one thing I know, Vic Rienz is not a weak bastard." His voice is icy with condemnation.

"Maybe if you stopped screaming like a crazy woman and let him talk, you might hear his side of the story."

"Here," Ike shoves the bottle and washcloth at me. "Why don't you quit yelling and see if he's okay. I'll stay right here in case you get crazy again."

Well, I guess I've been told. I find myself standing alone looking at Vic's back. He's leaning on the stonewall looking out over the ocean, trying to compose himself.

I walk over to him, not knowing what to do. "Here," I say pouring water from the bottle over the cloth.

"Thanks," he says without turning around, and wipes his face. He takes a drink from the bottle to rinse his mouth. "Sorry about that. I have this weird stomach thing, when I get upset, I heave. Simple as that. Damn pain in the ass and embarrassing too." He turns to face me. "Elle, we need to talk. Please believe me, I never left you."

The anger dissolved from my body, the ranting and raving served as a purge and now I feel empty. Hollow from the place where pain resided for so many years, erecting its own shrine. I feel emotionally drained, there's no fight left in me, either I listen or turn and walk away. It's rare for people to get a second chance in life. Was I going to turn my back on Vic? That undaunted love……. the pain over losing of him had never left me.

"Tell me what happened, Vic." I say in a hoarse voice ragged from screaming and crying. "Tell me what happened to you."

He throws a leg over the wall and sits, his eyes facing the ocean, not looking at me, pulling thoughts from the past. "Agghh, I tried to forget, it hurt too much to remember." he sighs, raking his hand through his hair.

"After I was dragged from the bus station, my father made sure I was locked in jail. I was charged with assaulting an officer of the law with a deadly weapon and illegal possession. He wouldn't even get me a lawyer, said I deserved the punishment. So I spent five months in a juvenile prison camp in Mexico."

I sit quietly on the wall and listen.

"When I was released he picked me up and said he was taking me to a place I needed to see. We flew to New York City, so I thought he was taking me to you and the baby. But we drove to a small private cemetery outside of

Syracuse, I didn't want to get out of the car, but he insisted he had something to show me. I knew what I was going to see even before I got out of the car. It was your family cemetery; there were gravestones with your family names etched on them." Here he pauses shaking his head, making an obvious effort to stay in control of his emotions. Remaining silent, I squeeze his hand in reassurance; I know the cemetery. "There in the back of the cemetery was a new gravestone with your name, date of birth and date of your death. Our baby daughter was buried with you." his voice raw with emotion, "You see, he told me you died in childbirth along with the baby." He snatches his hand from mine and pounds his fist onto the stone, "I believed him! What the hell was the matter with me?" He rages, "The sneakiest, most conniving bastard I have ever known and…..I trusted him!"

"He told you I was dead. Oh, my God." The horror over the duplicity of our parents washes over me. How could we have been so easily deceived? I slump down on the wall beside him, stunned. I just keep repeating, "Oh my God, oh my God…."

"What happened to the baby, Elle?" Anguish is written on his face.

"The baby was a boy, not a girl. Vic, we had a baby boy." I rest my head against him, and he kisses my hair repeatedly. "They stole him away. I never got to hold him."

"*Jesus*," I feel him murmur into my hair.

"Our parents signed the papers for adoption, stating we were under age and not fit to be parents. And the baby was gone, just gone. I tried to find him but the records are sealed and I finally had to let it go. But it still hurts knowing he is out there somewhere." Vic tugs my hand, and before I know it, I'm on his lap with his arms around me.

He breaths, "Elle, Elle, I'm so sorry." I feel his body trembling under the linen shirt. "So sorry, how can I ever make it up to you?"

I shake my head. "It wasn't our fault. I can't believe our parents were capable of such evil. They had the power, more than we realized."

He tightens his hold on me. "After all the betrayals from him in the past, I should have known. But the gravestone was real." He holds his wrist up to validate the truth to his words. "I have scars on my wrists from where I beat my hands bloody on it. He just stood there and watched." He shakes his head. "How do you fake such a thing? What kind of man fakes someone's death, complete with a gravestone? Who do you bribe or pay off to accomplish such a thing." The muscles in his cheek twitch as he tries to hold in the anger. "God, I hate him. I didn't think my hate could grow, but if he were standing here I'd kill him with my bare hands." Waves of rage pulse from his body.

"He took me back to Mexico. I was numb with grief, didn't care what I did or where I was going." Pausing he looks into my face, "I basically tried to kill myself." He says with an apologetic shrug of his shoulders.

"*Nooo*." I feel his pain, palpable in the night air; our families betrayed us, nearly destroying us in the process.

"I'd ride my motorcycle or the wildest horse on the ranch; I didn't care if I came back." He says, shaking his head over his stupidity. "I rode bareback with no saddle and the lightest bridle I could find. I drove too fast, took the curves too short And then one day, I got my wish I took a curve too sharp, spun off the road and landed thirty feet down a bank. I left half my face on the asphalt road and crushed half the bones in my body on the fall." He looks skyward, exhaling harshly. "But I didn't die. I was in so much pain, but I didn't die. I wanted to, but they wouldn't let me. I had several reconstructive surgeries on my face, which is why you didn't recognize me right away. Some people think I look better than I did before the surgeries." He gives a bitter smile. "I don't know."

"Let's just say it didn't hurt your looks." I murmur, caressing the hollows of his cheekbones.

"Thank you." He gives a wry smile. "The only good thing to come out of the whole mess was my mother stopped drinking. She roused out of her alcoholic stupor to nurse me back to life. The nurses weren't allowed to care for me unless it was something she wasn't capable of doing. After my recovery, she divorced my father and never drank again."

"Do you still see her?"

"Yes, actually we're fairly close. My father died five years ago of a heart attack. I hadn't seen or spoken to him in over twenty years so it was no great loss."

"What did you do, when you got better?" I ask softly, hugging his arm close to my body, his heat warming my skin.

"Drifted mostly, I had to get away. I signed on a freighter ship as a crew hand and basically traveled the world. The time in jail had hardened me. I was now one tough kid with an attitude, and the wandering lifestyle suited my mood. Ike and I met on an oil freighter bound out of Saudi Arabia." He shakes his head musing, "Ike and I have been together…a long time." He chuckles. "We were freighter tramps, young and dumb, moving from one ship to another. Whatever ship paid the most money. Both running away from the life we left behind. We've been watching each other's back ever since. Ike is my best friend and aside from my mother, my family. He stayed on to be my back up man once the movie business started; always hire a friend as a bodyguard. Can't trust anyone else."

"How in the world did you get into acting? Seems a far cry from being a freighter tramp?" I'm overwhelmed with questions.

"South America."

"South America?"

"Yeah, we were in Chili on a leave from the boat. A production company was filming a movie. As a joke we signed on as extras. The joke was on me because the camera liked my face. That and the fact I speak fluent Spanish and English led to larger parts and a few years later, I was in Hollywood, and now, in a film possibly nominated for an Academy Award. It's just nuts how it all happened."

"I'm sorry for going crazy on you, Vic." I slip out of his lap to stand in front of him. I let my eyes roam up and down the length of his body. I still can't wrap my mind around the fact he is here...... *Vic.* Leaning into him I enfold myself into his arms. "I guess you didn't run out on me. I've lived with the thought of you dead for so long, it was a shock seeing you standing there, this huge movie star, I jumped to the wrong conclusions."

"*Dios mio*," He shakes his head, his eyes soften with understanding. "I can see how you thought that."

His frown deepens as I continue, "It hasn't been easy for either of us, has it?" He takes my hand and kisses my knuckles tenderly; the touch of his lips on my skin resonates through me. I shrug my shoulders and the joy in finding him seeps through the pain of the past. "And yet for some strange magical reason, we're standing on a beach in California holding each other."

"I think it's called kismet." He says with a chuckle pulling me to him.

"Do you know what I want to do now?" I ask, tipping my head back looking into his eyes.

"No, but I think you're going to tell me."

"Look, what a beautiful night," I gesture toward the water and sky. "The ocean is calm, the moon and stars are out. A perfect night to take a romantic stroll down the beach with someone you once loved."

"Always the nature girl?" He smiles down at me.

"Yep," My lips twitch with laughter.

"Good, I've missed her."

Slipping off the wall, I hold out my hand to him. "Do you think we could just walk, hand and hand, no more talking of the past or the future........for a while." My mind is reeling from the enormity of this evening. "For now....I want to kick off my shoes, hold your hand and walk through the surf. No thinking, no talking.......just you and me..........I want this moment to last......because I found you."

Vic stands up, purses his lips, unable to hide his amusement and offers his arm. "My lady, shall we walk?"

Chapter 27

Redemption

Waves gently toss grains of sand back and forth, back and forth, the rhythm of the ocean lapping the shore. The moon overhead reflected in the surf. Constellations wink down from the sky above, calling out their names, Swan, Lion, Sirius and Leo. Tensions ease and familiarity sets in as we stroll down the beach. The slow easy motion of walking allows the events of the evening to fall in place, the pain and confusion of the past fade, and the magic that was ours reclaimed.

The beach deserted, no one in sight, the lights from the parking lot fade away replaced by the sporadic lighting of private residences. A blue lifeguard tower stands as a lonely sentinel to the sea.

"Think we can climb up there?" I ask, cocking my head, fluttering my eyelashes in a flirtatious manner. "I need to sit for a bit, and I've never been in a lifeguard's stand. Maybe you can give me a tour?"

"Sure, you might to want to leave those fancy shoes on the sand and hike up that dress for the climb." He leads me to the steps of the lifeguard tower. "But first," he reaches out, his hands warm and strong, hard on my wrists and pulls me into his embrace. I recognize the look. The sudden darkening of gold in those deep eyes before his clever hands run up my body and his mouth covers mine. I feel a shiver starting along my spine where he lays his hands. I'm weightless, floating above the sand, yet I feel every plane and line as his body presses against mine. It has been a long time since I've been held like this, and tonight I feel as though I'd ridden to the top of a crest and weakness floods me. "I've missed you so much, Elle." He breathes. Oh, I still affect him.

The dark of night has intensified; stars appear brighter in the sky, the wind died, and the sound of the sea a steady heartbeat in the distance. The moon sails overhead and around us the night shimmers with the echo of magic. And that is enough.

Weathered by the elements the lifeguard tower stands in need of paint, splinters stick out of the ragged wood planking. We climb up and sit on the small deck overlooking the Pacific Ocean.

"I was a lifeguard at a resort in Mexico for a while." Vic says, pulling me into the warmth of his chest.

"Really, I bet the girls loved you."

"It was the most boring job I've ever had, hot, lonely and just dull."

"Did you ever save anyone?"

"I swam out a few times with the surfboard because some stupid idiot over-estimated his swimming ability, usually aided by the help of too much alcohol."

"Very glamorous." I say, snuggling closer as the cool air blows in from the ocean.

"Here, you're shivering." He takes off his tuxedo jacket and wraps it around my shoulders. The bad girl in me thinks; I won't mind him shedding a few more of those clothes. God, is he gorgeous and in my defense...... it's been ...ummm....a while.

"Warm?" He asks, leaning over to kiss my forehead.

"Mmmm, very cozy." Our eyes lock, as silence settles around us, time enough for a warm flush to ignite my blood. I see my reaction reflected in his eyes.

"So are you ready to talk?" He kisses the back of my neck. I moan softly

"Nooo, not just yet." I catch my breath as he nibbles a sensitive spot below my ear. "I rather you continued with what you're doing. And I'm getting some very suggestive ideas." I giggle.

"That's fine with me." He murmurs. "Maybe you should tell me some of those suggestive thoughts." His hand wanders up and down the length of my body.

"Oh no, once we start……as you remember restraint was not our strong point." I sigh. "I'm not sure this flimsy lifeguard station is strong enough."

"I bet we wouldn't be the first ones to give it a try." His hand moves up to the swell of my breast. "It would be my happiest memory of lifeguarding."

"Mmmmm, maybe," I purr under the attention of his hands, his fingers caressing my nipple though the fabric of my dress. "First," I whisper, reason overcoming desire. "I have a few questions."

"Sure, fire away." He breathes into my ear as his hand slips under the fabric of my dress, moving in slow lazy circles.

I swallow and close my eyes, trying to keep my head above the tide of yearning snaking through my body. "Vic, are you married, engaged, in a serious relationship?" I manage to choke out as waves of heated desire shoot through me. "I need a few answers before this goes any farther."

"Whoa! Okay, serious stuff," he sits back, rubbing his chin with long fingers as he contemplates his answer. "I *was* married, about fifteen years ago. I met Sophia DeLong on a movie set in Mexico, she was the leading lady. I had a small role in the movie. What can I say but she was Spanish, beautiful and passionate. The sparks between us ignited into an explosive relationship. But that was it, once the initial desire waned; we fought like cats and dogs. It only lasted for about five years, and that was because of Hanna."

"Who is Hanna?"

"Sophia and I have a daughter named Hanna, who is thirteen going on thirty, much to her mother's and my dismay. She is a great kid, but still a teenage girl with way too many adult ideas."

"Teenage girls can be a handful." My finger toys with the button stud on his shirt. "I'm glad you have a child. I can't imagine life without my children."

"Hanna is the light of my life, which she knows and uses shamelessly against me to get her way. But Sophia and I have a pact that all major decisions have to go through both of us. Usually one of us is strong enough to be the disciplinarian." He nibbles on my ear. "How many children do you have?"

"Two, You met Lani, and my son, Trey, who is eighteen and will be starting college in two weeks."

"Your husband?"

"Jack died almost two years ago of a heart attack."

"Oh, I'm sorry."

"I miss him. But you know, finding you feels like destiny. I think Jack had a hand in it…up there playing the good angel, meddling around in people's lives."

"Who knows, I stopped trying to figure it out a long time ago."

"So you have no serious commitment to anyone?"

"No, honestly, there is no one special in my life at the moment." He grasps my hand squeezing it tightly.

"And truth be told, Elle, I never stopped loving you."

Good God! My mind spins with the enormity of what he just said. I squeak out, "Really?"

"Yeah, I don't know, they say you never forget your first love, maybe it was the tragic way we were separated." He shrugs; a wry smile crosses his face. "Who knows?"

"Vic, maybe after all these years, we've changed, and life has gone on. Was losing our baby and being separated a trial of some kind? Maybe it's too late."

"I hope not, I have no intention of letting you go." He tightens his hold on me. "You need to tell me the whole story, Elle. What happened?"

I sigh, and lean into him, gazing at the halo of the moon, conjuring up the past. "They took me to a home for wayward girls. It was run by the nastiest bunch of nuns that ever walked the face of the earth." I burrow my head into his chest, seeking comfort from the past. "I haven't stepped foot in a Catholic Church since I left that place. It was a walled fortress, made of brick and stone. We were made to work all day to atone for our sins and locked away in our single rooms at night. I would wake up with nightmares, crying for you to come, but they ignored my tears saying I should pray and find solace in the Lord."

"Jesus, I didn't think places like that existed, even thirty years ago."

"Oh, Helen did her homework; she found a home for unwed mothers that served as a prison in disguise."

His voice catches, "I'm so sorry, Elle."

I continue on, wanting to purge the pain, and put the past behind us. After the baby was born, they signed the adoption papers because I was under age. I never even held our son."

Vic shakes his head in disbelief. "Damn it..."

"After they took me home, I waited for you. And one day the phone rang, it was your aunt telling me you died in a motorcycle accident."

"My aunt? None of my aunts speak English," he shakes his head in disbelief. "That son of a bitch, he must have put Mariposa up to it, his mistress. She would do anything for him. Of course, he paid her well." Vic curses, "That deceitful old bastard, the lengths he'd go to get his way."

"Well, it worked. I got off the phone, went upstairs to my bedroom, wouldn't eat, drink or speak to anybody. I died inside."

"Oh, Elle," Vic murmurs, his body rocks me slowly back and forth, aching to dissipate the pain.

"After about two weeks, my father and Helen tried to place me in a mental institution because I was so depressed." I peek up at his face and smile. "Actually, this is my favorite part of the awful story. Just picture this, Gran and Burt storm the house with Gran banishing her cane. She holds my father and Helen at bay, calling them every curse word in the English language while Burt abducts me from my bedroom. He carried me down the stairs and out the door, while Gran threatened if anyone tried to stop them, there would be hell to pay."

Vic chuckles "I can just see the two of them. Burt isn't very big, but he is strong and wiry."

"Burt passed away about two years ago."

"Oh, no! God, I'd love to see him again."

"He had a massive heart attack. He was finishing up a nature program with a school group. It was a beautiful day; he had his dog by his side and one of his best friends with him. It was how he would have wanted to go."

"I'm so sorry to hear that."

"I miss him terribly; Gran passed away six years ago and then Jack. Those are gaps in my heart that will never be filled."

Vic nods sympathetically.

"Anyway, Burt carried me to the upstairs bedroom of Gran's house. They opened the windows to fresh air and sunshine, filled the room with wildflowers, read my favorite books, nursed me back to health. They wouldn't let me go, basically, forcing me back to life."

"Thank God," he says with a grateful half smile on his face.

"I was helpless to fight off the power of their love. They showed me life was worth living. Burt even brought a collie puppy home, knowing I needed something to love. Eventually, I went away to college, got a teaching degree, married Jack and had two children. I owe them my life."

"They were special people."

"And so here we are," Vic muses, "By the grace of God and the love of a few special people."

Overcome by the emotional turbulence of the evening, we doze in each other arms, content, wrapped in the presence of love reclaimed, until I'm rudely awakened.....

Chapter 28

Give Me Back My Manolo's

"Well, well, well. Looky, what we have here, Joe." A sneering voice followed by a blinding beam of light comes from below the lifeguard station. Vic mumbles an oath as he sits up shielding his eyes from the light.

"Looks like a pair of lovers got lost on the beach. That's what it looks like to me," answers a man hidden in the dark. The figures of two men come into view as the one holding the flashlight explores the lifeguard tower.

"I think they need help finding their way home. Don't you?"

"Dressed real fancy."

"Pretty lady, look at those boobs sticking out of her dress."

Vic growls a warning. "Gentlemen, I think we're capable of finding our way home without your assistance." He moves putting himself between me and the men on the beach. "I suggest you move along."

"Not until we help ourselves to your wallet and the lady's purse." A slightly built man who appears to be Asian chortles in the pale moonlight. He pulls a knife out of his pocket, a press of a button and out flashes a switchblade. The knife gleams in the meager moonlight.

I stifle a scream clutching Vic's jacket. I feel his body tense under my grasp. He eases himself over to the edge of the tower, poised to launch in my defense.

"Elle, let go of me," he hisses.

I tighten my grip. "They look dangerous."

"Listen to the smart lady, buddy, and no one will get hurt." The man with the knife warns. "Toss down your wallet and the purse."

"Gentlemen, there is a small fortune lying at your feet." Stalling for time, Vic points to my shoes tossed in the sand. "Those fancy shoes are probably worth $500 bucks."

"Absolutely not!" I protest. "Those are not my shoes; they have to be returned to the costume department tomorrow. Lani could lose her job!"

"Elle, quiet! I'll get you new shoes."

"But they have to be the same ones," I hiss in an admonitory voice.

"Shhhh," he cautions me. "No shoes are worth getting killed over." Spoken like a man I fume, sometimes they don't appreciate the finer things in life…like pretty shoes. I watch in regret as the stocky man bends over picking up the stilettos.

"Why aren't these pretty little bling-bling slippers." He holds a shoe up, glittering in the moonlight. Just as I feel Vic tense to hurl himself at the one holding the switchblade from behind the lifeguard tower comes a voice edged in steel, "I would leave those pretty little shoes just where you found them, my friends."

"What the hell?" says the smaller man, and swings his flashlight in the direction of the voice. Standing there in all of his six foot three, muscle bound, flaming russet hair, Celtic warrior glory was…..Ike, holding a hand gun pointed at the two vandals. I choke back a sob of relief. As strong as Vic may appear, there were two of them and only one of us; because you can count on me to be worthless. Hand to hand combat, not high on my list of talents, I've been reduced to tears by a broken nail.

"These good folks are friends of mine." Ike gestures down the beach with the gun. "I think the two of you had better high tail it out of here. I would hate to hurt anyone, dark beach, no witnesses. Who's to know? Two drifters left for dead."

He holds the gun up slightly higher and tenses as if to take aim. "It would be such a shame, probably not worth an investigation, especially with your past criminal records. I presume you boys have a rap sheet a mile long. Am I right?"

"Okay, okay, we're going, ease up on the gun, mister."

"Not until the two of you scum bags are out of my sight. Now run before I change my mind and start shooting."

With the threat echoing in their ears, the two men start running down the beach, one trips falling down in the sand. Ike shines a flashlight on their retreating backs. "Good riddance, you trash."

While his eyes are trained on the beach to pick up any suspicious movement, Ike calls out to Vic, "Hey buddy, I suggest you and the little lady get off this beach before we have any more friendly visits. Why don't you head up to the boardwalk, there is a restaurant where you can wait while I go back and get the car."

"Thank God, you were following us, Ike." Vic jumps down from the lifeguard tower and lifts me onto the sand. "I owe you one, man. It has been a long time since I've done any street fighting."

Ike chuckles, "The day I start cashing in your debt, I can retire on a private island with a harem of woman."

"In your dreams, Vic retorts.

"Yeah, probably more like a nightmare, all them

women squabbling over me, give a guy a headache." He sheathes the gun in a holster strapped to his back. "Are you all right?"

"I'm fine." Vic nods. "Elle, are you all right?"

"I'm fine," I lie, my knees still shaking. "But a cup of coffee, a glass of wine, food, lights, people…safety, would be very welcome right about now." I reach down to pick up my Manolo Blahniks' from the sand. "My Manolo's," I wail in disbelief, holding up one silver shoe twinkling in the moonlight. "He took my shoe. That rotten bum stole my shoe! What in the world is he going to do with one shoe? That's just spiteful!"

"Sorry, sweetheart, we'll get you a new pair." Vic says, tugging at my hand trying to move me down the beach. "But we need to get out of here, before they decide to come back for the other one."

Ike scrutinizes the lonely strip of beach. "I'll walk along with you to the boardwalk; it's about a half mile back. Just to make sure there are no more surprise visitors then I'll double back and get the car."

"Let's get the hell out of here." Vic claps Ike on the shoulder. Under the light of the moon a silent language of friendship passes between them, a kinship closer than most brothers.

…

Overlooking the Pacific Ocean is The Blue Mar, an upscale restaurant, specializing in sea air and overpriced cuisine. Being late, the usual sunset crowd has thinned, leaving Vic and I the privacy of a dimly lit corner booth. The waiter barely raises his eyebrows at our request for a pepperoni pizza and beer. Not the usual fare in this swanky bistro, but reminds us of summer nights in the Adirondacks, where Mac bribed the local pizzeria into delivering pizza and beer to camp. The food arrives, tasting wonderful, warm and rich with a hint of heat from the spicy pepperoni. The cold beer and pizza satisfy one craving, but another craving is not satisfied with food….

Desire tingles though my body, all the tension of the day seeking a channel, straining against him, wanting more. A hunger held in check, the longing, the lust……the electricity, if visible, would be an intense red haze around and between us, mounting into sweet, sweet desire.

"Elle, we need to leave. We're starting to attract attention, and the paparazzi are soon to follow." Vic says as his teeth catch the tender lobe of my ear.

"Yes, yes, yes." I breathe into his cheek, his voice barely audible over the pounding of my heart and the roar of lust coursing through my body.

Ike discreetly pulls the limousine up to the restaurant entrance and we fall into the privacy of the backseat. Not losing a beat, the petting and fondling becomes an erotic dance. In a daze, I can't help thinking if the girls back home could see me. Oh my goodness, I've still got it! *Yes!* After almost *two* years, I'm finally going to get *Lucky*!

"I think we should wait." Vic's lips find mine for a deep tongue probing kiss.

Wait….what! I almost bite off his tongue.

"What did you just say?!" My ears must be playing tricks. Did he just say…wait? Wait for what! My body is on fire, every nerve in my being screaming for his touch and he says: *Wait*. You've got to be kidding me. I've waited thirty years for him.

Vic heaves a sigh, pushing away from me. "I don't know how to say this, but I think it's best if we wait….before we make love."

"Why?" I croak like a lovesick frog.

"Trust me, I want to make love to you more than anything in the world, but I don't know if it's safe." His hand brushes the hair back from my face as he peers into my eyes.

"Safe?" I ask incredulously in a voice husky with desire. "It's not like we're jumping off a bridge. Since when has being with you ever been *safe*?"

"No, this is serious stuff." He runs a hand through his hair, oh; he looks just glorious, tousled hair, white shirt with a dark suit, eyes like melted chocolate, and a body that won't quit. He glances out the window, and I think I just moaned in frustration. "Elle, I'm sorry to admit, I've been with a lot of women, especially lately, they just came and I took them. And sometimes stupidly, I have not always taken precautions and practiced shall we say 'safe sex".

"You have got to be kidding me? You could have AIDs?!" After almost two years of living like a nun, reunited with him, and he may have an STD! "Are you kidding me?"

"I'm sorry, Elle," He throws himself back onto the leather seat, eyes riveted to the ceiling, saying over and over again, "Stupid, stupid, stupid."

"Are you sick?" Concern for his health throws a wet blanket over my desire.

"No, No, I'm fine, but I've hurt you so much in the past, I don't want to risk harming you again. It's one thing for me to be careless with my own heath, but I can't risk exposing you."

He continues, "I'll get Jules on the phone right now, she can set up a lab appointment first thing in the morning." He shakes his head. "Damn it! Tomorrow morning I have a huge meeting with a producer and some studio VIPs for my next movie project. I can't miss it; my entire career may be riding on it." He runs a hand through his thick hair, screwing up his mouth in concentration. "Maybe later in the day," he thinks out loud. "It might take a few days to get the results back. *Shit."* We gaze at each other, not touching. He groans. "But God, I want you now." He breathes against my mouth, and there's a desperate, passionate feel to his kiss.

"Who is Jules?" I ask, and why do I care who Jules is. I'm so hot in the confines of this limo, there is only one thought on my mind…I want him *now*. He can't be serious, wait days for test results to come back. I need to be home for school in a few days. I want to jump this man right here and now. Easy for him to say, he's been screwing every bimbo in Hollywood. I'm on the cusp of menopause! This could be it; I'm done waiting!

"Jules, is my personal assistant," he explains, speaking into a very expensive looking cell-phone. "Juls, it's Esteban, Yes, I know it's very late, but this is important." He nods, smiling, "Yes, I know you require eight hours of beauty sleep. But I need you to make a doctor's appointment for me, whatever it takes to screen me for STD's." He rolls his eyes in exasperation. "Yes, I need you to set this up for me either very early in the morning or after the meeting. Why now?" He snorts. "Very cute, no, I have not had an epiphany regarding my, as you call it, slutty lifestyle, and no, I am not applying for the priesthood." He leans over to kiss me and I hear Juls laughing on the phone. "You're right, they wouldn't have me. Yes, I've met someone. Very special." His eyes glitter warmly on me. "No, I'm not going into details now. You're awfully nosy for someone who was sound asleep just minutes ago."

I listen to this one sided conversation, the tone more like the banter between a brother and sister than a professional relationship. "So give me a call and let me know the details." Vic says. "Yes, I know this is going to cost me. Hey, I just gave you a raise. No, you're not indispensable. I'm sure a thousand girls would line up for your job. Yes, I know it would take a thousand women to replace you, love you too, go back to sleep."

"I'm sorry." He looks at me with a quizzical expression on his face, misinterpreting my disappointment for anger. "Are you mad at me?"

"You know," I sniff, "You made the assumption I would sleep with you. Maybe, I'm not that kind of girl. Mr. Rienz." I say half seriously, a bit chagrined at my passionate response to him and possibly being lumped into the one night stand bimbo category. He attracts woman like candy on Halloween. Yes, I want to sleep with him……*really bad*….. but the STD conversation, while responsible on his part, took the romance right out of the moment.

"Elle, I'm sorry. I didn't mean to assume, we're both available and it feels so right, I thought it would just happen." He kisses me gently on the cheek and moves along the bridge of my brow. "I've been in Hollywood too long. This town has no moral code, everyone is screwing around."

"Vic, I don't need to be courted, we're both adults. The idea of you showing up on my porch with a bouquet of flowers and a box of chocolates is ludicrous."

I smile at the thought. "I want to be with you. The whole STD business though….Vic, I'm done with sharing. My husband had affairs. I know he was *very* careful, for his sake and mine, but I don't want that fear hanging over my head anymore. This time I get to choose, with Jack, I had our children to consider. And truth be told, I did love him, as stupid as that may sound. I loved him, his family and our life, I wasn't about to ruin it just because Jack was a jerk."

"Elle," He says, placing his finger under my chin, tipping my head back forcing me to look into his eyes. "I can't change the past, but the future is a road we can map out together. In all honesty, I'm tired of waking up next to strange women. If I didn't have Hanna, I'd have no roots at all. I'm sorry your husband was unfaithful. And for me, the meaningless affairs are getting old. I'm ready to settle down. I know it's too early to have this conversation, but my gut says what you and I had as teenagers is still there."

I trace his lips with the tip of my finger. "I want to be with you, but I'm not a casual lover. I've only been with two men, you and my husband. By today's standards, I'm almost a virgin."

"For a virgin, you're a quick learner." he quips, a dimple plays in the corner of his cheek.

"Don't change the topic, but you understand what I'm saying? I don't think I can play the Hollywood game. So for now, you're right, we slow down and wait." I run my hand over the lapel of his tuxedo jacket, loving the feeling of his broad shoulders. With a giggle, I continue my exploration, adding, "But in the meantime, there are a few skills I've picked up along the way.....are you sure that glass separating us from Ike is see-proof? I'd hate for him to see......"

And so, on the drive to Lani's house we were like teenagers in heat, let loose in the back of a travel van with a six pack of beer. Ike discreetly raps at the window announcing we had arrived. With great reluctance, Vic helps me straighten my clothes while I try to still my racing heart."

"Walk me to the door?"

"As a gentleman, I insist. Nothing less will do. I'll even hold open the door."

"Perfect," I extend my hand to him as he exits the limo. Ike holds the door, making no attempt to hide his amusement over Vic's lustful state.

We stroll up the walkway to the house, hand and hand; I limp like a three legged dog on my one shoe. At the door, turning to face each other, he dips his head for a good-night kiss and the finality of the moment rockets a shot of fear through my heart. I've lost him before; I can't bear the thought of him walking away, even if only for a day. My hand trails out of his as he turns down the path, blowing a kiss from his fingertips. "Until tomorrow, I promise, Elle, I promise." Tears swim in my eyes; a cold ache of loneliness fills my being.

Watching his dark silhouette walk to the car, I have an idea, a flash of inspiration; a light bulb moment. I remember. "Vic, wait," I cry, reaching into my purse, limping down the walkway, pulling out the strip of pink condoms my girlfriends gave me as a dare….waving them like a pink flag of courage. They challenged me to live a little. And I'm ready to live, *boy am I ready to live*. "I've got boots!" I squeal.

"Boots?" He asks with a quizzical look on his face.

"Condoms, rubbers, safe sex! Dummy." I laugh. "I'm supposed to be the naïve one, Mr. Hollywood Hot Stuff." I hear a snort of laughter erupt from Ike.

Vic turns and slowly walks toward me, stopping just

outside my arm's reach. He whispers, "Elle, *caro*, you are making this so hard." He runs a hand through his hair, shaking his head in doubt. "I'm afraid to touch you the way I want to," he says, a quiet tremor in his voice. "I've hurt you enough for one lifetime."

"Vic, don't leave me here." I plead, holding out my hand to him. "I'm a big girl. And Cinder-Ella doesn't want to go home, she already lost the slipper, but Prince Charming is standing right in front of her, the carriage awaits," I take off my shoe, and hold it out to him as an offering, it winks and gleams in the moonlight. "It is past midnight, the clock bell has tolled.........take me home with you. Finish the story."

"Elle," his voice husky with emotion. He covers the distance between us in two short strides, sweeping me into his arms, as only Prince Charming can....and the shoe drops....... forgotten, sparkling like a jewel in the dew covered grass.

Chapter 29

The Heart Leads You Back……

Ike pulls the limo up a curved driveway leading to a Spanish style villa jutting out over the ocean. Vic's West Coast retreat. The entrance to the house is crowned in a gorgeous profusion of bougainvillea growing over the doorway, framed with pots of brightly colored flowers. Vic sweeps me into his arms and carries me over the threshold. As he gently places me down, my eyes are drawn to a doorway leading to a patio opening to a view beyond the boundaries of the house. A vista of sky and water as far as the eye can see. A small infinity pool tumbles over the edge, mimicking a river flowing to the ocean. The beach below the balcony is a sea of white sand leading to the surf of the frigid Pacific Ocean. The half-moon overhead casts a pearly glow to the beach. But the stars overhead are brilliant in the cloudless sky.

"Welcome home, Ella, my mia bella, welcome home." He runs the palms of his hands upward along my arms, so close I can feel his heat. "I can't believe you are here with me."

That's two of us….because once here in his home, I'm as nervous as a school girl on her first date. What have I started? Maybe I should have taken this more slowly. And then my attention is distracted, as he steps behind me, turning me toward the ocean view, placing kisses slowly up my spine, only stopping at the delicious, titillating hollow of my neck. His fingers caress the top of my dress, sliding against my skin, and his touch resonates through me. I moan, melting into his body.

Beguiled….if I ever doubted the word, now I understand. His touch embraces me with warmth, the fulfillment of a promise. With Vic, I'm beguiled, pulled along a current into depths beyond myself. No boundaries, no rules, just Vic. He tilts my head as he draws closer, his fingers a soft brush of warmth across my cheek, there is no escape. All I see are those compelling eyes. There is no delusion into believing any less, with Vic, it's only more.

A soft tug at the base of my French twist, hastily arranged when we walked on the beach releases a scattering of pins as my hair yields to his marauding hands. He slides his fingers upwards, releasing the restricting coils.

The soft graze of his firm lips quickens my blood until the pulse beating in my breast throbs in a delicious ache. He slips his arms around me, embracing me, pressing my breast against his hard chest. And, oh, it feels so wonderful, being held this way after so long. His mouth rolls off my lips and begins to trail a series of warm, moist kisses over my face. I feel myself tremble, the passion for him, once possessed, then stolen away, now resurrected. His lips move against mine, tasting my hunger, adding to his desire for me. My arms wind around his shoulders, holding him as my fingers tangle in his hair, his soft, silky hair. That primitive flame, dormant for so many years, thought never to be rekindled, leaps to life in a firestorm of passion, burning with a need I had nearly forgotten.

"Breathe," He whispers, his lips brushing mine. "Breathe, we have all night, nothing can disturb us here." My head falls back into the cradle of his arms, staring up at him, shocked by my response; dizzy from….lack of air and the consuming need for his touch.

I can see every feature, every line, every plane of his face etched in the dim light. He runs his hands over my shoulders, his soft palms sending shivers across my skin. And in one swift move, the zipper of my dress slides open, and the blue sheath rustles as it cascades down, a shimmering pool of color on the tile floor. He helps me step out of it, the cool night air strokes my fevered skin; and I feel his gaze lower to the swell of my breasts peeking above the lace-edged bra. He slips his hand around the base of my throat, pushing his thumb into the soft skin beneath my chin, forcing my head back until all I see are sparks of golden fire in his eyes, whirling in the shimmer of stars framed by the overhead skylight. His fingers deftly unhook the bra, as my breasts spill out; he unleashes his tongue on them. Groaning, I bury my hands into his hair, eyes closed against the onslaught of desire. Stopping, he looks up at me expectantly, and gently slips my panties down. He pauses, and stares for a moment, drinking me in, his eyes smolder. Removing his jacket, he tosses it to the mounting pile of clothes on the floor.

Rather clumsily, and with shaking fingers I fumble with the studs from his shirt, undoing the top three buttons. The contrast of white linen against bronzed skin hypnotic, and I rejoice in the smooth feel of his chest under the palm of my hand. And as much as I love a man in a tuxedo, I have a feeling that what is underneath….is better, *much better*………soon his trousers join my dress on the floor. I glance down at my body barely recognizing it in the gossamer of moonlight, his hand slips between my thighs. He presses his palm to the sensitive mound of flesh, his fingers sliding inside me.

As his fingers press into me, his thumb passes over the sensitive nub of nerves hidden beneath soft curls. My eyes close as my body moves against his hand. "Tell me," he whispers, his breath warm, his skin tasting faintly of the sea and salt beneath my lips. In a harsh whisper, his voice and eyes question, "Are you sure, Elle?"

The demands of his hands on my flesh cause a clawing hollow at my insides. I can't believe he's asking……the passion I feel for him is like a freight train running downhill without brakes.

"I want you." Slipping my arms around his neck, my voice comes almost in a whimper. "Please don't stop." He grabs my hips and pulls me into him; my hands reach for his neck and his mouth crashes down, his tongue finds mine. I moan into his mouth as we kiss savagely. He breaks free; scoops me into his arms, and carries me toward the bedroom. The trip a blur of touching, kissing, tongues, and tortuous desire aching to be fulfilled. He eases back slightly standing at the edge of the bed, "Are you sure?"

"Absolutely!" I'm frantic with desire to touch and explore every inch of his body. *Stop asking!* As we tumble onto the silk duvet covering the bed, he whispers,

"Smooth, warm, and beautiful," he makes me believe his words. He strokes my face with the back of his knuckles, bending he kisses my lips briefly. His hands move, slow and firm, it seems natural, and glorious, as our fingers link rolling over in the bed, to break apart, finding new secrets to explore. I clutch his shoulders as he kisses and nibbles along the undersides of my breasts, avoiding the two spots I'm desperate for him to touch. My breasts swell and ache for the fire of his mouth to claim them.

"You still smell like the forest." He says.

"The forest?" I ask dumbly, arching my back, tugging his head to where I want it…..his mouth closes over my nipple and I squirm in ecstasy. "The forest? I taste like the forest; you think I taste like……..*oh…my*!"

He lifts his head from my breast, my bones turning to mush as his fingers explore lower. "Ummm, yes, mountains… pine… sunshine…wildflowers," he breathes on the nipple before closing his teeth over it so gently. His touch feels like soft velvet brushing against my skin. He sinks one long finger into my waiting depths and he has me squirming and writhing beneath his hands and mouth. My body licked with flames of desire, so strong I'm surprised the smoke alarm doesn't go off. As I scream his name, glorious peaks of desire sweep through my body, spike, and clench all the muscles in my pelvis.

"Yes, Elle, let me hear you," he encourages.

I want him inside me now, I'm done with waiting, his breath hisses out as he teases me with his fingers.

"I want you," I beg…"Now, Vic, now."

His mouth joins mine, and I feel his desperate hunger. Keeping his eyes on me, he sits up, reaches over to the nightstand and grabs a foil packet, and rips it open with his teeth. Together we slowly roll the condom onto him. He grabs my hands and moves me onto my back as he eases himself into me. He closes his eyes and flexes his hips to meet mine, filling me. It feels so good, it has been so *long*. He rocks his head back, his mouth forming a perfect O as he exhales.

I move with his rhythm, numbing all thought and reason, lost in the sensations of pleasure rioting through my body. My breath ragged as I open my eyes in disbelief this is Vic…..truly Vic. With open eyes, I see he's staring back at me, eyes glowing, "Ella, Ella, my bella," he groans through clenched teeth. I roll over on top of him, taking control of my pleasure, and I cry out his name, spinning up….and up…then crumpling on top of him.

"Oh, *Elle!*" he groans, holding me still, letting go and finds his release.

…

Exhausted, I sleep until the edge of dawn breaks through the window. Propping my head up on the pillow, I see Vic sprawled across the bed, dead to the world. The Hollywood ladies may be young and buff…..

Careful not to wake him, I walk barefoot across the room and pick up a white button down shirt left discarded on the floor. Holding it to my face I inhale his scent ……*uummmmm*, but before any more erotic ideas pop into my head………I need a bathroom.

Refreshed from a hot shower, I explore the house, searching…the morning mantra of c*offee, coffee, coffee,* running through my head. I gasp in delight crossing the threshold into the kitchen. The room is awash with color, brightly hued Mexican mosaic tiles in blues, greens, and yellows explode over an arched cooking area. The center island covered in the contrasting tiles and the walls are painted the color of a warm pumpkin burnished by the autumn sun. Stepping out on to the terrace framed by the ocean view, I momentarily forget my pressing need for coffee; the view is breathtaking. A light breeze carries the early morning chill off the ocean, the sound of pounding surf and salty sea air intoxicates my senses. Sunlight spreads across the rippling water like a blanket of shimmering gold. I stretch, take a deep breath and exhale. With a shiver, I hug his shirt closer enjoying the view until the cold morning air sends me inside.

A quick search of the kitchen reveals an unopened can of coffee and some powdered creamer. Well, better than nothing. The cupboard and refrigerator hold no fresh foods, only canned or frozen convenience foods. The personification of a bachelor pad: a king size bed, Jacuzzi bathtub, stocked bar and no food.

Climbing the stairs to the bedroom, two steaming mugs of black coffee in my hands, I can't believe I'm standing here, in a house overlooking the Pacific Ocean, and best of all, Vic sprawled across the bed. I take a sip of the scalding hot coffee, and gawk, yep, still here and *naked, naked, naked.* He's sound asleep, only the bottom half of his body covered by the sheet, his broad chest and arms splayed across the bed, one leg poking out of the quilt. I enjoy the view for a few moments, thinking it would be nice to kiss the back of his neck, his bare shoulder, the small of his back….and then…...

Under the heat of my gaze, Vic rolls over with a yawn, an appreciative smile lights up his face as he reaches for the coffee. "Beautiful, sexy, and she makes coffee. The ideal woman." He takes a sip and throws back the sheet, inviting me to slip in beside him.

"Just don't ask me to cook." I place my mug on the nightstand and slide in next to him.

"That's what restaurants are for," He chuckles into my ear. In the recesses of my mind, an ugly thought comes ……Hollywood stars don't date fifth grade school teachers and take them out to expensive restaurants in lieu of beautiful starlets for long. *Be careful.*

"Come here and let me see you in the light of day." He puts his coffee down and opens his arms.

Oh…. not a good idea…!' My mind screams. This is not the same body it was thirty years ago. My hand clenches the collar of his shirt tightly against my body, warding off his probing eyes. He's dated Vanessa Leason, and married Sophia DeLong, just to mention a few. Having him see me naked in the dark and slightly drunk is one thing, but sober and in the light of day…..is *totally* another.

"Maybe, we should just leave the shirt on," I say, trying to distract him with a trail of kisses punctuated with nibbles along his jaw line.

"Elle," he whispers huskily into my ear. "I've waited thirty years to see you again. Don't make me wait any longer." *Crap…*

"*Ummm*, this is not exactly the same body you knew thirty years ago," I plead with desperation, thinking of the stretch marks here and the stretch marks there with a few pounds thrown in……….just for extra measure. Botox and liposuction are not on my list of vocabulary of words. "Let's just crawl down under these nice soft sheets. Egyptian cotton, 400 count. They're lovely."

The words coming out of my mouth are cut off as he kisses me to silence. He kisses my forehead, my eyelids, my lips then my nose, even my fingertips, rolling back onto his side so he can look into my eyes.

"Trust me, Elle," he gently pried my fingers off the shirt, slowly undoing each button, his mouth and tongue create a trail of desire as my skin is unveiled under his searching eyes. "Your breasts are beautiful," he says kissing the nipples into taut peaks.

"Stop, stop, really you should stop." I laugh trying to wiggle out of his embrace. "I've reached the point where sheets and clothes are my friends."

Not to be out done, he reaches and hauls me back into his arms, sliding the shirt off.

"You're just being a little tease." He holds my arms

over my head and skillfully kisses my protests away. Sweeping the sheet away; he trails kisses down my back, and stops at my backside and starts laughing. An incredulous expression crosses his face as he stares at my bottom.

"*What*?" I wince. "I told you it wasn't so pretty anymore."

"No, no, your butt is beautiful, especially with the little turtle tattooed on it. Let me get a closer look." Crawling across the bed, he straddles my legs to get a better view.

"What? Tattoo? Ohhhh.......*damn it!* I'd forgotten about that stupid tattoo. Jack talked me into getting it on our trip to Aruba. Propped up on both elbows, I look over my shoulder as he examines the little sea turtle done in aqua green ink.

"I didn't take you for the tattoo type. I like this naughty Ellen." He's fairly purring as he stretches out......his finger tracing the outline of the tattoo, completely distracting my thoughts. "How long have you had it?" He plants a smacking kiss on the turtle.

"Ummmm......Jack?" I blurt out, trying to ignore the racing of my heart.

"Your husband was a tattoo artist?" His other hand joins the first one, caressing, exploring and titillating the lower region of my body.

"No, no, not really." I hear the sound of my breath gasping at the back of my throat, then exhaling into a low moan. "We were on vacation.......*ahhhhhh*..........and drunk....*oh my goodness*.......and he talked me into getting that ridiculous tattoo on my ass."

"I love it." And he takes a playful nip at my butt. *Ouch!* "And your shoulders are exquisite too."

A trail of kisses moves up my spine to the hollows of my shoulder blades.

As I try to squirm out of his embrace, embarrassment becomes replaced with desire. *Oh, don't stop.* Who am I to argue with the man? Maybe I fulfill some soccer mom/school teacher notch on his list of lovers. Personally, I think poor vision and lousy judgment clouded by lack of sleep explain his questionable perception skills. *But, oh,* I really don't care, a groan of pleasure escapes my lips, his tongue licks the hollow of my hip…....*and* he knows stuff too.

"This body has given birth to three children, one of them, mine. I want to see every inch of you." He rips the sheet from the bed, and pauses to gaze with unabashed desire at me. The inner princess in me gives a whoop of relief and joy. "Your body is more beautiful and real than all those plastic women I have been with for the past five years. With them, you can't tell where fake ends and real begins. It's superficial, and all for show." Looking into my eyes, he runs his thumb along the plane of my cheek and jaw. "I've missed you, Elle. This is what I want." With that statement he rolls on top of me, hard and ready to give proof to his desire, my breathing accelerates as his steady rhythm pushes me higher and higher, my hips meet his thrust for thrust, he stares down at me in adoring wonder, and I lose myself in him.

…

Wide awake after our own personal sunrise salute, the sound of the ocean surf beckons for an early morning walk on the beach. "Do you have a sweatshirt or shorts; I could borrow?" A dubious glance at my discarded blue gown lying next to his crumpled tuxedo shirt shows a wardrobe seriously lacking in beach attire.

I look doubtfully from his long, lean torso to my pitiful pile of clothes scattered across the hallway. He rolls over onto his back, looking rough, restless and disheveled. The way a man should look after a night of unrivaled debauchery.

"Come on, I'm sure I have something that will work for you." He gets out of bed and heads down the hallway, pulling on a pair of sweatpants.

I follow him into an adjoining dressing room; the entire wall on one side is a built-in armoire. He opens a cabinet door with a flourish to reveal neatly arranged shelves of clothing. "Keep these on hand for my overnight guests." He says with a proud grin. Inside the cupboard are approximately twenty soft terry cloth jogging suits in a variety of pastel hues, arranged according to size with matching tank tops and flip-flops.

"What's this?" I ask, confused by the wide range of size and selection.

"I keep these on hand for...*uhhhhh.......ohhhhhhh....*" He suddenly looks contrite and realizes he divulged more information than needed.

You have got to be kidding me! I'm horrified. "These.....these are replacement clothes for your various one night stands, unfortunate ladies who wake up and find their clothes in tatters the next morning? You have morning-after *bimbo* clothes! How convenient." I pronounce scathingly. Instinctively, I can't help but reach out and caress the soft terry material, thinking how comfortable it would be to slip one on right now. *Over my dead body!* My subconscious screams. The possibility of being lumped into a one night stand-booty call firms my resolve. I fume, "And you, the congenial host, ready to meet the ladies every need, supply new clothes to replace the sullied ones. Where are the toothbrushes?"

He looks chagrined, pointing to the bathroom. I shake my head in disbelief. I can't believe what I'm seeing. "Just how many women have you been with, Vic? You have more clothes in here than the Gap." In the light of day, my beguiling of the night before suddenly seems irresponsible and potentially dangerous.

"I'm sorry, Elle," he sighs, looking away with hands on his hips. "I tried to warn you last night, I haven't exactly been a saint. The women were, basically meaningless affairs, I'm ashamed to admit, diversions of pleasure. I've been reasonably careful, but I've been with a lot of women the past few years." He shrugs his shoulders. "They just come." *great.*

I feel the breath in my chest catch against rising panic. I know I can't expect our little affair to go far, considering our different lifestyles. I'm just a distraction to please him until the next one comes along. And against my will, a sob escapes.

"Don't cry, Elle." He pleads, running his hands up and down my arms instinctively willing the blood back into my numb limbs. "I'm so sorry. I'm such an idiot, and it's been so long since I've been with someone who is real, not some Hollywood version of morality." He pulls me into his arms. "I didn't think. The house came equipped like this and the housekeeper just keeps things in order and well supplied. I'm sorry.......Welcome to Hollywood." He shrugs his shoulders.

"Vic, was I just another in a long list of women last night?" I ask, trying to keep the hurt out of my voice. I'm a big girl; I think to myself, I knew what I was getting myself into, hey, I supplied the boots. Oh, *dear God,* I supplied the condoms. My face turns crimson at the memory and a tear slips unchecked down my cheek. I furiously wipe it away and steel myself for the answer. "It's okay, I realize…." I caress his chest to reassure him that I understand. "Last night was fun; it doesn't have to be anything more than that."

"Elle, no, no, no," he groans, gently wiping away my tears. "I never stopped looking for you. Maybe in part that explains the womanizing. I entered into a disastrous marriage; there were qualities in Sophia that reminded me of you."

"What about…Vanessa?" I hug my arms, willing myself not to touch him, just the scent of his skin beckons, drawing me closer until the urge to move into him overpowers me. I desperately want to believe him, but do I even know him anymore? He's obviously charming; these women didn't end up in his bed without a little persuasive pressure on his part. I'm sure he knows all the lines, all the right moves. A serial seducer of women.

"Who?" He asks, confusion clouding his eyes.

"I'm sorry. I have no right to question who you date." My heart feels ready to burst, shattering into a thousand pieces and scatter like broken glitter across the tile floor.

"You mean Vanessa Leason from the premier?" A frown etches shallow lines into his brow.

"Yes, she was your date." I take a deep breath. "The two of you looked quite cozy when you came in together." I hold my breath, waiting.

"Okay," he nods with a faint smile on his face. "And if you noticed, that was the last time we were together the entire night. I'll admit for the sake of honesty, we had a brief fling at the beginning of the movie shoot."

"It was good for chemistry, but now we can't stand the sight of each other." His voice gentle, soothing. "She's dating the director's son."

"Oh," Twin spots of color rise in my cheeks. I've never been good at playing the jealous shrew, even with all the opportunities my marriage to Jack provided. But because of Jack and his philandering ways, I'm overly sensitive to infidelity in a relationship, trust doesn't come easy. Turning my back to him, I bite down on my lower lip to prevent it from trembling.

"Ella, Ella," he turns me in his arms, enfolding my body into his embrace. I can't help it. I'm trembling and the shattering has begun. "Shhhh, *querida,*" He caresses my cheek with the back of his hand, his fingers a soft brush of warmth. "You have to trust me on this. I've dated a lot of women, but never forgot you," he smiles. "When I saw you yesterday, surrounded by broken glass and that frustrated waiter in all of your Klutz-Ellen glory, something inside of me leapt to life, a hope that love is still a possibility. I don't want to lose that feeling."

Seriously, with all the women running around in his life….I can't believe he had any time to think of me. "But Vic, I'm not beautiful like those other women." I feel naked and vulnerable before him in the light of day.

"I'm approaching middle age."

"If you remember correctly, so am I." He says dryly. "We're the same age."

"But it's different for men." I respond, my mind turbulent with emotion. "You don't get wrinkles or stretch marks and whatever." And boy, *whatever*…….has not happened to him. Life is not fair.

"Silly girl," his lips curve into a compelling smile. "Men go bald; get beer bellies, bad backs and weak knees.

And need erectile dysfunction medicine." *Not you!* My mind screams, at least not recently.

He continues, "Remember that stupid cocky kid in the leather jacket who followed you around like a love sick puppy for all his machismo. Well, he never left; you have remained a part of his heart."

Silently I make a wish, a plea with God, because at some deep gut level I know he wouldn't deliberately hurt me…but if he does, and I lose my heart to him again…….

…

Heading down the timber stairway to the beach, defiantly wearing his hoodie and a pair of cut-off sweats; I look more like his little brother than his lover. And while I'm trying not to watch the way his butt moves under those tight shorts……..the view causes me to miss a step…..and fall….careening into his back, almost taking him down the stairs with me. "Whoa, you okay back there?" He says catching me in his arms.

"Sorry, just got momentarily distracted." I quip trying to cover up my clumsiness.

"It is a beautiful sight, isn't it?" He asks, pausing to admire the morning sun over the ocean.

"Oh, yes, it's a beautiful sight," I say, arching my eyebrows at him. But I'm not looking at the ocean.

The sand feels soft and cool under our bare feet after the rough wooden stairs. Sunlight spreads across the rippling water; it *is* beautiful, and this time I'm looking at the ocean. The waves whisper softly from the retreating tide; and the breeze lifts the stray ends of hair escaping my ponytail, teasing and tickling my neck, still tender from the stubble of his beard.

Vic stops just above the wrack line of the beach and

arches one dark brow in my direction, "I don't suppose you meditate?" *Meditate?........seriously?*

"For some reason," he continues, "When I stay at the beach, I like to get up with the sun. It's as if I'm drawn to the beach at dawn, and I've found meditation centers me. Ike taught me."

"You meditate? And Ike taught you?" I ask with skepticism. My idea of Ike as some kind of Celtic warrior crumbles in the wake of him in the down dog position. "That is so Hollywood of you." And with those words I slip my hand from his grasp and assume the mountain pose, hands folded at my heart center.

"Well, look at you, Miss Yogi." Vic assumes the stance of tree pose, wobbles, and falls to a sitting position on the sand. "Why don't you come down here and sit in the circle of my lap and we'll thank the higher powers for bringing us together." He crosses his legs into the lotus position, holding out his arms in invitation.

"I would love to meditate with you on this glorious morning, sir." I slip down onto the sand and settle into the protective cover of his body, placing my hands palms up, on top of his knees. "Meditation is so calming," I wiggle to get more comfortable. "I wish I had more time to mediate but something always seems to get in the way. Busy here, busy there."

"I can see why, shut up." He says; a deep chuckle rumbling from his chest. "Close your eyes and take a deep breath, inhale for the count of six, hold for two and exhale for eight counts. Let's try together."

"Inhale, one, two, three, four, five, six, …." As much as the idea of meditation appeals to me, at this particular moment, concentrating on the minds third eye just isn't a priority. The hard plane of his ribs pushing in rhythm against my back, the firm line of his jaw resting just above my hair, the slight lingering fragrance of sandalwood, spices and man…breathe…….okay just breathe in Vic, glory in the feel of his arms around me, the whisper of his breath as he exhales against my cheek and neck. One, two, three, *Vic*, four, five, six, seven, eight, *Vic*…….exhale.

"Hey you, Diago guy." A gravelly voice breaks into our morning salutation.

"Hey, Jonathan," Vic answers, barely breaking stride in his breathing. I look up and see none other than Jonathan Hunter standing in the halo of morning sun, wearing a bathrobe, baseball hat and smoking a cigar. Oh, my *God!* Biggest actor in Hollywood, winner of numerous Academy Awards.

"Pretty girlfriend." He says, stopping to peer at me from under the brim of his hat. *Thank you.* "She needs some new clothes; those are too big for her." He pushes his hat back, cocking his head to the side for closer scrutiny. "I bet she has a pretty little shape under that sweatshirt, a little skinny for my taste, but not bad."

"What!" I squeak in outrage by his blunt but fairly accurate assessment.

"Told you, gorgeous." Vic murmurs in my ear. "We'll get right on that, first thing this morning." Vic answers Jonathan in a trance like tone.

"Great, see you around Diago guy." Jonathan knots the bathrobe tighter around his waist and continues his way down the beach. "And congratulations on the movie, hear it's a hit."

"Was that Jonathan Hunter, *the* Jonathan Hunter?!" I ask in awe, never having seen a real celebrity outside of a concert or movie screen.

"Yep," Vic says quietly. "I meditate and Jonathan walks the beach with his cigar, we have a morning routine."

Really, I think to myself, you mediate and Jonathan Hunter walks the beach, ah, yeah, no big deal.

Ten minutes later, as I start to doze in his arms, he whispers in my ear. "I hate to say this, but I have to go or I'll be late for the studio appointment." His voice muffled as his lips brush against the collar of the sweatshirt, his face buried in the folds of the hood.

Stay, stay, stay, my mind and body scream, but reality forces me to say, "Sure, I'll see if I can find us some breakfast while you dress."

"Will you stay until I get back?" he asks, pulling me to my feet. "Or should I have Ike drop you off at your daughter's house?"

"I think it's best if I go back to Lani's. She may be frantic with worry or more likely curiosity. I can shower and find some real clothes so Jonathan won't be upset over my appearance."

"I don't want to leave you." His mouth opens over mine, gentle kisses, tasting my skin, I lean into him like a ship finding a safe port in a storm.

"Viccc……….." The sonorous voice of Ike calls from the top of the staircase. "Come on, man, you got to get ready. Now! We'll be late and there'll be hell to pay. *Vamonos!*"

"Shit! Told you he watches my back."

We sprint to the top of the stairs where Ike stands watching, an amused expression on his face. Dressed in faded jeans with a close fitting T-shirt, he looks showered, tan and *very* fit, his russet red hair glows in the morning sun. The Celtic warrior rises again. With a wry smile on his face, he tilts his head looking me up and down, arching an eyebrow he says, teasingly, "Nice duds." Barely suppressing his laughter, he looks innocently at Vic, "Nothing fit from the bootie stash?" Vic flashes a warning look at Ike. I glare up at him, slapping his arm. "I told you it was a bimbo sleepover care package." Ike erupts into laughter as he heads back into the house, calling over his shoulder, "Breakfast is on the island in the kitchen; car leaves in a half hour. Don't be late."

A glance down at my clothes has me second guessing my decision to refuse the bimbo kit. I'm wearing what can only be called……I just got sex….and I *liked* it attire. His oversized sweatshirt, cut off shorts and that just got laid look about my hair with cheeks reddened by his morning stubble. I think I have a hickey……..and I'm not wearing underwear. What happened to fastidious Ellen O'Connor….the bad girl in me gives a whoop and says………it's about time!

Chapter 30

The Invitation

Lingering on the sidewalk, I watch the black limousine pull away from the curb. My lips still warm from our parting kiss. Barely out of sight; and I miss him.

This morning he wore a well-tailored black suit accentuating the long lean lines of his body, the top button of his white shirt open, revealing a healthy expanse of sun-darkened skin, and a hint of black curls peeking through. The slim athletic build of his youth has given promise to a taller, more rugged man. Handsome doesn't begin to describe him; he is in my blood…I stand on the sidewalk, momentarily stunned, I love him. *I'm in love with him….again…*with the same intensity as when I was seventeen. My world turned upside down in less than twenty-four hours and spun backwards. *What just happened to me?*

The front door of the house whips open and Lani explodes onto the front porch hopping up and down in her excitement.

"Mom! Mom!" Lani's voice cuts through my thoughts. I look across the lawn at her in a daze.

"Ellie Jane!" Lani calls out concern flooding her voice. "Are you all right? Get in here before the neighbors start talking or the paparazzi shows up."

I grimace, calling out to her, "Hi, Honey, I'm fine." Slowly walking up the path to her house, gown in one hand, dragging the hem of his sweatpants in the other, I see Lani standing on the porch holding my shoe. My Manolo dangling from her hand. *Oh boy…*

She asks in a mocking voice, "Well, well, well, missy, how did this end up on the front lawn this morning?" She holds the door open for me, her face lit up with glee like a Christmas tree wrapped in twinkle lights. "I think you have some explaining to do, young lady."

I catch a glimpse of my reflection in her hall mirror and freeze in horror. Because I still look like…….I just got…..well, you know. The bad girl in me says, Yahoo, that was fun! And the good girl in me has both hands clamped over her mouth with her eyes wide open in shock and horror. And truth be told, I'm hedging toward the bad girl. I've been living by the good girl rule book for a long time…and being with Vic has rekindled a bit of that teenage wild girl streak but …… *oh, my God*…look at me. The quick fix in the limo on the ride over did little to repair the damage. And now in front of my daughter…...I look like a woman who spent the night in wicked passion with a hot man…..and *loved* every minute of it. *And again*…I regret not taking that cute jogging suit or at least wearing the blue gown home, would you look at this outfit. It's one thing to wear your boyfriend's sweatshirt at seventeen, but at my age wearing your lover's oversized sweatshirt and pants while carrying last night clothes says only one thing………..*tramp.*

Me and my high minded morality did not think this through, in one of those jogging suits, I would look cute……like I had just came back from a run……instead of looking like I had a roll in the sheets with some guy and wore his clothes home……*even* if it is the truth. Sometimes righteous idealism is highly overrated.

I turn away from the reflection in the mirror to the amused and delighted stares of Lani and Jason. Oh, how the tables have turned, they're shaking with mirth, taking great satisfaction in shall we say, my delicate situation.

"Mom, look at you." Lani says, pointing a finger at me. "*What* are you wearing?"

"Ummmm, just a sweatshirt and pants." I lay the dress over the back of the couch, blowing a lock of errant hair out of my face. "Stylish, aren't I?"

"Nooooo, not really," my daughter barely able to conceal her merriment. "Just whose sweatpants are you wearing? Let me get this correct, *my* mother is wearing Esteban Diago's sweatpants."

I nod mutely.

"Boy, I've heard he was good, but to seduce my straight laced mother in less than twenty-four hours, wow, he must be something." She sits on the edge of the couch hugging her knees, eyes agog. "So, Ellie Jane, what exactly happened to your clothes last night? You were properly attired when I last saw you."

"And by the way, how did you lose your shoe?" Jason holds up the shoe.

Someone just shoot me now. I flop down on the couch, propping my feet up on the coffee table and give the two of them a condescending look. "Weren't you even a little bit worried about me?" I reprimand. "Some strange man whisks me off into the night?"

"Well, we would have worried except for that nice man, Ike. He is Vic, Esteban, oh, whatever's his name is, bodyguard and friend."

"Yes, I know Ike," I nod wearily, stifling a yawn.

"He called from the beach house to say where you were, and explained the connection between you and Vic. He also said I could call his cell phone anytime if I wanted to speak with you. And he gave us the address of Vic's house. But he did add that he didn't think the two of you wanted to be disturbed."

Terrific. I stretch out on the couch, so tired. It's only nine thirty, but it feels like two in the morning. Stifling a yawn, exhaustion sets in as the excitement of the past twenty-four hours finally catches up with me. But the next words out of Lani's mouth have me fully awake.

"Aunt Kat called." She says, looking smug.

"What?" I sit up looking surprised. "Why would she call?"

"Well," Lani enthusiastically launches into the account of her phone conversation with Kat.

"Apparently, she tried to call your cell-phone earlier this morning but you didn't answer." Lani looks innocently at the ceiling. "Ummm, I wonder why. Preoccupied, were you? So she called me asking about the premier and if you enjoyed your night out on the town."

"And *what* did you tell her?" My voice dripping with icicles as trepidation washes over me.

"I said you had a lovely time." Lani answers primly.

"And?" I ask suspiciously.

"She said she wanted to speak with you."

"And?"

"I said you were unavailable."

"And?"

"She asked why."

"And?"

"Well, you know how persistent she can be at times."

"If you told her, she will tell that gossiping pack of jackals I call my girlfriends." I groan. "And the whole town will know. Ohhhhh……"

"Oh, some of them were with her."

"It just gets better." I whisper, massaging my temple where a dull pain has grown into a full-blown headache.

"I said you were not home."

"And?" I ask faintly, knowing fully well how the conversation had gone.

"I said you ran into an old boyfriend and never came home last night."

"You didn't tell her who it was, did you?"

"No, I know his identity needs to be kept quiet."

"And she let it go at that?" I can't imagine what Kat and Emi Jo's reaction will be when they learn the old boyfriend is Vic. But that's one piece of information I want to deliver in person, just to see the expression on their faces.

"Yes, she didn't care who it was, she just started howling with laughter. Emi Jo was with her. I heard her voice in the background." Lani pauses for effect, and raises her voice several octaves, imitating Emi Jo's falsetto voice. "Did she use the boots? She wanted to know something about if you used your boots."

"The boots?" I ask weakly, feeling faint.

"You know the little pink ones." She lowers her voice. "They wanted to know if you packed them in that pretty little evening bag you took last night? What kind of boots were they talking about, Mom?" Lani looks positively devilish. "And by the way Trey called, remember your son?"

God *only* knows what she told him………

…

The repeated ringing of a doorbell wakes me from my nap. My slumber plagued by feelings repressed in the past and dormant, now sprung to life in the limitless boundaries of dreams. My body alive in ways I thought forgotten. Tossing back the restrictive sheets; I find his sweatshirt lying on the floor next to the bed. It wasn't a dream. A glance at the clock on the nightstand shows it's early afternoon………....he said his meeting would last until late in the day. Can I wait that long?

Feeling like a high school girl with an adolescent crush, I pull on a pair of jeans, jeans long grown old and comfortable, frayed in a manner now considered chic, jeans carelessly tossed on a chair in the haste of dressing less than twenty four hours ago. As I rub the worn material, I feel my life tumbling away, no longer straight-forward and simple. I've always prided myself on being prepared, planning for the unexpected, having goals, knowing where my life is going. But this chance meeting with Vic causes the world as I know it to take an abrupt turn to a place I don't know or understand. Ordinary moms don't fall in love with movie stars. The realities are worlds apart.

Mothers warn their daughters about men like Vic; sensual, indecently handsome, full of dark passions. My love for him burned me once, and yet again, I'm lured to those smoldering fires burning deep within him.

"Mom, come here!" As I walk down the staircase, Lani swings her head around the doorsill of the outside patio motioning impatiently for me to join her. "Look what just came for you."

On a table underneath a striped awning stands a huge vase of black-eyed Susans. Next to the vase are two boxes wrapped in exquisite buttery yellow satin paper, topped with a cascade of ribbons in matching stripes and polka-dots. The wrapping complements the flowers in the vase.

"Oh, how beautiful," I exclaim, reaching out to touch the yellow flower petals. "Where did these come from?"

"Duh, Mom! How long have you been out of the dating circle?" She shakes her head in exasperation.

"Your loverrrrr!" She says in an exaggerated tone.

"Oh," I reach for the card stuck in the profusion of flowers. "It has been so long since I've received flowers from anyone. When we were first married your father sent them on Valentine's Day or our anniversary, and then as money got tight when I was home raising you kids, I told him not to bother."

"These are just beautiful," I bend down to breathe in their fragrance and come up disappointed. "I forgot black-eyed Susans don't have much smell. But it looks like a mountain meadow in a vase, doesn't it."

"Why black-eyed Susans?" Lani asks mystified. "I could understand if your name was Susan."

A slow fluttering of remembrance tugs at the recesses of my mind, opening a flood gate of memories. A mountain meadow blanketed in black-eyed Susans.

"*Oh, my God,* he can't possibly have remembered that, could he?" I whisper, sliding the card from its diminutive envelope. Written in his bold script are the words,

My Daisy girl,

Remember the meadow of black-eyed Susans on Wolf Mountain……..to many more afternoons of loving you.

Always yours, Vic.

Plucking a flower from the vase, I stare into the dark center and remember that hot August afternoon where we made love under the late summer sky, blanketed in a field of daisies. Drunk on love, sun, and cheap beer. It was the last time we were together and happy. I bite my lip at the bittersweet memory.

"Mom, are you okay?" Lani asks, "Flowers are supposed to make you happy, not sad."

"They do, sweetie, they do." I say with a shaky laugh holding the card close to my heart. "I can't believe he remembered that day. It was so long ago."

"So, can you tell me or is it private?"

"It was last day of camp before we were to go home," I say with a faraway look in my eyes. "We took off for a picnic on a nearby mountain. It was a beautiful sunny August afternoon. It was the last good memory I have of him."

"It's so romantic he remembered the day and sent the exact flowers. What does the card say?" I silently hand the card to her.

"Wow," Lani says looking impressed. "I can't wait to see what the boxes hold." She expectantly pushes a box in my direction causing me to smile at her impatience.

I slowly ease the ribbons from the package taking care not to destroy the pretty curls and bows. Once open, the box reveals a pair of delicate silver shoes with the name *Monolo Blahnik* written down the instep.

"Oh, my God," Lani gasps. "Those are *Monolo's ....Monolo Blahnik's!* Worth, like a thousand dollars. I didn't tell you, the ones you had on last night were fake, made up for the costume department. The real ones never leave the department."

I risked my life for fake shoes!!

I hold the exquisite shoe in my hand, and watch it shimmer in the sunlight, and trace the delicate straps with my finger. "These are gorgeous," I say, my voice thick with reverence. "It looks like the one I lost last night. How did he find ones so closely matched?"

"Mom, there's a note." Lani points at the box, barely able to contain her excitement. "I can't wait to hear what this one has to say."

I slide the card out of the yellow envelope and read:

Ella, Ella, my mia bella, my Cinderella,

How appropriate you lost a shoe last night. I'm sorry Prince Charming was unable to return the original one but please accept this humble pair as a replacement. I can't wait to see you tonight.

Always, Vic

"Oh, my," I silently hand the card to Lani. I've heard of being swept off your feet, I thought it was a figure of speech, until now. I couldn't find my feet if I wanted too. I feel like I'm walking on clouds.

Lani looks over at me, her eyes huge saucers in her face as she shakes the card in front of my face. "This guy is good, *real* good."

'Pinch me. No seriously, pinch me, I must be dreaming. This kind of thing doesn't happen to real people."

"Pinch me first," Lani says. "Most people don't even know people this kind of thing happens too."

"I'm almost afraid to open the last box. This is already too much." I pick up the package and gently shake, the motion reveals no clues. "I can't wait, the suspense is killing me." I raise my eyebrows in delicious anticipation.

"Open it, open it." Lani commands.

Larger and slightly heavier than the first box, no obvious clues to be found, I can only speculate on its contents. "With all this talk about Prince Charming, I'm afraid a magic castle will appear complete with a moat and turrets." I say with a laugh, slipping the box from its sheath of paper. "After all, Cinderella must have a castle.

What proper princess doesn't have a castle?"

Opening the box, I push the tissue paper aside and reveal the shining gleam of something leather winking up from its nestled cocoon. "Ohhh……." Awe causes me to catch my breath in a gasp. "Cowboy boots." Not just any cowboy boots, but intricately tooled leather pieces that only loosely resemble the clumsy boots worn by frontier cowboys. These boots, a work of art fashioned in leather, graceful and elegant. From the top of the curved calf to the finely molded heel, swirls of stitching over colored leather, made to accentuate a woman's feminine foot in supple leather, soft enough for a baby to wear.

"They're exquisite." Lani says in awe. "Here, try one on." She hands me a boot. "How did he remember your foot size?"

"I have no idea. But I think his assistant, Juls, is *very* good at her job." I slip my foot into a perfectly sized boot. "I'm beginning to think this man has super-hero seduction charms, do they teach this stuff in Hollywood hot guy school or is he just incredibly sweet." *Wow.* I sit back fanning myself with the unopened card, feeling a warm glow cloak my body at the mere thought of him. "I'm completely lost. He had me the minute his hand touched mine last night." I look over to see Lani holding a boot in one hand and a *Monolo* the other. "I can see you're not going to be any help keeping me grounded. If your eyes bug out any farther you'll be mistaken for an alien."

"He had me with the flowers." Lani says with a deprecating shrug. "What does this card say?"

"I'm almost afraid to look." My finger traces the bold outline of his handwriting on the face of the card. I take a deep breath and slide the card from the envelope.

Dear Elle,

These boots come with the invitation to join me at my ranch this weekend. Please say yes. Mi casa es su casa. My house is not a home without you. Come home to me, Elle.

Vic

"*Ohhh*, it's the castle," I moan, falling back into the chair cushion.

"Let me see that," Lani snatches the card from my hand; her eyes quickly scan the handwriting. "Oh dear God, it is the castle."

With a dubious look in my direction, her eyes roam up and down, assessing my appearance, causing me to cry out, "*What*!" in self-defense. "I don't look that bad, do I?"

She shakes her head in disgust, "I can only hope he is coming to pick you up in a coach pulled by an old, slow pony, driven by a blind coachman who gets lost on the way. Even then I'm not sure there is enough time." She stands up pulling me to my feet. "First, we start with the wardrobe," she rolls her eyes, muttering under her breath, "And that old stretched-out sweatshirt isn't going to get you laid." *Hmm*…I muse to myself and smugly shrug my shoulders…*seemed to work this morning*………

Chapter 31

The Birds

Topping Lani's list of essentials for a romantic evening, in bold print, was something about a push up bra being critical. Hey, I have breasts……just not big ones.

And……because the art of seduction sometimes requires *more* than high heels, boobs and a good personality, the secret path to a man's heart is often through his stomach……so when you combine a nice set of boobs atop a pair of high heels, throw in some food……. you can't go wrong, it's female magic.

Unfortunately, I can't cook…...Julia Childs, I'm not. Maybe if I had more French blood in me. As a working mom, I relied on frozen entrees complemented with salad from a bag and frozen vegetables. Hosting a dinner party sent me into a panic for weeks. Then I learned a little trick, meet the caterer at the back door, transfer the food onto my own serving dishes and china, *voila,* instant dinner party. Took Jack years to figure out why I was such a fantastic cook on special occasions, but a lousy one on weekdays. In my defense, I do have a few dishes I can whip up to impress the unsuspecting, but if Vic wants more than two meals, I'm screwed. Remind me to google catering/Los Angeles/delivery/fast!

…

Rather than have Ike pick me up, Lani drops me off at the front entrance to Vic's house, staying only long enough to ogle the beautiful Spanish façade and view of the ocean. As she pulls away, the car stops and she sticks her head out of the window, hesitating before speaking, "Ummmm, Mom…..are you wearing underwear?"

"What! Of course I'm wearing underwear. Why? Are they showing?" I try peering behind to look at my butt.

"No, just a little panty line, but you might want to get rid of them."

"Get rid of them, why?" I sneak another look at my butt.

"Well……men think it's sexy when women don't wear underwear."

"Oh, that sounds slutty to me."

"I'm just trying to help," she says defensively. "I know you've been out of the dating loop for a while and…….."

"I know what men like! I was married for like twenty five years." *Jeez.*

"Yeah, but that was just Dad. Not like going out with a real guy."

Right, not a real guy, just the biggest horn dog around, complete with a set of pilot wings pinned to his chest. I keep this thought to myself. It's bad karma to speak ill of the dead, especially to his daughter.

"I imagine it's difficult to date again, being old and all. I thought I'd give you a few hints." She shrugs her shoulders, squinting at me over the top of her sunglasses.

Old and all! I can't believe I'm having this conversation with my daughter. Pointing to the street, I shout, "Go!" She gives a devilish grin and with a wave of her hand, she's gone.

Ungrateful child. And to think I suffered through twenty-three hours of labor bringing her into the world.

…

Still contemplating the question, is it a panties

on....or a panties off night....in creeps the insidious idea that maybe, just maybe Vic's a vegetarian. Worse, yet *vegan.* And the fillet mignon in my grocery bag is so beautiful; the cow's mother would stand in line to eat it. But maybe he doesn't eat meat. How could I be so stupid not think of a back-up meal? The whole state of California is practically vegan. Maybe he eats tofu now? Bean curd? Anything that ends in the word curd can't be good.

Caught up in my thoughts, I jump at the sound of the garage door opening, followed by the rumble of a motorcycle. A yellow Harley Davidson motorcycle with flames painted on the front and back bumpers slowly inches out onto the driveway. Even in my confused state of mind, I can't help but think, *way cool!* The motorcycle pulls up and Ike cuts the engine, extinguishing the deep rumbling thunder.

"Wow, hi."

"Hey, *chica,*" he says, pulling off his helmet and running a hand through his thick unruly hair. "I didn't know what time you were arriving, so I left the side door open. There are a couple bottles of wine in the refrigerator and Vic should be home soon. I'm taking off for a few of days, so the house is yours."

"Oh, thank you. Please don't feel you need to leave on my account." I protest. "This is your home."

"Ahhh, yeah, I do." He laughs and rolls his eyes. He pushes the bike back onto its kickstand and dismounts. *Holy moly* I always thought cowboys lived out on the prairies, riding horses, and herding cows. But watching Ike Adamsen wearing a black leather jacket and chaps dismount his motorcycle in the setting sun, russet hair burnished to copper, his tawny skin with a smattering of freckles, hooded hazel eyes sparkling with humor. This guy is some kind of handsome. Older than Vic by about ten years, but good looking in a Robert Redford craggy, outdoorsy kind of way. Everything about him is autumn; all brown, reds, gold and bronze. He exudes strength and security, like a towering oak crowned in the glory of fall. What is it about the men in California? Is it the sun, the sea air, closer proximity to the equator…..*wow!*

"Ellen?" I look into hazel eyes alight with humor. *Oh*……I wasn't paying attention to a word he said.

"Oh, sorry, I was just distracted by the…..ummmm………ocean view. The one behind your back." I add lamely, pointing to the garage, which blocks the view of the ocean.

"Sure," he says, arching his eyebrows at me as he takes the grocery bag from my hand. "Come on in and I'll show you the kitchen." I follow behind, wondering how Vic would look in leather chaps. Just the thought makes my body temperature rise……it must be the close proximity to the equator….the intense sunlight…lack of clouds…*whew*…whatever.

"Vic doesn't cook much," Ike continues, innocently unaware of the scrutiny his ass is receiving. "If we eat in, I usually throw something together. Do you cook?"

"What? Yes, all the time." *Liar, liar, pants on fire.*

…

The brightly colored kitchen tiles glow in the setting sun, adding a festive air. A cool breeze comes through the open French doors bringing the scent of bougainvillea and ocean.

While short on food items, the "bachelor" kitchen is stocked with every culinary gadget or tool available to

turn even the lowliest cook into a gourmet chef. ......
and I need all the help I can get. Ike and I inspected the pantry and found a tablecloth, china, wineglasses and even taper candles. Standing back with pride, I survey the small table on the terrace set with a white tablecloth, china, and candles of assorted sizes. Flowers cut from the small garden add a touch of color to the romantic setting. Off in the distance the low rhythmic wash of ocean waves coupled with the call of seabirds provides all the acoustics needed for an evening of al fresco dining.

Satisfied with my efforts, I pause to admire the ocean view, the heat of the day ebbing as the sun begins its slow descent bringing the promise of a cool evening. As I stand sipping a glass of chardonnay from the Napa Valley the tantalizing aroma of dinner cooking in the kitchen wafts through the French doors.

What to wear for dinner...had been the question of the afternoon......*sexy or sophisticated?* Lani ambushed her wardrobe to create a sophisticated *sexy* beach look. A snug-fitting coral print dress and the push-up bra...doing wonders......instant boob job. The dress clings in the right spots, and floats over the not-so-right spots, falling just below the knees. A simple pair of silver hoop earrings add in a few bangle bracelets and, of course, the locket completes the outfit. Smiling ruefully, I look down at my choice in footwear. Lani had a fit, but I insisted. Nothing but the cowboy boots would do. Hey, they almost match, there is coral thread running through the stitching....*and* the boots say *yes* to his invitation to the ranch. And I definitely want to say *yes* to a weekend of Vic.

Shifting my shoulders to glance at the front door, a sigh escapes my lips. I'm impatient for his return, yet anxious. In the light of day will the thrill of our reunion be dulled by the reality of life? My mind traces back to the memory of him this morning, his face relaxed in the innocence of sleep, a thick wave of dark hair falling across his brow. Am I naive to think I can have him? Me, Ellen O'Connor, fifth grade teacher from a small town…..how can I compete with Hollywood?

Taking a sip of wine, I watch the magic of the tides at work, slowly swallowing the beach until a thin spit of sand remains. The sinking sun mutes the turquoise blue sky into a soft mauve, painting the terrace in a wash of gold. A lone surfer paddles out to catch one last wave before sunset. The large umbrellas that earlier in the day scattered across the beach like brightly colored starfish are packed and gone home. Along with them the children, buckets and shovels, leaving behind only sculpted mounds of sand decorated with bits of shells and beach debris.

Setting down the wine glass, I lean over the railing, squinting at a bird feeding on the beach, moving up and down the surf line, feasting on the leftovers from the ocean and afternoon picnickers. My attention riveted by the bird. *Holy jumping John James Audubon.* Is that a Glaucous Gull? Before leaving home, I had made a list of possible birds in California that I might add to my life list. New bird sightings……. I remember seeing this particular gull, it's rare, not normally found in this part of California. I can't be sure without binoculars, but I think I see the small red dot on its bill. The bird works its way over to a trash barrel picking at stray crumbs littering the beach. Maybe if I threw out some food, it might wander over. I can imagine the lecture from Burt preaching the evils of feeding wild animals. Just this one time, I promise. What can it hurt to toss out a little piece of bread? How often can you add a new bird to your life list?

I quietly sneak into the kitchen, find a loaf of bread and dash back outside. So intent on luring in the rare bird, I don't notice the other resident gulls perk up at the sight of a plastic bag full of gull nirvana. An open invitation, clueless, I start throwing small pieces of bread in the direction of the Glaucous Gull, and before I can blink my eyes, I'm in a scene from Alfred Hitchcock's movie, *The Birds*. Out of nowhere hundreds of gulls descend on me, wings flapping, feathers dropping, noisy raucous calls, the patio littered with them. My beautiful table has four of them perched on the china plates, the railing looks like a call back for *Chorus Line*. Two land on the gutter above my head. I wave my hands to shoo them away but the swaying bag of bread only entices them closer. One pecks at my feet. *Ouch!* "Shoo, go away, shoo," I yell at them. "What is wrong with you birds? Didn't anyone teach you any manners? Shoo means go!" To scare off a mountain lion or black bear, the idea is to look intimidating. Stand tall, wave and flap your hands, make a lot of noise, works like a charm with huge ferocious predators, with these damn gulls……..not so much. The more I flap and yell, the more they come….and come. This is ridiculous. I'm trapped in a corner by a brazen horde of hungry birds, beady little eyes watching my every move. My beautiful dinner table ruined, the terrace floor covered with birds, feathers and *Oh, my God.* I watch in horror as one unceremoniously flips his butt up, and a white glob of poop splashes down the side of a wine glass...*euuuuu*…. That's it. I've got to get out of here. As I prepare to launch myself into the foray of beaks and feathers, and battle my way to the house, I hear the sound of Vic's voice calling from the front hall. I panic. *I can't let him see me like this; I look like an idiot held hostage by a band marauding of birds.* I'm the nature girl!! But I can't move; held paralyzed against the stucco walls by fear, intense mortification and the insane hope he won't see me. As I inch along the wall, I hear the sound of a door closing followed by the sound of shoes hitting the floor. Vic hates wearing shoes, sheds them at every opportunity.

"Elle? Ella, Ella, mia bella, where are you?" His voice calls from the kitchen. *Oh crap and double crap.* Now I'm really screwed.

"Out here! On the terrace, Vic." My pulse quickens at the sound of his voice. The gulls have quieted, their beady eyes never leaving the bag of bread clutched in my hand, ready to pounce if I move.

"God, I thought this day would never end, sitting in one boring meeting after another, missing you." He stops short; pausing at the doorway, a bewildered expression on his face at the sight of dozens of seagulls perched on his patio. "What the *hell*?!" My heart does a flip-flop....he's a vision of male perfection, wearing only a pair of dark trousers and looking impossibly cool in a white shirt. And he's barefoot.

"Elle?" He calls, tossing his jacket over a rattan chair by the door. "Are you out there?"

His voice sends the gulls into mass of shrieking, flapping confusion.

"Yes," I call out to him, humiliation sweeps through me. "I'm trapped; the gulls won't let me move."

"What the hell?" he repeats again. "Buttercup, hold on. I know how to get rid of them. Damn nuisance birds." He disappears from the doorway and returns with a bullhorn in his hand. He steps out into the squawking, screaming mass of birds and releases a blast from the horn. The gulls are momentary stunned by the noise, a second blast sends them to the sky like a band of drunken pirates fleeing with their plunder.

"Are you all right?" He turns to me in concern after chasing the last of the birds away.

"I'm fine."

"What happened?"

"Nothing."

"They just came?"

"Kind of …"

"They are getting bolder by the day, nothing but a pack of flying rats."

Feeling guilty, I hold out the bag of bread, proof of my crime.

"You fed the seagulls?" he asks, incredulously. I nod mutely.

"Don't you know you never, ever feed birds on the beach, they are nothing but a horde of roving beggars, ready to attack any stray piece of food and fight each other to the death for it?"

"No!" I whimper defensively. "I've never lived anywhere near the ocean. I didn't know how aggressive they get over food." And feeling the need to stand up for the birds, I continue on, "Burt said everyone needs garbage men and gulls act as nature's garbage men or something like that." I offer lamely, remembering one of Burt lectures on scavengers. "And I thought I saw a rare gull, one to add to my bird list." I choke back a sob. "I'm so sorry, Vic, I didn't mean to ruin your house." I bite my lip and tears well in my eyes as I survey the damage.

Broken wine glasses lay scattered across the table; flowers hang in limp disarray, feathers and bird droppings everywhere. Maybe this isn't going work, I can't even put together a simple dinner.

"Elle, don't cry." He whispers, his eyes crinkle with laughter, taking in my appearance, bag of bread still clutched in my hand. His body starts shaking with mirth, a wide grin splits his face, "Oh God, how I've missed you, Klutz-Ellen." Laughter rumbles from deep within his chest. "Just let me look at you." Our eyes meet, hold for a moment, the breeze does nothing to cool the heat building between us. A muscle at the corner of his mouth twitches. "Bella, Bella, mia bella, you look like a goddess of summer even with feathers and bird poop on your shoulder."

"Aggggh, No!" I feel the blush rising to stain my cheeks and drop the bread, furiously brushing at the glob of poop on my dress. *Damn it.* He collapses into a chair, laughing, tears running down his face.

"Look, now you just sat in it!" I point accusingly at him.

"I don't care; this is the most fun I've had in years." And he goes off into peals of laughter.

I stare at him and giggle, leave it to me to have bird poop in my fairy tale. How is this happening? I don't care as long as the happily ever after……is ending up in his arms.

He stands up, pulls me into his embrace, pausing he tenderly lifts his hand to cup my face, my cheek rests against his palm. He murmurs, "I hope your battle with the gulls didn't sap your energy. I'm not planning on sleeping much tonight. My test results came back, I'm clean. Clean as a newborn babe."

"Well first......we need a shower, with *lots* of soap………" I brush a feather off his shirt, he raises an eyebrow. "And by the way," I whisper against the tender flesh of his ear. "I had a nap ………so don't plan on getting *any* sleep tonight."

Lifting me in his arms, he crosses the terrace to the open portico of the bedroom, stopping at the doorway; he looks down at my feet with a bemused expression. "By the way, nice boots."

Chapter 32

California Dreaming

The gray Land Rover speeds along the freeway, leaving behind the smog and congestion of Los Angeles. Sunlight streams through an open sunroof. Vic expertly weaves in and out of the traffic maze, one hand on the wheel, the other resting on my knee.

"Are you comfortable?" He peers at me over the top of his aviator sunglasses.

"I'm good, thank you, in fact *very* good." In actuality……I'm purring, after an evening of …..*well*, you know…..followed by a morning walk on the beach, breakfast on the terrace overlooking the ocean. *No seagulls.* And now with his hand on my knee, warm and reassuring, sending pleasurable sensations to other parts of my body, what more could a girl want.

"It will take several hours to reach the ranch. Instead of chartering a plane; I thought you might enjoy a tour of the countryside."

"Definitely, I can't wait to see more of California." I stretch out my legs, admiring how long and lean they look in jeans and cowboy boots. "I'm not much of a city girl. Two or three days in a city and I start longing for trees and green space. I'm looking forward to visiting your ranch."

"If you are looking for trees and green, the ranch should be to your liking. And I can throw in a mountain or two for a slight extra charge." His hand caresses the inside of my thigh, suggesting what he has in mind for payment.

"That price might be negotiable." I wiggle my bottom on the seat in appreciation of his attention.

The valley and hills rise on either side of the highway. Rolling hills of brown grass dotted with sparse trees stretch mile after mile, dry and thirsty after a summer of meager rainfall.

Turning off the freeway, the SUV hugs a two-lane country road weaving through foothills. The houses and towns fade, replaced by trees and rolling grasslands. The grass on either side of the roads turns from the color of straw to a cool shade of green as the vehicle climbs higher in elevation. The air becomes fragrant with pine, cedar, and fir, the faint smell of salty sea air is carried by a breeze from the distant coast.

"We're almost there." Vic stifles a yawn. Stretching, I'm guilty of dozing off on the ride. "Soon we'll be coming to the small town where we shop and get most of the supplies for the ranch. It's rather quaint and old fashioned. I think you'll enjoy exploring it when you have a chance."

"The scenery is beautiful." I have this feeling in my chest, I'm coming home. But that's not possible; I've never been north of Los Angeles. Maybe it's a spiritual aura, coming to a house, maybe…..coming to our home.

"Here's the entrance gate." He says, flipping on the turn signal. The Land Rover turns onto a driveway of crushed white pebbles, passing under an adobe arch, perfectly aged to the golden patina of old Mexico or a villa in Tuscany.

"*Oh!*" My eyes widen at the sight of the tree lined drive, the house nowhere in sight.

"Where's the house?" I ask, leaning forward, looking out both sides of the windshield, seeing only a lane of trees and still no house. On one side of the trees is a wooded area, and on the other there's a vast grassland. I imagine a meadow abound with wildflowers in the spring.

"The house is about a mile down the road. Are you feeling okay?" He asks with concern in his voice. "You look pale, car sick?"

"No, no." *Are you fricking crazy, look at this driveway!* My mind screams. "You're mistaking envy for nausea." I say. "It's just a different shade of green."

You haven't seen the house yet."

"I know, and if this driveway is any inkling of what is to come, I'm going to be an even deeper shade of green."

Craning my neck to get a better look at the row of trees lining the driveway, I exclaim, "Who needs a house, this is so beautiful, just pitch a tent and live here. It's lovely, utterly tranquil.......and suddenly, the unbidden image of him standing outside a sultan's nomadic tent, chest bare, dressed only in a tunic and turban, while inside I lay reclined on a bed of pillows, dressed in the filmy costume of a belly dancer, waiting for his attention........*whoa*, wait a minute.......belly dancer, sheer costume.... belly........belly exposed...........after three children........oh, no.......that's not going to happen. *Poof*, image gone.

Ignoring my distraction into the world of fantasy, he continues on, "Pitching a tent won't be necessary, we have running water, flush toilets, and all the conveniences of modern life." He squeezes my hand. "It's not huge by today's standards, just three bedrooms, kitchen, dining room, living room and of course, a pool. I didn't want to go into debt buying a sprawling mansion. The movie business is very fickle. One day the public loves you and the next they can't remember your name. I wanted a home with enough room to take care of my family, but at the same time have character and charm."

He stops the Land Rover in the middle of the driveway, putting it in park before turning to me. Laying an arm across my shoulder, he looks serious. "I want to talk to you before we get to the house." Pausing, his gaze slides over my face. He seems to struggle with his thoughts for a moment then releases his breath in a long sigh. "I hope you like the house. Elle, it's the first place I've ever felt at home. And I hope this house could be your home too. Again, I know it's too early to be talking like this, but this is how I feel. I usually don't bring my so-called "dates" to La Posada Lobo. This property is for family and close friends, kind of a sanctuary for us," he grimaces. "In fact, I'll have to do some quick explaining to Bridget when she sees you. She is my housekeeper, a cousin of Ike's from Ireland and *very* old school. Bridget and her husband Hank virtually run the place for me. They have a small home just down the road from the main house. I don't know what I would do without them and Ike. Through thick and thin, they are my family."

"What exactly is Ike's story, how did he end up on the freighter with you?" I ask, dodging the very scary subject of our future, *where, when and how I was going to fit into his life.*

"Ike," Vic muses, thinking for a moment, looking out the windshield at the trees forming a canopy overhead. "Ike is Canadian, grew up in Toronto, he got a girl pregnant. They got married too young, it was a disastrous marriage."

"Like us without the marriage part?"

"No, this was totally different. Ike admits he was a stupid kid who got drunk, and she was a one-night stand that ended up pregnant. We were in love, no parallels to our story."

"Right."

"Anyway, he felt trapped, so he started drinking and gambling as an escape. He ended up in jail for assaulting a cop. And his wife threw him out and refused him visitation rights to his daughter. In jail he realized he was on his way to becoming an alcoholic and a jailbird. Soo…..he rationalized a plan to get away from it all. He knew he screwed up and wanted to get his life back on track. And what better place than on a boat stuck in the middle of the ocean. He became a freighter tramp. By the time I met him, he was sober, invested in his art and a certified yogi."

"His art?"

"He does detail painting on motorcycles, vans, motorhomes, he likes painting things that move. Next to taking care of me which is a full time job in itself," he chuckles. "That's his job. And once or twice a year he takes a motorcycle trip across the country, always ending up in Pittsburgh to watch a Pirates baseball game."

"I know the Pirates. Jack was a baseball nut, dragged me all over the country to watch games. Ike is a Pirates fan?"

"Actually, he'd be the first to admit how crazy this sounds. He met a woman at a game, years ago, but he never got her name. And for some reason he can't get her out of his head. Every year he goes to Pittsburgh in hopes that maybe, someday he will see her again. And it's a destination for him, he has friends there and his daughter lives in Delaware."

"Poor Ike. No woman in his life?"

Vic quirks his eyebrows up. "He dates now and then

but no one for very long. Maybe he's waiting for that lady from Pittsburgh, the impossible dream and thereby his excuse to avoid commitment."

He slides his thumb over the curve of my bottom lip, as he lowers his head. "I never stopped loving you, Elle." The look in his eyes takes my breath away. So full of heat, so full of sensual promise.

. . .

Much later, a sprawling house appears as we round a curve in the driveway. A two-story adobe house stands at the edge of the woods, shaded and cool on one side while the other half basks in afternoon sunlight. Colorful waves of flowers grow up the walls of the house to bend over windows framed in sage green shutters. A juniper beam portico covers the wide stone steps leading to an enormous entranceway. The massive wooden doors stand hospitably open, revealing a glimpse of terra cotta tiles covering the courtyard floor.

"Vic, it's beautiful." I murmur sincerely as he brings the car to a halt before the wooden doors. The tinkling of water flowing into a small circular-shaped pool in the courtyard beckons visitors into the house. A peaceful place, a house of sanctuary.

An exclamation of delight escapes my lips as we walk through the doorway, high walls covered with flowering vines give the appearance of an old world garden. Clusters of flowers spill over large pots set next to a small wrought iron café table. At the far end of the courtyard tucked into the shade, rattan lounge chairs beg for an afternoon nap, velvety eggplant colored blankets are draped across the headrest, soft and cozy made for snuggling.

"Do you like it?" Vic asks anxiously.

"Vic," I say in breathless awe. "This is unbelievable!"

The courtyard flows into the living room, designed around a huge stone fireplace flanked by walls of warm Tuscan stucco. Rustic furniture in rich earth tones provides a lived-in comfortable feel to the room, and heavy wooden doors flanked by floor-to-ceiling windows open to the outdoors. Timber beams support the ceiling rafters, punctuated by large skylights. Beams of sunlight splash across the mahogany floors covered with rugs done in patterns of the southwest.

Patio tiles of red canyon rock lead outside to a terrace dominated by a waterfall cascading into the pool. The terrace is bordered by trees, flowering bushes and pots of citrus trees and flowers. Under a roofed pergola sits a heavy wooden table surrounded by cushioned chairs. In anticipation of the next repast, the table is set with china and crystal goblets skirted by gleaming silverware and candles. Wall sconces tucked into the corner posts stand ready to pour shimmering light against the dark night. A couch with deep cushions and two matching chairs circle an outdoor fireplace.

I pirouette in a full circle. "It's like living outside." I exclaim. "The entire house flows around the courtyard or the pool. How can you ever leave it?"

"I try to spend as much time as possible here. Hanna lives about five miles away, so it's convenient to be with her." He leans against an adobe column, pulling me into his arms; the musky man smell of him fills my senses as I wrap my arms around his waist. "The beach house and the limo in Los Angeles are rentals, this is my home." He shifts his weight to the other foot, kissing the top of my head. "The pool area was added when we first moved here. Unfortunately, the house was too rustic for Sophia,

Hanna's mother. She prefers a more formal house." I nod in understanding, my head on his chest, loving the rumbling sound of his voice against my ear. "The house was the first of many arguments. But Hanna loves it as much as I do. I hope you will too."

As we head towards the bedroom, Vic pauses on the landing of the curved staircase, looking down at my suitcase. "What the hell happened to the wheel of your suitcase?" he asks. I cringe, thinking how can I tell him about the "luggage episode" after my encounter with the seagulls. Just how much nuts can one man handle in a few days?

From the back of the house a door bangs open followed by a strident voice calling out, "Vic, Mr. Vic, would that be you? The security system says it was your code entered at the gate. If it's not Mr. Vic, you had better run; my husband is on the way with a shotgun." The voice threatens.

"Oh boy, here she comes, my Irish banshee," he mutters under his breath. "Bridget, it's me. I'm here in the living room." He calls out to her.

"Why didn't you call?" A small diminutive woman with a heavy Irish brogue accuses as she comes whipping through the entranceway like a locomotive around a steep curve. "Ya know you supposed to call ahead, so that I can be getting the house tidy and ready for yea."

Bridget is the model of Irish breeding; barely 5 foot tall in stature with a shock of short red curls and skin the color of pale cream kissed by rose petals. Across the bridge of her nose is a dusting of faint freckles.

While her appearance suggests a sweet disposition, her sea green eyes spark with fury when she sees me...... standing next to Vic on the stairs, heading to the bedroom. Her eyes glitter with suppressed rage.

"Ooooh, ho, so I see, why you couldn't be bothering yourself to call," her chin juts out, hands on her hips, clinched into fists of anger. "So it's finally come to this, you've brought one of your floozy girlfriends home to the house."

"Whoa, whoa, Bridget, wait, you've got the wrong idea." Vic holds his hand up to stop the flow of her words. "This is Ellen. You know my Elle."

"Sure, sure, today it's Ellen, tomorrow its Tammy, and so on and so on. It's all over those disgusting tabloid newspapers." She says, waving her hands at him in disgust. "When we set up this household, it was agreed this property was for family. The Hollywood business stays down there, in the land of Sodom and Gomorrah. You would not be bringing it home to taint your daughter. What will Miss Sophia say if she sees you with this tart?"

At the word tart directed in my direction on the heels of being called a floozy, I let out a squeal of indignation. "Excuse me!"

"Bridget!" Vic reprimands her. "What the hell!"

"I didn't hire on to run no playboy bunny house like that, that, Hugh Iffler, Stiffer, oh, whatever that man whore is called," she says, turning on her heels, heading to the kitchen in a huff. "If this is the way it's going to be, Hank and I will be leaving." The faint whoosh of the kitchen door swinging is the only sound left in the room. Vic and I stare at each other in stunned silence.

"Is she always like that?" I whisper, casting a fearful glance at the door, dreading a re-appearance of the apparition that went flying through it.

"Good Lord, no! I think she's lost her mind," he

shakes his head in disbelief, raking a hand through his tumbling mass of hair. "Let me see if I can straighten this out."

I follow Vic to the kitchen, pausing at the door as he confronts Bridget who's slamming cupboard doors with as much vehemence as a barely five foot tall body can muster. She throws a green pepper on the chopping block and attacks it with vengeance.

"Bridget, please put down the knife and talk to me." Vic says in the same soothing voice he would use with a spooked horse.

"And what do you want me to be a saying," she shakes the knife in his direction. "Oh, sure, come and bring all the little whores and doxies home, Bridget will cook and take care of us. We're the beautiful people of Hollywood. We can do what we want and who cares about the consequences. So what if your soul burns in hell!"

"What are you talking about? Where are these crazy ideas coming from?" Vic takes a half step backward as she points the knife menacingly in his direction. Then with a determined look on his face, he places his hands on his hips, leans over her slight form and demands, "What the hell is going on here? Have you lost your mind attacking Ellen like that!"

"Me!, It's you that is losing his mind." She drops the knife with a clatter, yanking open a drawer, throwing five tabloid newspapers on the center island. "Look at that, I can't even go to the grocery store to do my shopping without that trash staring me in the face. I'm ashamed to be working for a man of such loose morals." She wipes a tear from her eye and stifles a sob. "I thought you were a good man, Mr. Vic. What's happened to you?"

"Bridget, you know these rag sheets exaggerate the truth." He says with a dismissive shrug of his shoulders.

"So you mean you were never with these women?" She challenges.

"I'm sure…." his voice trails off as he studies the contents of the photos. "Well, yeah I did date Nicole for a couple of months, and Laura only lasted one night. Shit, Vanessa was only a publicity stunt for the movie and Kate was just plain fun. And this one is Ellen when she fainted in my arms the other night. A good thing her face was hidden." *I'm in the tabloids……*I snatch the paper out of his hands. *Good God, I can never step foot in the grocery store again….what will the neighbors think?*

"So you don't deny it."

Vic sits on a stool with a pensive look on his face. "No, I guess I never stopped to think about how it looked. The stardom went to my head. I was riding the tide of Hollywood good times, thinking it won't last forever, so why not enjoy it now."

"Mr. Vic," Bridget shakes her head. "This is not you. You've never been a womanizer. I can count on one hand the number of woman you dated over the years, but after this last movie, this celebrity business has gone to your head. You have a teenage daughter to think about."

"You're right. I never thought about Hanna seeing these trumped up newspapers, peddling their lies and exaggerations. It's mostly publicity for the movie." Vic says holding up the latest tabloid. "But you have to listen to me, Ellen is different."

"Why? Because she fainted in your arms?!"

"Well, yes, she fainted from shock. She thought I was dead. You've seen her before. Wait a second." Vic gets up off the stool, and pulls me further into the room.

"Elle, come here, I have to revive Bridget's memory."

"Why in the world would I remember this woman?" Bridget replies indigently.

"You'll see. Elle, come here."

Peering cautiously around the corner with the tabloid crushed against my chest like armor, I see Bridget holding a knife pointed in my direction. For safety I duck under the protective cover of Vic's arm.

"Bridget, look at Elle closely," he turns me in his arms towards her. "Think of my studio."

"*Ohhhhhhhhh,* my stars," she looks at me in mounting horror. "It's the Daisy girl, the one hanging in the…."

She makes the sign of the cross on her chest. "Saints preserve me. I've called the love of your life, a whore!" She looks at Vic and accuses, "You said she was dead."

"She was, no! Our parents lied to us." He says defensively. "My father even went so far as to buy a gravestone and engrave Elle and the baby's names on it."

"Oh, Lord," Bridget says, bringing her hands up to her face in disbelief. "What happened to the babe?"

"They signed our baby away for adoption at birth." I say; a bitter edge to my voice. Vic's arms tighten around me, understanding my pain.

"Oh, you poor darlings," Bridget reaches out touching my arm in sympathy. "And now you have gone and found each other after all this time. It's like a miracle." She sniffs, pulling a handkerchief from her apron pocket, blowing her nose with a *honk*. "By the mercy of the good Lord, how did you meet?"

"At the movie premiere, Ellen's daughter was a costume designer on the film. She invited her mother as her guest. I saw Elle and thought I'd lost my mind. But then I saw the locket I'd given her so many years ago and

I knew it was her."

"So you have a daughter?" Bridget asks suspiciously. "Are ye married?"

"I have a daughter and a son. My husband died of a heart attack almost two years ago." The memories of my life with Jack seem a world away.

"So you are both free......to be together at last." Bridget claps her hands in happiness for us. "It's like something out of a fairy tale or one of them *Hallmark* movies."

Holding up an arm in mock defense, Vic says, "It was a fairy tale until we walked through the door and ran into an Irish hellcat."

"I'm sorry about that," she says, a chagrined look on her face. "Hank accuses me of getting too worked up about things. But you can see why I had my concerns."

"I understand, but Elle is different." Vic says with authority. "So, no more doxy talk." With a hoot of laugher, he shakes his head and asks, "What the hell is a doxy? Is that some old Irish term or did you just make that up?"

"Just you never mind, I'm so sorry, Miss Ellen," Bridget says, contritely. "I didn't mean to hurt your feelings. To apologize I'm going to make you a lovely dinner and retire to my quarters until late tomorrow morning, leaving the house to the two of you, so you can be reacquainting yourselves."

...

In a dark sky with no city lights, the stars vie only with the half-moon casting dappled shadows throughout the woods. Strands of white lights wrapped around the branches of a large oak tree twinkle and wink like so many small woodland fairies flirting amongst the leaves.

The pool glows like an aquamarine gem illuminated by the underwater lights. The magnificent dinner Bridget prepared, reduced to a scattering of crumbs littering the table.

Swaying gently back and forth on the patio swing, we sip our coffee in companionable silence. A plate with the remains of a chocolate torte rests on the table next to a French press coffee pot. Firelight flickers from a pit built out of rough hued rocks that complements the natural design of the pool area. Feeling content and half-asleep, we sway back and forth on the swing.

"I can't eat another bite." I moan, desperately wanting to unsnap the top button of my jeans, only vanity prevents me from doing so…….and fear of what will pop out.

"I'm stuffed." He twirls a piece of my hair around his finger.

"Bridget may have a temper, but she sure can cook. And as far as I'm concerned she can call me a doxy all she wants as long as I don't have to go near the kitchen." He chuckles and kisses the top of my head as I lament, "The pots and pans are much safer in her capable hands."

"That's fine with me." His hand caresses my leg. "I can't afford to eat like this every day; I'll have to run five miles tomorrow morning to work off this meal."

He cocks his head looking at me. "Do you run?"

Run….Do I run?!….is he nuts? I haven't run since……oh, boy, a long time. I played volleyball in high school because I didn't have to run. I hike, bike, and paddle because *no* running is involved. "Look at us," I squeak, hoping to divert him from the idea of a morning jog. "No family, students, movie people, paparazzi. Just sitting here, swinging along sipping our coffee."

"I could stay like this for a very long time." The look in his eyes sends my heart careening into the wall of my chest.

"Oh, you'd get bored with me." My voice husky, slightly breathless; secretly hoping he vows he can't live a day without me.

"I don't think so," He sighs and smiles, reflexively drawing me closer. "Never, I feel so comfortable with you, like we never parted."

"Yes," I agree slowly, "But our lives are so different. All that Hollywood glamour, huge houses, drivers with limos and paparazzi, it's overwhelming. I feel out of place. It's a world I don't know or understand."

"It's just me, Elle. None of that matters. It's the trappings of the industry."

"But it's your life."

"Yes, but with proper security measures, you can protect your family."

"It's a different lifestyle. All those beautiful woman throwing themselves at you, I can't bear the thought of sharing you with anyone. I'm greedy, I want all of you. Will one woman be enough?" And I can't help but think, a woman who is twice as old as his recent dates, and double the cellulite.

"Elle, I'm not going anywhere. Wild horses couldn't drag me away."

"Sophia?"

"There was passion in the beginning. I mistook passion for love. And honestly, at the time, she was good for my career. We drifted apart and I admit to cheating on her. Hanna keeps us connected. We have occasional family dinners, sometimes even vacations with Hanna. We replaced passion with mutual respect and friendship."

"You cheated on her and she forgave you?"

"I wouldn't call divorce forgiveness. Her fury at me made tabloid headlines. A case of wounded pride, how dare anyone cheat on the fabulous Sophia, even though she was sleeping with her leading man. "

"Vic, I have no more tolerance for affairs. I've lived that life and I'm done with it."

"Elle, I'm not Jack."

"No, but you're *Esteban Diago,* Mr. Hot Stuff, sex on a stick, every woman's fantasy."

"Not every woman, polls say only about thirty percent."

"Not funny!"

"You're right, but seriously, I'm not Jack. Give me time and I'll prove it to you." He refills our glasses with a pinot noir from the Sonoma area of California. He stares pensively at the stars overhead, swirling the liquid in the glass before giving me a half smile over the rim. "I'm in no position to talk, I'm not an angel," he says. "But I'm tired of being lonely." His intense gaze darkens suddenly and he blinks. "Sharing is not an option for me, I'm done wandering." Taking my hand, he holds it over his heart; I flex my fingers slightly, feeling the warmth of his skin beneath the thin fabric of his shirt. "I love you, Elle; please, stay with me."

I desperately want to believe him and trust he wants a lasting relationship. But I have doubts, his track record with women suggests otherwise. For now, it's easier to be in the moment, I slowly undo the buttons of his shirt, tricky with one hand, better to concentrate on having him in my life again and not dwell on the future, it's too soon. My heart needs time...because to love and possibly lose him again….would shatter me into pieces, beyond repair.

Chapter 33

A Slippery Slide

"Leave the breakfast dishes, Bridget will take care of them." Vic grabs my arm heading me toward the kitchen door. We had spent the morning sleeping in on a luxuriously soft king size bed followed by a sumptuous breakfast feast, which I somehow managed to cook… only because Bridget left behind detailed instructions.

"I have something I want to show you." He insists. I look at the countertop and table, in my attempt to cook breakfast; I demolished the immaculate kitchen, completely. Dirty pots and pans, a bowl with pancake batter spilling down the side, toast crumbs and coffee grounds litter the countertops. Is he *nuts*? Bridget will have an Irish coronary if she sees this mess, and she'll know I can't cook for beans. The breakfast was edible, in fact, delicious; but the entire process of preparing the meal was tortuous ……and the poor kitchen bears the scars of that pain.

"I can't leave a dirty kitchen." I stop, digging my heels in to prevent his forward motion. "I wouldn't feel right expecting Bridget to clean up after us. That's not fair."

"It's her job," he says, pulling me toward the door. "And if you touch those dishes, both our heads will roll. Trust me on this."

"Just let me straighten up a bit; put the dirty dishes in the sink and the food in the refrigerator."

"Not a good idea," he says with an ominous tone to his voice.

"*Bang ,bang, bang*.......comes the sound of pounding on the back door, followed by Bridget's bright green eyes peeking through the curtains. Attila the Hun would have made less noise. "Yoohoo, are ye in there. Can I come in? Are you decent?"

"Come in," Vic calls out, walking over to open the door. "And as you can see, we are more than decent." His voice sounds disappointed, looking at our fleece and jean clad bodies, not an inch of flesh showing.

"Well, I would hope you'd be up and about. It's almost ten o'clock. Half the day is gone." She fusses good-naturedly, heading for the coffeepot and stops, a stunned expression on her face. "I....see....you had your breakfast...." Her eyes travel over the countertop and stove, taking in the dripping pancake batter, spilled coffee grounds, and pan of half burnt bacon. "Oh my Lord in heaven," she crosses herself. "It looks like you were very......hungry." She trails off weakly. Scratching her head with one hand, surveying the damage, she offers, "It must be difficult, cooking in a strange kitchen......not knowing where things are kept." With an ill-concealed *hump,* she reaches for the apron hanging on a peg near the back door. *Yeah,* that's the reason, I mentally groan.

"Bridget, let me help you clean up." I start picking up the egg carton and milk, heading toward the refrigerator. *Smack,* the sound of a spatula hitting the countertop causes me to jump. *Holy shit!* She's pissed!

"Don't you dare touch a dirty dish in this house!" she glares at me over the top of the spatula, wielding it like an assault weapon. "It's one thing for you to be mucking around in *my* kitchen, cooking for Mr. Vic and all, but don't you go and think you'll be putting me out of me job and start cleaning up. *I* clean this house. *Understood?!*"

"Yes, of course, I just want to help."

"I don't be needing your help. Do I look like a feeble old woman who can't be keeping up with her chores." She glowers at me.

"No, no, absolutely not!" I think I just cowered. *chicken.*

"Good, then we understand each other. You can help cook and care for Mr. Vic, but I do the cleaning in this house."

"Yes, yes, understood, and I appreciated the note with instructions for cooking breakfast. It was helpful." I start twisting a lank of hair around my finger and offer lamely, "I don't cook much."

"Really," Bridget says dryly, looking over the kitchen, hands on her hips. "I wouldn't have guessed." She shakes her head and rolls her eyes. "Go on now, get out of my hair and let me be doing my job."

"*Told you.*" Vic hisses in my ear, as we escape out the back door, pots and pans rattling and banging in the kitchen behind us. "Don't worry; her bark is worse than her bite."

I'm beginning to think she has the bite of a man-eating Bengal tiger.

...

"Where are we going?" I ask. He squeezes my hand in response, leading me down a flagstone path towards the stable area, stopping before a large adobe barn. Except for the heavy timbers supporting the barn-like structure, the architecture and color scheme match the main house. A driveway of hard packed gravel leads from the main entrance of the house and loops back around to the stable. Through the open top half of the stall doors, comes the sound of horses munching hay and hoofs stamping against wooden floors. A huge black horse sticks his head out, and nickers to Vic.

"Hey, Diablo, you greedy devil, I'll bring you a carrot later." Vic calls out to the horse, walking to a door on the far end of the barn. The horse whines in protest.

The building appears to be divided into three sections. Vic points out that the barn contains a stable for the horses, a small apartment for Ike and the rear of the building is for his office and tack room. Inside the tack room, saddles of polished leather hang from tack racks mounted on the walls. Bridles and halters along with lead ropes fill the empty spaces. The scent of leather, saddle soap, horses and hay permeates the air. I've always loved the smell of a horse barn.

A staircase in the tack room leads to the upper level. Vic puts a hand on my back and propels me up the steps. At the top he pauses, taking a key from his pocket, unlocking the door, steering me into a huge vaulted room. A loft. A bank of windows showers the room in sunlight with a magnificent view of rolling hills stretching across the valley. Several easels with art projects in various stages of completion stand next to the windows. One is an oil painting, another holds a charcoal study, and the third, a water color. Dominating the center of the room is a circular bed placed directly under a skylight; covered with a comforter of midnight blue embossed with patterns of stars and planets. Deep piles of pillows rest in the middle of the bed, to be tossed about in any or all directions, depending on the whim of the sleeper. A vast sofa covered in a woodsy plaid sits at an angle to the windows. On the far wall a black granite bar completes a mini-kitchen. As I walk around, I'm awestruck….again.

"Oh my ……..what is this place?" I breath in the

scent of leather and horses; pausing to run my hand along the plush fabric of the sofa.

"Well," Vic explains, holding out his hands, "It's my gallery, studio, darkroom, and observatory, all under one roof." he points to a telescope by the window. "It's my sanctuary, I come here to create and unwind. I keep it locked, no one is allowed in. Not that there is any reason to keep anyone out, I just like the idea of my own private world. I let Bridget in a few times a year to clean, other than that it's my space."

He points to a series of oil paintings on the wall, "I've had the occasional invitation to present my work in a few galleries across the country, even before the movie thing started, which is very gratifying."

"It's impressive. I've forgotten how artistic you are." I turn three hundred and sixty degrees……and that's when I see them. In the back corner of the loft…….are several pictures, portraits actually………hanging by invisible wire, as if floating in the air…………and all of them are of me….*Nude*! There I am….bare assed naked, wearing nothing but my birthday suit and a few daisies. Black-eyed Susans are artfully placed to prevent the pictures from being X-rated, yet at the same time, very provocative. The only color in the dim corner of the loft is the brilliant yellow of the daisies waving against a blue sky…and the amount of exposed flesh on my body. The air leaves my lungs in a *whoosh*……I feel faint…..somewhat nauseous….and yet slightly complemented at the same time, as I stare at the pictures in horror and envy………because…...*damn, I looked good back then.* But secondly and the more important question is…*what the hell is my naked ass doing hanging from his ceiling!!*

"*What* is this?" I venture cautiously. I had never seen

the pictures. I knew they existed, but *oh, my God.* How many people have seen them? My stomach churns in dread. I clutch his arm so hard; the blood throbs in my fingertips.

"Remember our picnic that last day in the Adirondacks. Well, this is some of my best work. I won a citation for lighting effects in this series of photographs. My ex-wife, on the other hand, wasn't so fond of them, accused me using the gallery showings as a means of flaunting my old girlfriend in her face. She always had a jealous streak. When Sophia enters a room, she holds reign like a queen, leaving other women to fade into the background."

I can't speak. All I can do is gaze up at the portraits. My face staring back at me, a bubble of disbelief rising inside me. Bridget's……. *daisy girl*………..my face flushes at the thought of her seeing me like this……so young…..so in love………and so naked.

"How many people have seen these pictures?" My voice comes out as a squeak…….*oh, God.*

"Gosh, I don't know, thousands. And that one there," he points to a smaller one in the far corner, "is the back cover for a *Thirsty Mad Dogs* album, huge hit."

I groan in mortification. The album cover of a heavy metal rock band…….it just gets better.

"What? Elle, you still don't get how beautiful you are?" Vic looks slightly mystified. "I don't understand; I was the envy of every man who saw those pictures, and half the women."

"Because they knew you screwed her!" I hissed at him. "I look like a horny playboy bunny let out for a romp in the meadow. Those pictures were private, Vic, not for the whole world to see."

"I guess," he shrugs sheepishly. "I thought you died, so I took my grief to the dark room and set out to show the world how beautiful you were."

Well, when you put it like that, how is a girl to argue.........he thinks I'm beautiful......okay, it was a while ago, but still, he thinks I'm beautiful. That doesn't get him off the hook for exposing my naked butt for anyone to see.

"That was the last time we were together." He tries diffusing my anger with memories of that afternoon overlooking the lake, how we were so in love that nothing else in the world mattered. To have such innocence again.

"Seems like ages ago, doesn't it?" I muse.

"Yes and no, sometimes it seems like yesterday."

He continues, "We could bring out the camera and recreate the scene for old time's sake." His hands start doing that magical thing underneath my blouse, making my righteous indignation dissolve in the wake of rising passion....why does he affect me so, I slightly resent how easily I fall under his spell, how I come unglued at his touch......I've never been considered a prude but with him, my inhibitions melt away, replaced by reckless abandon.....a glance around the room reveals no black eyed Susans or a meadow in sight.....well, I guess we'll just have to improvise.

...

Under the oversized skylight of the loft, the rhythmic melody of rain lulls us into an afternoon of unhurried lovemaking. Overhead clouds scuttle by, punctuated by the drum of raindrops on the roof; the sound of horses stomping below; a perfect afternoon for cuddling and napping. Contentment purrs in my veins. Curled up in a warm naked ball, there's no place in the world I'd rather be than in this bed. I run my hand down his thigh marveling in the contrast between smooth skin and sinew muscle. I pull the soft fleece throw tighter and snuggle deeper into his embrace, half asleep.

"*Mr. Vic!*" Bridget's voice screeches over the intercom system that links the house to the barn. Generally Vic uses the system, rarely Bridget, as she respects his privacy when working in the loft.

Jolted from our nap by the urgency in her voice, Vic groans, "What could she possibly want?"

"Mr. Viccc!" Again, the shrill voice of Bridget shouts into the intercom as if she were calling from the other side of the mountain. "Hanna is *here*. Now! She's heading to the loft at this very moment. I tried to stall her, but she's all worked up over some teenage thing, and insists on speaking with you, immediately! Do you hear me?!"

"Ohhh, holy shit! Quick, Elle, we got to get you out of here, fast." He jumps to his feet pulling on a pair of faded jeans and a rumbled t-shirt, knocking me off the bed and onto the floor. *Thump….ouch!*

"Come on, come on!" He tosses my jeans at me, and the rough fabric smacks me in the face. "Shit, shit, shit! I need time to explain to her." He sweeps the rest of my clothes onto the floor as he straightens the comforter.

Hopping on one foot as I hastily attempt to dress, I can't help but wonder what happened to the *I love you and you are the most precious thing in my life?*

I scramble around the floor on my knees gathering my underwear and shirt scattered by his frantic cleaning, and I hear footstep coming up the steps.

"Dad! Dad! Where are you? I need you! *Daadddy!*" Vic's daughter, Hanna comes running up the stairs.

Vic grabs my arm, propels my half-naked body through a side door out onto the platform of the hayloft.

"Hey! What the hell!" I protest, surrounded by hay bales, underwear clutched to my naked breasts. The hay loft is a U-shaped floor following the outline of the horses' stalls below, the center of the elevated deck is cut out so hay can be tossed down next to the stall, leaving only a very narrow ledge to maneuver around.

"I'm soo sorry; just give me a few minutes. Forgive me." He places a quick kiss on my forehead and not waiting for my forgiveness, slams the door in my face.

I stare at the closed door as his daughter's voice vibrates off the loft rafters. "Dadddd!" *Jeez,* she's a noisy one.

"Hanna, darling, what are you doing here?" I hear Vic's breathless voice through the wall. "I wasn't expecting you."

"You always say I can come anytime I want," she whines. "Why are you acting so strange? You look like you just woke up, what are you doing sleeping in the afternoon? What a geezer."

"I worked late last night and was catching up on my sleep." He offers the lame excuse.

"Fine then, *whatever,*" Hanna's voice edged in teenage contempt. "Mom won't let me go out with Trevor." Feeling only slightly guilty, I press my ear against the door.

"Why don't we go in the house? I think Bridget just made some cookies. We'll have cookies and milk and discuss the issue." I hear Vic opening the door to the stairway, trying to coax her out. I see a knothole in one of the wall boards; and shamelessly eavesdrop.

I button my shirt and squat down to watch the show,

with my past experience of raising two teenagers I can appreciate the drama.

"Milk and cookies!" She sputters. "What do you think I am? Five! I need an answer now! I told Trevor I'd go to the movies with him and a bunch of his friends. Mom is acting so lame. You could call, and tell her you're fine with me going out with Trevor."

"Hanna," Vic takes her elbow, steering her away from the rumpled bed, still warm from our lovemaking. "Are you sure we can't go *in* the house?"

"No, I like it up here, it's so horsey." She plops herself down on the couch where I see the edge of my bra sticking out…….this could get real interesting. "Besides if we go in the house Bridget will butt in with her old world British ideals."

"Bridget is Irish, I'd be careful calling her British. It tends to make her cranky." He says with a sigh, stealing a peek at the door leading to the loft. "Now what is the problem?"

"Uhh, No one listens to me!" she says, throwing her hands up in disgust. Boy, you can tell she's the child of two actors. *Phew*, drama queen. "I *just* told you, Mom won't let me go to the movies with Trevor."

"Hanna," Vic begins slowly with patience. "How old are you?"

"Dad! You know very well how old I am. Fourteen."

"And what was the age your mother and I decided acceptable for you to go on a car date? He says with the practiced air of someone who's had this conversation before.

"Sixteen! Come on! That is so lame! Everyone else can go, why can't I?"

"Those are the rules of this family."

"You and Mom are divorced; we're not a real family."

"When it comes to you, your mother and I are a family, united in what's best for you." He pushes a stray lock of hair behind her ear. "We love you, and I agree with your mother that no dates with boys in a car before sixteen. And isn't Trevor that Millnor kid who is what, seventeen or eighteen. Sorry sweetheart, not going to happen."

Crouched in my position against the wall, I silently applaud Vic for sticking to his rules where his daughter is concerned. Lord knows, Jack and I were tested by our two teenagers. Jack the more lenient; leaving me to play the bad cop, and trust me, it's not a popular position. I shift my body, wiggling, trying to dislodge loose pieces of hay. Somehow the chaff worked its way into the material of my shirt. I itch like hell. I squirm around looking for a means of escape. There must be a way down from here, a set stairs or a ladder somewhere.

"Oh, Dad, come on! I thought you would be cool about this." Sensing defeat, Hanna changes her battle tactics. With a voice like silvered honey she says. "Daddy, you're like the cool Dad, all the girls think you're such a hunk. I promise I'll be careful. Pleaseee."

"No."

"I never get to do anything."

"You're right."

"You and Mom are such loser parents"

"Yep, it's your lot in life to have loser parents. Sweetie, you will date, you will go in cars……..with boys, and there are many adventures in life waiting for you. Just not at fourteen."

"I can pout and scream all I want but you're not going to change your mind, are you?" she sulks.

I spy a ladder leading down to the ground floor but it's on the other side of the barn, forcing me to crawl on the narrow ledge to reach it. *Damn.* My knees ache and I have an overpowering urge to itch my entire body.

"I'm in total agreement with your mother." Vic says. "But I appreciate you coming to us, there may be circumstances where we bend the rules, but night driving with older kids on mountain roads, isn't one of them. Okay?"

"Fine, I hate my life." I hear her open the door to the stairway. "I'm hungry. Did you say Bridget made cookies?" The kid has the attention span of a gnat…

"I'm sure of it, let's go see." I hear the relief in Vic's voice as he opens the stairway door. "Come on."

"No, first I want to see Moon Star."

Really, I'm hiding in plain sight of the stalls. Now where do I go? Maybe I can beat them to the ladder. Ehhhh….too many decisions. I hear their voices on the stairwell. I'd better hurry.

"What? Moon Star?" he says, confused.

"My horse, what is wrong with you? Why are you in such a hurry to get me in the house? I thought you liked it out here, all the quiet and privacy." They stop on the stairs.

"I do but I'm starving, I missed lunch."

"It will take just a minute. Don't be so impatient."

"I'm sure Moon Star is fine. I checked on the horses before I came upstairs."

"I'll meet you in the house. I want to say hello," she says, clattering down the wooden stairway.

"Wait, wait for me. We'll go together." Vic calls out, raising his voice, hoping I hear and take cover. *Great....* I flatten myself against the hay bales praying my blonde hair and pale skin act as camouflage.

"There's my pretty boy." Hanna croons from the doorway of Moonstar's stall. "Dad, do we have any apples for him?"

"Yeah, sure, I'll go and get a few." Vic rushes to the feed room and back in a matter of seconds. "Here's a couple……..okay, let's go."

"Just a minute, let me feed him," she says with a laugh. "Can we go for a ride later?"

"Umm, sure, sure. Whatever you….. want….." his eyes widen in disbelief at the sight of me creeping along the edge of the wooden platform. I give him the thumbs up and point to a pile of loose hay, a perfect hiding spot. With Hanna intent on feeding her horse, he steps out of her line of vision and starts waving frantically at me.

What?

"Dad, what are you doing now?" Hanna asks, a perplexed look on her face. "Maybe you should go back and finish that nap."

"Ahhhh………chasing flies." He swats at imaginary flies. At that moment I erupt with an explosive sneeze……*I'm so screwed.* I've always been suspicious that I'm allergic to hay, explains the itching.

"What was that?" Hanna walks to the middle of the aisle looking up in the haymow.

"What?" Vic grabs her arm, pulling her toward the door. "I didn't hear anything."

"That sound." Hanna repeats. "Is Hank working upstairs?"

"No one is up there." Vic says, desperation creeping into his voice. "Come on, Hanna, let's go."

"What are you deaf? Someone is up there." Hanna grabs a pitchfork pointing to the upper level.

I tuck myself into the pile of loose hay. She can't see me; it's dark in this corner of the loft. If I don't move, she'll leave. I think I hate this kid already……..*just* go in the house.

"Who's up there?" she calls out. "I know someone is up there. My Dad has a gun and he's not afraid to shoot."

"Hanna!"

"Dad! Maybe it's some crazy stalker fan."

To avoid detection, I burrow deeper into the pile of hay and realize too late……there's no floor underneath; I'm free falling….down a drop hay chute.

Ahhhhhhhh……..

I'm a screaming, tumbling human bale of hay. Flying down a twenty-foot hay chute, landing with a *whomp!*

"What the HELL!" Hanna cries, jumping back at the apparition sprawled on the ground before her.

"*Elle!* Elle, are you hurt? Buttercup….?" Vic drops to his knees and scans my face, pulling hay out of my eyes and mouth so I can breathe. I'm covered head to toe, where the hay stops and I begin is difficult to determine. And by dressing in haste, I missed a few buttons and snaps, the result….my breasts spilling out of my shirt, jeans slid half way down my hips, more off than on…and panties falling out of my back pocket. I looked like a scarecrow gone stripper.

"Who the hell is this!" Hanna's screech pierces my shocked wits. Dressed in a flirty flowered skirt and matching tank, her gorgeous chestnut hair twisted in a messy knot at the nape of her neck, she looks a younger female version of Vic. Through the hay plastered to my face, I see the same decisive chin as her father, straight nose, chiseled high cheek bones and her mother's aqua green eyes and hair. She's stunning, at fourteen, tall, model thin, yet voluptuous in all the right parts. I feel sympathy for Vic, between her fiery temper and beauty, his hell has just begun.

"Elle, seriously, are you hurt?" Vic helps me to my feet, his voice edged with concern, checking me up and down for injuries.

"I'm fine, really, just a little shaken up." I give him a tremulous smile, trying not to wince as I straighten my back. "Whew, what a ride!" I chime, trying to lighten the mood. I wiggle my fingers and legs. "Everything seems to be working."

"Dad! Is this one of your one night stands?" she points an accusing finger at me, demanding an explanation. "Mom is going to have a fit. You know the rules; the mountain house is our home. Family and close friends, none of the Hollywood stuff. No wonder you wanted me out of the barn. You're disgusting. How dare you talk to me about family rules! Look at you hiding one of your "girlfriends" in the hayloft." She uses her fingers to make quotation marks around girlfriends, letting me know she really means "slut". "You were not napping, you were doing it! Ughh! So…. gross!"

"*Hanna!*" Vic spins around, silencing her with a glance. "I can explain. This is not what you think." I make a vain attempt at straightening my clothing, buttoning and zipping things that need to be closed up and put away. Lost cause, I'm a mess. I do look like a slut.

"Why was she hiding then? Her clothes are half off." Hanna rants on, "I'm not stupid. Anyone with half a brain can see you were screwing her." She stamps her foot. "Mom's already pissed at you, every magazine in the market is plastered with your picture and every week it's a new woman. That part of your life is supposed to stay in

L.A. This is our home, where I can come and go between the two houses…….and not worry about interrupting your little flings." She throws her fingers in my direction as if I were a speck of garbage to be disposed. She pauses a moment to catch her breath, her words filled with hurt, betrayal and anger. "How do you think I feel? My Dad's some steamy sex symbol? All the girls at school gush about how hot you are. *Gross*, I want to scream at them. That's my father you're talking about; he's old enough to be your grandfather!

"I am *not*!" Vic snorts in shocked denial.

"Really….Dad." she shakes her head in disgust. "What are you, like, fifty? You could easily be a grandfather. Talk about me needing to grow up, maybe you should take some of your own advice. Stop screwing every woman who crosses your path."

Okay, now I like this kid. You go, girl, tell him he needs to settle down with a nice moderately attractive school teacher, someone who knows how to be a good wife and mother.

Vic's concern bounces from me to Hanna, as he grips her arms to still her quaking anger. "Hanna, Ellen is different." he says, desperate to calm her down. "We knew each other as teenagers. We worked at the same camp in the Adirondacks."

No sooner were the words out of his mouth, when Hanna's head snaps back and she stares intently into my face. The blood drains from her cheeks and she cries, "It's her! That woman in the pictures! The ones you and mom argued about, I heard you fighting. You said she was dead. Dead……..you lied! She's alive! Where have you been hiding her?" Hanna cries out, sobbing. "Mom begged you to get rid of those pictures; she said you could never love her until that other woman was gone."

Oh my God...I cringe. The pictures in the loft. *Was he nuts?* The thought of his wife and daughter seeing me in a moment of teenage lust brings a flush of embarrassment to my face. I flop down on a hay bale and rest my head in my hands. This is not how I wanted to meet Vic's daughter……*crap*.

"Hanna, *listen* to me." Vic says, working to keep the panic out of his voice, knowing his daughter feels betrayed. "I thought Ellen was dead. Our parents deceived us. You must believe me. My father purchased a gravesite and engraved Ellen's name on a headstone. Dates and everything. He took me there, showed me her grave. I was so young and stupid I believed him. Then he had a woman impersonate my aunt and call Ellen, telling her I died in a motorcycle accident."

"I don't believe you." Hanna says, her voice choked with tears. "You said she was dead. You lied to us, Dad!" The look on her face cuts Vic to the quick; she turns on her heel and runs out of the barn, sobbing.

"*Shit*, that didn't go well." He sits and leans back against the stall, running both hands through his hair. "I think I'm going to be sick."

"Deep breathe." I suggest. "Vic, I'm so sorry. If I had been more careful, this wouldn't have happened." My voice filled with remorse. "I feel terrible. I would never hurt your daughter."

He pulls me into a hug. "It's no one's fault. And on a scale of one to ten, your entrance into the barn was one of your best Klutz-Ellen's. God, you should have seen your face, it was pretty damn funny, if I were in a laughing mood." He blows out a long sigh.

"It's not funny. I could have been killed." I give him a

playful punch on the arm. "You'd better go to her. I'll slip up to our room and stay out of sight until the coast is clear. Go, go, I understand. I've raised two teenagers, I know how sensitive they are about……..*everything*."

He pulls me into his arms for a slow lingering kiss, tracing the outline of my lips with his finger and growls, "I'll deal with you later. Maybe even give you a little spanking as punishment for getting me in all this trouble."

"Me! Punished! You got yourself into this mess, Mr. Casanova. If anyone deserves to be punished, it's you. How dare you throw me out of a warm cozy bed, half naked into a hay pile, force me to crawl around in the dark and nearly fall to my death. Just wait and see what I have planned for you. I'm thinking of something with whips and leather." I point to the riding crop hanging on the wall with a wicked leer on my face.

He raises his eyebrows. "Ummm, I think we have a date."

"I'm not afraid of you." I call out scornfully to his retreating back.

"Buttercup, you should be."

…

"Good God, you look like something the cat dragged in off the street." Bridget exclaims, as I tip-toe through the kitchen door, hoping to advert any further disasters. *Drat.*

"Are you hurt?" she asks.

"I think I twisted my back a little. Nothing a hot bath and a muscle rub won't cure. Oh, Bridget, I've gone and done it this time." I plop down on a kitchen stool with a wince. "Hanna is so upset, heaven knows, I can't blame her. Her father's latest lover tumbling down at her feet, screaming, half dressed and covered with straw."

"Ohhh, I heard all about it." Bridget mouth twitches and she dissolves into laughter. "You flying down that hay chute with your knickers half off, landing at her feet. I can just imagine the look on Hanna's face. Priceless!" Laughing she sits down on a stool next to me, mopping the tears from her face with a handkerchief. "Oh, Lord have mercy on my soul, I can see it now. Mr. Vic standing there his mouth hanging open caught between the two of you." Oh, she is enjoying this way *too* much.

"Wait until Miss Sophia hears about this one. She was not in love with those pictures hanging in the gallery. Mr. Vic said they were art, she said they were pornography."

I groan. "I'm worried about Hanna."

"Don't be."

"Bridget! How can you say that? She's very upset." I look at her incredulously.

"Hanna's parents are actors; she is well versed in the fine art of melodrama. She's been practicing for this role since she was two years old. Luckily, her parents recognize the symptoms and treat her accordingly." Bridget says dryly. "Trust me, Hanna will live, that child is a survivor."

"If you say so," I rise from the stool holding my sore back. "I think it's best if I make myself scarce. A hot bath and a cup of tea is all the medicine I need right now."

"Run along and pour your bath." Bridget says. "I'll bring the tea up to you in a minute."

"Are you sure? I don't want to bother you." I ask, leaning against the door jam.

"Go, I'll bring up the tea." Bridget makes shooing motions with her hands, erupting into peals of laughter.

...

It's almost seven o'clock when I come down for dinner. Pausing at the doorway, I chew on my lower lip working up enough nerve to go in and face Hanna. Hey, it's no big deal, I tell myself. She's a fourteen year old kid, not like I'm going to face Attila the Hun. Think positive, what's the worst she could do to me...poison, switchblades, hand grenades….

When I reach the door to the outside veranda, I stop and listen. Very still. Has Vic miraculously managed to deflate Hanna's raging anger? Entering the dining room, she's seated in quiet conversation with her father.

"Elle, come join us." Vic says, rising from the table, pulling me into his arms for a quick kiss. I cast a glance at Hanna, prepared to duck the poison dart aimed at my heart. Nothing, just a withering glance of dismissal cast in my direction. Vic continues, "You seemed to have recovered from your fall. How are you feeling?"

"Ummmm……. Amazing! A hot bath, a cup of Bridget's Irish tea and a little nap, I feel like a new woman." I say, slipping into the chair he's pulled out for me, checking the seat for protruding nails….. live grenades…...spiny sea urchins. When assured my life's not in jeopardy, I extend my hand to Hanna. "Hanna, I'm Ellen O'Connor, I hope you will forgive the circumstances of our earlier meeting." I continue, "I don't make it a habit of introducing myself to people half dressed with underwear hanging out my pocket."

Vic snorts with laughter, my eyes shoot daggers at him. *You're not helping!*

Hanna views my extended hand with suspicion but good manners and breeding force her to accept the gesture of apology. "Yeah, it's a pleasure to meet you." What her voice lacks in enthusiasm is further covered by a cloak of teenage disdain she wears like a mantle. She adds under her breath, "I guess."

Vic takes my hand and turns it over, tracing the line of scar running from my wrist to index finger, encircling my hand in his, our eyes meet across the table. He leans in and kisses me lightly on the lips. Reaching across the table to caress Hanna's arm, he entreats, "Elle is important to me, Hanna, I'm hoping you can be open minded about our relationship."

"Eewww, enough already, Dad." She rolls her eyes. "Seriously, if she makes you happy and you stop screwing the rest of the world, I'm all for it, but enough of the romancy stuff." Hanna grumbles slouching in her chair. "If you two can suck face at the table, then I can text." She casts a disparaging look in our direction and picks up her phone. "When I get as old and lame as you, just shoot me."

Vic leans his forehead against mine and moans, "God help me." And I can't help but think; he's going to need it…

Chapter 34

Giddyap Cowgirl

Strains of rock music rouse me from slumber. "What the hell?" I mumble into the pillow, peering through the mass of hair falling over my eyes. And realize I'm naked, I never sleep naked. What happened to pajamas, I *always* wear pajamas? At least the old Ellen did.......this new amorous Ellen....maybe not...I sigh....too much wine and too much.....*oh, yes*.....

For a moment I lie still. My head is pounding with rhythmic pain, like some sort of massive jack-hammer drilling music with deep bass notes into it, and I realize it's not my head, but the music pouring through the house............Is that *Inagoda divida* , blaring from God knows where? I'm transported back to the 70's. I've died and gone to Rock and Roll hell as *War, what is it good for, absolutely nothing,* thumps through the walls. Wiggling off my stomach onto my back like a beached turtle, I see a vision standing in the doorway. Okay, maybe hell just turned into heaven.

"Hey, sleepyhead, time to get up. The day is wasting away." He shoves a mug of steaming coffee in my face. "I've got big plans for us today, mia, mia."

Struggling into a sitting position, I gratefully accept the mug, take a sip, and snuggle back into the pillows with a contented sigh, blowing him a kiss of gratitude. He flops down next to me, planting a quick kiss on my cheek. "Great view, huh?" He asks, pointing at the windows framing the forest below. Outside a stream meanders through the woodland understory, beams of sunshine break through the tree branches on a path bordered with wildflowers.

"This house is magical, Vic." I nestle deeper into the feather down comforter. "Except for that awful music, it's perfect. I'd never leave."

"The music is my morning wake up mojo, gets me charged for the day." *Really,* what happened to quiet morning meditation, no sweating, cuddling up against him in the lotus position……worked for me. He is a complex man. Stealing a peek at him over the rim of my cup, I admit, complex or not, he is *really cute*. Day old beard stubble, hair tossed back in casual disarray, T-shirt under an open flannel shirt, artfully worn jeans; he looks as if he stepped out of a high-end outdoor catalog.

"Speaking of leaving," he drains his cup, setting it down on the nightstand. "Hank is waiting down at the barn, he saddled a couple of horses and Bridget packed a picnic for us. Come on, girl, *vamonos*! Get your cute little ass out of bed."

"What time is it?" I ask, stifling a yawn, still not comprehending the get out of bed, horses, outdoors, picnic stuff.

"Six-thirty."

"*Oh, good God,* I forgot you're a morning person." I crawl back under the covers. "This relationship is doomed. You can't keep me up all night and then wake me at the crack of dawn."

"Sure I can, watch." With a laugh, he yanks the comforter off my naked body, and playfully slaps my butt. "Bridget packed *Twinkies* for you."

Twinkies…okay, now that's more like it, food and the promise of *him*….I'm up.

…

While Bridget is perpetual energy in motion, her husband, Hank is like a quiet, slow moving stream, more comfortable with animals than people. The stable area of the ranch is his domain. He prefers spending time in the barn, and working a small herd of cattle. He is tall, sparse and lean, steel gray hair cut short with piercing blue eyes, and his skin is the color of worn leather.

"Morning, Ms. Ellen," Hank greets me respectfully, touching the rim of his hat. "I picked out a nice quiet mare for you. Vic said you had a couple of bad falls, making you a little skittish around horses."

Skittish is an understatement. We had horses for years while the kids were growing up. Jack and the kids were natural born riders. I, on the other hand, not so much. I always loved the grace and beauty of horses, but they didn't love me back. I tried riding with the kids, but the minute I put my foot in a stirrup, the horse knew they had a sucker on their back, and the bucking, jumping, and running away games began. After a few falls, I hung up my spurs, until today. Maybe I should have taken up running, less distance between me and the ground.

"Thanks, Hank," Taking a deep gulp, I approach the horse, petting its soft muzzle, introducing myself. "What's her name?"

"Why, we just call her, Pretty Girl, because she is so dainty and pretty." Hank says with a chuckle, looping the reins over the horse's neck. "Do you need a leg up?"

"No, thanks, I'm good. Well, here we go, Pretty Girl. Just take it easy with me." I pat her neck, putting my foot in the stirrup, and swing my leg over the horse's back. Settling my butt in the saddle…… *Ouch.* Squirming, I get the lady parts situated; I'm going to have to pace myself. I think I've had more sex in the past few days than the last three years of my marriage. And Jack was a horn dog. Wiggling a bit more, finally, everything settles in place.

"Are you okay up there, Ms. Ellen?" Hank looks at me, a pained expression on his face. "You're jiggling around up there like there's a burdock on your butt. Can I fix something for you? Shorten the stirrups?......his voice trails off.

"No, no, this is fine." I answer brightly, reaching for the reins in Hank's hand. Straightening, I see Vic lead a massive black horse out of the barn. *Holy Man O'War.* Look at that brute. Pretty Girl and I instinctively shy away.

"You look like a natural up there," Vic says, mounting the sleek black stallion. "Diablo will help keep her in line. Won't you, boy?" I bet he will. I mutter to myself, giving Pretty Girl a sympathetic pat on her neck.

"Are you sure you're comfortable with this?" Vic reins in Diablo next to Pretty Girl, his eyes inquiring. "Absolutely!" I say with false bravado. *Liar, liar, pants on fire......again.* I'm going to need an audience with the Pope to confess all the sins I've committed this weekend.

...

Chaparral and wild oats blanket the foothills as the horses trot leisurely toward the cathedral-like groves of conifers growing up the mountain slope. A few deciduous trees are turning red and gold bringing in the first colors of autumn. Sparkling drops of dew cling to the leaves, glittering like jewels. The sun on our back chases away the early morning chill. The air is crisp, clean and refreshing. Relaxing, I enjoy the rhythm of the horse moving beneath me, the creak of saddle leather, and the muffled sound of hoof beats on the trail. Turning from the foothills, the path climbs deeper into the mountains coming out in a small clearing with a slow moving stream veiled in a canopy of cottonwood trees and willow bushes.

Vic reins his horse to a stop near the rushing stream. "I thought we'd stop here. This is one of my favorite places on the ranch."

"Perfect." Sighing, I settle back in my saddle, appreciating the view of pine covered foothills and mountain meadows. Smiling at Vic from my perch atop the horse, I admit, "I enjoyed the ride. I think Pretty Girl and I are going to be great friends. Look, I'm still on her back." I flick my hand at a stray fly buzzing the horse's ear.

Vic dismounts and comes to stand at the left side of my saddle, "Here, let me help you down." Placing my hands on his shoulders, my body scrapes against the rough material of his jacket in a slow abrasive slide down his torso, a wave of sensation shoots through me as he pulls me astride his steel-muscled thigh in an erotic glide, *oh giddyap*........my fingers dig into the muscles of his arm. His lips come down feasting hungrily on mine and before I know it, he slips his hand between our bodies, flipping open the buttons on my shirt, and slowly unzips my jeans. I protest only when he breaks our kiss, and steps back. *Holy cow or holy horse.*

"Where are you going?" I whisper, grabbing his forearms.

"Nowhere without you." He loops his finger into the strap of my tank top, gliding it down my shoulder. Pulling me closer, he trails kisses down my neck to the sheer silk of the shirt, stabbing at the pink crests with his tongue. I close my eyes; and a sigh escapes my parted lips. *Oh, he is so....good, even if I don't want it........I want it!* With infinite care he undresses me, kissing every inch of my body, drawing soft, pleasured sounds from my throat. He pulls the boots and socks from my feet, lowering jeans and lacy panties from my hips, his hands, his lips, and his tongue, lap, nip and tease the soft sensitive inner thigh, coming to rest and nuzzling the hollow of my hip…….*ummmmmm*

He steps back suddenly, slowly undoing the buttons of his flannel shirt, tossing it onto the pile of clothes. Reaching down he lifts the hem of his T-shirt and flips it over his head, revealing his chest, never taking his dark eyes off mine. His boots and socks follow before he grasps the top snap of his jeans.

"Let me." I whisper, reaching over, slipping my bold fingers inside the waistband of his jeans, and tug so he's forced to take a step closer to me. He gasps, and then smiles down at me. I undo the button, but before I slid the zipper down, I let my fingers find him through the denim of his jeans. His hips thrust forward into the palm of my hand, relishing my touch.

He exhales his breath with a hiss, "Oh, Elle, you make me crazy." Stepping back, he removes his jeans in one swift, agile move…...

Taking my hand, he leads me into the stream, the cool water licking at my fevered skin. Branches and leaves arch above us. The trees on opposite banks try to reach their mates from the other shore, falling short, a narrow shaft of brilliant blue sky slicing between them. Not a sound to be heard except the buzz of insects and rush of water tumbling over rock. Walking into the pool, I lower myself in, submerge, come up, water streaming, smoothing my hair back. Like moving through liquid silk, holding out my hands to him, I beckon and he walks into my arms. Taking my outstretched hand; he puts my fingers in his mouth, sucking as if to taste the water.

He cups my buttocks and pulls me hard against him, so I feel the heat of him pulsing against me. His mouth hot and hungry on mine, then in one swift motion, he turns and slides my legs around his waist, pulling us back to shore.

Carrying me to a blanket spread on the ground, his mouth never leaves mine, hands twist into my hair, our tongues entwined, as he gently lowers me down, following, so he's lying next to me, flesh to flesh.

"You are so beautiful," he murmurs, and I believe him. His hand trails down along my waist, and I rejoice in the feel of his touch, his hungry mouth at my breasts and his skilled fingers caressing, stroking and loving me. Hands moving over my hips, my bottom, down my leg and back up again to rest at the apex of my thighs….*oh, he's soo good.*

Grasping my knee, he hitches my leg up, curling it over his hip, making me gasp, and he chuckles at my reaction. *Ohhhh,* I gaze at him; he's breathless, his dark eyes locked on mine, as I slowly lay claim to his body. He places his hands on my hips and pushes into me. The peace and quiet of the stream broken only by our mingled breath, as he rolls over taking me with him, and leisurely he starts to move, closing his eyes, he moans softly. My breathing accelerates as his steady rhythm pushes me higher and higher. He's kissing my mouth, my chin, my jaw, his breath harsh against my ear with each gentle thrust of his body.

"*Quierda,*" He gasps and my body starts to quiver, his words my undoing, as we both come together.

Oh……my!

…

The banked pool in the stream creates an outdoor Jacuzzi, washing away trail dust and heat of the day. Locusts hum in the trees above as the temperature rises, water ripples over smooth river rocks, glittering in the late morning sun. Floating on my back, the sun overhead reminds me……I'm starving. What can I say, I'm easily distracted.

"Hey, where is the food, I'm famished!" Standing up from the stream, water drips off my naked body along with my inhibitions. Wrapping a soft sun-warmed towel around me, I rummage through the saddlebags, looking for food. Vic joins me, wearing jeans with the top button undone and nothing else. *Nice, very, very, nice.*

Bridget outdid herself, in addition to the *Twinkies,* she packed a tablecloth, thermos of coffee, hard boiled eggs, crusty bread, a fruit salad and mouth-watering little meat pasties.

We wrestled for the last one, and I won. Hey, a girl has to keep up her strength.

"What day is it?" I ask, brushing the crumbs off my stomach.

"Who cares?"

"I know, but I'm going home on Friday. I promised Trey I'd be back in time to take him to college. And my contact with school says I have to be back to work on Monday." Thoughts of reality flood through me, I don't want to leave this fantasy. A few days with Vic and my old life is a distant memory. It's like I've walked through the looking glass, entering into someone else's existence. Who am I? I muse, looking down at myself, sitting naked on a blanket, munching a cookie, washing it down with a shot of tequila from a flask found in Vic's saddlebag. I barely recognize myself; and since when do cookies and tequila mix…..

I have a son, a job, a dog………responsibilities back in New York. As much as my heart is consumed with Vic, my inner voice of reason says, easy girl, slow down. Let's take this one-day at a time. I'm an organized person, always have a plan, and believe it or not, I've grown more conservative by the year. I wouldn't describe myself as prim and proper but…….. the sudden appearance of Vic; blew my neat, organized world to pieces. Million and millions of beautiful little Vic pieces.

"I'm not letting you go." He pulls me into the protective circle of his arms. "Don't go."

"Can't I take you home with me?" I giggle at the thought. "Look, my souvenir from California. Oh, what I wouldn't give to show you off. Especially to that prig faced Joanne Goodwin. I'd love to see the expression on her face. She does nothing but brag about her perfect husband, children, house, country club, thriving law practice, and on and on. Just once." I sigh with regret.

"Are you suggesting I be your boy toy, an object of sexual fantasy for your girlfriends?"

"Umm, yeah, something like that." I say with a self-deprecating laugh, nuzzling his neck greedily with my lips.

"Why thank you, I'm flattered."

"Spoken, like a true male. And yet part of me wants to keep you a secret, a precious secret held close to my heart." I heave a deep sigh.

"Stay here with me, don't go home."

"Don't you start filming a new movie soon?" I nudge him gently, reminding him of his obligations. "On the plane coming here, I read a magazine article about the new movie." I reach up and stroke his face, running my hands over the stubble on his cheek. I trace the line of his bottom lip then trail my fingers down his throat, leaning over to kiss his collarbone.

"Yeah, next week, I need to leave for the South Pacific." He makes a low sound in his throat, his breath washes over me, and he kisses me, lovingly, "I don't want to go without you…wait, I have an idea," he sits up, enthused with inspiration. "Go home, take Trey to school, then quit your job and come join me on the movie set. You don't need to work, Elle, I have enough money, as long as we're not stupid. My business manager keeps an investment portfolio for me. Even if I don't score any more movie roles, we'll be fine. What do you say?"

"Vic," I pause, choosing my words carefully, realizing the importance of this conversation. "I don't want to leave or lose you, but we've been together for less than a week."

"But it feels like we've never been apart."

"I know. I feel the same way too." Placing my hand on the side of his face, I gently kiss the prominence of his incredible cheekbones. "But we have children, jobs, families, responsible adult stuff. I have to rescue my poor dog from the kennel. Maybe if we had been more cautious as kids, we'd have escaped some of the consequences of our actions. We were so in love, so impetuous. "

"But that was then and this is now. And you can bring the dog with you." His finger traces the curve of my breast, followed by the warmth of his mouth, licking, kissing trying to distract me from the conversation. And it almost worked.

"*Amigo*," Taking a deep breath, I push him away, "Let's go slow…give ourselves time……get used to the idea of being together……time to figure how to blend our lives and families together. I love you, but it's complicated."

"So what?" He fumes. "You go home and that's it? We see each other when it's convenient?" Vic stands up, pulls on his shirt and a wall of hurt builds between us. "I thought…" he stalks to the stream bank, stops and turns his back to me, fists pushed into his pockets, eyes pressed shut, craning his head toward the sun, jaw muscle twitching. "The thought of you leaving makes me crazy, it's eating me up inside. I know it's only been a few days, but this is me. I'm the same. I understand you have responsibilities, but I *need* you, Elle. I didn't realize how much, until you came back into my life."

Following him to the water's edge, I slip my arms around his waist, hugging the warmth of his sun baked flannel shirt, a flicker of fear grips my heart. "I need you too," leaning into his body, I lay my head on his chest. He closes his eyes, and his face creases as if he's in pain. "Do you think I'm going home and leave behind Esteban Diago? Do I look like an idiot? I've been a nun for almost two years; it wasn't fun." I start a little enchantment of my own, playfully nipping and kissing at his neck and chest. "I love you, but if our teenage years taught us anything, we need to be cautious. I have a son waiting for me, a classroom of students, Jack's family, please don't rush me." My hand teases the waistband of his jeans, hinting of more magic to come. "In two years I can quit with twenty five years of service. I've worked hard to earn that bonus. I love my job but now I have……options." I run my hands up and down the muscled plane of his chest. "Some *very* nice options."

"Two years!" He explodes.

"I'm not saying we stay apart for two years. Let's take it month by month. You go to your movie shoot. I'll return home, get Trey off to college and start the school year. When you finish filming, I'll meet you or you come to New York. I have Gran's cabin, no chance of the paparazzi lurking in the woods there."

"That is such a long time. Come on location with me." He pleads.

"I don't want to distract you. The article I read on the airplane said….." I pause, "When you take a part in a movie, you immerse yourself in the role. You think, talk, dress and literally become the character."

"I have a good mind to immerse you as one of my wenches," he leers at me. "And *that* will be an Oscar winning performance."

Chapter 35

The Unthinkable

Not two weeks; or four …our long distance romance turned into a ten week separation.Seventy days with *no Vic.* Vic's filming schedule put him on some remote island. God only knows where; with no cell phone connection…...is there *really* such a place left on earth?

To be apart so soon after our explosive reunion has put me in a tailspin. One minute I'm ecstatic in love, then paranoid he's fallen for his new co-star, to outright panic over a future with a movie star, who happens to be incredibly *hot.* The problem is…he wants me to leave my family, my friends, my home, and the only life I've ever known to build a future with him. *Whew!*

Not only is this taking an emotional toll but also a physical one as well. I have no appetite; the sight of food makes me nauseous. I'm exhausted, yet toss and turn, sleepless at night, then drag my tortured body to school only to come home and crash on the couch for three hour power naps, waking up at seven p.m., disoriented and starving for ice cream and *Twinkies.* I'm a lovesick teenager living in a middle-aged body. This can't go on……. I don't have the stamina.

As fall merges into winter, Thanksgiving week was circled on our calendars, no matter what, we would meet at the ranch. With Trey off on a ski trip with friends and Lani spending the holiday with Jason's family, I'm free to join Vic. So after ten weeks of separation the plane descends into the small private airport near the ranch. As the wheels hit the tarmac Ike comes into view leaning against the Land Rover, arms folded, legs crossed, face shaded under a cowboy hat. To avoid the paparazzi and protect my privacy, Ike will drive me to the ranch. And...there is nothing like the sight of a Celtic warrior cowboy to dash away the memory of a turbulent flight over the Rockies. It's the Irish and cowboy together......that rare eclectic combination that sets any girl's radar on high alert. *Giddyap.*

"Ahh, there she is, at last." Ike envelopes me in a one arm hug while taking my bag from the flight attendant. "Good flight, ehhh?" Growing up near the border one learns the charming Canadian quirk of adding "ehh" to the end of their sentences. It makes me feel at home.

"It was a bumpy ride over the mountains, but two glasses of wine and half a box of imported chocolates took the edge off my nerves." I brush loose strands of hair out of my eyes, feeling the delicious warmth of the California sun on my shoulders. A welcome change from the cold rainy weather back East. "And I've never flown on a private jet, and not wanting to offend the hostess, when she offered, I said yes......to everything." Which explains my queasy stomach, I feel a little green. I pray I don't look green, green woman don't turn men on.

Ike chuckles and takes me by the elbow, steering me across the parking lot.

"Boy, have we missed you."

"Oh, thank you." Ike likes me...I think.... I wasn't sure after our meeting on the beach that first night.

"Listen, living with Vic this past week has been hell; he's like a polecat with a burr in his paw." Ike launches into his explanation, propelling me along like he can't get me to the car fast enough. "Bridget threatened to quit, I'm thinking of joining up on a freighter again, Hank hides in the back shed, and Vic's ridden Diablo to exhaustion. Even the horse avoids him. We can't take it anymore, you have to save us." He tilts his hat back revealing a brush burn down the side of his lean face. "I got this four wheeling with him the other day, just trying to keep up. I'd rather face a grizzly bear in early spring than go back to the ranch without you."

"So he really missed me?"

Ike stops dead in his tracks, peers at me over the top of his sunglasses, eyes narrowed, looking at me like I'm deaf, dumb, or just plain stupid. "Did you not hear a word I just said?" He asks, an incredulous look on his face.

"Well, yes, but I'm still a little insecure about his feelings for me. He's surrounded by beautiful sophisticated women. I don't know how to compete in that world. I'm a middle age school teacher, and the only cosmetic work I've ever had done was a pedicure."

Ike laughs, causing his amber eyes to sparkle. He is so handsome when he smiles. "Ellen, he loves you. Don't sell yourself short; you're a beautiful talented woman. And not everything that glitters in Hollywood is gold. Underneath all the hype, it can get real ugly."

"Oh," I smile, feeling some of my insecurity fall away. *Vic loves me, Vic loves me;* plays over and over in my head.

"Come on, we don't want to keep him waiting, and Hanna is coming this weekend. Then all hell will break loose. I'm her godfather and love her to pieces, but God, that girl's a whirlwind."

Ike tosses my bag in to the back hatch and walks around the vehicle to open my door, he hesitates before asking, "You're here to stay? Right?" He points to my luggage. "That's an awful little bag. The rest of your things….are being shipped?"

"Ummmm……no."

His eyes shoot daggers at me. "What do you mean; no?"

"I'm just here through the weekend. I have to go back after the Thanksgiving break."

"What!....... oh, no way, you have to stay or you're taking him with you. We can't take anymore of him mooning about, snapping everyone's head off."

"Ah……we haven't worked out the details yet. I want to finish out the school year. And I was hoping for us to slowly transition into each other's lives." I shrug my shoulders as I click the seat belt in place. "Go back and forth for a while……...?"

"Shit..." The expletive hangs in the air as he climbs into the driver's seat and throws the car into gear. Tires screech as he guns the accelerator, the force throws me back onto the seat as he executes a U-turn on the tarmac. Abruptly he signals and pulls onto the highway. His hands are white knuckled as he grips the wheel. He seems angry. So much for him liking me…..and I think I have whiplash.

There's silence in the car as Ike concentrates on driving the curving road as it twists and turns through canyons and mountain passes. I sit quietly, chewing on my thumbnail, dying to ask a thousand questions. Finally I break the ice, slowly asking…… "So how is he?"

Ike shrugs, "What do you mean?"

"Aside from all the mooning around business, is he okay?"

"Never been healthier, never looked better, never had so much money." He looks at me suspiciously. "You aren't one of them gold diggers, are you?"

"Good God, no!" I retort indignantly.

"Only teasing." Ike's head doesn't turn, but the corner of his mouth twitches up ever so slightly.

Whew "I just need time, to get to know him again, it's……been awhile. You've lived with him for years. Maybe you can help me understand him."

"I'm sorry. I didn't mean to bite your head off, not much of a welcome." Ike's voice softens. "Vic and I, we go way back…we watch out for each other, so when I see him upset, it bothers me." He looks over at me and grins ruefully. "And I haven't seen him this worked up over a woman; in I can't remember when, I just don't want him to get hurt." He pats my knee, and for a fleeting second, his amber eyes burn into mine. "He needs you, Ellen. That's all you need to know."

I nod. No one can answer my questions but Vic. But Ike says *he loves me*…and for now that's enough.

We drive for a while without speaking; golden hills punctuated with green trees sprawl out into the distance on either side of us. At length Ike turns on the radio. The Beach Boys are playing "California Girl"…how appropriate, California girls are more *fun* than east coast girls…*great*…and as we zip along with sunlight glinting off the windshield, I suddenly feel like we're in another country and for me another life.

The drive seems endless and my excitement grows with each passing mile, finally the gate to the ranch comes into view. Pulling down the visor mirror, I check my makeup, add a touch of lip gloss and fluff my hair to look deceptively casual. Not exactly cover girl material, but not ready for AARP either, I'll look spectacular in candlelight.

My "she's too hot for me, mama" pink nail polish

peeks out of open toe sandals with three inch heels. The tight skinny jeans have spandex, clinging in just the right places. A slinky red sweater with a push up bra…......bottom line….this is as good as it gets.

My heart's hammering in my chest. I feel faint, either overcome with desire or nerves. I'm not sure which one. With maddening slowness, we pull in front of the massive wooden doors leading into the house. And I see Vic… standing silhouetted in the doorway…looking impossibly handsome in a white linen shirt half tucked into jeans that hug his hips like a second skin, bare feet, hair tousled, just on the edge of disheveled…God, he looks good. A wave of longing hits me like a punch in the gut, and I realize how much, how very much I've missed him…

I fling open the door, and sprint up the steps before Ike comes to a complete stop.

"Dang it, woman!" I hear Ike yell, the car skidding to a halt. "You're going to kill yourself."

I run through the entrance and jump onto Vic, wrapping my legs around his waist. In one swift movement his hands cup my butt, lifting me, and as my arms cling to his neck, he slowly whirls me around and around, his lips searing my skin with desire. All the pent up frustration of the past ten weeks lies forgotten in the wild spontaneity of our reunion. Between kisses, he breathes, "Elle, Elle," touching my lips, neck, eyes, ears, anointing me in his love.

The scent of him is turning me inside out. We stumble into the hallway of the empty house, laughing and kissing, gasping for breath in a state of unbridled passion. His hands slides under my sweater and my fingers fumble with the buttons on his shirt feeling the hard ridge of muscle beneath my hand. With one deft movement he pulls the sweater over my head and releases my bra. The sweater falls in a jumble to the floor. He slowly spins us around in small circles, my hair forming a shimmering veil down my back in the dim light. The warmth of his skin on my breasts causes my nipples to tighten and tingle, my mouth peppers his face, neck and shoulders, tasting and devouring every inch of him.

"Vic, what about Bridget, shouldn't we…um…..go somewhere more private?"

"Gave her the afternoon off, she and Hank went to town for a movie." His kisses trail down the side of my neck.

"Oh, I've missed you so much." I brush back his dark hair, basking in the glow from his eyes. "But what about Ike?"

"Missed you more," And not missing a beat, he continues, "Ike plans to spend the evening in his apartment out in the barn; there's some Canadian hockey game he wants to watch." He stops the slow turning to kiss me. His clever hands run up my body, I'm weightless, floating above the ground. He is so close I feel every part of him, pressed against me.

"I can't believe it's been ten weeks." His warm breath trails down my throat to dwell in the curve above my breasts. "I've waited so long for you, I was going crazy." He buries his face in my hair, "I missed the smell of your hair, the sound of your voice, your cute little butt."

He laughs, giving my ass a squeeze.

"I know," I caress his cheek. "Just hold me, promise you won't let me go. For the next nine days, I'm going to eat, sleep, and do other *naughty* things in your arms. We'll be attached at the hip."

"Maybe we should investigate those possibilities in

the bedroom, or I'll just take you here on the floor." He threatens. I grind my hips into his torso; his body stiffens as he groans in my ear. "Bring on the naughty; and I especially like the attached at the hip part."

"Look how long your hair is," I lean back in his arms, tucking a stray lock behind his ear. "Very warrior like." I pull the silky length into a ponytail. "Can I tie it back with a leather thong? Mmm, very sexy. I've never been ravaged by a warrior."

"It was for the movie, it fit the character. I left it for you to see. I thought you could help me cut it."

"I don't know." I'm intrigued with the idea of the sun bronzed warrior returning from a successful campaign, the fair maiden clutched to his chest as the spoils of war, astride his battle hardened stallion. "Let's leave it long for a while." I push the hair away from his neck finding the sweet spot on his collarbone with my tongue. Dark, deep, chocolate, with a hint of bourbon, some things get better with age.

Then to our shock and horror, comes..."Mr. Vic, when Ms. Ellen arrives, just to let you know, dinner is in the refrigggggg……..." The whirling dervish known as Bridget comes flying around the corner. "Oh, my good Lord! Would you look at the two of you! Can you not wait until ye get into a bedroom, and protect the rest of us from your philandering ways?" Bridget shrieks, throwing her hands up in the air. *Shit.* That woman has got to slow down. She stops frozen in shock at the sight of Vic and I entwined, half naked in the foyer.

"Hello, Bridget." I call out to her, my laughter muffled against Vic's shoulder. "How are you?"

"Oh, just wonderful, Ms. Ellen," she says, her voice laden with sarcasm, standing with her hands on her hips shaking her head. "Welcome back, it's good to see you…..I just don't need to see as much of you as I do at this moment." She makes a harrumphing noise in her throat. "I'll leave the two of you…to whatever. Food is in the kitchen, help yourselves. Hank and I are leaving…….after I scrub out me eyeballs." She calls, vanishing toward the back of the house, the heels of her shoes making disapproving clicks on the tile floor. The sound of her voice trailing behind her, "Saints preserve us, the way the two of them go at it, tis worse than a band of horny monkeys, titch."

We dissolve into laughter. "I think we had better move this party upstairs." Vic chuckles against my hair.

"Horny monkeys."

And the laughter starts again. I cradle his face in my hands, "Hey, take this monkey upstairs." And as he carries me up the stairs, two at a time, being in his arms, in this house, feels right………like I've come home.

…

It was one of those days, Thanksgiving morning dawned cold and rainy. A day to start with muffins, fresh from the oven, coffee, strong and hot, laced with Irish crème. A lazy day spent curled up by the television watching the Thanksgiving Day Parade, cheering when Santa dressed in royal red comes waving down Fifth Avenue. With the muffins and coffee in hand, Vic and I planned a long morning on the couch, playing peek-a-boo under each other's clothing during commercial breaks.

But no. Bridget fully recovered from the shock of seeing my nearly naked body……insisted I help her cook the Thanksgiving dinner. Complete with *all* the trimmings. *What?* Somehow she decided my cooking skills or lack thereof, to be a disability and rehabilitation started this morning. *rats*

So instead of a morning lounging on the couch, Hanna and I spent the day slaving away in the kitchen. I mean, a Stoffer's turkey dinner and a bag salad, constituted Thanksgiving in my house.

The holiday season is off to a shaky start, missing the first official viewing of Santa is unheard of in my world ....and I *hate* to miss a good game of peek-a-boo.

The table groans under the weight of our efforts, yet after all the work to prepare the meal, I'm left with no appetite. In fact, the sight of the table laden with food makes me nauseous. Ordinarily, I have an excellent appetite and I'm seldom fussy about what I eat. Maybe that's why I don't cook; all that energy goes into making food and not enough left to eat it.

After the last piece of pumpkin pie disappears, Bridget refuses to allow anyone help with the dishes. She didn't want anyone mucking up her kitchen. She and Hank have plans to go over to a friend's house for the evening and she has no time for amateurs getting in her way. *Thank God.* Surviving a day with Bridget has formed a common bond between Hanna and me, a shaky truce at best, but a start.

Vic and Ike are sprawled out on the sofa, beer in hand, enjoying a friendly argument over a football game on television. Ike stands up and points his beer bottle at Vic saying, "I don't care how long your hair is or how dark your skin is, you ain't no Indian. And you don't know shit, sorry Hanna, about the Washington Red Skins. I've got the stats on my computer, I'll be back to prove you wrong." He turns to leave the room. Vic signs the letter L over his forehead at Ike's retreating back.

"I saw that, and just for that you can get your own

beer. Who's the loser now?" He sets his beer bottle down, and holding up his hand, he rubs his fingers together, "Want to put a little money where your mouth is, Kemosabee?"

"You're on." Vic calls out to him. "I know I'm right…looooser! Detroit's going to win anyway."

Outside a cold autumn rain slashes against the windowpanes, a fire in the hearth crackles in the background. As I rest my head in the curve of Vic's shoulder, I can't keep my eyes open. I'm exhausted for some reason, a morning with Bridget? And then I feel a slow tightening across my abdomen….*You have got to be kidding me!* Of all the luck, my weekend with Vic and I have my period. Racking my brain, I can't remember the last time I've had one, my cycle's been very erratic to nonexistent the past few years, and irregular is the new norm at my age. I stopped worrying about it, *ouch,* didn't miss the cramps. I squirm in an attempt to get comfortable. Maybe I should take something for the pain.

"What's the matter, love?" Vic asks in a drowsy post-thanksgiving dinner voice. "You're squirming like a two year old. Can't get comfortable?" He pulls me closer, even a game of peek-a-boo doesn't sound fun.

"No," I reply, grimacing. "Maybe I'll go change into something more comfortable."

"Sure, Vic says, giving my butt a little swat as I gingerly stand up.

"Ohhh," I groan as another cramp rips my belly.

"Elle, What is it?" Vic sits up, his face creased with concern. "Sweetheart, what's wrong?"

"I…I don't know." I gasp; this is not ordinary cramps. I sink back onto the couch feeling a rush of blood seeping between my legs. I'm bleeding…really bleeding. Oh Lord, what's happening?

Vic's face goes pale beneath his swarthy skin, his eyes blink rapidly as he watches the growing circle of blood seeping into the couch. "Elle," his breath coming in gasps as panic seizes him "Oh my God, Elle." He stands bewitched by the sight of the blood. "Hanna! Ike, call 911!"

Call 911! Let's not get crazy here, hospitals are for sick people, it's just a period. Really. And there's no way I'm going to the hospital because……even in the grips of pain, I recall in horror, I put on pair of Betty Boop underpants as a joke this morning. No ER team is going to see me in Betty Boop underpants…I vaguely remember my mother warning me to wear clean underwear, what if you get in an car accident. Great, I'm in an accident and I'm wearing Betty Boop…….. and I think there's a hole in the crotch. I can just see the tabloids now; *Esteban Diago's current lover comes to the ER wearing Betty Boop underwear. Kinky*…then another cramp hits and I don't care if I'm wearing Bozo the Clown panties and a matching red nose……

I hear Hanna cry out as she comes running in from the kitchen. "Dad, *Oh, my God*, what's happening to her?" Hanna grabs Vic by the arm and shakes him. But Vic is frozen in terror. His eyes fixated on me.

"Dad, Dad!" Hanna screams in panic. I see Vic start, like he's been slapped in the face.

"Hanna, where's Ike?" Vic looks to the back of the house in desperation. "We have to get her to the hospital."

"I don't know where he went, I don't know," she says in a quavering voice. "What should we do?" She starts crying.

Vic grabs her by the shoulders, "Hanna, don't freak out on me now. Run down to the barn and find Ike. Tell him to bring the Land Rover to the front door."

He pushes her toward the stable. "You can do this, hurry. Toss me that blanket on your way out." Vic points to a fleece throw hanging over the back of an arm chair. With her lower lip clenched between her teeth, Hanna nods and tosses the blanket in Vic's direction as she races out of the room.

He squats down next to me on the couch. "Elle, what can I do for you?"

Through the haze of pain, I look him straight in the eye. "A shot of bourbon and a beer." A weak attempt at a joke.

"Not funny!"

"I don't know." I say, taking a deep breath. "I'm so sorry for being such a bother, but I think I need a doctor." I hasten to add, "I'm sure it's just some female thing, I've heard of something like this happening to women." But why am I bleeding so much? *Oh no*….a sudden horrible suspicion enters my mind……..tell me I'm not this stupid………why does that seem to be my mantra. I try counting back to my last period…….it's not possible, I can't be pregnant…. I'm like old…… in menopause……..or so I thought.

Vic brushes the hair back from my face. "I'll call the hospital and alert them that we are on our way and see if they have any instructions for us." He gently lifts me, slipping the blanket underneath. "It's okay, mia." Vic gives my arm a reassuring squeeze, though his face is clenched in fear. "We can do this, we'll do it together."

…

I don't remember much of the drive to the small community hospital. I feel Vic's arms holding me tight as he rocks back and forth, saying over and over, "It will be okay, it will be okay." Echoed by Ike from the driver's seat saying, "She's going to be fine, man. We'll get her to the hospital in record time."

At one point I glance up to see Hanna, turned in the front seat watching us, her eyes huge in her pale face. I give her a reassuring smile, touched by her concern for me……or more likely she's terrified at the speed Ike's negotiating the curving mountain roads. Through pouring rain, slick roads, and tortuous turns, Ike drives swiftly and competently down the canyon road. Vic mentioned he drove stock cars many years ago, if this drive is any indication of his ability….. Jeff Gordon, move over.

As we pull up to the hospital, I'm suddenly surrounded by bright lights, and people yelling directions. Vic lays me on a gurney, and then everything goes black.

…

Oww….I wake up, groggy, disoriented, not knowing where I am. Is it morning yet? I feel so rough. What happened? I try to sit up and feel a dull pain in my abdomen, ugh….the cramps are still there.

With a huge effort I open my eyes and see I'm lying in a dim room on a hospital bed. There's a panel of buttons to my right, and a bunch of flowers, black-eyed Susans to be exact, on the nightstand.

With an inward gulp, I see an IV needle taped to my right hand. Boy, I've had bad cramps before, but these were doozies. This is unreal. I'm in a hospital.

Trying to sit up, I give a little moan and see Vic asleep, half sitting in a chair, half slumped over the bed, one hand clutching my leg.

"Hello?" I call out feebly. My voice sounds dry and raspy. His eyes fly open at the sound.

"Hey," he says, running a hand over a two day stubble of beard growth. "How are you?"

"I don't know, you tell me." I say, wiggling to get more comfortable, he leans over to help me to sit up.

Taking a small step back from the bed, he looks at me, shaking his head, his face a mask of sorrow, two small tears roll down his cheek. I can't help thinking, *what?!* Am I dying…is it cancer…some rare incurable disease. Tell me….!

"Elle," He starts to speak, then looks away, struggling to maintain his composure, his lips clenched to hold back the grief. His voice wavers as he speaks, "You had a miscarriage, Elle."

"*What!*"

He says in a barely audible whisper. "You had a miscarriage and I was too fucking stupid to realize what was happening to you. I lost the last baby……and I lost this one too." He rocks back on his feet, rubbing the heel of his palms into his eyes as his fingers clutch his hair. "Why can't I protect you? Why is it every time I am with you, everything gets so screwed up. Here we are again, the same story. What is wrong with us?" His voice a tormented rasp, tears flow down his face, he hastily wipes them away, but the pain is etched on his face.

"No," I whisper. "It can't be possible." I'm stunned with shock.

"Why didn't you tell me you were pregnant?"

Oh my God, How could I be *so* stupid? I feel like someone gut punched me, and then threw me into a vat of ice-cold water. A miscarriage, this can't be possible.

"Vic, there must be some mistake." I shake my head

in disbelief. "There is no way I was pregnant. They told me years ago, there would be no more children, something to do with a mild form of endometriosis. I barely have a period anymore. Jack wanted a large Irish family and it was a miracle we had two children. They must be wrong."

"You had a D&C, *quierda*,," he gently tucks a lock of hair behind my ear, giving me a tender kiss on the forehead. "The doctor said the baby was about twelve weeks old. The timing fits the last time we were together. Elle, we conceived another child." He gives a weak laugh and shakes his head. "Remember Bridget's comment about the horny monkeys?" He bites his lower lip, rolling his eyes. "We'd fill an entire zoo with them. It seems every time I touch you……" His voice turns bitter. "And we never get to keep our babies." He walks to the window, and stands with hands on his hips, chest heaving in anger. "Son of a bitch."

My head is whirling; I can't believe it. A baby? Pregnant again? I'm like…..*old*. Boy, talk about miracles….or not.

Vic turns to me, holding up his hands in consolation. "I know this doesn't help, but the doctor said it was probably a good thing you lost the baby. At your age, it would have been difficult to carry the baby to term and there's a very high risk of birth defects."

I feel the creeping tendrils of depression and loss curl through my gut. At my age, I really don't want another child, but the thought of losing a baby is crushing. Tears flow down my face, deep sobs rack my body. All the anguish of losing our first child comes back with a stabbing pain. I feel the bed compress under the weight of his body as he lies down, gathering me close to the warmth and safety of his arms.

"I'm sorry, Ella, my bella, bella," his lips brush tenderly against my hair. "I'm so sorry, darling."

"Vic," I reach my hand up to caress the beard stubble covering his face, only enhancing his rugged beauty.

"Yes, love," he answers his voice gravelly with fatigue.

"I want my baby."

"I know, sweetheart," he leans into me, sighing. "I'll be honest; the thought of having a child never crossed my mind. I just assumed we were beyond that stage in our lives. You had said you were no longer….you know…. So we were careless." He shakes his head.

"No, Vic…"

"You want to try again?" He rolls onto his elbow peering intently into my eyes. "I'll be honest, mia," he caresses my face. "I think it's too risky, I'm terrified of losing you."

"Vic," I touch his lips with my finger, stopping the torrent of words, smoothing back the long lank of hair tied back with a strip of leather, I never did cut his hair this weekend. I sigh; a wistful smile plays across my face. I pull his face down to brush his lips with a whisper of a kiss. "No, I want our son."

"Our son?" He questions, a confused expression on his face.

"Yes, our son, the one who was taken away from us."

"I thought you tried to find him."

"I did, but my resources were limited, and Jack wasn't keen on finding another man's baby. Jack's philosophy on life; what's done is done, move on, live in the moment." I look out the window, and muse, "As much as I tried to forget, sometimes…when Jack was away flying, the house all quiet and lonely, the thoughts and the wondering came. Did his adoptive parents tuck him in at night, read stories, take him on walks in the woods; did he play soccer or love baseball? I tortured myself with doubt. Did they love him?"

Vic blows out a sigh. "I understand your feelings," he says, leaning back on the pillow. "Shit, I was a mess over the whole thing," he says, shaking his head.

"I think Jack was jealous of you." I say with a sniff. "He claimed a piece of my heart belonged to you and that drove him crazy." I take a deep breath. "He once used that as an excuse for his affairs, that I never stopped loving another man." I caress his arm that lay slung over my hip. "I did love him, maybe in a different way, but he never let me talk about you or the baby."

"They say you never forget your first love." Vic murmurs softly. "I never have, she always lingered at the fringes of my mind." The weak morning sun filters through the diaphanous curtains blurring the outline of trees bordering the hospital grounds.

"I know this sounds crazy, but Vic, could we…hire a private investigator to find our son?"

He nods, thinking. "No, it doesn't sound crazy at all, in fact, it sounds sane……. very sane."

As I drift off to sleep, the oddest thought floats through my mind, whatever happened to the Betty Boop underpants? Are they stashed with my clothes or hopefully, a little pile of ash in the hospital incinerator? After all this and I'm worrying about what I was wearing…..that's called female resilience.

Chapter 36

Lost and Found

Seated behind a mahogany desk in one of the most prestigious law firms of New York City, Tee looks good; maturing into her vision of the tall, sophisticated, beautiful executive. The view from her office overlooks the Manhattan skyline. Leaning back in a leather chair that costs more than my car, her appearance exudes poise and confidence. At ease in the corporate world, secure in her stature earned by hard work and a dogged determination to succeed. Vestiges of the gangly teenage girl from Camp High Point, in pressed pink shorts and button down shirts, vanquished into a polished professional woman. She graduated at the top of her class from Cornell Law School, never married and dates infrequently. As Lani's godmother, she dotes on my children, insisting they call her, Auntie Tee. At birthdays and holidays, she satisfies her maternal urges through extravagant gifts and afternoon outings …..with returnable children.

Over lunch a few months ago, after a glass of wine…or two, I confided in her that the search for our son had reached a dead end. The adoption laws years ago protected the adoptive parents not the birth parents. The records were sealed. As one of my closest friends during the emotional turmoil of losing Vic and the baby, Tee understood my frustration. She listened with a sympathetic ear, nodding as I filled her in on the details. I turned to her, hoping for a loophole, were there any legal paths for us to pursue, do birth parents have rights?

Tee suggested before we start legal proceedings to contact the private detective employed by her law firm. She assured me the man was tenacious at ferreting out information. The firm used him exclusively due to his high rate of success. But he was very expensive.

With a little luck and good timing, I hired Richard Harsonge on retainer…and not only was he expensive…..he was *very* expensive. Even Vic's eyes widened at the cost. No Jimmy Choo shoes for me.

And finally, one night about a week ago, as Vic and I relaxed in front of the fireplace at the ranch, the phone rang. It was Harsonge, informing us he obtained the requested information. He refused to go over his findings on the phone, suggesting an appointment be made with Tee in New York City. A copy of his investigation would be forwarded to the Manhattan office by courier. In addition, he proposed we allow Tee to open the paperwork, and review the contents from a legal perspective before our meeting.

Since the phone call, Vic and I can't eat, can't sleep and had our first fight. Over what flavor of ice cream to buy! We're going nuts. He started running, I stopped eating, I lost three pounds, he lost five……..except he lost the weight off his stomach, I lost it off my boobs……life isn't fair.

At last the day arrives and Tee ushers us into her office wearing her professional lawyer demeanor, all business until she relaxes back in her chair, a barely suppressed smile on her face, eyes twinkling with eager anticipation.

I take one look at the file on her desk and want to launch myself at it. Vic must have read my mind because he places a restraining hand on my arm.

"Actually, if you want to wait, we can do this some…other time?" She says, pointing to the file with a nonchalant air, a puckish grin on her face. "Hey, I heard of this new bistro on 25th, what about lunch first?"

"Tee, I love you, but if you don't open that immediately," I say, between clenched teeth. "I may have to kill you."

Vic puts both hands on the desk, looks her in the eye and growls, "Tell us for Christ sake!"

"Sorry," she says, looking contrite, "I'm just so excited, I don't know where to start."

"Teeee," Vic says, his voice raising an octave.

"Are you ready?"

"Yes!" We shout in unison.

"Okay, here we go," she opens the file, arranges the papers to her satisfaction, picks up a pair of reading glasses, and begins………she's either going to break my heart or make my life complete in the next few minutes. "Richard Harsonge delivered this to me a few days ago." She places a protective hand over the paperwork. "I did review the information, as requested from a legal stand point. I know how important this is to you."

I cast a worried glance at Vic, and he gives my hand a reassuring squeeze. Our lives and the life of our son forever changed based on some papers in an envelope; just a small thin envelope. Would he want to see us? How will our children react to a half-brother? Will the adoption parents feel threatened? Should the past have remained buried? A litany of doubts plays in my head, I'm clenching Vic's hand so tight; my nails dig into the soft flesh of his palm. A wave of anxiety sweeps over me. So many years of asking…where are you? Do they love you? Emotion overwhelms me, a sob escapes my throat.

Vic glances nervously at me. "*Mia,* are you all right? We said we wanted this no matter what." I mutely nod. Taking a deep breath he gives Tee the nod to proceed

"Ellen, relax, I'm happy to report, it's all good news." Tee's face finally breaks into a grin as she holds out the first sheet of paper. "We've waited a long time to find this baby. And now here he is…a fully grown man."

Did she say a man? I've always thought of him as a baby, a little boy. A surreal feeling washes over me.

"Joshua Westland," she looks up, tucking a lock of sleekly coifed hair behind her ear. "Your son's name is Joshua Westland. Ironically, he lives near Old Forge in the Adirondacks." Tee says with a glimmer of mischief in her eyes. "Not far from where he was conceived." She wiggles a finger at us, a goofy grin on her face. "Yes?" Sometimes……Tee's sense of timing is not the best, her comments occasionally off the mark, creating awkward moments, like now. She stops short at the look on our faces. "Okay then……to continue on," She reverts back to her professional demeanor, "He's a biology teacher at Blue Mountain High School. In addition to his teaching duties, he heads up the ecology and photography clubs at school. *Hmmmmm.*" She taps the side of her face with a finger. "I wonder how he inherited those talents. His adoptive father is a civil engineer, working for the Army Corp of Engineers. Together he and his wife ran Westland's Canoe Outfitters in Old Forge. They are avid backpackers and members of the family compete in the Adirondack Canoe Classic held every September."

I vaguely remember hearing about the ADK Canoe Classic, it's some ninety mile race held over a three day period in September. One of Jack's nephews competed in it a few years back. Vic and I dare not look at each other for fear of breaking this spell of good fortune. The grip I have on his hand is crushing.

"He is married," she looks up removing her glasses, and smiles. "This is the best part. He has two children." She gushes, "A girl named Isabella, who they call Izzy, she is five and the little boy just turned three, his name is Ansel, like the photographer." Tee pauses for dramatic effect, with a flourish of her hands, she announces. "You're grandparents! Get it, Grandma and Grandpa!"

I'm stunned. I look at Vic shaking my head, not comprehending this information. A son……and two grandchildren magically appear and most likely a daughter-in-law too. We never thought any farther than finding our son, the fact our child was close to thirty, and married with children never occurred to us. It's quite feasible and logical; we're just unprepared for this bounty of blessings. Vic releases my hand, leans back, rapidly blinking in an effort to control the deep well of emotion breaking to the surface from a core of hurt and misplaced guilt. He hurriedly wipes a tear from his eye, while I unabashedly weep. This can't be happening. Am I dreaming? For good measure I pinch my arm, this is reality, we've found our son. It's true. The puzzle pieces from the past, fall into place, and fit so perfectly.

"Tee," Vic pauses in askance. "How can we be sure this is our son? The paper trail for finding adopted children is often vague and full of speculation, not facts. Without a DNA test, how can we be positive Joshua is our son?"

Not saying a word, a small secretive smile plays across her face as Tee reaches into the envelope and removes a photograph. Slowly and deliberately she pushes it toward us. In a quiet voice she asks, "What do you think?"

I stare at the image of our son on her desk, as the air is sucked from my lungs.

"Sweet Jesus!" I hear Vic expel, leaping up to get a closer look at the picture on the desk. "It can't be; it just can't be." Oh, but it is……there smiling up at us from the glossy eight by ten photo is a picture of our son, looking slightly older than Vic when I met him the summer of my seventeenth year. The face is Vic, the square lean jaw accented by chiseled cheekbones, the same tousled dark hair…….and the eyes…….. deep with amber lights of gold. No denying whose son this is…and no need for DNA testing.

A cold clammy sweat breaks out over my body. My heart's racing, and those little stars that dance in front of your eyes before passing out, are twinkling and whirling in the foreground. The room spins and fades before going dark. And for someone who has never fainted before, this is twice in six months……thank God for strong arms to fall into………but as I go down I take out Tee's prized Oak Wood Country Club Tennis Award of 2005……….Vic catches me…… but the trophy falls and shatters into pieces………..it was made of Swarovsky crystal. *Oh boy……..*

Chapter 37

It's Just Hormones

Once recovered from the shock of finding Josh, the reality of contacting him occupied long discussions into the night. I wanted to jump on the first plane and throw myself on his doorstep as his long, lost mother. Vic on the other hand, cynical from many years of celebrity status suggested we proceed slowly, showing up on his doorstep announcing ourselves as Mom and Dad seemed radical and preposterous. And he cautioned, while Josh may be our son, we don't know anything about him. We need to protect ourselves. As far as we know, he never tried finding us; maybe he has no interest in meeting his biological parents.

In the end, we opted for a plan that will give us time to acquaint ourselves with him from a distance, let him meet us as people before introducing the fact we're his parents. And pray he doesn't think we're creepy stalkers.

We contacted a real estate agent in the Old Forge area inquiring about rental property. The owners of the camp called it Camp Sky Haven. We called it perfect for our needs. The camp was forty-five minutes outside of Old Forge, located within close proximity of the town but far enough away for privacy.

We rented Sky Haven from May through September. The camp overlooks a private lake with a gargantuan kitchen, four bedrooms, multiple porches, balconies, a boat house with an antique Chris Craft boat, a canoe, two kayaks and the lake comes with a licensed pilot on call for the….*seaplane*………*with pontoons! A fricking Seaplane!*

The camp, new by Adirondack standards was constructed 50 years ago in the tradition of the Great Camps. As much as I loved the mystic of renting an older historic camp, the reality of drafty rooms, erratic electrical service and limited communication lines enticed us to rent a modern version of a Great Camp. Face it, I'm all for going nature girl. Give me a backpack, some stout hiking boots and let's head for the back country. Otherwise, a hot shower, down feather beds and a fully stocked refrigerator set the standard. I believe the hand lettered sign over my bed reads, *Former Purist……gone soft.*

Well off the main road, nestled in a forest of balsam fir, the house sits on a small rise facing the mountain lake. The two-story timber frame lodge was built using logs and indigenous stone work from the local area. A shingled roof with broad overhangs covers multiple porches. A large expanse of windows overlooks a shoreline bordered with mountain laurel, alder and clumps of willow. Loons call out over the water at dusk and dawn, and the wings of osprey flash as they dive for fish in the afternoon sun.

Ferns and shade loving plants landscape the gardens surrounding the house while the decks boast a mixture of Adirondack chairs and tables built from twisted twigs and branches.

The kitchen is a gourmet cook's paradise; at least, I think it is…I don't recognize half of the appliances or culinary gadgets in there…sooo, it could be a hardware store for all I know.

Holding a steaming mug of coffee, I lean against the porch railing watching the sun rise over the lake. Beams of golden light glitter through the trees, the riparian plants growing along the water's edge glisten in the morning sun. The month of May in the mountains is a time of rebirth after the long Adirondack winters.

My recovery from the miscarriage in November was neither swift nor easy. There are reasons women in their forties don't get pregnant…our bodies suck at it…..it's kind of been there….done that…..and *not* going there again. So exhausted and emotionally spent, I've taken a leave of absence from my job at school and moved myself into Camp Sky Haven. Standing on the balcony overlooking the lake, breathing in the crisp spring air, I'm reminded of the tuberculosis patients at the turn of the century coming to the Adirondacks in hopes of finding a cure. The mountains hold a healing power.

And while renting a camp in the mountains for an entire summer may seem drastic, the idea involves us moving into the Old Forge area and becoming part of the community. Actually, I become part of the community. After Vic's last movie, half the magazine covers in America carry his picture. And despite the fact he had plastic surgery after the motorcycle accident years ago, the resemblance between Vic and our son remains astonishing. He needs to stay undercover…..for a while. With my leave of absence from school, I have time to walk the dog through town, join in on town events, and volunteer for a committee or two.

Hence, the idea of renting a house, where I can live full time, instill myself in town while getting acquainted with Josh and his family. Vic will commute back and forth depending on his schedule.

Due to a PR event in Miami, Vic left camp this morning at first light on the seaplane. Pressing business, his publicist said, it couldn't wait. *Really?* Florida, the font of unlimited sun, oceans of retired people, mecca of the early bird special…can't wait. Since when is anything pressing in Florida, I once saw a gopher tortoise beat an old lady riding a three wheel bike across the road. If they have anything…..it's time…..they can wait. I miss him already. *Selfish.*

Setting the mug on the railing, I inhale deeply raising my arms in a yoga stretch, enjoying the luxury of the serene mountain morning. A sense of peace and contentment pervades my body. Alone in the mountains. Tranquility, until a wet nose followed by a thumping tail nearly knocks me over. About a year ago, my children suggested, Jack's parents insisted, and finally, the family took matters into their own hands….and bought me a dog. A big scruffy tri-colored collie named Cyrus. After Jack's death, everyone decided I was spending too much time alone. Trey involved in school and sports, Lani on the West Coast, I needed companionship. No one gave me credit for having a life of my own. And none of us bargained on Cyrus. Seventy-five pounds of boundless energy, unfettered by the multiple dog obedience classes we attended. The last one asked us to leave after Cyrus tried humping a Pekinese. It was like trying to wedge a compact car under a moving semi-truck. As the instructor pointed to the door, she suggested tranquilizers, I wasn't sure if she meant for me or the dog.

Cyrus entertains himself by galloping from one end of the house to the other, the black, tan and white of his fur a blur as he whirls down the hall and around the kitchen counter. And he loves the water, collies historically hate being wet, a holdover from generations of tending sheep in the cold soggy fields of Scotland. But Cyrus thinks he's part Labrador retriever and he's part of our plan to connect with Josh. No one can resist him.

...

After all of my initial doubts over Vic's fidelity, he's proven he wants a permanent relationship, and I'm the one hesitating…the entire lifestyle of the rich and gorgeous is foreign to me. While the beautiful homes, lovely restaurants and designer clothes complemented by a boat load of money is nice, this way of life feels extravagant to my middle class upbringing. I'm uneasy with the fans clamoring for autographs, his extended time away; coupled with the lack of privacy…I find the whole thing a bit disconcerting. Even the simplest of outings require careful planning and a constant need to be on alert.

I'm unnerved by the fact he carries a handgun when away from security and bodyguards. The price of fame puts you in the public eye, making you vulnerable to unsavory individuals. After our brush with the muggers on the beach that first night, he vowed he'd never be defenseless again. He and Ike have pistol permits and are excellent marksmen. He thinks I need a gun. Is he *nuts?!* I can barely walk straight let alone shoot a gun. I'd be menace to society.

Luckily for us, we are content with simple dinners at home with friends or family. Long walks in the woods, overnight trail rides with the horses, or paddling the canoe on the lakes and streams bordering his ranch.

Limbo, that old left over term from Catholic school days, describes my feelings…I'm between…my old life as wife, mother and teacher no longer seems to fit…yet it's hard to move across the country, away from all that is familiar.

I love him but can I step into the abyss of his waiting arms, trusting our love is enough. Transition…….life changes, ever shifting, never staying constant. It's part of the journey. For me, this time in the mountains is a chance to rest, reconnect with the past, while moving forward to create a new future. And seriously, am I crazy? I'm in love with a hot guy who worships the ground I walk on, and just for kicks…….throw in a wealthy lifestyle. I chide myself…stop being cautious Ellen…take a leap of faith.

Musing, I take a sip of coffee feeling the warmth infuse my body through the damp morning chill. I hug Vic's flannel shirt closer, the smell of him lingers, my favorite perfume…….an earthy spicy scent evocative of man. Aside from the wool socks and his shirt, I'm basically naked. Another lifestyle change…I *always* wore clothes.

Before first light, Vic greeted the seaplane pilot, reviewed the departure details, and then closed the door in the surprised pilot's face to say his good-bye in private. Pinned against the wall, he kissed me, when he was done I looked myself over to make sure the few clothes I had on were still intact. The kiss sizzled all the way down to my toes. I thought my socks self-combusted.

Nine months we've been together, well actually, it's only four months, we were apart most of September through November, no sex during the recovery after my miscarriage, then in January I resumed my teaching job for a few weeks to tie up loose ends…….so it's only been a few months. So, we're still on our honeymoon, which explains the lust……I blow out a sigh and look heavenward. No doubt about it, I'm a slut, a selective slut. But I think, technically, to be a slut you have to be doing it with more than one guy…..so actually, I'm just addicted... And the lustful object of my addiction….. is six-three, has ebony hair, dark gorgeous eyes, broad shoulders, narrow waist, skin the color of cafe au latte, and his name.......*Vicente*. "Who could blame me, seriously, its hormones," I say to the loons passing on the lake. "It's not my fault. I have too many hormones....and way too little restraint."

With a start and a shake of my head, I realize the coffee in my mug has grown cold and the morning is slipping away. While my mind is lost in the glow of last night, the reality of today sends me into Old Forge, time to start learning the community. First stop, the hardware store in town to pick up a copy of the Old Forge Times. The local newspaper is a gem of information about happenings in the area, along with recipes, restaurant reviews and tips for the best fishing spots. Check out the want ads, maybe a job...I could be a tour guide, work in a gift shop, maybe a short order cook... okay, now that's just ridiculous.

Chapter 38

A Paddle Down the River

Old Forge remained a sleepy mountain hamlet until an influx of snowmobiles in the winter coupled with summer money turned this quiet town into a tourist mecca. The shop lined streets boast gifts from whirly-gig lawn ornaments to costly hand-hewn Adirondack furniture. Bars, restaurants and taverns stand poised to meet the needs of the most finicky palate. Diners can find a burger and beer at the blue-sided Landmark overlooking the water to a posh meal from "The Inn at Three Corners" serving lobster ravioli with a wine bar. A traditional start to the day begins at Locke's Diner on the outskirts of town, where a photo display of Adirondack wildlife is offered along with maple syrup on your stack of pancakes.

When mountain temperatures soar above the necessity of flannel shirts and wool socks, the parking lot at the water slide park is filled to capacity with the happy shouts of water enthusiasts.

A ride on the ski lift at McCauley Mountain presents a panoramic view of the surrounding mountains and lakes. If one is of the athletic persuasion, the area is rich in hiking/biking paths and canoe routes.

I love the Adirondacks, all my favorite activities wrapped up in the largest state park in the country and where I found Vic. Yummmm……my favorite flavor of the mountains. That reminds me, I'm hungry. The question remains, do I want…pancakes….eggs… muffins… waffles…. or a cappuccino. I want them all.

After a quick stop at the hardware store to pick up the newspaper, I stroll down the street, enjoying the preseason quiet. I left Cyrus at home, wanting to explore the village, without his exuberant approach to life, which includes, but not limited to, peeing on every street sign and sniffing any passing crotch. Male or female, he doesn't care, he's not discriminating. What he lacks in manners, he makes up for with enthusiasm.

A charming coffee shop entices me inside with the smell of freshly baked cinnamon buns wafting out the screen door. I'll be healthy tomorrow….how often does one get hot right out of the oven cinnamon rolls. In my house…never, unless they come out of a Pillsbury Dough Boy can.

Ohhhh…ummmm…….and they taste divine. I squirm in my chair, boy, these are good ….I'm going to need a takeout box. Once every bit of gooey cinnamon goodness is licked off my fingers, I refill my coffee cup and begin perusing the Old Forge Times. Yes! Perfect! In the middle of the paper is an advertisement for Westland's Canoe Outfitters offering a preseason coupon for 20% off the rental of a canoe or kayak.

I think this will work……my heart begins pounding as excitement courses through me. I'm dying to meet Josh and his family. Armed with the coupon, I present myself at the store posing as an innocent bargain hunter wishing to learn more about local canoe routes and the purchase of a kayak or canoe.

Looking down at my clothing, I note my choice of attire is appropriate for outdoor activity. Above average temperatures for mid-May compelled me to wear a pair of river sandals, a plaid shirt over a tank top and hiking capris. A messy ponytail peeks out the back of a baseball cap, and loose wisps of curls frame my face. A quick glance at my compact mirror shows the makeup basics in place, a swipe of lipstick and a touch of mascara and...I look as good....... well..... I tried.

Taking a final sip of coffee, I wipe the few remaining crumbs off the table, resisting the urge to pop them in my mouth for one last taste. With the newspaper tucked under my arm, I head for the door, firmly resolved *not* to get a takeout box of cinnamon rolls. As I walk away, I repeat the mantra, *om*. My ass is big enough....*om*, my ass is big enough. See meditation helps......it comes in many forms.

Westland's Canoe Rental follows the Moose River, about a mile from the town center. The ad in the paper feels like an omen. In addition to renting water equipment, Westland's serves fresh donuts every morning in the summer months along with specialty coffee. In the evenings, the deck overlooking the river is a hangout for locals and tourists sampling regional beer from the local breweries.

Nestled in a grove of willow trees, the rental shop is a small cabin constructed of local hemlock logs perched precariously on the river's edge. Tuffs of green moss form a velvet carpet covering the roof. Small ferns and delicate spring wildflowers compete for sunlight in the tree-shaded yard. The brick path leading up to the main building is lined with bright yellow pots full of red geraniums and an eclectic collection of birdhouses.

The porch railing and boundary fencing are crafted from twisted tree branches in traditional Adirondack styling. If not for the colorful canoes and kayaks dotting the lawn and poking out of storage sheds, the yard looks perfect for a hobbit community.

I stop, enchanted by the scene, wondering why Jack and I never visited this canoe shop. Our equipment was purchased from outfitters further north and our trips were generally on the lakes and rivers closer to Raquette Lake. Pausing a moment to calm my racing heart, I hear the sound of childish laughter coming from behind the building. A little girl comes running around the corner giggling as her younger brother chases her with a butterfly net.

"Zizzi, stop!" He calls out as his chubby legs furiously pump to keep up with his older sister. "You promised be ma flutter fly!"

The little girl whirls around dancing in the sunbeams filtering though the half open leaves, and with a flute like laughter, she calls out to her brother. "Ansel, only the queen of the fairies can catch a butterfly. You know that, don't you remember the story?" Just as the little boy closes in to make a swoop with the net, she twirls and disappears between the storage sheds.

"Zizzi!" the little boy squeals in disappointment, swinging the net through the air in a vain attempt to catch her.

"Oh God. I have grandchildren." I whisper. My heart swells with joy. I have grandchildren, they're real. They run, jump, play and laugh. What a miracle of life. It takes all my willpower to resist the urge to pull these beautiful children into my embrace.

Okay, I can do this. Forget the shaking legs and sweaty palms. Breathe, Ellen, breathe, step in and trust the future. Slow...... and easy.

Entering the cabin that houses the store, I see two large screen doors opening onto a balcony overlooking the river. The wooden floors are worn and smooth, burnished from years of wear. The walls above the wainscoting are draped with T-shirts depicting scenes of canoeing in the mountains. An assortment of hats, maps and water sport equipment fill the tables and racks throughout the room. An old canoe propped in the corner is put to use as a shelf and a moose head hangs above the doorway. A map of the major canoe routes in Old Forge covers a wall behind the counter. Seated on a high stool munching an apple sits Claire, Josh's wife. I recognize her immediately from the photographs Richard Harsonge sent us.

I see how Josh fell in love with her…… her hair. We call it mermaid hair. Tumbling locks of glorious auburn, cascading in soft ringlets down her back. Tall and lanky, she looks like a mother earth child. She needs no makeup; her complexion is flawless, one wonders if a piece of candy, drop of alcohol or red meat ever touched her lips. The rewards of a good life……..the way I eat, I should look a hundred.

Claire is beautiful in an understated way, her clothing a mixture of eclectic peasant with a nod to the outdoors. She looks like she stepped out of Robert Redford's *Sundance* catalog. Twisted rope and metal bracelets embellish her arms and artsy earrings dangle from her ears. A long chain with a pendant hangs between her breasts over a peasant blouse embroidered with tatting and beading. On the floor, the children with ruddy red cheeks from playing outside are engrossed in emptying a toy box, oblivious to my entrance.

"Hi," Claire says in a casual friendly voice. "Welcome to Westland's. Can I help you find something?"

"Yes." I say, my voice tremulous with nerves. I hold up the newspaper. "I was hoping to take advantage of your pre-season discount."

"Absolutely," she puts down her apple and picks up an invoice form. "What were you looking to rent, a canoe or kayak?"

"It's such a beautiful day. I thought I might take a small kayak out on the river for a quick paddle." I tilt my head as if asking permission.

"That sounds like a lovely idea. It's is a gorgeous day for a paddle." She comments pushing a rental form towards me, holding out a pen. "Fill out the information and I'll just need to make a copy of your driver's license and we will have you on the river in no time."

A squeal and crash come from the corner where the children are playing. "Izzy and Ansel!" She admonishes looking over at the children. Ansel with his jacket half over his head, trips over the blocks on the floor, and crashes in a giggling, wiggling heap.

"Ansel, not again," Claire looks fondly at the little boy as she untangles him from his jacket. "I don't know how he does it," she laughs. "He's always tripping and falling over himself. It's just one scrape after another." She leans closer to me and whispers, "Sometimes, he's such a klutz."

Oh, dear God, the child inherited Klutz-Ellen, only he's Klutz-Ansel. I look at Ansel with empathy and bite my lower lip to quell the laughter threatening to erupt; Klutz-Ellen is an inherited trait. The poor thing. Claire turns back to me apologizing, "I swear they get wilder as the day goes on. Thank goodness, Daddy will be home soon to wrestle some of that energy out of them."

"Oh, please, don't make them stop." I smile, hugging my arms; only sheer will prevents me from dropping to the floor and entering into the squirming, giggling foray.

"I'm enjoying their laughter. My children are grown and I miss the company of young ones."

"No grandchildren?" she asks politely. "Not that you look old enough to be a grandmother." She adds hastily.

Already I love her; she thinks I look young… I'm a sucker for flattery.

"No, not yet," I answer, a note of hesitation in my voice. How am I ever going to explain to her, that her husband is my son and those are my grandchildren.

"You look familiar," she says, looking earnestly at me. I freeze, praying she doesn't recognize any resemblance between me and Josh. It's too early.

"I've just moved into town for the season." I explain in a rush, "My husband and I rented a house north of Old Forge. Maybe you saw me at the store or church." The husband part… just a *little* fib.

"Maybe," she says with a pensive look on her face. "It's early in the season so generally it's only the locals, so any new face sticks out. But something about you seems so familiar, I just can't place it."

"Oh, *shit*, I think to myself. Just act cool. "Funny how things like that happen, usually it's just a coincidence." I say in a nonchalant tone of voice.

"I'm sure it will come to me," she says with a bright smile. "Now do you need any help or instruction with the kayak, especially if you are taking it out alone?"

"I have the basic idea. I don't plan on going too far, just to the bridge and back." I point to the map on the wall. "I brought my binoculars and camera. Hopefully, I'll see a few spring migrating birds."

Just by luck I had remembered to put my binoculars and camera equipment in the car trunk.

"Do you have a cell phone?" she asks, swiping my

credit card through the machine.

"Yes."

"Good, we have decent coverage around town, so you can call if you have any trouble." Claire reaches across the counter and hands me a business card. "Here is our number should you need assistance. We can't afford to lose a customer this early in the season," she jokes. "We usually wait until later in the summer before we let people wander off. And you look capable so I don't think you'll be our first."

"I'm sure I'll be fine." I assure her. "I'm used to doing things on my own. My husband's job takes him away for long periods of time, so I've become quite competent at taking care of myself."

"Well, you're in good hands." She picks up a lifejacket and paddle from a shelf behind the counter. "Josh, my husband is an EMT on the Search and Rescue squad in town. Actually, things have been slow around here. The boys on the squad are eager for a good man *or* lady hunt, gives them bragging rights over beer at the bar. And just think of the gossip you'd generate in town, the first in a long list of local summer legends."

Little do I realize how prophetic her joking banter will prove to be, a foretelling of things to come.

"Thanks, but no." I say with a laugh. "I have enough embarrassing stories to my credit already. I don't need to add any more. Someday when I know you better, I'll tell you about my high heel getting caught in the luggage conveyor belt at LAX airport. I think my picture still hangs on the bulletin board in the baggage handlers break room. The caption reads, "Dumb blonde stunt of the Year."

"I'll buy your glass of wine to hear that one," she

smiles and calls over her shoulder to the children. "Hey, my little darlings, come help Mommy put this nice lady in the water."

. . .

It's a beautiful day to be on the river; and the only place to be in late spring, the dreaded black fly season. Those annoying creatures buzz your ears; fly up your nose, zoom behind your glasses and land in your mouth should you be foolish enough to open it. But for some reason they're less aggressive on the water. Hiking in late spring is for the hardy or hapless, unless armed with bug netting, insect repellant and clothing built like a suit of armor.

I haven't been on the water since Jack died. The serenity of drifting with the current, the slow dip and pull of the paddle, works like a moving meditation, calming me. The warmth of the afternoon sun seeps into my bones, like a gentle massage.

Water striders skate away from the kayak's path and turtles reluctantly abandon their perch in the sun, sliding down slippery logs into the murky river. A male green frog vocalizes the sound of a plucked banjo string from the shallow banks. Old trees topple inward toward the stream as the undercurrent cuts their roots, causing them to lean ever inward and eventually fall. Beneath the water surface is an intricate spider web of roots and branches that stop and tug as boats float by. Tucked into a curtain of pine trees, small cottages populate the water's edge, often only detectable by the docks jutting out into the river. Frayed edges of a rope swing beckon from an overhanging branch, lazily waiting for school to end and summer vacation to begin.

A great blue heron gives a raucous call of alarm as he

lifts his oversized wings, smoothly gliding downstream in search of quieter hunting grounds. With my binoculars, I spot yellow throated warblers flitting between the bushes of willow and mountain laurel calling out, "*Wichita, Wichita*".

Reaching an expanse of open marsh on the river, I stop to admire the view. With a sigh, I lay back, resting the paddle across the gunnels of the boat and drift, closing my eyes, enjoying this simple pleasure, allowing my thoughts to move with the current, freely, unimpeded, and simply living in the moment…...

…

With a start, I jerk awake, dazed and bewildered; the bow of the kayak rests against the riverbank. Pushing a willow branch out of my face, I look around. *Oh noo*……I must have dozed off, where am I?

The sun is sinking in the western sky and the air has cooled off considerably. A glance at my watch confirms the time, almost five o'clock. *Oh my God!* I slept for forty-five minutes….. and I still have to paddle back!

Pulling my cramped legs back into the boat, I grab my fleece jacket and slip it over my head, grateful for the warmth. I need to get back to the shop before Claire fears I've fall overboard or stolen her boat.

My return trip to the dock looks like something out of a cartoon, my arms a blur of paddling motion, the speed causing a small wake to form behind the boat. Smoke bellows out my ears because I'm so mad at myself. After a half an hour of frantic paddling, the dock is finally in sight. Maybe I can surreptitiously pull the kayak up on the landing area, wave good-bye and be on my way before anyone realizes the time. I'm sure Claire's worried. I can't believe I fell asleep. How stupid can I be?

Ohhhhh….no! My mind frantically intones as I watch a tall figure come out of a storage shed and head down the path toward the dock. Who is it? As the shadowed silhouette comes into view I see the dark hair and angular jaw line. *Josh!*

Shit, shit and double *shit.* I *am* not ready to meet him. Not like this. Some strange, forgetful woman…*Oh God.* Look at me, I'm a mess, clothes wrinkled, hair shoved in a hasty ponytail. What am I to say? Hey, I'm your mother and I'm *nuts*. For the *fricking* love of God. I can't believe this is happening. That's it. I'm coloring my hair tomorrow. It must be the blonde hair short circuiting my brain…or something. I'll look fabulous as a brunette.

Maybe I'll paddle home. Forty-five minutes by car, four days by kayak. Not a problem. I'll just yell out as I go by, thanks I'm good, practicing for the Ninety Mile Canoe Classic. Yep, that's me, super-duper marathon canoe woman. Just put the extra charge on my credit card……*yeah,* that sounds sane.

What will I say to him? Think, think….don't panic. This is only your long lost son, who you've not seen in…forever. No big deal.

He is probably furious at me for worrying his wife and interrupting dinner. *How could I be so careless?*

Ellen, don't you dare panic……whatever you do……..*don't* panic! Remember the less you say the better, don't *babble*. Maybe if I tip the kayak over and drown………*Ohhh*, here he is!

Josh comes striding down the dock with that black cat grace reserved for athletes and those blessed by the gods.

And the panic leaves my body in a whoosh of air. Oh...oh…oh….he is so wonderful. Look, my son. Like a mother with a newborn baby, I'm instantly in love with him. Momentarily shaken, I keep one hand clasped to my chest, trying to hold my racing heart in place.

His dark hair curls lazily along the nape of his collar. Gosh, he looks so much like Vic. While he's pure Vic in essence, there is still a hint of me, shadowed around his eyes and mouth. He stops by the water's edge with his hands on his hips and calls out in an amused voice, "Hey, kayak lady, we thought we lost you." He laughs, crouching down to guide my boat up to the launch. His eyes are his father's dark, dark eyes with lovely little flecks of gold. "Claire was only kidding when she said the emergency squad needed practice."

"I am *so, so* sorry." I manage to gasp out. "Would you believe I fell asleep?" I can't breathe. Oh God, I'm having a heart attack.

"It, it….was such a beautiful day." I eke out in a rush. "The sun lulled me to sleep." No, not a heart attack, no shooting pain down my left arm; just pure panic. I continue on bravely. "Ummmm, I was drifting along with my camera taking pictures….and the next thing I know, I woke up with the bow of the boat stuck in the river bank."

"Not a problem; happens to the best of us," he says. The lines around his eyes crinkle slightly as he gives a dismissive shake of his head. "We're just glad you're back safe and sound. Claire was afraid something happened to you."

"I'm so sorry to bother you. I'm usually very responsible." *Liar, liar, pants on fire.*

So much for slipping quietly into his life. But oh, with a mother's unconditional love, I'm enamored with him. There is an air of quiet confidence about him, and he obviously has patience with idiotic woman. Regaining my senses, I say, "I'm sure it must be past closing time and I'm interrupting your dinner."

"We tend to eat late around here. I come home and play outside with the kids before it gets dark. It gives Claire a chance to start dinner and have a few moments of peace." A considerate husband. Someone raised him well. "They just went up to the house. Hand me your gear and we'll get you up onto dry ground and headed home." I hand him my backpack and place the camera gently on the dock.

"Let me help you." He offers; taking my hand in his, the kayak wobbles as I shift my weight to climb out, his fingers strong and warm as he pulls me up. Standing in the evening twilight with his hand in mine, I give him a polite smile for the assistance, but fear I'm staring at him like I've seen the coming of the next Messiah.

"Thank you." My wellspring of conversation dries up as my gaze drops to his hand. My son's hand, I am standing here holding my son's hand. A few scars stand out white against his bronze skin, giving his hand depth and character.

Let go of his hand. Now! I admonish myself. Release your grip, before you look like the village idiot or an old lady on the make. Reluctantly, I let go of his hand and transfer my stare to his face.

"So," I say, rallying the few wits I have left, "Where do you store the kayaks at night?" And cringe at the inanity of the question.

"We just prop them against the building or in a shed," he says, waving a hand to the surrounding area.

"Do you need any help?" I ask, realizing I'm grabbing at any excuse to prolong the conversation. Like this well-muscled young man needs any help from the likes of me, to offer is an insult to his masculinity.

"I'm good, but thanks." He gives me an amused grin as he effortlessly hoists the kayak onto his shoulders; his attention diverted to my camera lying on the ground. "Do you like photography?"

"Actually, yes," I answer, praying he doesn't ask any in-depth camera questions. "My husband is the camera buff. I'm more of a shoot and go girl, strictly amateur. I wanted to take a few pictures so I could email them to him. He's in Miami on business. I thought he'd enjoy seeing the marsh and river."

"I'm sure he would." Josh nods in agreement. "Say, if you're interested in photography and kayaking, this Saturday, I'm running a clinic. We're going to take an informal paddle down the river, stop along the way to discuss aperture settings, lighting, and just general aspects of photography. Maybe you'd be interested in joining us? I think there's still a few spots open. Check with Claire."

"Yes! That sounds wonderful, I'd love to come." I reply, trying to contain my joy at the prospect of seeing him again.

"Excellent, call Claire tomorrow and she'll give you the details." Josh says leading me up the path toward the parking lot. "And we will see you on Saturday."

I mentally chide myself to say good bye…..and no, don't shake his hand again… just…*go*.

"Yes, see you then." I call out with a wave.

Wait….don't start……no, don't twirl around and dance with joy until I'm home, alone, in the woods. If he sees me joyously cavorting in the parking lot and finds out I'm his mother…he'll fear insanity runs in the family.

Chapter 39

The Fine Art of Skinny Dipping

"Cleaning is the process of making something clean, either in a domestic or commercial environment."

Webster Dictionary

I don't cook, I clean. Cleaning is a legacy from my stepmother, Helen, the *only* common bond in our tortuous relationship. They didn't call me *Cinder-Ellen* in high school for nothing. Helen's idea of a prom dress was an apron paired with a toilet brush.

Yet, surprisingly, I like to clean. Cleaning is therapeutic, when life knocks me off balance and the universe sends me into a whirl, I clean. A broom, a mop, a dust cloth slick with lemon oil, these tangible symbols of domestic stability give me a purpose, a reason to move forward, if you keep moving trouble can't catch you. I tried jogging for stress relief, but after ten minutes of running, I'd collapse in a heap alongside the road begging for Para-medics and oxygen.

But cleaning, a person starts early in the morning and can still be working by nightfall. Exhausted, replete, spent, you've made it through another day. Cleanliness is next to Godliness, so they say. My way of praying when Jack died......well, it was better than eating my way through grief.

Not that I'm troubled or upset at the moment, just restless. With Vic gone and little to occupy my time until Saturday, I need a project. I thought of making a batch of muffins for Claire and the children to apologize for being late. Then I come to my senses……. I'll stop at the bakery on my way into town on Saturday.

Unfortunately for me, the Adirondack lodge was left in immaculate condition. Not a cobweb, not a dust bunny, not a slick on the windows, but…… the attic of the old boat house situated on the water's edge proved to be a veritable treasure of collectibles, some *less* collectable than others.

I called the owners and they were delighted to let me "straighten up". Apparently over the years, what the family didn't want in the main lodge, ended up stashed in the boat house. Old sports equipment, lawn furniture, gardening tools, lifejackets covered in mildew, and cardboard boxes full of outdated clothing. Bursting at the seams and starting to smell. Untouched for years, the boathouse was the dream of every fanatic cleaner.

…

Standing on the dock after a long day of cleaning, I stretch and tentatively flex my aching back while surveying my progress. Not bad for a day's work, I'd applaud my efforts but my arms ache too much. Scattered across the lawn are three piles; one goes to the garbage dump, one to the fire pit and one box of articles still usable.

Pulling the dusty bandana off my head, I study the boathouse edifice. While one can't help being impressed by the grandeur of the great camps sitting like crown jewels at the edge of a mountain lake, I've secretly coveted the tiny boathouses clinging to the shore. Designed to match the main lodge, the boathouse acted as a garage for boats, while the second story serves as a guesthouse for visitors. Many great camps require a boat or water taxi, being accessible only by water. Seen from afar, the boathouse with the camp's signature flag flying, announces the family is in residence.

Walking around the building, I imagine it painted a deep brown with red trim, window boxes spilling over with bright crimson geraniums and Adirondack chairs dotting the overhanging porch. The leaded glass windows, washed and open, with curtains billowing in the summer breeze. Climbing the steps, I envision the upstairs room decked out in vivid reds, greens and orange, colors symbolic of the Adirondack Great Camps. Casting a wistful glance out the window at the lake, I realize how hot, tired and dirty I feel from hours of crawling through cobwebs, musty lifejackets, rotten wood, and a conglomeration of dirt and unidentifiable smells. Though the temperature is dropping, I long for a quick dip in the velvet cool of the lake, to sink below the surface and feel the cleansing waters wash away the grime.

Wiping the sweat from my brow with the corner of Vic's old shirt, I think, why not? All I need is a towel; since there is no one around for miles, why bother with a bathing suit. It's just me, Cyrus and the deer. So before the sun sets any further and I lose my nerve, I sprint to the house. Dropping my dirty clothes on the bathroom floor, I grab a towel and lock Cyrus in the kitchen. Otherwise, he'll follow me into the water and I'll have a wet smelly dog in my bed. Poor substitute for Vic.

I dive off the dock into water the color of black ink, slicing through like an otter on a hunt. Surfacing, I float on my back, watching the last rays of sun sink below the hedge of pines rimming the mountain range. My initial euphoria over the invigorating cool water is quickly replaced by a slow body-numbing chill. Scooting up the ladder of the dock, I hastily wrap a towel around me, and dash across the lawn to the house, questioning the wisdom of skinny-dipping in May. Am I *stupid?* I know how cold the water can be, even at the height of summer, anything more than a brief swim is for the hardy.

Leaving a trail of wet footprints across the deck, I yank on the handle of the sliding glass door and almost pull my shoulder joint out of its socket. The door's stuck. I yank again. Still stuck. Pull harder. *Oh, my God, it's locked.*

What, *no!* I used that door only minutes ago, how can it be locked? Did the latch accidentally fall into the locked position, did Cyrus lock it? *ehhhhh*............the security code! The owners programmed the security system to lock the doors at 7 p.m. The wife's father has Alzheimer's and tended to wander at sundown. Vic and I left it in place, using the keypad to let ourselves in, only he punched in the code and apparently I paid no attention. *Bloody hell, where is the code!!* Inside the house on a little piece of paper, stuck to the refrigerator, is the entry code. Behind the locked door.

I hear Cyrus barking in the kitchen. Okay, don't panic; one of the windows or doors must be open. I always leave a window open. After a quick survey of the ground floor entrances to the house, I panic. All of them are locked. *Shit, shit, shit, and double shit!* Temperatures are predicted to be in the forties tonight. Resting my head against the door jam, I imagine the newspaper headlines, middle aged blonde woman found dead, outside her palatial mountain home, naked and frozen, cause of death: stupidity combined with pre-season skinny dipping.

I can't even get into my car; the keys are in the house. In desperation, I try wedging the handle of the hose under the windowsill in a vain attempt to pry it open. No luck, closed up tighter than a drum. In utter and absolute hysteria, I start beating the hose handle against the window, but to no avail. Constructed of high tech security glass, the windows are shatter proof to prevent vandalism. The house is miles from any other residence. Peering fearfully at the darkening woods, I don't relish the idea of running barefoot through miles of wilderness roads, clad only in a towel.

Oh, boy, I'm really starting to get cold, I can't stop shivering and my teeth are chattering. Ummm, think Ellen, think. You've taken survival courses, what did they teach you……. Nothing!!

Making a shelter out of sticks, doesn't work well in a pine forest without a hatchet. Very little scattered branches and leaves needed for building materials. I'm going to die, Oh, sweet Jesus, I'm going to die of hypothermia. Vic is going to kill me, even if I'm dead, he'll resurrect my corpse and kill me again for being so stupid.

First rule of survival; *don't panic!* Not working, I think I just ran in a circle chasing my tail. How much time has passed? Fifteen minutes? Twenty? Judging from the darkening sky…..a half hour? There must be something I can use to get warm. The boathouse!! Maybe some of those old smelly clothes. I think I saw a gas tank; maybe I can start a fire. Matches, I don't know if I saw matches. But I have to look, I'm desperate with cold.

Without the aid of a flashlight and relying on the meager moonlight filtering through the trees, I pick my way gingerly down the path to the boathouse. Reaching the building, I realize I padlocked the door. I can't believe I locked this stupid building full of worthless junk. It's all trash. Just because the owners locked it, doesn't mean I needed to lock it too. From what? The raccoons!!

Shivering with cold, I squat down and twirl the dial, trying to remember the combination numbers. Just as I hear the tumblers click into place and release the lock, I hear a twig snap behind me. Wheeling around to see what creature wants to eat my frozen carcass, I'm blinded by a sudden flood of light. Screaming in terror, I throw my hands up shielding my eyes against the glare of a spotlight....... *And* my towel slips to the ground. And I'm standing butt naked with nothing but what God gave me, caught in the glare of a search light, screaming hysterically.

"Excuse me, Ma'am." I hear a disembodied voice calling from the dark reaches behind the light. "*Lady!* It's okay. It's the *Police!* We're not going to hurt you."

"The police?" My mind frantically wonders. What the hell! How in God's name did the police show up?

"Here, you dropped.....ahhhh.......your towel." Another voice comes from the dark. Good Lord, how many of them are there? I see the towel, but before giving it to me, the shadow of the man stands up, and settles back on his heels, as if enjoying the view. *Jerk!*

"Give me that!" I snatch the towel from his hand. "Put down the light, you're blinding me." I yell through chattering teeth. I'm shivering convulsively with a mixture of cold and fear. "Who are you?" I demand, not sure if I'm relieved to be rescued or embarrassed at being found in such a ridiculous situation.

"Old Forge Police, ma'am." the first voice answers, as he lowers the blinding light away from my face. "The security alarm at the house was tripped and a call came into the station. We came out to investigate a burglary."

"Hey Frank, give her your jacket," says the second voice in the dark. "She looks like she's freezing. Just look at the goose bumps on her, she can't stop shivering."

Oh, yeah, I'm sure it's my goose bumps the two of them are looking at, oh hell, what does it matter, I've reached a new level of mortification, just give me the jacket before I freeze to death.

"Ma'am, what are you doing out here?" The voice named Frank asks as he hands me his jacket.

"Do I look like I'm committing a burglary?" I snap at them, trying to slip my arm into the jacket without losing my grip on the towel. One strip tease a night is enough. I wrap my arms around my body, holding in the warmth, inhaling the faint scent of the man's aftershave. Smells like my father. Old man cologne.

"No, Ma'am, you do not," replies the police officer in a calm even tone reserved for soothing raving lunatics. "But Ma'am, the alarm has been tripped and we're not aware of anyone in residence. Usually the owner contacts us when the house is rented. We have not received any communication as to the occupancy of the house."

"My husband and I are renting the house from the Bellamys for the summer." I say through chattering teeth. "I can't help it if they didn't contact you." I throw back at him. I'm tired, hungry and convinced I'm turning into a human Popsicle. "Listen, I went for a late swim and accidentally locked myself out of the house. Pleaaasee, help me get in, I'm freezing."

"I'm sorry, Ma'am. We don't have the authorization to open the house without the owner's consent. We have access to the code for the key pad, but first we need to contact the owner."

"Seriously?" I ask querulously, now I'm getting riled

up. "Are you insane?" I stomp my foot and point an accusing finger at them. "Do you really think I decided to come out here and try to break into a house not wearing any clothes, and carrying no weapons or tools? I just happened to be wandering through the woods naked, so I could break into a vacant house and steal a new wardrobe." My voice raises several octaves, I'm on a roll…… and *nothing* is going to stop me. Fueled by fatigue and numb with cold, I launch into the two police officers.

"Do you two narrow minded, small town, Barney Fifes really think that is what I was doing? Really! Do you have nothing better to do than harass a freezing woman locked out of her house? Is your small town life so pathetic this is how you get your kicks on a Monday night?" *Oh, please*…..someone gag me *now*….anything…. shut me up…..but I keep on going… "If you lived in the real world, away from this two bit backwater town, you'd be arresting criminals committing *real* crimes, rape, murder, gang warfare, but no, you are so pathetic for excitement that bullying a defenseless woman is your idea of entertainment. Just how stupid can you be?!" Apparently not as stupid as I am at this moment, because a freezing, naked woman should not insult her would-be rescuers. First rule of survival.

"Excuse me! What did you just say?" Asks the incredulous voice of the one named Brian.

"I think the little lady just called us Barney Fife, living in a two bit back water town," says the second cop. "Maybe we should leave her in the cold, and go up to our warm patrol car and investigate what's really going on here. Excuse me, ma'am, I'll be needing my coat back. It's getting a little nippy out here, wouldn't you agree?" His hand reaches for the coat. I slap it away.

"Frank, that was assaulting an officer. Right?"

"Absolutely Brian, boy howdy, when the sun goes down in these here mountains, a body sure could freeze to death. We, country bumpkin cops, don't want to catch our death of the cold. So little lady, why don't you just wait here, all bundled up in that little towel while we figure out the situation. Sometimes these matters can take hours to straighten out. I know you big city types don't mind waiting around. After all, you come up to the mountains to get away from all that hustle and bustle, so why don't you just sit back, relax and enjoy the view. We'll call you when we have the information, might be tomorrow morning. Will that be fine with you? We hate to inconvenience you with our small town investigation process."

This was just too much for me at this point, in horror I feel myself burst into great heaving sobs of frustration. "No, no, I'm so sorry. Please don't go." I cry. "I'm freezing. Please don't leave me here to die." A moan escapes my blue lips, as I clutch the jacket with a death grip. "I didn't mean what I said. I'm just so cold; I wasn't thinking straight, my brain is frozen. I love Old Forge."

"Well, seeing as how you put it that way. Am I to understand that was an apology?" The taller one asks.

"Yes, yes, please, please, help me get into my house." I plead, vowing to never take my clothes off again or venture into the woods after dark.

"We did swear an oath to be servants of the people. Be a shame, leaving the lady out here on a cold night."

"Let's go up to the patrol car. We'll contact the station and access the files for the entry code." says Officer Frank in an amused voice. The two policemen clearly enjoying my discomfort. If I wasn't so desperate

I'd go after them with the baseball bat left discarded on the "to be burned" pile.

"I don't think she was really breaking and entering, do you, Brian?"

"Na." says Brian. I swear one of them snickered. This is not funny. The taller one presses the button on a radio attached to his shirt, reporting into headquarters their location then nods in my direction. "We'll put her in the patrol car with the heater on while we clear this up. There's a blanket in the emergency kit she can use."

After what seemed like an eternity, the Bellamys were contacted and clearance given to open the house, along with profuse apologies for the inconvenience. *Apologies my ass.*

Once I was deemed no longer a threat to the security of the North Country, Officer Frank entered the security code and the house miraculously opened.

Calling out my thanks and good byes to the police, I dash up stairs for a hot shower and the warmest snuggly pajamas I can find.

Imagine my astonishment when descending the stairs wrapped in a fleece robe; I smell coffee brewing and the distinct crackle of a wood burning fire in the hearth. A rush of warm air rises from the furnace ducts followed by the smell of bacon sizzling on the stove. Who's here?

I peer cautiously around the corner and see the two policemen sitting around the kitchen island holding steaming mugs of coffee. The island is set with three place settings, and a mug of coffee waiting for me!

"We didn't want to leave until we were certain you were okay." Officer Brian comments holding up his mug. "So we helped ourselves to your kitchen, we thought you could use some hot food."

"For me?" I accept the hot coffee with gratitude. "You are my heroes, you probably saved my life."

"All in a day's work for us, narrow-minded small town Barney Fifes, ma'am." Frank chuckles.

Over sunny side up eggs, hot buttered toast and a steaming mug of coffee laced with brandy for me; the next hour passes in a pleasant exchange of apologies for the misunderstandings perceived by both parties. We laughed over the hilarity of my situation while not underscoring the dangers of hypothermia in the North Woods. The officers good naturedly poked fun at me, claiming I was the first woman in fifteen years of service they almost arrested wearing only a dragonfly necklace.

Unable to keep my eyes open as exhaustion settles in, I assure the officers I no longer need their services, and send them forth into the dark night, to save more damsels in distress. This damsel, after locking the door, shall head straight to bed with dreams of the alarm code swirling in her head, never to be forgotten, again.

Chapter 40

Splash!

"You what?!"

"Ummmm, you know, what I just said."

"I know what you just said." Vic's voice sounds grim coming through the phone. "And I can't believe what I just heard."

"It's no big deal, over and done with, let's forget I even mentioned it."

"Forget!" Oh boy, now he sounds agitated. "Forget! How the hell do I forget my girlfriend almost kills herself by skinny dipping on a forty degree night, gets locked out of the house, and if that is not enough, she's found by the cops, naked, half frozen and nearly arrested for assaulting an officer.

"Oh, that cop was such a big baby, I just slapped his hand away, he wanted his jacket back and I was cold."

"Ellen!" Now I know he's really mad, he *never* calls me, Ellen.

"What!"

"How the hell did you lock yourself out?"

"It's not my fault!"

"So you're saying some woodland creature came along and locked the door on you."

"No!"

"Enlighten me." His voice low and flat, I can feel the volcano about to erupt. Suddenly, I'm thankful for the thousands of miles separating us.

"I was hot from cleaning the boathouse…"

"*Cleaning* the boathouse?" His voice sounds

exasperated, and I hear him heave a sigh that sounds like a moan. "Go on, I won't even ask why you were cleaning the boathouse."

"It was filthy." I say defensively.

"Yeah, I'm sure it was...."

"Anyway, I was hot and tired and the lake looked so inviting, I wanted to take a swim."

"And forgot about the timer for the locks?"

"Y-yeah, it's not my fault, stupid idea locking all the doors and windows."

"And you forgot the code?"

"Yeaaahhh........I threw Cyrus in the house, grabbed a towel and forgot about the code."

Thunk, thunk, thunk.......and nothing but silence on the phone connection.

"What are you doing?" I ask, fearful of the answer.

Thunk, thunk, thunk.............

"Vic?"

"I'm bashing my head against the wall."

"What! Why?"

"Because how could I have been so stupid as to leave you and Cyrus in the middle of the woods and not expect you to find trouble."

Thunk, thunk, thunk...... "Stupid, stupid, stupid."

"I resent that." I say, defensively, knowing fully well I don't have a leg to stand on.

"I'm coming home."

"No,no,no! I can do this, I have the code memorized, everything is fine, no need to worry." Famous last words.

"You know, I'm not getting any younger. My father had a weak heart and I think I just had three heart attacks." *Jeez.*

"Ike was coming up for a visit, he can come early. I'll

feel better if someone is with you."

"No!" While the idea of someone staying in the house with me is attractive ....the *last* thing I need is the incredibly hot Celtic Warrior Cowboy, who will be bored, moody and brooding following me around like an overprotective nanny. No thank you.

"Please, promise to be more careful." He pleads.

"Absolutely."

...

Saturday, the day of the kayak clinic with Josh dawned cloudy and overcast. Temperatures hover in the high fifties. Armed with my camera, lunch...... and a *watch*, my stomach is aflutter with nerves at the prospect of seeing Josh again. A swing by the bakery for a dozen cinnamon buns and I'm on my way to the river.

A flotilla of brightly colored kayaks bobbles along the water's edge. A few people are kayaking up and down the stream, practicing their paddling skills, eager to start the day's adventure. The rest of the boats remain lined up on shore, patiently waiting.

Jogging down the launch ramp, a quick glance reveals an eclectic group of people, mixed ages, physical characteristics and a host of probable personalities. Josh takes a moment to introduce everyone. Two middle-aged men dressed in hiking gear, listen intently as Josh explains the kayak route. Engineer types, all fact and no fiction.

George and Irene Irish, recently retired college professors, confide their eagerness to learn the basic elements of taking good pictures. They look the part of retired academia, lean to the point of thin. Routine and proper decorum defining their lives, most likely breakfast consists of oatmeal and yogurt, lunch, a turkey sandwich on whole grain bread, the indulgence of the day is a tumbler of scotch on the rocks enjoyed while relaxing on their veranda overlooking the manicured garden of their one acre home…. I like to make stuff up about people. They have a trip to South America planned in the fall, where they hope to climb Machu Picchu and bring home some amazing photos. Brag bait, they call it. "Most of our friends scoff at the idea of retirement." Irene said. "We want to show them there is life after retirement, in fact, a very adventurous life."

"Keep the bow pointed downstream." Josh instructs as we push off from the shore. "You can paddle, but also use the paddle blade as a rudder." I set my paddle to water and the kayak follows the river as it meanders through cattails and reeds, the current slow and lazy. A kingfisher calls off in the distance and we pass a blue heron, its body still, standing in knee deep water, silent, watchful.

At our first stop, Josh explains the differences between contemplative photography and conceptual photography. Rather than focus on the conceptual discipline of photography where the emphasis is on visual texture, color, and play of light, he encourages us to focus on taking pictures that appeal to us, looking at life from a different angle. Don't worry too much about technique, he suggests.

The next half hour is spent wandering through marsh grasses and combing the shoreline for just the right angle. Instead of capturing pictures to share a view with the world, take pictures to inspire meditation and contemplation.

My personal favorites on the trip are Dick and Midge Hamish. Slightly overweight, dressed in matching jeans, sweatshirts and sneakers, they resemble a pair of oversized twins. And they don't have a clue about photography or kayaking….and could care less. Their children bought them a camera and the class for their fortieth wedding anniversary. But they'd rather tell jokes than take pictures and after almost rolling their double kayak, they launch into a series of jokes about canoeing. As Dick talks, Midge passes around a Tupperware container filled with the best oatmeal cookies, ever. I'm a sucker for homemade cookies……I love this woman. When I decide to let myself go, this is how I want to be….plump, happy……with a cookie in my hand.

Completely unashamed of the fact that less than an hour ago, I polished off a cinnamon roll with Claire, I unabashedly ate one, okay two, and…stashed a third cookie in my pocket for later. Hey, a girl has to keep up her strength.

Watching from the edge of the group, I notice two younger women, hugging close to Josh's kayak and hanging on every word he says. It's difficult to decide who has the bigger crush. The local librarian trying to conceal the fact she wants him. Or the beautiful leggy seventeen year old girl……..who hasn't quite mastered the sophisticated art of seduction. And she is beautiful, face it, it's difficult to find a seventeen year old girl who isn't gorgeous. It's part of the master plan to tempt stupid young males away from the lure of sports and beer. Her name is Veronica and she takes his advanced placement biology class. Long chestnut brown hair caught up in a twisted knot at the base of her neck, and soft brown doe eyes. She dragged her equally long legged, skinny stomach, beautiful girlfriend with her. And in theory……..I think I hate them both…its called middle age female envy over our lost nubile bodies.

Veronica's girlfriend shows no interest in taking pictures. It's doubtful she knows where to find the camera lens and apparently has no desire to learn. Her short-cropped black hair is tipped with shocking pink ends. A nose ring and layers of black mascara are the only adornments to her attire. She's wearing a rock band t-shirt, faded jeans, and a pair of scruffy red high laced sneakers.

Squinting at the t-shirt, I wonder if she wears it to school, the name of the rock group is rather offensive. *Hmm*...she is interesting to watch. She spent the first part of the trip floating down the river with her legs hanging over the gunnels of the kayak, filing her nails between burst of dogged paddling to keep up. Veronica, on the other hand, smitten with Josh, keeps within a paddle's reach of his kayak, hanging onto his every word. I remember those painful high school crushes. Where you walk by a boy's house, in hopes he was outside mowing the lawn, squeak out a brave hello and he….looks at you….like you have three heads. I shudder in sympathy for Veronica, looking at Josh with Vic's dark good looks, who could blame her….except for the fact……he's married!

Jen the librarian; admits to a recent divorce and wants to improve her photography skills, hoping to give free-lance work a try. Looking closely at her hand, there is a faint pale line of flesh on her ring finger. Obviously, a very recent divorce, her face has the predatory look of a love starved female. Husband probably cheated on her. It's tough to meet a man in the mountains. For one, the year-round population of males is sparse and not many of them interested in discussing literature classics on long winter nights. She'd be considered plain except for her vivid green eyes and the voluptuous figure spilling out of her hiking shirt. *Gee*....if I angle a little closer....give that kayak a shove, it's going over. Serves her right........she knows better.

The clouds scuttle across the sky and occasional bursts of sun break through the diaphanous cover, jackets get stuffed in rucksacks and winter pale skin warms in the basking rays of spring sunshine. I wish the day to last forever, skirting the edge of the group, I take utter delight in watching Josh.

Growing up on Fourth Lake, he fell in love with the mountains, choosing to make his home here. A natural teacher, he possesses a wealth of knowledge about the local area, photography and the flora and fauna of the Moose River. How ironic, I muse, he was so close....

Patient with the girls, he maintains a safe distance between them, obviously well versed in holding young women at bay. With the older couples, he swaps jokes while munching on Midge's cookies, brushing away stray crumbs as he points out aperture settings on the camera. Midge is more interested in feeding him than learning about the workings of her camera. The golden light of his dark brown eyes twinkle with mischief and humor over the fumbling of Dick and Midge. Dick repeatedly questions the wisdom of their children for not purchasing a fully automatic digital camera. "What were they thinking?" He asks with a baffled look on his face.

As I lounge on the riverbank feigning interest in the class...it's Josh who holds my attention. And I fall in love with our son more and more with each passing minute. He gives forth the quiet grace and ease of someone who's spent time in the woods.....there is a serenity about him.

And the edge of pain and longing I've worn over the

years lessens; he is everything I could ask for in a son. Poised, self-assured, gentle with an amazing sense of humor. Maybe this is how life was supposed to work out. Maybe he was meant to be raised by his adopted parents. Vic and I were so young; maybe God had a better plan than mine. I shake my head as a very small shard of hatred falls away, having my own children and watching them grow and make mistakes enlightened me to the horror our parents felt when they discovered I was pregnant at such a young age. But I will *never* forgive how callously they handled us, there was no love involved.

I can't wait for Vic to meet Josh. Just knowing our son has turned into an accomplished young man will help dispel his anguish over the past. *And*… I even picked up a few photography tips….

…

The damp cold of a spring evening settles over the water as we glide up to the shore, shoulders aching and tired from the day's paddle, it's good to see land. The kayaks bump against the dock as everyone unloads their gear, careful to exit the shaky crafts without tipping. Quiet laughter and groans of pleasure float across the air as cramped muscles are stretched and massaged. Names and email addresses are exchanged as the group prepares to depart for the comforts of home, a hot shower and dinner. I hold back, not wanting the day to end. All I have waiting back at camp is a cold empty house and the prospect of a lonely dinner. Thank goodness for Cyrus, I can't wait for Vic to return on Monday. I long for the warmth of his arms, the feel of his lips against mine, but mostly I just….miss…him. This time apart has been a reality check of life without Vic.

I bob contently on the water watching the others

disembark from their kayaks, waving goodbye, one by one, departing as the sun sinks slowly into the horizon. I secretly hope to be the last one on the dock, maybe even help close up, just to gain a few extra minutes. I don't want to let go of him, enjoying the sweet pleasure of my son. Is that too much to ask…

Finally, I can wait no more, I'm the last one left on the water and he's standing there a tall silhouette against the setting sun.

"Y'all coming in?" He calls out in an amused voice. "Sun's setting and I'm getting hungry. Or are you hoping to meet the search and rescue team? Saturday night, the boys will be down at the local bar just champing at the bit for some action."

Good Lord, no! That's all I need; the blue light bennies charging out in full force searching for me.

"No, not necessary." I say. "Sorry, I was just waiting for everyone to finish, I'm in no hurry." My kayak moves smoothly across the water, bumping into the dock with a *thunk*. I hand him my pack and camera bag. Accepting his hand I exit the kayak being mindful of not tipping it over. As I lean into his arm, my dragonfly necklace swings away from my shirt. Josh looks at the necklace quizzically, than at me. A dawning light of compression causes his eyebrows to arch up in surprise and a look of astonishment crosses his face.

"Oh, my God! I know who you are." He exclaims in excitement as we stand up, his hands on my elbows holding me steady. His eyes meet mine. He knows who I am!

Yes! Yes! Yes! My son recognizes me! Thank you, God! There must be some vestige of mother child bond linking us through the years. The invisible umbilical cord of emotions is too strong to sever. Neither time, nor space or distance can separate a mother's love from her son. He knows I'm his mother. Reunited at last!

"You're that *naked* lady! The one Frank and Brian helped out the other night." He exclaims in the delight of a child figuring out the last clue of a puzzle. "You're that poor frozen woman locked out of her house; aren't you?" *What!*

"Noooo!! I howl in despair. As the wail erupts from my throat, I instinctively shove against his chest in horror that he now knows me as the "naked lady!"

The nightmare continues……the shove at the precarious edge of the dock…… coupled with the force of the push…..sends him…….. propelling backwards……...arms flailing……whirling like a windmill ………..and in slow motion. ………..falling……falling…… backwards off the dock……into the frigid…… snow fed water of the Moose River….on a cold spring evening in May. *Splash…….Ooooh….. My…… God!!*

Chapter 41

Vic........Unglued

"Elle, buttercup, I can't understand you. You have to stop crying."

"I know you're upset. Are you sick? Are the kids sick?"

"Ella, Ella, my mia bella, whatever it is, we'll fix it together."

"No, calm down, take a deep breath and tell me."

"Yes."

"Yes."

"Yes, I'll love you no matter what."

"*What!?*"

"You what! You pushed him off the dock!"

"How the hell did you push our son off the dock."

"What were you thinking?"

"I know it's not your fault."

Thunk, thunk, thunk.

"Yes, that's my head."

"No, I'm not having a heart attack."

"He recognized the dragonfly necklace?"

"The cops told the story around the local bar about rescuing a naked lady wearing a dragonfly necklace."

"And he put two and two together and came up with you as the naked lady."

"He's okay, He's not hurt?"

"What do you *mean* not exactly?"

"He cut his hand on a mussel shell."

Thunk, thunk, thunk.

"Yes, that's my head."

"But because his wife was gone, you stayed, bandaged his hand and made him dinner?"

"So everything is fine?"

"Why the hell didn't you say so in the beginning?"

"No, I'm not mad."

"I always mutter under my breath in Spanish."

"No, not just when I'm angry!"

"That's it. I'm coming home before the spirit of *Lucille Ball* channels your body or you end up on the most wanted list in the post office."

"Yes, of course, I still love you, always."

Thunk, thunk, thunk.

Chapter 42

The Curse Returns

The plane lands in Albany, a short drive through the mountains and he's home. And Esteban Diago came home, looking good…….real good.

His skin buff, bronzed and glowing from days in South Beach working on a promo shoot for the sequel to *FireBrand.* Cosmetologists skilled in skin therapy and exercise physiologists turned him into a gleaming six-pack package of manhood. Ohh, mama, he is fine. Makes me wish I had spent a little more time buffing and toning myself while he was away. As far as I'm concerned any sequel that has him playing Sentar, warrior king of the underworld works for me. There will be no complaints...none…at *all!*

After three days of total preoccupation with each other, still heady under the sweet fumes of infatuation, our love mellows to a place of calm. A place of comfort, moving beyond the frantic groping of lust, that first seed of attraction to a true love spreading roots, growing to weather the storms of life to fulfillment. A fulfillment forged by a commitment between two people. I'm beginning to trust the idea of marriage and starting a new life with him……...

…

The destination for our first outing is the Adirondack Museum on Blue Mountain Lake. Paying homage to the mountains and culture of the Adirondacks, this is my favorite museum in the world and I've been to the Louvre.

From a sailboat under a glass dome to a furnished railroad car, floating antique dory boats to replica cabins from the Great Camps, all set amid lush gardens brimming with native plants and trees. The museum is the sum total of the Adirondack experience.

Attired in hiking pants, a light weight khaki shirt and a wide brim hat, Vic resembles Indiana Jones gone Adirondack….one of my favorite disguises to detract from his identity. Only it doesn't seem to be working. He's attracting attention. What woman doesn't have a thing for Harrison Ford as Indiana Jones….and if she doesn't, check her pulse, she's dead. With his hair pulled back in a sleek ponytail, bronze skin, dark eyes shaded with aviator glasses, he's making Harrison Ford look like Chewbacca. The Hollywood veneer is showing. Out of the corner of my eye, I see the ladies giving him appraising looks. It's time to take pretty boy home.

Grabbing his hand I steer him in the direction of the museum bookstore, to the disappointed faces of the women lingering too close for comfort. What is it up here? Is it the mountain air, the long winter nights, the overabundance of pine trees, too many lakes and rivers, a surplus of flannel and denim? Is the scent of balsam in the spring an aphrodisiac causing woman to stalk and grab the nearest male?

"What?" He questions me in innocence, ignorant of the attention flowing in his direction.

"We're done."

"But the tour isn't over."

"It is for you. The ladies were getting too close."

"You just want to shop." He accuses, holding open the door to the gift shop.

"Brains and brawn, every woman's dream." I quip,

ducking under his arm through the doorway.

The museum store is a virtual treasure of books, jewelry, gifts and home decorating items geared to the Adirondack mountain theme. Walls covered with prints of Adirondack landscape, shelves stacked with blankets, pottery, food, and coffee mugs crafted in enough designs to have a different one for every day of the week.

"Of course, I want to shop. Woman are genetically programmed to shop, it's in our DNA. While the men were off hunting, the women gathered in the fields and forest. Shopping is simply the modern day woman's form of gathering." I reply impishly. "Instead of fields, we gather in stores."

"Oh, boy, this could be trouble." He teases as he looks around at the wall displays and tables covered with retail goods. "I'm not getting out of here anytime soon, am I?"

"I won't take long. I just want to check and see if they have any new additions for my Adirondack book collection. You wander around a bit. Hey, they have a hat section; maybe you can buy yourself a new *chapeau*." I prompt. "Something a little less Indy and a lot more old man of the mountain."

"I like the one I have, thank you very much." He says, meandering over to inspect a photographic print, tugging his hat lower.

Perusing the books on the shelf I take down a title I don't recognize, *Myths, Mysteries and Weird Phenomena of the Adirondacks.* Placing the book on top of a glass display case, I thumb through the pages with interest, until my hand halts by its own accord and a tremor of fear courses through my body. *Oh*, this can't be possible. It can't be the same one.

I stare in disbelief at the picture of a glittering pin. The brooch. That stupid evil brooch the crazy hermit insisted Vic and I accept. I thought it was a piece of costume jewelry or a cheap imitation. It can't be the same one……..or *could* it?

The brooch gleams up from the picture, sparkling in a rainbow of colors, shimmering and glittering, pulling the unsuspecting into a web of unfulfilled promises, deception and despair. I read the text with growing horror, the same story the hermit recanted to Vic and I so many years ago about the Freeport family. But the hermit failed to mention the brooch was cursed. The brooch that so unwittingly fell into my possession……was the same one. It can't be the same brooch. But it is…...

The passage of the text states William George Freeport, a wealthy lumber baron of the late 1800's had commissioned the brooch for his wife, throwing a lavish dinner party in his Adirondack home to show off the piece of jewelry. But it was one of the last parties William George Freeport hosted, from that point in history the family was plagued with great tragedy, houses burning down, mysterious deaths, fortunes lost……and suicide. Just to name a few. The brooch was lost, sold or simply thrown away…to this day no one knows it's whereabouts, but the author of the book claims the object was cursed and the reason for the families downfall.

Breaking out in a cold sweat, the room starts to spin, I feel faint and dizzy. The little boy at camp who almost drowned the day we came down the mountain with the brooch. I remember the brooch pinned to the inside of my jacket the day Vic and I run away so many years ago. Young, desperate and very pregnant, I placed the pin on the inside of my jacket thinking it might be valuable.

Then later, forgotten for years, I found the brooch in my jewelry box and wore it on an anniversary date with Jack, the next morning I miscarried our first child. Without consciously thinking about it, I thrust the brooch out of my life, wrapped in faded velvet covering, hidden in the dark recesses of my jewelry box.

Not a suspicious person by nature, I didn't fully grasp the connection of evil, until Jack suggested I wear it to a function at the country club in honor of his brother. I had completely forgotten about it, and I was fussing as women are wont to do, that my simple black dress needed something. Jack remembered the brooch for some reason. Being in a hurry, I didn't think, just pinned it to my dress and it looked perfect.

Giddy on the champagne served to toast his brother, we made mad love that night, and he died of a heart attack. Returning from the hospital, alone and bereft, I found the crumpled black dress on the floor, tossed in haste to satisfy our lust. And the jewels glittered and mocked me. It scared the bejeezus out of me.

This time I made the connection, the brooch was evil, the hermit's story ringing in my ears. A week after Jack's burial, I drove into the mountains. Digging deep into the rocky soil, scraping my hands raw, heaving sobs of grief, I buried the brooch. I covered it for all time, forgotten, to harm no more. Or so I thought….

"I knew it!" I cry out, jabbing a finger at the picture of the brooch in the book. "I knew that thing was evil."

At my outburst everyone in the store stops and stares at me. Vic shoots me a look of concern, rushing over to see the source of my distress.

"Elle?" His hand runs lightly down my back and I

instinctively move closer to him, seeking his protective embrace. "What's wrong?"

"Look, look, do you remember this?" I say, smoothing the pages of the book flat, gesturing with my finger to the picture of the brooch.

Leaning over, he studies the picture but no look of comprehension crosses his face. Shrugging his shoulders, he asks, "Should I?"

"Yes, don't you remember the day…." And I launch into the story about the wild man who scared us half to death and insisted we take the brooch back to camp.

Vic looks at the picture more closely. "I guess? I forgot about that ugly thing, are you sure this is the same brooch?"

As I start to answer him, I sense the presence of someone moving closer, staring, and eavesdropping on our conservation. I glance up; feeling uneasy and see a very large man, one of the employees working behind the counter feigning a disinterested posture. But I know he's edged closer, pretending to rearrange the jewelry in the display case. I know……he's listening. I lower my voice to a whisper, "Yes, I would recognize it anywhere and according to the book that ugly thing is worth a quarter of a million dollars!"

"Get out of here. You don't still have it, do you?" Vic asks in an incredulous voice not the least bit hushed.

"*Shhhhh…..*" I notice the large man's head snap up, as he leans in even closer, pretending to straighten his tie in the mirror on the counter next to us. There is something vaguely familiar about him, his size, the dark mane of hair pulled back into a braid that reaches down the middle of his back. His one hand has a jagged scar running up his wrist disappearing under his shirt sleeve. I have this feeling, I'm missing something, some piece of a puzzle, a sinking feeling in my gut……but I just can't place it.

"I'm sorry, but I just have to ask," interrupts a slightly overweight middle aged woman with hair too black to be real. Only her hairdresser, a bottle of Miss Clairol and a long line of Italian ancestors could produce hair that shade of black. Teased into a bouffant style and held in place with a long scarf, she looks like a gypsy fortune teller. "I will never forgive myself if I don't ask, but you look so much like Esteban Diego. I mean, who would expect to find a movie star in the Adirondack museum, but really, you look just like him. You are him, aren't you? My girlfriends will be *soo* jealous. Please sign my museum guidebook."

I stare at her incredulously….*sign* your museum guidebook? My mind screams……I'm thinking of placing the guidebook somewhere where the sun don't shine, lady….your girlfriends won't be so jealous then……

"You know, I had someone ask me that last month." Vic answers smoothly. "Who is this guy, did you say he was some baseball player?" He shrugs. "I don't think I could even spell his name? What was it again?"

"Oh, come on, really? Your girlfriend must know who he is, that hot Latino actor who plays Sentar in the movie, *FireBrand*." She insists in a wheedling voice.

I frown. Girlfriend, *girlfriend*?…. how does she know I'm not his wife…hey, he's asked me……..lots of times….maybe I better start saying yes……..I need a wedding ring with a *big* rock to keep away his horde of circling female vultures.

"Vic, darling, let's take this book. It's getting late and we need to head home." I cajole him, knowing he feels bad lying about his identity, but before you know it, there would be a swarm of autograph hunters. Rude or not, I want out of here. "We have plans for dinner, so if you'll please excuse us." I nod to her, pulling him toward the exit. *Liar, liar, pants on fire…..again. Boy*, when I finally get in that confessional, the priest better have a lunch, a six pack of beer, and a blanket…it's going to be a long day.

"I'm sorry," he says, taking the woman's guidebook, signing his name. "This is the best I can do."

"Vic Rienz," she scowls at the piece of paper. "Thanks for nothing." She stalks off in a snit throwing the pamphlet into the nearest trash bin.

"Little does she know," he shakes his head. "She had the real thing; a true fan would know my family name." This is his way of separating the sincere fan from the autograph hunters.

"Come on, hot stuff; let's get you out of here." I mutter under my breath.

In my haste to leave the museum, I fail to notice the large dark man from the gift shop running across the parking lot, and slide into a grey van with darkened windows. The van merges onto Route 28, and stays a few car lengths behind us, surreptitiously following, but not too close. But close enough to make the turn onto the deserted road, stopping short of our driveway, watching and waiting. Who has the stalker now?

Chapter 43

Jolib

The rain, razor-thin and mean with cold produces a miserable drizzle slicing through bones and into the spirit. More telling for a day in early April; and certainly unseasonable for Memorial Day weekend. The sort of morning when a reasonable person snuggles in bed; or at the very least, lingers over a second cup of coffee. But Cyrus, whining and scratching at the door has other ideas. A glance out the window reveals dark swirling mists hovering in the pines; the raindrops cling, sliding down bent tree branches, stretching closer to the ground like shadows behind a silver curtain.

Rather than disturb Vic, I silently creep out of the bedroom, closing the door behind me. He's exhausted from the tedious all day publicity shoots and interviews necessary for the launch of the new movie. Along with the predawn work out sessions to maintain his physical conditioning, he needs his beauty sleep.

In the kitchen, I turn on the coffee pot, looking forward to a hot cup of coffee after my walk. Grabbing Cyrus's leash from a hook by the door, I slip out onto the porch, inhaling the fresh damp morning air. Checking to ensure the security code is clear, I head down the dirt road at a brisk pace. Cyrus gives an excited bark and picks up a stick chasing after me, insisting we play fetch. Scanning the trees, I see songbirds flitting back and forth between the branches. In the distance, the sweet whistle of the white-throated sparrow calling *Sam, Peabody, Peabody, Peabody* anchors one to the mountains in spring.

Only the steady crunch of my feet on the gravel road punctuates the stillness of the deep woods. Lani and Jason along with Trey and Hanna are coming for the long weekend. It will be the first time the family has been together since Christmas where someway, somehow……everyone got along famously. I can't wait to see them again. I wish Josh were joining us. Maybe next time. I need to be patient, good things come to those who wait…but I'm tired of waiting……

Hitching up the collar of my jacket against the damp, I divert my attention to the preparations for the weekend ahead. The beds are made with fresh sheets, small bouquets of wildflowers are strategically placed in each bedroom. Pillows stuffed with balsam fir needles are tucked into nooks and crannies throughout the house giving a pungent welcome to the Adirondacks. As my feet move along the road, my mind runs through the menu I've planned for the weekend, mentally checking my list to ensure everything is in place to create sumptuous feasts for my family. I'm in way over my head, but I've been practicing some of the recipes Bridget gave me. The Barefoot Contessa, I'm not, but with a marathon of cooking shows to my credit, I might pull it off.

I'm so preoccupied with preparations for the weekend; I don't hear the branches cracking in the undergrowth behind me until Cyrus growls and barks. I whirl to catch a blur of movement and a vicious yank on my arm slams me against the rock hard chest of an unseen assailant. A rag with a disgustingly sweet cloying smell is shoved against my mouth and nose cutting off the flow of fresh air. Ether, my rapidly fogging brain manages to register. I hear Cyrus barking frantically.

My heels skid across the gravel, the light fades as I'm

dragged into the woods away from home and safety.

...

Damp wood smoke, the acrid smell of a fireplace left unattended, half burned logs lying in a bed of soggy ashes brings me to consciousness. Simply turning my head produces a shearing pain radiating from the base of my skull to slam into the back of my eyes. A small whimper escapes my throat. Dear God, where am I.... what's happened to me? A numbing, stabbing pain screams up my arms and legs as I try to move, my hands and feet are tied. Opening my eyes, I see the sheen of duct tape in the faint light binding my hands tightly in front of me, cutting off circulation and any hope of moving freely. Screaming will do no good as my mouth is taped closed. Rolling to a half seated position, I see dust motes float in the wane light filtering through windows streaked with grime, half hidden by shades tattered and ripped through years of hard use. Walls of rough-cut lumber painted an insipid green popular in the 1950's stare back at me. From my limited viewpoint, the room is furnished with a table and three badly battered chairs; the bed I'm lying on is pushed against the wall farthest from the hearth. A rudely constructed cupboard and countertop hold a meager assortment of food items, neatly stacked. Who lives here....and why am I here? Why would someone want to do this to me? What time is it? Has Vic missed me yet? Surely he must realize something's wrong.

Pain and despair nearly spiral me back into the oblivious peace of unconsciousness. I close my eyes and listen, paying attention for any sound indicating I'm not alone. Moments of silence follow. I will my legs to swing over the side of the bed, sitting up gives me a better vantage point to survey the surroundings in hopes of finding a way to escape or seek help.

The door is ten feet away from the bed. Can I hop or roll to the door with my hands and legs tied? I need to free my hands. Frantically searching for any object to slice through the duct tape, I spy an ax lying next to the hearth. Hopping slowly, icicles of pain shoot up my legs, yet I manage to reach the hearth. Crouching down, I wiggle my fingers to place the small ax in position between my feet, and slowly and painfully saw at the tape wrapped around my wrists, gasping in panic at the thought of my abductor returning. At last my hands break free of the bonds, I almost scream as the blood rushes into my fingers bringing blessed pain and relief. Choked with fear, I claw at the tape holding my legs prisoner. As the last piece falls away, I streak for the door, only to have it flung open before I can reach the knob. The force of the door opening sends me crashing into the table, scattering chairs across the room.

A huge dark man with a mane of black hair flowing down to his waist fills the doorway with his presence. His eyes glitter with malevolence, his beard spattered with spittle as he screams, "You, stupid bitch!"

His long arm snakes out, cruelly grabbing my elbow yanking me to my feet. "What the hell do you think you are doing?" Dropping my arm, he rears back, slashes the air with his huge paw of a hand, and slaps me across the face, sending me careening back, smacking my head against the wall. An explosion of violent color and pain blind me, as my body goes slack in shock at the assault upon it. I've never felt such pain in my entire life. The room spins, his voice a distant throbbing against my ears, muted, muffled like a tape recorder played in slow motion. I start sinking into the abyss of unconsciousness, only to be cruelly pulled to my feet, tossed like a rag doll on to the bed with a wrenching jolt.

His fetid breath hisses in my ear, "You will not die until you tell me what I need to know, you lying stealing whore! Do you hear me?" He shakes my body in cadence with his fury. "Do…you…hear…me!"

"Wh…what are you talking about?" I manage to rasp out of a throat, parched by fear, ether fumes, and lack of water. God knows how long I've laid here. Fear permeates the very core of my being. What does this insane man want from me? Is he some depraved fan of Vic's, jealous over his wife or girlfriends' obsession, one of my student's parents or a family member? Wild speculations run rampant through my head. Desperation causes me to grasp at any idea explaining this man's crazy behavior. Who drugs a person, kidnaps and holds someone hostage, especially me. Seriously, I'm a fifth grade school teacher; this must somehow be connected to Vic or a random act of violence.

"You know what I'm talking about!" My vision diminished due to the rapid swelling of my eye, takes in this wild apparition of a man, and recognition shoots through my brain, sending fear, and dread cascading in a rush of adrenalin. Oh, my God, it's the man from the museum. Gone is the neat and tidy appearance of the bookstore employee. It's the man leaning over the counter, listening in on my conversation with Vic.

"Answer me!" He says, threading his hand through my hair, twisting my head so my face is posed just inches below him, his breath reeking of alcohol and rage.

I barely recognize him, his hair unbound, the wild look in his eyes, clothes dirty and disheveled.

"Stop," I plead. "I can't breathe."

"You're not giving the orders here, you lying thief!" He rolls off me to tower above the bed. A black hulking hallucination from hell. "I've waited too long for this day. You will tell me where you put it ….now! He rages, grabbing my chin between his powerful hands; squeezing with enough force to break my jaw.

I sob, "I, I don't know…..I don't know what you want." I pause, my lungs burning as I drag in much needed air, desperately willing my brain to think. What does he want? "Please don't hit me again….please." I whimper, ashamed of the fear paralyzing me. "If you tell me, maybe I can give you what you want."

"The brooch, you stupid woman." He lurches to the head of the bed, shaking the footboard with fury, causing the bed to buck and roll, sending a wave of nausea through me.

The brooch, of course. That accursed thing has come back to haunt me again, this time to kill me. In the foggy recesses of my brain, I try to piece together what he wants to know about the brooch.

"The one in the book?" I ask, instinctively bracing myself for another blow.

"Yes, you have it, I know you have it." He glowers down at me with a twisted sneer on his face. "I heard the two of you talking when you didn't think I was listening."

With my mind racing, I try to remember, did I tell Vic about this man? I was so upset over finding a picture of the brooch in the book; I just wanted to block out the whole incident. I don't think I told him. I don't know….I don't remember…..why didn't I listen to my gut. If Vic remembers my suspicions then he may have a clue of where to start searching for me. If I tell this mad man the brooch is no longer in my possession, he'll kill me and leave me here. No one will find me.

Think….think…think… I press a fingertip against my temple, willing my brain to work. I have to stall him long enough for Vic to find me. How did I get here, where are we? I can smell the scent of balsam trees in the air, so we must still be in the mountains. But where?

"Why do you think I have it?" I question him hoping to buy time, feverishly thinking of ways to delay my untimely death.

"I gave it to you and that stupid smartass boyfriend of yours, years ago. I've spent the last thirty years of my life searching for it." He screams at me, lurching closer to my huddled form on the bed. He grabs my throat, pinning my body to the headboard as he slowly closes his hand over my windpipe. "Give it back to me. Where do you have it?" He growls. "Shall I keep choking you? I can easily snap your neck. Just a little pressure here." He exerts more force on my throat. "Are you going to cooperate with me?"

I claw frantically at his hand while trying to nod my head held in his death grip. I collapse, coughing and gasping as he releases his hold. "It's buried." I choke out, chest heaving with the effort of breathing. I study the face of this man holding me hostage through a haze of pain. Jolib! That crazy hermit Vic and I met in the woods so many years ago. The man who stuffed the brooch in my pack. How could I have been so stupid, not to recognize him. The familiar nagging feeling I had yesterday, the premonition of foreboding. I merely shrugged it off as a silly woman's intuition, now has come back to haunt me.

"What do you mean it's buried? Where did you put it?" He roars at me.

"Why do you want it, the thing is cursed. You know that. The brooch caused me nothing but heartache, so I got rid of it." I sob, pleading with him. "You saw the book, it's true."

"It's mine; I never should have given it to you." He stumbles around the room, clutching fistfuls of hair in his hands. Moaning, "It's mine, mine, it belongs to my family. Give it back, give it back."

"But you have a job and a life. Aren't you afraid of the curse? I lost my boyfriend, a baby and husband because of that damned thing." He lifts his head from his hands, eyes bleary with obsession, greed and lust. I hesitate in the face of such madness. "I can try to find where I buried it, or just let me go. I promise I won't tell anyone. This will be our little secret. If you need money, I'm sure I could come up with….

"No! Stop!" He screams, dropping his trembling hands to his side. "It's not about money." He halts his pacing to glare at me. "Where did you bury it?"

"Off a hiking trail, about two years ago." I feel the sting of pain in my heart. The memories come flooding back. The grief and agony of loss I felt as I scrabbled in the earth, digging, deeper and deeper praying never to see that damned brooch again. And now this man wants me to find it.

"Where?!" He roars shaking the bed. I glance out the grimy windows; twilight has set in, the light gone from the day. The gloaming hour, despair fills me. Panic threatens to overwhelm me.

"I can find it." I lie, my mind scrambling back to the day I buried the brooch. I purposely put it in an obscure spot, where temptation would not beckon me back. "Let me think a minute, it's dark now, I can't find it in the dark." The thought of spending the night alone with him is terrifying, but buys time for a search team. They must be looking for me. Vic will be relentless in his search. And the children arrived today, I feel disheartened to know how worried they must be, yet the thought of my loved ones looking for me is comforting.

His shadow looms in the fading light. "What town is it near?" He demands "Think you, stupid bitch, think."

A plan comes to me; the odds of being found are slim to none; no one knows where I am. I buried the brooch on a seldom used path leading off the main trail up Blue Mountain. As the children were growing up, the trail to the top of Blue Mountain was a favorite family hike. One day we decided to try a new route by diverting off the main trail, it turned out to be a dangerous decision. The trail narrowed to a thin ledge along the mountain pass, I wanted to turn back, but Jack and the kids were caught up in the adrenalin rush of adventure. At a narrow point on the trail Lani's foot slipped on a loose rock, fortunately a tree growing out of the rocky ledge saved her from a serious fall down the precipitous. The adventure lost its luster; and we never took that trail again. Until the day I brought the brooch back to the mountains, some sense of calamity must have called me back to that rocky ledge. I scrambled up the steep summit, and once assured that no one was around; I buried the brooch, hoping never see it again. Maybe, just maybe, if I took him up the mountain; he'd have to free my legs, opening the possibly for escape or give me the opportunity to push him off the ledge. An icy chill runs up my back. Do I have the courage to shove him over the edge? Could I kill someone?........Do I have a choice?

Chapter 44

Nightmare

Night passes in bouts of fitful sleep; exhaustion fueled by terror pushes my body to survival mode. Easier to succumb to sleep then the horror of reality, so unbelievably, I slept.

Dinner, a bottle of water and two stale granola bars. Not having eaten all day, I devoured them like a starving animal. Trying to sleep with my legs and arms bound by strips of duct tape is agony. Movement brings on spasms of muscle pain, lying still, a torment of numbness and shooting pain. Screaming or crying, a waste of effort, another strip of tape stretches across my mouth, preventing any sound from escaping. Awake, I lay with ears straining for any sound of rescue, hearing only the silent forest. There's nothing to do but wait and hope. I lost count of how many times I recited the rosary in my head, using pressure on my fingertips as counting beads. The fingers of my one hand throb with pain, I think I broke them falling against the hearth. Praying the mindless manta of Hail Marys helps sooth my frayed nerves and offers a glimmer of hope.

He sleeps in a tattered recliner next to the fireplace, pieces of stuffing fall out of holes in the worn corduroy. His snores echo in the still of the cabin, he sleeps secure in the knowledge I have no chance of escape. In addition to the duct tape bonds, I'm tied to the bed frame. The threadbare quilt covering me provides little warmth. I'm freezing. The night passes in a misery of dreams, and the dreams distort into nightmares.

"Get up, you lazy bitch." The quilt snatched away, as a rough hand jerks my body upright. The stench of evil called Jolib Freeport wakes me, bringing harsh reality, a wash of pain, hunger and cold. Consciousness comes in a welter of confusion. Angry cramped muscles screamed for relief and I needed to use the bathroom…now!

A slight graying in the east separates the trees from an overcast sky as feeble morning light filters through the windows. The morning chorus of songbirds announces a new day, a new chance at life. Will I survive this day? Fear engulfs me.

Twenty minutes later he rudely thrusts me out the cabin door, the cold morning air snaps my senses awake. Parked next to the dilapidated cabin sits a new white panel van; tires sunk in muddy tracks. The van stands in sharp contrast to the squalor of the yard strewn with rusted lawn furniture, old appliances and bags of trash piled against a woodshed.

"Stand still." He orders pushing me against the side of the van. My arms cruelly yanked behind my back and tied again. A red handkerchief is tied across my eyes, followed by the ripping sound of another piece of duct tape to silence me.

Through the night, my clamoring mind pieced together a plan, shaky at best, but having few other options, there is little I can do. On a map, I pointed out the trailhead for Blue Mountain, refusing to give him more information until we reached this destination. Claiming not to remember all the details of the trail, I assured him once there it would all come back to me. Realizing by holding back information, giving only bits and pieces at a time, I increase my chances of survival. My hope is someone will see us at the trailhead, I can scream for help or escape. If I go up the trail with him, locate the brooch and in his eagerness to have it in his possession, the distraction may give me an opportunity to shove him over the edge and escape. Maybe....God... I don't want to die.

Lying on the floor of the van, I feel every bump and jar of the rough road. The drive takes about 40 minutes, twenty minutes on a dirt road and another twenty on the highway, then a left turn. A left turn onto Route 28? Where in God's name were we?

The van tires crunch to a stop on a gravel drive of some sort, the engine idles then stills, the only sound is his labored breathing. He must have some kind of respiratory ailment; I've seen him use a medication inhaler of some sort. This could work to my advantage, I'm in good shape, a strenuous uphill hike over rough terrain, and maybe I can out run him.

I hear the click of his seat belt release; he stumbles back to where I lie on the floor of the van. I feel something hard, metallic and cold press into my back. It......can't....be....but I know it is.......a gun. How can I out run a gun?

"Listen, and listen good," he grabs my hair and pulls me into a sitting position. "We're at the trail head for Blue Mountain. It's early I don't see anyone around. The only other cars here are probably hikers in the back country."

I whimper. My heart sinks at the news the parking lot is deserted. I had hopes of making contact with someone before heading into the woods with this madman. "I'm going to take this gag off so you can tell me where we have to go." He shoves the gun into my ribs, I groan with pain as a new bruise joins the kaleidoscope of red, green and purple on my body. "Don't think of screaming, there is no one here, you scream or try to escape, you'll be sorry."

Was it only yesterday I had a family who loved me, a home? I was safe and secure, decisions no larger than what to wear or cook for dinner. With his free hand, the tape covering my mouth is ripped away.

The nausea from the bumpy ride comes flooding over me, the gag reflex repressed for so long will not be denied. My stomach heaves, I retch as I have never retched before, rolling to my side in gut wrenching spasms.

"Stop, what are you doing?" He screams in alarm. "Not in my van, for Christ sake!" Without thinking, he flings open the door, and shoves my body onto the gravel parking lot. Stones scrape my tender bruised skin and vomit pools from the side of my mouth. There can be no greater misery. When finished, he hauls me to my feet and uses the pistol as a pivot, shoving me back into the van. Removing the blindfold, he hisses, "What the hell kind of stunt was that!"

"I couldn't help it," I rasp out, trying to wipe my mouth on the sleeve of my jacket. "Water, please!" He cuts the duct tape away and using both hands, trembling, I lift the water bottle to purge the taste from my mouth.

He looks out the front window, "I don't see anyone, you're lucky."

"Let's go before someone comes," he cuts the ties binding my feet. "I'll get out first. You don't come until I tell you." He shoves the gun into my rib cage. "Got it? No funny business." I nod miserably.

The trees filter out the sunlight overhead as we head up the trail made of hard packed-dirt and rock.

Barely able to walk, I push my bruised and beaten body. Cramped muscles cry out in pain, and I feel faint from lack of food and water. Yet, the haunting beauty of the mountain morning touches my soul. If this is my last morning, I'm glad it's in the mountains. Stumbling on an exposed tree root, I fall to my knees, only to have the butt of the pistol thrust into my back as he hauls me to my feet.

"Get up, thieving bitch." He grunts. I hear his labored breathing behind me. I feel a sense of satisfaction, as much as I'm hurting, he's struggling to keep up. I hear him stop periodically to use his inhaler. In hopes of exhausting him, I've taken the steeper longer path, circling around to the top of the ledge instead of heading directly there. He stops often to rest, his breath coming in ragged gasps. "How much farther?" He wheezes. "I'm starting to think you're bluffing me."

"It's at the top of the ridge; see those boulders to the right." I gesture frantically, bracing myself against the bark of an old hemlock tree. I can feel the sticky pine sap ooze onto my hands. *Wait*….is that my imagination, or did I hear the crack of a tree branch?

"Get moving; I'm losing patience." He threatens, pointing to the path with his gun.

Reaching the tree line, climbing over waist high boulders, we scramble to the top. I hear his heavy breathing and the sound of his boots slipping, as they fail to find hold on the algae covered rock. I survey the rise of the rocky contours, searching for the crevice I had dug out a few years ago. I pause and listen, pretending I'm searching for the hiding spot, and I think I hear another muffled sound in the woods. Is it my imagination or is someone out there? Stealthy creeping, following, waiting for the opportunity to strike when Jolib's not watching. Can I dare hope? Over his labored breathing, he'll never hear the background noise. If I'm right, maybe I can help by creating a diversion. The brooch; I have to find it. His obsession will be his undoing.

"God damn it, where are you taking me? You said it was here." He demands, chest heaving.

"Give me a second to catch my breath and look around." I inhale and exhale loudly, mimicking his labored breathing. Using the noise of our combined breathing to cover the faint sounds I hear approaching, moving behind the cover of the tree line. I have to act quickly while he is winded. I hear the *hiss* of his inhaler.

Choosing a rock crevice where the brooch may have been buried I reach up, closing my hand over a large branch. My fingers pluck and poke though the soft place on the rock ledge, creating a pile of loose dirt, grit and stone. Finding a sizeable stone, I place it on top of the pile. Digging deeper; reveals…*nothing*. My plan involved finding the brooch and throwing at his face to distract him. *Damn it…….where is it?* A glance over the side of the ledge shows nothing. The faint noise I heard earlier must have been the longings of my desperate imagination. I have to act now, it's my only chance.

"Here, I think I have it." I position the branch near the crevice opening, cradling the rock in one hand, while taking a scoop of loose dirt in the other.

"Damn it, about time!" He leans over toward me, excitement causing his voice to quaver. "Show me, show me!"

Soon….a few seconds more, I tell myself. Having him so fiendishly close makes the back of my neck tighten, my whole body quivers in fear.

"Here it is." I yell, tossing the large stone into the air.

He cries out and lunges, trying to grab the flying object.

Quick as a snake I strike. Using the branch I swat at the hand holding the gun and it goes off. My other hand flings dirt and rock into his eyes. Jolib screams, clawing at his eyes.

The sound of a gunshot deafens me. The shot from Jolib's gun went wild, but the bullet fired by the State Trooper S.W.A.T. team hit its target. Jolib staggers, shrieking obscenities, arms flailing as the force of the bullet pushes him over the edge.

I crumble. Whatever courage and bravado I possessed earlier, now spent, as I collapse in a shivering, sobbing heap on the ground

Chapter 45

The Proposal

Jolib's death scream echoes across the ridge as his body plunges over the cliff. My body folds in on itself and I lay huddled like a limp rag doll, crying with heart wrenching sobs. The sound of heavy boots comes crashing through the underbrush. The vague impression of men in khaki uniforms, their words drifting through heavy layers of exhausted relief. The pain in my fingers aches with a pulsing need for attention. I'm afraid to move. Fear paralyzes me as I cling to the ledge where I'm so precariously balanced.

From above, voices call, sounding so strained, so sharp. A man kneels down beside me, his voice softening, "Ellen, its over. I'm Officer McNeil." He touches my shoulder. "Mrs. O'Connor, we're here to help you. You're going to be fine."

"Are you hurt?" he asks.

Through the dull roar in my head his voice comes again, but the words don't make sense. Unable to respond, my barely conscious mind wants to answer, but I can't find lucid words in the whirling haze of my dazed brain.

He leans in, pulling my body away from the ledge to rest against him. His hands are swift and efficient as he reaches for a blanket to swaddle my quaking limbs. Muscles shudder uncontrollably beneath his touch as he swings me up in his arms, striding to a flat area of the exposed mountaintop. With my head bobbing against his shoulder, I catch a glimpse of camouflage men peering over the edge into the abyss below.

Laying me gently on the ground, "Ellen, does this hurt?" he asks, competently running his hands over my body assessing for injuries. I wince as he taps on my rib cage. "Does this hurt? His hand slips under my shirt for more careful examination. "I'm not sure about this rib." The probing causes me to moan. He's saying something important, something I should comprehend…if only I could think straight. I feel the world whirl around me in slow revolutions that leaves me nauseous. My good hand clutches fistfuls of wool, searching for something solid, an anchor. I lay atop the blanket, shivering in the morning cold. The harsh fabric against my battered face makes me cringe.

A voice I don't recognize as my own rasps, "Vic, my children?" My throat parched, I can barely speak, but I need to know where they are.

He hesitates a moment, then chuckles. "Eh…that would be Rambo II. I suspect he and your children are crashing up the mountainside right now, heedless of a trail or not when they saw the all clear flair go up."

"Rambo II?" What is he talking about? There is such a pounding in my head, a steady roaring, drowning out his words so that I only hear a few at a time.

"Your husband, boyfriend, whatever, has been over the top frantic to find you. He insisted on joining us in the apprehension of your kidnapper." I nod wordlessly imagining the scene Vic would have made in his panic to find me.

"He claims he played a S.W.A.T. team member in one of his movies. In fact, he spent actual time with the team to prepare for his role, so therefore, that qualified him to come along with us." Officer McNeil chuckles as he wipes fine beads of sweat from his brow, sitting back on his heels to visually assess me. "I think one of your ribs might be cracked. Does it hurt to breathe?"

I nod, aware of the sharp pain on my left side. I lift my crumbled hand for his inspection. I inhale sharply as he gently examines each digit. To take my mind off the pain, I picture Vic charging up the mountain followed by Lani, Jason, Trey and Hanna in tow. I take great comfort and a little humor in the thought. That's my man-all brash and bravado.

"Yeah, this hand needs attention." He reaches into a medical bag at his side pulling out a splint device.

Officer McNeil rambles on as my feeble brain spins to keep up with him. "We told Mr. Diago that spending a day or two with a S.W.A.T. team does not qualify him to join in the apprehension, especially when the apprehension concerns a loved one. We don't allow our own officers to participle if a family member is involved. Your judgment's clouded and you're not thinking rationally. It's just not done." He nods matter of factly. He looks up from his ministering, his right hand holding the splint securely in place. "Even in light of the seriousness of the situation, we couldn't help calling him Rambo II."

"He still insisted, didn't he?" Somehow it was reassuring to know the depth of his fear and concern.

"Insist is putting it mildly; if his daughter hadn't calmed him down, physical restraint would have been necessary. Hey, Tom, pass me over a bottle of water." He deftly catches a plastic bottle tossed in his direction, a quick twist of his wrist, and he's holding precious relief in his hand. "Now, you look kind of parched. So we are going to take it slow, too much will make you sick."

I nod feebly as he eases me into a sitting position. Only the pressure of his strong hand prevents me from gulping the entire bottle. Leaning back into his muscular arms, I start to feel better. Hey, he's actually kind of cute….okay….now I know I'm feeling better.

"So you didn't have to tie him down?" I ask, my stiff muscles starting to relax as the warmth of his chest seeps into the cocoon of the wool blanket.

"No, you have good kids. Anxious as they were, they understood the logic behind our decision. And they reasoned with him. Your future son-in-law managed to keep everyone organized and cooperate with us." *Jason.* Officer McNeil continues, "I would expect Rambo any second. This mountain isn't going to slow him down. He looks to be in pretty good shape." He gives a rueful laugh, adjusting the blanket, pulling it closer. "I don't think I'll be carrying you down."

Another man clad in khaki kneels down beside us and asks, "How's our lady doing?"

"I think she's going to be just fine, a little rest and some readjustment of bones, she'll be fit as a fiddle." He eases his head back to peer into my face. "You doing okay?" I nod weakly.

"This is Officer Tom Pulanski, Ellen." Officer McNeil gestures toward a freckled face police officer who doesn't look old enough to drive. His uniform baseball cap perched backwards on his head, a thatch of red hair sticking out the front. With an impish grin, he looks like one of Trey's friends waiting for pizza in my family room. "Tom's the head of our tracking operation." McNeil adds.

Really….God, I feel old. I smile in his direction and whisper, "How did you find me?"

"A lady was walking her dog at the trailhead this morning, and saw you lying on the ground with your hands tied behind your back. Freeport was holding you at gun point. And because your kidnapper wasn't very smart and left evidence at the point of abduction, we were able to release an A.P.B. last night and the woman recognized the situation. Lucky for you, she was able to use her cell phone. A helicopter response team coupled with search and rescue dogs, and we were tracking you in no time." Officer Pulanski grins with unabashed pride over his part in the rescue. "Rambo remembered your suspicions about the man from the museum so we were able to track down some information about the suspect. The local search and rescue team knew the area which allowed us to zero in on a target zone. Oh, by the way, one of the guys on the S & R team seems to know you."

Oh, God……Josh. What must he be thinking….here she goes….again. First, the skinny dipping incident with the cops followed by shoving him in the river and now a S.W.A.T. team with the entire county on alert. Yeah, this kid's going to love me. Who wants a resident wacko for a mother? I nod, locking eyes with Pulanski, not feeling so good again.

"I think his name is Josh," he screws his face up in thought. "You know, he looks an awful lot like your Rambo friend."

I close my eyes and nod, attempting to stem the fresh wave of nausea washing over me. I clutch McNeil's shirt to anchor my spinning head. Josh and Vic…together that had to be some reunion, like looking in the mirror. Is Josh suspicious?

The sound of pounding feet, an explosion of cracking branches, accompanied by heavy breathing and someone frantically calling my name……Vic has arrived.

"Elle!" He cries, running towards me, his face taut with concern. "Ella, Ella, mia, are you hurt? Is she all right?" His eyes search the police officers faces, fear and worry radiate from him.

Officer Pulanski holds out a hand, slowing him down, "Easy sir, she's going to be fine. But we have to take care; she has a few broken bones."

"Are you sure? Elle, look at me, baby." His eyes beseech me, "How can she be all right, look at her?"

"Elle…" his voice cracks with emotion. "What did he do to you?" He holds out a trembling hand to caress my cheek, but pulls back at the last second; afraid his touch will cause me pain.

"Vic," I thought I screamed his name, but the sound emerging from my lips, no more than a croak.

"Sweet Jesus, Ellen." He's pissed, he's calling me Ellen again, that means he's mad. A single tear cascades down his cheek, the muscles in his jaw twitch. "This is it, Elle, I can't take it anymore. Do you hear me! When I get you down this mountain, I'm grabbing the first minister, justice of the peace, or whatever the hell I can find.… and once the doctors give you clearance…. *You* are fucking going to marry me! Ike and I will be your bodyguards 24/7. I've almost lost you three times. I can't take this anymore….No more bullshit about where we are going to live, old lives, new lives, children, and who the hell gives a flying shit!!…..You're killing me. I'm never letting you out of my sight. Ever! Ever! Again! Do you hear me?!

He looks exhausted, the worry of the past few days erupting in a volley of emotion. I long to touch his face, and ease the lines of tension bracketing his lips; smooth away the deep crevice of worry between his black brows.

"Dad, was that a proposal?" Vic glances over his shoulder at the sight of Hanna, Lani, Jason and Trey. Faces scratched, hair flying in all directions, clothes ripped and marred by dirt streaks. *Boy*, are they going to make me pay for this…..Lani and Hanna hate wilderness experiences, their idea of the outdoors is having their nails done in the suburbs.

"Mom!" Lani sobs, falling to her knees, eyes blurred and red from exhaustion and crying. "Mom, tell us you're all right. Mom, please say something?" I try lifting my crippled hand, and nod weakly in her direction.

"It's over, sweetie." I whisper. "I'll be fine." Lani breaks down into gasping sobs of relief. Trey kneels beside her, his hands kneading the curve of her shoulder, his face a tight wall of concern… his eyes never leave my face.

"Mom?" He utters in a hoarse whisper. A broken smile slides across my lips, our eyes lock and I nod.

"Dad," Hanna crouches down, placing an arm over her father's shoulders. "I think you need to rephrase that proposal. *You're fucking going to marry me,* boy, what a declaration of love. I can only hope my future husband is such a romantic. Not!" She laughs, kneeling down to give her father an affectionate hug. "Thank God, we found you, Ellen. I can't imagine living with this lunatic for the rest of my life if he lost you. He was like, *totally* insane." Jason nods vigorously in agreement.

"I was not!" Vic insists defensively glaring at the group. Everyone, including the S.W.A.T. team; roll their eyes, and snort with laughter.

"Yeah….right." Lani says with a knowing wink at Officer McNeil. "So about that proposal?"

"Of course, I mean it. Damn it to hell!" He shakes his head in exasperation. "I've been trying to marry her for the last six months. And since she's come up here, she's done nothing but get herself into trouble." *Holy moly, don't have a cow.*

And the thought of spending the rest of my life sheltered in his arms, always and forever…my dull mind wraps around one word, *bliss.*

"Can I hold her?" Vic opens his arms, reaching for me. Officer McNeil slowly releases his hold, transferring me to Vic who locks me in his strong arms. I press my cheek to his chest, listening to the steady beat of his heart. Over the throbbing in my head, I hear him whisper my name, over and over, like a prayer.

"Are you really okay?" He brushes his thumb across the corner of my lips. "I was so afraid he would kill you."

"Yeah, I had the same thought." I say, snuggling against his chest, drawing comfort from his body.

"Tell me, what can I do?" He slides his hand along the length of my body, the heat of his palm radiating through the blanket.

"Hold me, Vic." I whisper. "Hold me, and never let me go."

"Ella, Ella, my bella," He murmurs, burrowing his head into my dirty tangled hair. He pushes back a stray lock, gently tucking it behind my ear.

He strokes my face with the back of his fingers, wishing to take away the fear and terror. "My mia bella…..marry me, tomorrow."

"No."

I smile as his expression pulls into a frown, confusion clouds his face, he looks askance to the children, as if he heard wrong.

"Elle?" he questions.

I press a fingertip to his lips, a mischievous light twinkles in my eyes. I love him. I will always love him. "Soon," I say, "I want to marry you, but at the Camp with our friends and family surrounding us." He smiles, his lips curve beneath my fingertips. My voice raspy from disuse continues, "I want champagne, fireworks and I want to wear white. Just because. And I want our son there."

A tall figure casts a shadow as he crouches down beside us. "I would be honored to be included, and quite frankly," he chuckles, "It's about time the two of you got married and made me legitimate." *Josh…..*

Josh more than suspects, he knows.

"Like I was saying," Josh continues, "It's about time the two of you made me legal. I've always known I was adopted and Claire picked up immediately on the resemblance between Ellen and my son, Ansel. And when I saw Mr. Diago yesterday, up close and in person, the physical resemblance, well, I thought I was looking in the mirror. So?…do you have something to tell me?"

Vic and I start babbling at once. Yes, he is our son. We didn't want to give him up for adoption; he was taken from us at birth. And now that we found him, we thought if he got to know us first, it would be less of a shock when he learned we were his biological parents.

"Please don't think we're crazy stalker people." I beg him.

"Are you kidding? I'm touched by the care and concern you have for my feelings. And if the last few weeks prove to be any indication of the future, between the two of you, there'll never be a dull moment. Throw in a few new brothers and sisters…I think life is going to get much more interesting."

My voice tremulous, "Can I ask just one thing?"

Josh smiles; emotion softens his face, "Anything."

I open my arms and ask, "May I hug you?" Broken finger and bruised ribs forgotten, I engulf my son and hold him as I've so desperately longed to do....and feel the very being of him seep into my soul, his strength and goodness beneath my hands, and know I've found my son....*at last.*

Chapter 46

Home, Sweet Home

My nose twitches like a rabbit. Something smells good, a smell so divine, it pulls me from deep slumber. Sprawled on my stomach, head stuffed into the pillow with just my nose peeking out, I smell it. And it's coming closer, pushing aside tousled hair I see a mug thrust into my face. With a happy sigh, I roll over to a cup of coffee, followed by a plate with a cinnamon bun fresh from the oven. Pulling myself into a setting position, I see Vic standing next to the bed, dressed only in a pair of low slung jeans hugging his hips in all the right places, and low enough to expose those six-pack abs. And I find myself humming along with Julie Andrews……girls in white dresses with blue satin sashes, snowflakes that fall on my nose and eyelashes, silver white winters that melt into spring…….these are a few of my favorite things and standing before me ……..is one of my favorite things. If I died now…….. it would be a happy death.

"Wow!" I smile at him in appreciation.

"You're welcome, now get up."

"Up? I'm happy here. And I'd be a lot happier if you came and joined me." I lift the blanket in invitation.

"Nope. I've got plans." He says and starts rummaging through the dresser tossing out a pair of jeans, t-shirt and sweater, followed by a bra and panties.

"What plans? Hey!" I protest as he takes the mug and plate putting them out of my reach. "What are you doing?"

"Getting you out of bed." He replies, pulling a shirt

over his head. I feign a pout. There's nothing like the sight of a taut abdomen and well defined biceps with your morning coffee. *Who needs doughnuts?*

"I'll be down on the dock and I expect you in twenty minutes."

"What.....why?"

"And don't be late." *Bossy, bossy, bossy.* I grumble as my feet hit the cold hardwood floor. You'd think after all I've been through he would be more considerate......just because he's hovered over me for the last ten days after shooing our children home, he'd continue taking care of me ....indefinitely. I liked having my own personal stud butler. Complete with dark hair, gorgeous eyes, and a *very fine butt.* After all, it's not every day a person is kidnapped by a maniac and needs to be rescued. That deserves extra attention... I wasn't kidding about the invitation between the sheets. Sighing, I pick up my clothes from the foot of the bed, noticing he didn't choose very sexy underwear. Granny panties! What's wrong with him, he *always* notices my underwear.

...

Hopping down the lawn while trying to put on sandals takes all my concentration until I stop, gawking at the sight in front of me. An old wooden canoe riding high in the water is tied to the dock. Its varnished sides gleam in the morning sun, and a bouquet of white daisies rests against the gunnels. A wicker picnic basket sits in the bow while a caned-back seat cushioned with a life jacket takes up the middle of the boat.

"Wow!" I exclaim halting, one foot in my hand, amazed at the sight before me. "What's this? *Wow and double wow!*

He's standing on the dock holding out his hand, "I

thought we'd take a picnic lunch, head down the lake."

"But the canoe, it's beautiful. Did you do this?"

"No, woodland fairies." Vic says, his mouth twitching. "I keep a crew on standby."

"Really? I thought Ike was visiting his sister in Montreal?"

Vic snorts, "Ike's been called a lot of things, but I want to be there when someone calls him a fairy."

He beckons me toward the boat. "Hop in." He nods at the canoe. "Sit in the middle seat."

"I can't paddle from there."

"That's the plan."

"What if I feel like paddling," I whine. "I'm well enough to paddle a canoe. Oh, come on! It's not like I'm an invalid or something."

"No."

"Just a little bit."

"You have two broken fingers and a bruised rib."

"So?"

"You need to take it easy for a while." He shakes his head. "Besides, this way I can keep an eye on you, make sure you stay out of trouble."

"But I feel like moving, I'm tired of being cooped up in the house. I can only read and do puzzles for so long. I need to move before I go crazy.......and I think I'm ready for *other* activities." I waggle my eyebrows at him in a suggestive manner.

Vic rests his head against the paddle, muttering in rapid fire Spanish, shoulders heaving, head shaking back and forth in agitation. A smart woman would know better than to argue with him once he gets going, but then again, no one has ever accused me of being smart.

"Hey, I don't understand much Spanish, but I think

you said I'm driving you crazy."

"I did." He lifts his head from its perch atop the paddle and peers at me, his eyebrows drawing together. "Ella, Ella, mia. I love you but I can't keep up this pace, I'll be an old man before my time."

"You keep doing that with your eyebrows, and you're going to need Botox."

"Buttercup, there won't be enough Botox in all of Hollywood to put me together if your antics continue."

"Very funny." I say, lifting my chin. "It wasn't my fault."

"It never is, darling, it never is."

...

Large puffy clouds scuttle across the sky. A light breeze kicks up small waves, riffling the water's mirror-like surface, and the sun plays peek-a-boo with the clouds. My fingers dangle in the water as I watch Vic paddle down the lake....... being lazy does have its advantages......being able to enjoy the scenery.....mainly him....... and realize the enormity of my good fortune. Kidnapped by a mentally deranged man, I came away with only minor injuries and a brief hospital stay. Due to the quick thinking of Juls, Vic's assistant, we escaped the media spotlight and after a short investigation by the police, the hospital released me... home to the care of my family, who literally tried killing me with kindness ...seriously......the lodge house turned into a three ring circus of well-meaning helpers, tripping over each other to please me, to the point I didn't have a moment of peace.

Vic tried organizing a routine, but chaos ensued, everyone thought they knew what I needed. Finally, Ike fled to his hide-out in the boathouse and placed an emergency call to Bridget. Within 24 hours she was at our doorstep.... she flew in.......rumor has it she came by broom. Standing at the entrance to the kitchen, she dared anyone to cross her threshold. She had that Wicked Witch of the West look on her face, the one that says, I have flying monkeys and I'm not afraid to use them. And we believed her. Soon she had a schedule of family visits, meals and like a well-adjusted happy family, we played cards in the evening, shared books, watched movies, and popped popcorn over the fire. She even coerced Izzy and Ansel....the children loved her........they thought she was Mary Poppins with attitude. I'm sure the kitchen table laden with crayons, markers, stickers and just about any kind of craft supply desired....along with milk and warm cookies from the oven didn't hurt.

And through the grace of God, Josh, Claire, and the children became a part of our family. At first it was awkward, but sometimes blood is thicker than water. Ancestry and personality quirks passed down through generations prove to be the glue holding the fragile web we know as family together.

Although Josh's adoption parents never hid the fact he was adopted, he was shocked to learn the circumstances behind his placement. He always wondered if he had another family somewhere, and was delighted to meet his new siblings.

And as much as Vic and I suffered when we lost him; I could not have chosen better people to raise my son. The Westlands loved him unconditionally and were very supportive of him reuniting with us...as long as they got Christmas, seriously, generosity only goes so far.

So under Bridget's direction, for seven loud, amazing days we hosted all four of our children and grandchildren.

Everyone had a grand time. Hanna claimed she had the best time of her life....even if Cyrus ate her cell phone.....the cellular reception in the mountains isn't very good anyway......then Ansel spilled red wine on a blouse Lani designed as part of her fashion week collection.......personally it looked like a tattered bed sheet, best put out of its misery before it went to the runway at Fashion week. Ike taught Josh how to ride a motor cycle........a Harley Davidson....every mother's dream.

Jason and Josh enjoy reading mystery novels, Claire and Lani are alma maters of the same college, Vic and Trey share a passion for football and Claire taught me how to knit. *Sort of.....is it knitting or knotting.* And it is freaky scary how much Josh and Vic are alike.....*freaky scary*....who ever said blood is thicker than water was right. So all and all, we're on the way to being a delightfully, quirky dysfunctional mixed family.

...

Vic pulls me out of my happy memories of the past week by pointing out a loon diving for a fish. I notice the canoe is drifting into a small cove, the boggy shoreline ringed with shoots of pickerel mixed in with yellow and purple water iris. Pond lilies poke through the water's surface, buds held in tight floating orbs, ready to burst open as the lengthening days bathe them in sunlight. Turtles perch on a fallen log while fish float near the water's surface, basking in the morning sun. Taking two sweeping strokes through the tea-colored water, he glides the canoe into the center of the cove and we drift, lulled by the warmth of the sun and serenaded by the call of a hermit thrush off in the distance.

Vic leans his paddle on the canoe gunnels, and he

gazes at me for a long moment, the wind riffles through his hair. Looking up, squinting into the sun, he seems to be thinking. I tilt my head watching him, waiting, enjoying the tranquility of the lake, the birds calling back and forth across the cove. An ovenbird trills *teacher, teacher,* from the forest floor. And from the muddy shore a bullfrog bellows *jug a rum, jug a rum,* followed by the familiar banjo twang of the green frog. Sensing the need to be quiet, I wait…. and wait…… and wait. He hasn't brought up his marriage proposal since my rescue on the mountain…. maybe… he's changed his mind. Life with me can be pretty chaotic to say the least. When I saw the canoe I thought…….well, I thought maybe……..you know.

"Is this the picnic spot?" My patience wears thin.

"Nope."

"Oh…..it's so beautiful."

"Yep, but the shoreline is that spongy sphagnum moss, a little damp for a picnic. I just wanted to stop here and enjoy the view."

"I see, but you seem to be looking at me as much as the scenery."

"Yep."

"Why?"

"Making sure you don't get into trouble." With a sigh, he rakes a hand through his hair.

"How can I get into trouble?" I huff indignantly. "I'm sitting in a canoe with a life jacket underneath me in water that barely reaches my waist. We have a picnic basket full of food, sunscreen with an SPF of 80 and a lifeguard watching over me. There is a canister of bear mace in the pack along with two bottles of wine, so if something should happen, I can die happy. And I'm wearing granny panties." I finish with a flourish. "What could possibly go wrong?"

"Trust me," he says, shaking his head wearily. "I'm not letting my guard down for a second, I've learned the hard way."

"You can't stand guard over me for the rest of my life." I fume. "That's crazy, I wouldn't be surprised to see Ike positioned on that ridge armed with a satellite walkie-talkie."

"I think he's just a little to the right of the white pine." Vic chuckles as he points to the line of trees.

"Very funny." I mutter, thinking so much for a marriage proposal. See what happens when you wait too long. *Oh no*……. what if he brought me out here to *dump* me, telling me he can't take it anymore. The price of bodyguards and S.W.A.T. teams are too expensive, even for him. Maybe he wants out, maybe that's why he picked out the granny panties…he doesn't want to be tempted. *Oh, God.*

In a state of confusion and dread, a host of questions breaks free, fluttering through my mind like confetti in a parade. I barely notice the canoe enter a narrow channel leading back into the main part of the lake. Trying to tame my runaway thoughts, I nervously tug on my lower lip, searching for a topic of conversation to dispel my anxiety. "Hungry?"

"Yep."

So much for opening the lines of communication, I try again. "Maybe we should peek in that picnic basket. Did Bridget make lunch before she left this morning?"

"Yep."

Why won't he talk? I'm confused; no one has ever broken up with me. Limited opportunities due to the fact

I've only had two boyfriends and a pathetic love life.

Vic stops paddling and points over my shoulder. "We're here."

"Here? Where?" I crane my neck to catch a glimpse and nearly tip the boat.

"Look." He angles the canoe so I see a small island dotted with pine trees where clumps of blueberry and hobble bush hug the rugged shoreline. A bank of woodland ferns lead down to the water's edge and a lone columbine pokes its pink head through the green fronds. Nestled in the pines with a view down the lake sits a lean-to, constructed of freshly cut lumbar, the clean surface of the wood gleams against the dark pines.

"Oh, what a darling little island. I wonder who owns it?" I ask, enchanted by the sight.

He places the paddle inside the canoe pointing to the island, and nods at me. "It could belong to you."

"Me?" I look between him and the island in confusion. "What do you mean…..me? Only the Rockefellers and Donald Trump own islands."

"I would like to give it to you." He says. *Oh, no, this is it.* He's going to leave me on this island like the lepers on Molokai. I'm a menace to society, a person to be ostracized for the safety of the general public. But I don't like being alone, I'm afraid of the dark. What will I eat…….how long can a person live on blueberries?

He clears his throat and starts to speak, oblivious to the turmoil running through my head, he hesitates and starts again. "I screwed this up the last time. I want to get it right. You deserve to have this done properly." He takes my hand in his, looking deeply into my eyes, he says, "Elle," He stops and smiles. "Ella, Ella, my mia bella." And reaching into his pocket, he takes out a ring and slips it onto my finger; an exquisite sapphire set in woven strands of silver surrounded by diamonds shimmering like tiny rainbows in the sun.

"Will you marry me?"

What did he just say? Did I hear him correctly?

"Elle, marry me, I promise there will be benefits."

Marry......he definitely said marry. Thank goodness, the uncertainty was just my imagination running away with me....*how unusual.* I open my mouth to speak, nothing comes out.

He stares down at his feet and mutters something indiscernible, probably in Spanish. He holds up a hand. "Don't say anything, let me finish."

His thumb caresses my wrist, "Elle, I promise you a lifetime of Twinkies, a full-time cook, no matter where we live-and that may be self-serving on my part." He chuckles, shrugging his shoulders. "I promise to be true to you in good times and in bad, life is full of ups and downs but let me be your constant." I try to speak but only croak.

"I spoke with the owners of the Camp," he continues. "And if we want, Camp Sky Haven can be ours. They are moving to Seattle to be closer to their daughter and grandchildren. They fell in love with Puget Sound and the San Juan islands. The lodge no longer works for them. It could be our summer home, close to Josh, and a place for the family to come and visit. The property comes with this island. I told them the final decision was up to my wife. What do you say, will you be my wife?" He cocks his head, smiles at me, his white teeth blazing against his bronze skin, and he says, "Come on, how many people can say they own an island?"

Me!! I can own an island and live happily ever after

with Vic. Even after all the insanity, he still wants to *marry* me! I launch myself full bore into his arms, yelling, "Yes, yes, yes! I will marry you." And in the blink of an eye, the force of my catapult causes the canoe to roll to its side.......tilt and tip over......into the water....*Splash! Oh my God*.....they say when you're drowning your life flashes before you........but flashing through my mind is the thought, if he lets me drown...he'd never be convicted, no judge or jury in its right mind would pronounce him guilty, it would be ruled justifiable homicide. She had it coming.

Coming to the water's surface, gasping for air, I see him draped over the canoe. "Elle, buttercup, are you all right?" His voice edged with concern.

"I'm fine, oh Vic, I'm so, so sorry; I've ruined everything. Again! You can change your mind. I understand. How could you possibly want to marry me? I'm a disaster."

He starts laughing, his body shaking and heaving with the force of it, causing the canoe to rock in the water. "Elle, I can't imagine a life without you, what would I do for adventure and drama?"

"But I've ruined the picnic, we have no food, and we'll freeze to death in these wet clothes."

"Nope, I've learned. I packed the food and a blanket along with extra clothes in canoe dry bags, just in case something like this happened. I've been with you long enough to know that I need to Klutz-Ellen proof.

And what can I say..........I've found my soul mate.

Chapter 47

Mountain Twilight

A few weeks later……..

Today was our wedding day. The completion of a story…a story that began so long ago in the mountains….once upon a time boy meets girl at summer camp…...and ends miraculously with……they lived happily ever after. Today I married Vic at our camp surrounded by family and friends. It was the most perfect of days.

Pausing at the open window of our bedroom, I watch the sun sink into the horizon. Cool mountain air pushes back the heat of the day. With a shiver, I search through a pile of gifts stacked on the bed and find the angora shawl Claire gave me this morning………a wedding present from my daughter-in-law.

Throwing the shawl over my shoulders, I step out onto the balcony, needing a moment of quiet, to reflect back on the day, to savor the precious memories of our wedding.

I love the earth best at twilight; mountain peaks muted in the dying light, the depths of the lake lie dark and deep. Lingering, I watch the sky deepen; pink tinted clouds fade to lavender and the shoreline reflects the colors of the mountains. Profound contentment sweeps over me in a moment of serendipity. Tilting my head to one side, I listen to the sounds drifting over the lawn of stubby mountain grass, the resonance of ice clinking against glass, the ebb and flow of quiet conversation playing as background music for the giggling laughter of children and barking dogs. These are the sounds of contentment, of dreams fulfilled, of a family found and a curse lost. Unconsciously I exhale, letting go of the fear and uncertainty of the past, and send an unspoken prayer of gratitude towards the heavens.

...

One word describes our wedding....magical. We stood under the brilliant June sun, surrounded by loved ones. Even though we were not married in a church, we wanted the sanction of a Christian marriage, a holdover from my Catholic school days and Vic's devout Mexican family. The ceremony was a blend of traditional wedding rites and Native American rituals. A mix of customs and cultures we hold dear in God's cathedral of the forest. Ironically, Vic's mother has Native American blood. She looks like her Swedish grandfather but her beloved grandmother, Bema was a Lakota Sioux.

Our wedding started on the water, we arrived in separate canoes from opposite ends of the lake. I came from the south in a hand crafted wooden canoe, sides burnished to a golden yellow hue. Lani and Hanna manned the paddles, with strict orders *not* to tip the canoe. White birch and ribbon along with ferns and wild roses were woven into the gunnels of the boat. It looked like a small barge for a Viking princess. I wore a white dress, long and flowing, delicate embroidery on the hem and a wreath of wildflowers in my hair.......daisies. In my lap rested a bouquet, a cluster of June blooming wildflowers, mimicking the blossoms dotting the meadows and roadsides throughout the mountains. Tall spikes of purple lupine, ox-eyed daisies, pink mountain laurel and yellow bird's foot trefoil held together by a border of ferns. My hair unbound, fell freely down my back, a deep caramel color, lying in wait for the sun to paint in the streaks of summer copper. On my feet, a delicate pair of sandals, the hand tooled flowers encircling my ankles held with a thin strap. Around my neck, the locket Vic gave me so long ago, the filigree heart, edges worn with tarnish, a familiar weight to anchor my overflowing heart. The choice of clothes reminiscent of a seventies flower child, but truth be told……. that's how I feel, young, fresh, embarking on a new beginning……. while reclaiming the past. It's never too late…

Paddling alone, Vic arrived from the north, in an aluminum canoe, a nostalgic rendition of the one we used at Camp High Point. He was dressed in a tuxedo, minus the bow tie. He wore the tuxedo because…. I love a man in a tuxedo. And he looked impossibly handsome. Waiting at the dock, Ike helped us disembark from the canoes. Following a Native American ritual, he placed a blue blanket on Vic's shoulders and then one on mine, representing our past sorrows and disappointments. Standing between us, he led us up the bank to the plateau of grassy lawn, under the shade of a large white birch tree where our family and friends gathered forming a tight circle. Aside from one of my brothers and our friends from Camp High Point, ironically, most of my family was Jack's. Jack may be gone, but the love of his family lives on; and I've never loved them more than on the day I married a man….other than their son. Their presence showed the generosity and goodness of their hearts. They stood in a tight knot, beaming at me from all directions; his mom and dad, brothers and sisters with assorted nieces and nephews. Individually, they're nice people, it's when you get them in a herd; they can be slightly, let's just say…. overwhelming. And if there is one thing Jack's family never misses, it's a party. When they accepted our invitation, I was concerned that one look at them would send Vic running for the hills, fearful they were a lynch mob in disguise. And yet quite the opposite happened, with the common bond of beer and poker, Vic, Ike and the brothers played cards until the wee hours of the morning. They wanted to make sure Vic was good enough for me. Can't be trusting those Hollywood types, Jack's Da whispered in my ear the night before the wedding …..and they heard we were serving top shelf whiskey.

Vic's mother arrived for the ceremony wearing a pale blue suit; and a very handsome older gentleman on her arm. After divorcing Vic's father she stopped drinking and started painting again, even garnered a few private showings of her work. In fact, the silver haired fox escorting her was the owner of one of the galleries hosting her paintings. And he looked quite smitten with her. Looking tall and elegant in her blonde patrician beauty, it's hard to believe Vic is her son; they look nothing alike except he inherited her height and elegant bearing along with her loving heart.

Waiting for us under the shade of the birch tree stood the minister from the little stone chapel overlooking Pine Lake. As we approached the center of the circle, our children aligned themselves on the lawn, standing at the four cardinal directions; north, south, east and west. It is a Native American belief the cardinal directions bring blessings to a marriage.

Lani stood holding a hawk's feather, symbolizing the element of air, and in a clear strong voice she invoked the blessings of the east; the bringing of openness, the gift of breath and communication to our marriage. From the east we receive the gift of a new beginning with each rising sun. Trey held a burning flame in a birch bark vessel representing the south: energy, passion, and the warmth of a loving home. Hanna faced west and cradled in her hands a vase of water, filled with river rocks, the element of water. In marriage one must offer absolute trust in each other and vow to keep your hearts open in sorrow as well as joy. And from the North, our Josh; a pottery bowl rests in his hands brimming over with rich black soil, the element of the earth. Earth which provides sustenance, fertility and security, earth which feeds and enriches one, and helps build a stable home, where one may always return.

After our children offered their blessings on our marriage, the minister stepped forward welcoming our guests to the mountains on such a beautiful day, stating our intention to make a solemn eternal covenant before God. His glasses glint in the afternoon sun as he asked the assembled congregation to join in the celebration reflecting our love and joy. Directing us to face each other, we exchanged vows, choosing the traditional Christian rite, time honored, tested and true. Holding hands we pledged our promise to be true from this day forward, for better, for worse, for richer, for poorer, in sickness and in health, to love and to cherish, for as long as we both shall live. A solemn vow held in our hearts, finalized and consummated through the simple exchange of silver rings.

The minister placed his hands over ours, and looking out over our friends and family he said, "My friends as we gather here, I want you to reflect on why the birch tree we stand under is the perfect symbol for marriage.

This tree is rooted in the ground, yet it still reaches to the heavens above, weathering the storms of life. It flexes and bends with the winds, static but always changing, adapting to whatever comes its way, as a husband and wife must bend and give. And always reach for heaven to our Almighty Father from whom all good things come."

Grasping our hands tightly in his, he continued, "I'm sure everyone gathered here today knows the story of Vic and Ellen's love, the trials, tragedy and separation they endured, and yet within the divine mercy of God, they stand before us professing their love. And lest we forget, their time apart was not for naught. Through Vic's travels he earned the loyalty of a trusted and invaluable friend. He married and was blessed with his beloved daughter, Hanna." Here the minister pauses and nods at Hanna who beams a smile at her father. "And somewhere along the way, Vic, I don't know how or why, but the camera fell in love with your face and you fell in love with the profession of acting." Reverend Stephans laughs at his little joke before moving on, "And Ellen, you became a teacher, and someone earlier today told me you were named one of New York State's Outstanding Environmental Educators a few years ago. Very impressive." I feel a slow blush creeping to my face, and cut my eyes to Jack's Dad, who I'm sure was the blabber mouth. He loves to extol the virtues of his children. And I'm blessed to be counted as one of his children. And of course, he smiled back at me with a completely angelic look on his face.

"Ellen, you were a loyal and loving wife to Jack for twenty five years, and in your marriage you and Jack raised these beautiful children, or I should say young adults." He smiles at Lani and Trey. Reverend Stephans sweeps his hand to encompass all of Jack's family. "And the depth of your commitment to Jack is evident by the loving support of his family. But life changes and we move on to new beginnings or maybe in this case, to finish a story started so long ago, and bring a happy ending."

"Vic and Ellen, God had a greater plan for you. A story with many chapters, but the conclusion included the love for a child so great it could not be ignored, a burning desire to be reunited with your son, Josh. And God saw fit to bless you with four children and two grandchildren. I'm sure today, your cup runneth over." At this point Vic and I were overcome with emotion, our foreheads touching as tears unabashedly rolled down our cheeks.

Reverend Stephans continued, "But that is the past and now you embark on the adventure of a new beginning, a new life, and a future designed by the two of you. Standing under this birch tree, I'm reminded of a Robert Frost poem, *Birches*. The first line of the poem talks about the birch trees bending to the left and right, across a line of darker trees. Such a lovely analogy of life and our need to bend and flex in the darkest hours, to be able to withstand the ice and rain storms and then live in joy, the kind of joy that allows little boys to climb and swing away from the earth for a while.

Vic and Ellen, our wish for you today is......that you may bend and flex as the trees through the hardships of life and yet like a child, climb up snow white bark toward the heavens in joy, till the tree can bear no more and dips to swing back safely to the earth. May the Lord bless you and keep you all the days of your life."

After the minister's blessing, Ike removed the blue blankets, wrapping us in a white blanket representing our new life together. We kissed as man and wife…*finally*.

…

Woof! The sight of Lani's fiancé, Jason engaged in a playful tug of war on the lawn with Cyrus pulls me back to the present, allowing my memories to slip away, hidden yet safe for another day. Even from my vantage point it's questionable who will win the contest. A sharp tug from Cyrus causes Jason to slip on the dew covered grass, falling hard on his butt and Cyrus sprints off in search of another hapless victim. Shaking my head with amusement and affection, I watch Lani help Jason to his feet, suggestively brushing off his butt. Which he rewards by pulling her into a passionate embrace; two silhouettes become one in the fading evening light.

And then I sense more than feel his presence come up from behind, sinewy arms pull me into enveloping warmth, causing my skin to tingle, come alive and turn velvet in the lavender light of evening. The day old stubble of his chin tickles the soft side of my jaw sending tremors of delight down my spine. *Vic*…..

"Penny for your thoughts, mia." his husky voice drawls as his breath caresses the lobe of my ear. His arms tighten around me, and I feel safe, cherished, and loved.

"Oh, they're much more expensive than that," I whisper, leaning my full weight into his embrace sighing in disappointment when the delicious kisses at the nape of my neck cease. He whispers hoarsely, "The best things in life are free, my love, or haven't you heard."

My face softens as my gaze travels over the Adirondack cedar house surrounded by porches, peppered with brightly cushioned furniture. Pure false gold winks from the shuttered windows, the light held within spilling out the windowpanes.

Two dormer windows peek through the roofline, capped with flower boxes, each box a cascade of geraniums and ivy. My heart rings with the truth of his words, for it is not the house nor the contents, but the voices of loved ones spread out across the lawn that beckons us, to come and draw near.

"You smell heavenly, like the forest on a summer day." He kisses my hair and inhales deeply.

"So do you,' I whisper, wrapping my arms around his waist and kiss the dark patch of skin peeking out from the collar of his shirt.

"Look," he points down to the fire pits spread out along the shoreline, two smaller fire circles flanking a large tower of stacked wood. "I told them to go ahead and light the fires. We can watch from up here, the view is better."

In slow motion our guests gather around the campfires and we watch as Josh and Claire help the children light the smaller fires then ignite the kindling at the base of the main fire. Claire pulls Izzy and Ansel close within the protective folds of her skirt, their curiosity outweighs caution. Jack's brothers spent the better part of the morning building the main bonfire. Over seven feet tall, it is a towering pyre. Within minutes a sweeping cluster of flames reaches to the stars, sparks popping and cracking, the night sky obliterated by the blaze.

"Hey, are you hiding away up here? There will be none of that." It's Lani standing at the doorway to the balcony, carrying a tray with champagne flutes. "A toast to the newlyweds." She places the tray on a small table by the railing. "But don't drink it until Trey gives the toast." She admonishes as she hurries back down the stairs.

Our guests gather around the campfire, faces dappled

by the firelight, turn as one holding their glasses in salute to us. Trey lifts his glass, and his clear baritone voice cuts through the night air, "To Mom and my new Dad, Sentar, the warrior king," this comment elicits laughter from the assembled group as he continues, "We love you and wish you mountains of happiness, a love as deep as the lakes, and may your joy soar like the song of birds on a spring morning. We wish you peace and a life ruled by contentment. And may you be blessed by the abundance of joy that life has to offer." As we sip our champagne, from the far corner of the lawn comes, "Knock, knock!" followed by a chorus of groans. Emi Jo, Ben, Tee and the ever unflappable Mac continue, "Knock, knock!" And the resounding response is "Who's there?" Mac answers, "Ewe!" And in the spirit of fun, everyone calls back, "Ewe Who?" And Mac with great flourish raises his glass in our direction shouting, "We love ewe!"

The night is magical……..with a sense of euphoria in the air, drunk on the freely flowing champagne, or perhaps, from the glow of firelight competing with the moon, leaving little space for stars to fill in the gaps of the darkened sky.

"I can't believe they are all here." Vic murmurs, shaking his head in wonder.

"Except for Gran and Burt." I say, laying my head against his chest, feeling the beat of his heart. "I miss them so much."

"Oh, I think they're here," he says. "I feel their presence. For instance, Burt is perched up in that red maple tree by the water." He motions to a maple tree skirting the shoreline. "And Gran is down by the dock trying to con Jack's brothers into a poker game."

"You think so?"

"Definitely, I know so. Here, you're getting cold." He opens his jacket so I can slip my arms around his waist, wrapping me in the cocoon of his body heat. "Better?"

"Much. It's blissful." Closing my eyes, I enjoy the feel of his arms around me.

Strains of music drift from the band playing under a tent. Sounds that filter through the night air, to mingle and merge with the chorus of frogs and early crickets in the reeds along the shoreline. Humming along with the music, the band playing an old favorite, I watch Jack's parents twirl around the dance floor. "Look at them, how much in love they are, after all these years. That will be us in thirty years, won't it?"

"Absolutely, and I think we should start by taking a spin under the stars, see if your dancing skills can keep up with the competition." He sways to the beat of the music, pausing for a moment, "I like Jack's family. I know how much they mean to you. It was generous of them to come and be part of our wedding."

"They're special people. Oh, look, over there." I point to a couple dancing under the shadows of the birch tree. "It's Siobhan, Jack's sister, dancing with Ike."

"You're right." Vic leans over the railing to get a better view. "They look pretty cozy."

"Siobhan recently divorced a man she should have sent packing years ago. And…" I pause for dramatic effect. "She took one look at Ike, it was like watching a starving cat in front of an open bird cage, topped with catnip."

"Ahhh, the ladies do like Ike, he just isn't one for keeping them around too long."

"True, but they haven't taken their eyes off each other since they met." I point out to him.

"I agree. He does appear smitten. He left the poker game last night to take a walk with her. That's unheard of in the world of Ike." Vic sighs and tilts his head. "Who knows, maybe, this year he won't take that trip to Pittsburgh looking for his lost love. I'd like for him to find someone. No one deserves to be alone."

Actually, I think he's perfect for Siobhan. She needs to have a little fun and I know Ike will be kind to her. And I……..I have a teensy tiny confession to make."

"Oh boy…mortal, venal or sin of the white lie category?"

"Well….ummmmmm……I put something in her purse." I blush even thinking about it.

"And what did you put in her purse?"

"Aaaah….the pink ones."

"The pink ones.......what pink ones?" Then comprehension dawns on him. "Seriously, you put pink condoms in her purse?"

"Well……you see, she's out of practice," I pause for a breath, blurting out, "And not exactly the type to be toting her own."

"Kind of like you, when your girlfriends forced them upon you." He chuckles.

I arch my eyebrows at him coyly, "Just returning the favor. It worked *very* well for me."

"That it did, my darling; that it did. But I hate to tell you, I think Ike usually packs his own, and pink isn't his color."

"It will be dark; he won't be caring if they're pink or royal red with polka dots."

Suddenly the sky overhead explodes into a burst of color and a loud boom resonates throughout the valley. "Ohhh……ohhhh……fireworks!" I clap my hands in glee, doing an imitation of a five-year old girl at her first parade. My eyes shine in the reflective glare, I *love* fireworks.

"For you, my mia bella, happy wedding day, *quierda*."

"But….but….how did you do this?"

"I filed a petition with the town council. They balked, but your hero status after the kidnapping helped, they felt sorry for you and gave us a permit for five minutes of fireworks, so don't blink or you'll miss the show."

"Oh, no, that's just enough; I feel guilty disturbing the mountain peace, but what a guilty pleasure." I leave the sanctuary of his body, craning my head to watch the collusion of fire and gun power ignite the sky. "Look…. look, I love the white ones that rain down gold." A series of green and pink embers explode, "No, maybe it's the green ones or the red, white and blue spinners…..Oh, I don't know…….. I love them all! Thank you, thank you, thank you, you are the best husband ever!" I pepper his face with kisses.

"And don't you forget it." He growls in my ear, his hands sliding down my body possessively. He kisses the back of my neck and his fingers do some clever maneuvers along the sensitive secret hollow of my hips. Those magic fingers have my full attention with the promise of things to come……

"Are those roving hands a promise, or are you just teasing me?"

"Buttercup, there are teases, threats, and certainties, this is definitely a certainty."

Once the fireworks fade to falling embers of ash, and the bonfires reduced to a bed of glowing coals, a soft twinkling spreads across the meadows surrounding the house, blinking on and off. The twinkling repeats in the trees and bushes hugging the fields. *Fireflies.* The fireflies of June. Beautiful tiny, blinking orbs of greenish white light, the glow emitted from the abdomen of the female. In the tall grass the female signals for her mate, *blink, blink, blink,* I'm here, over here, come find me. A call of love, so simple in its purity.

Releasing a breath in silence, my entire being comes alive in the perfection of the moment. These rare serendipitous moments we live for, that space in time……precious, singular, wondrous…bordering on divine.

"It will just be you and me, babe, spending the entire summer on this beautiful mountain lake," he whispers. "Being lazy, sleeping in till noon, cook or not cook, eat whenever and whatever we want; stay up all night watching the fireflies, skinny dip off the dock, paddle to the island, or lounge in the sun doing absolutely nothing. That's my idea of heaven, right here with you. Going nowhere, doing nothing."

"Really?" I ask, holding my breath and blink my eyes rapidly, already knowing the answer to the query. "Won't that be boring?"

"Nope, you, me, Cyrus, and the kids now and then, that's it."

"*Oh, boy……*"

"What do you mean…..Oh boy?" He cocks his head to one side, and his lips twitch in amusement.

"Maybe we want to do a *little* something?" I rub my hand along his chest in a soothing motion, thinking it's not like I can't get the registration fee back, and no one is counting on us or anything like that. I guess I should have thought this one through or asked him before I signed us up. At the time it seemed like a great idea.

Okay, I got caught up in the excitement of the moment and the idea of a challenge. What was I to do? *Ask him*........so I should have asked him. But he's *not* going to like it.

Steeling myself for our first fight as a married couple, I plunge in..."I signed us up for the 90 Mile Adirondack Canoe Classic in September." I rush on before he can protest. "We start practice tomorrow; the trainer arrives at 9:00 a.m. sharp. He's German or something, we don't dare be late."

"*What!*"

"You love me, right?"

"*Thunk, thunk, thunk.*"

"That was your head?"

"Yes...."

"Still love me?" I hear him muttering away in Spanish.

"Always, Elle, always. Forever and ever more. I did say for better or worse, good times and bad. How far is this race?"

"Ninety miles."

"*Wow*...we have a lot of practicing to do; did you say this trainer is German?"

"Ummmm....yes."

"I hope he comes with super powers and is a licensed miracle maker. With your athletic prowess and talent for tipping boats along with my penchant for being lazy, this guy needs a direct line to the gods."

"It was that damn snotty lady at the registration desk, she goaded me into it. I was just asking about the race and she said I was too old to participate." I say indignantly. "What was I to do? It wasn't my fault!"

He kisses the top of my head. "It never is, darling, it

never is."

"*Whew.*" I love this man. I love his strength, his sense of humor, his innate honorability, the intoxicating hold he has over me and I love that he *gets* me. I burrow my head into his chest, knowing I will love him always, a love born in these mountains, once lost…….and now…..forever found.

The End

About the Author

L.R. Smolarek and her husband are self-proclaimed gypsies. Their caravan, a 24 foot RV with two kayaks hanging off the back is home for a good portion of the year. In the company of two very spoiled little dogs, they travel across the country, coming to rest in the Adirondacks, along the beaches of Florida or hiking the canyons and mountains of the west. But for winter, home is a cabin, once her grandfather's sugar shack tucked in the woods of Western New York. Her writing has appeared in *Country Living magazine, National PTA* and for eight years she wrote a monthly column called *Nature's Corner* for *Western New York Family* magazine where she drew on her experiences as a naturalist encouraging families to spend more time learning and exploring the great outdoors.

32999137R00268

Made in the USA
Middletown, DE
25 June 2016